Don't judge a book by its cover! Nothing, and no one, is EVER what they seem.

Ellen Christenson escapes from an abusive life, but does one ever escape the scars that are left on their soul? One must move on, one must try. But life has a tendency to circle back to what one once knew, and one finds that her life choices bring her back to the scenes of her abuse to deal with it finally and fully, in ways she had never thought she would. It is then that the healing can begin, as she repairs her soul and the people she has devastated along the way.

Ellen hadn't intended to end up in Silicon Valley and its high-tech world, but due to life and its circumstances she finds herself the head of a startup tech company. Cool, calculating, efficient – she shows the world a side of her that she doesn't have, and few if any know the real Ellen. Nearby San Francisco provides her with plenty of girlfriends. That elusive one, that soulmate, she has a hard time recognizing due to the scars within.

For years, she has lived with her decision of letting someone die for their sins, and Ellen is blown away by the feelings and emotions she has bottled up for so long....

A K'Anne Meinel novel

Also by K'Anne Meinel:

Novels in Paperback:

SHIPS *CompanionSHIP, FriendSHIP, RelationSHIP*
Long Distance Romance
Children of Another Mother
Erotica
The Claim
Bikini's Are Dangerous
The Complete Series
Germanic
Malice Masterpieces 1
The First Five Books
Represented
Timed Romance
Malice Masterpieces 2
Books Six through Ten
The Journey Home
Out at the Inn
Shorts

Anthology Volume 1
Lawyered
Malice Masterpieces 3
Books Eleven through Fifteen
Blown Away
Blown Away
The Alternate Cover
Small Town Angel
Pirated Love
Doctored
Veil of Silence
Malice Masterpieces 4
Books Sixteen through Twenty
The Outsider
Pirated Heart
Vetted
Recombinant Love

Novellas in Paperback:

Mysterious Malice (Book 1)
Meticulous Malice (Book 2)
Mistaken Malice (Book 3)
Malicious Malice (Book 4)
Masterful Malice (Book 5)
Matrimonial Malice (Book 6)
Mourning Malice (Book 7)
Murderous Malice (Book 8)
Mental Malice (Book 9)
Menacing Malice (Book 10)
Minor Malice (Book 11)
Morally Malice (Book 12)
Morose Malice (Book 13)

Melancholy Malice (Book 14)
Mad Malice (Book 15)
Macabre Malice (Book 16)
Marinating Malice (Book 17)
Macerating Malice (Book 18)
Minacious Malice (Book 19)
Meddlesome Malice (Book 20)
Meandering Malice (Book 21)
Vaquera Safica (Spanish)
Surfista Safica (Spanish)
ケーアンヌ・マイネル (Japanese)
Maniacal Malice (Book 22)

Pocket Paperbacks:

Mysterious Malice (Book 1)
Sapphic Surfer
Sapphic Cowgirl
Meticulous Malice (Book 2)
Mistaken Malice (Book 3)
Malicious Malice (Book 4)
Masterful Malice (Book 5)
Matrimonial Malice (Book 6)
Mourning Malice (Book 7)
Murderous Malice (Book 8)

Mental Malice (Book 9)
Menacing Malice (Book 10)
Minor Malice (Book 11)
Morally Malice (Book 12)
Morose Malice (Book 13)
Melancholy Malice (Book 14)
Mad Malice (Book 15)
Macabre Malice (Book 16)
Marinating Malice (Book 17)

In E-Book Format:
Short Stories

Fantasy
Wet & Wet Again
Family Night
Quickie ~ Against the Car
Quickie ~ Against the Wall
Quickie ~ Over the Couch
Mile High Club
Quickie ~ Under the Pier
Heel or Heal
Kiss
Family Night 2
Beach Dreams
Internet Dreamers

Snoggered
The Rockhound
Stolen
Agitated
Love of my LIFE
Quickie in an Elevator,
GOING DOWN?
Into the Garden
The Book Case
The Other Women
Menage a WHAT?

Novellas

Bikini's are Dangerous
Kept
Ghostly Love
Bikini's are Dangerous 2
On the Parkway
Stable Affair
Sapphic Surfer
Bikini's are Dangerous 3
Bikini's are Dangerous 4
Bikini's are Dangerous 5
Mysterious Malice (Book 1)
Meticulous Malice (Book 2)
Mistaken Malice (Book 3)
Malicious Malice (Book 4)
Masterful Malice (Book 5)
Matrimonial Malice (Book 6)
Mourning Malice (Book 7)
Murderous Malice (Book 8)
Sapphic Cowgirl
Sapphic Cowboi

Mental Malice (Book 9)
Menacing Malice (Book 10)
Charming Thief
~Snake Island~
Charming Thief
~Diamonds are a Girls Best Friend~
Minor Malice (Book 11)
Morally Malice (Book 12)
Morose Malice (Book 13)
Melancholy Malice (Book 14)
Mad Malice (Book 15)
Macabre Malice (Book 16)
Marinating Malice (Book 17)
Macerating Malice (Book 18)
Minacious Malice (Book 19)
Sayyida
Meddlesome Malice (Book 20)
Meandering Malice (Book 21)
Maniacal Malice (Book 22)

E-Book Novels

SHIPS *CompanionSHIP, FriendSHIP,
RelationSHIP*
Erotica Volume 1
Long Distance Romance
Bikini's Are Dangerous
The Complete Series
Malice Masterpieces
The First Five Books
To Love a Shooting Star
Children of Another Mother
Germanic
Blown Away
Blown Away
The Alternate Cover
Small Town Angel

The Claim
Represented
Timed Romance
Malice Masterpieces 2
Books Six through Ten
The Journey Home
Out at the Inn
Anthology Volume 1
Lawyered
Malice Masterpieces 3
Books Eleven through Fifteen
Pirated Love
Doctored
Veil of Silence

E-Book Novels Continued

Malice Masterpieces 4
Books Sixteen through Twenty
The Outsider
Pirated Heart
Vetted
Recombinant Love

Videos

Biography of Books
Ships
Sapphic Surfer
Ghostly Love
Long Distance Romance
Germanic
Sensual Sapphic
Sapphic Cowgirl
Couples
Lie Next To Me

Sapphic Cowboi
Timed Romance
Readings (SHIPS)
Doctored
Veil of Silence
She's Coming (The Outsider short)
It's Coming (The Outsider short)
The Outsider
Vetted

Dedicated to anyone who
thinks I'm writing about them.
I am.

K'A. M.

K'ANNE MEINEL

BLOWN AWAY

Published by:
Shadoe Publishing
Copyright © February 2018 by K'Anne Meinel

ISBN-13: 978-0692460863
ISBN-10: 0692460861

K'Anne Meinel is available for comments at KAnneMeinel@aim.com as well as on Facebook @ http://www.facebook.com/K.Anne.Meinel.Fan.Page, Google + @ https://plus.google.com/u/2/+KAnneMeinel, LinkedIn @ https://www.linkedin.com/in/k-anne-meinel-a026385a, or her blog @ http://kannemeinel.wordpress.com/ or on Twitter @ https://twitter.com/KAnneMeinel, or on her website @ www.kannemeinel.com if you would like to follow her to find out about stories and book's releases.

www.shadoepublishing.com

ShadoePublishing@gmail.com

Shadoe Publishing is a United States of America company

Cover by: K'Anne Meinel @ Shadoe Publishing

❊ CHAPTER ONE ❊

REMEMBRANCES

She stared at the ruins of a once beautiful farm house. Memories came, flashing back in an instant yet spanning years. There once stood a beautiful pair of oak trees with a swing between them for her to play on. She could still hear the echoes of her mother telling her to be careful as she climbed them. Skinned knees and scraped palms; she never complained about the slivers her mother had to remove because of her tomboyish activities. The shade of those oak trees provided her with endless hours of escape from the relentless sun but still she would burn from it. The wind would part the leaves and beams of sunlight would beat down between them, making her red hair shimmer. Her imagination could play for hours as she gazed up through them, envisioning them as towering giants and she a mere mortal. She loved those trees.

"I can't believe you climb like a monkey, and in a dress, too!" her mother would scold. She remembered that fondly – the inflections – the lilt in her mother's voice was still in her consciousness despite the span of years.

The house still tilted haphazardly. Weather and time hadn't pulled it to the ground and for this she was surprised as she stared at its sturdy build. Her great-grandparents had been among the first to build in this area and had used good wood and stone to construct their sturdy home. Their son and granddaughter had both raised families in this house. She scowled as she remembered she had been the last raised there.

It looked well picked over. The weeds around the place were elbow high and although she hadn't seen it in over twenty years, she couldn't help but wonder why it hadn't yet been torn down, which was why she was now there.

"Ms. Avril?" a voice asked her respectfully. She started in surprise as she hadn't heard anyone approach. The man who had spoken began to apologize. "Oh, I'm sorry miss, I was expecting...."

"It's okay, you just startled me," she said in precise and clear tones without a hint of the accent that was unique to this part of the country and that was so apparent in his voice. That accent brought back other memories, ones she had tried to quash and couldn't. Ones that she'd known needed exorcising, which could only be done by coming here. It was why she had come. She needed to stop the dreams that had returned. Her feeling was that they were in the past and they should remain there. Her psyche, though, was haunting her and she had to face it one last time.

"I was expecting Ms. Avril," he began again, peering at her intently and wondering who she was. He was shorter than she, his skin brown from the winds that blew there, and he was stooped from a lifetime of work.

She smiled, not realizing the beauty that was apparent in her face. Her pale white skin hid the freckles that came out in the sun, but no tan touched her creamy milk-white skin anymore. "I'm A...Avril," she answered, hesitating over the name for only a millisecond. '*Or, I was,*' she mentally corrected herself, but not aloud, as he wouldn't understand.

"You're Ms. Avril?" he asked, puzzled. He peered at her for a long time while shaking his head, trying to see some semblance of the youth he had known. As her smile faded, he saw a glimmer of recognition. Not of her but of her mother and that was when he took on a relieved look. His hat came off his head in an instant and his weathered face wreathed a smile showing several missing teeth. "Why, Ms. Avril, you've all growed up!" he drawled, pleased at his discovery.

"How are you, Mr. Davidson?" she asked pleasantly. The smile didn't quite reach her eyes. Not with the memories pushing at her temples begging her to remember, to relive them, and she tried hard once again to suppress them.

"Poorly," he said honestly. "Right poorly, but I aim to do the job you is needing done. I shorely do. Just like I promised." He gestured

to the truck that was parked at the end of the drive. On the trailer attached to it sat a front-end loader, securely chained to its bed.

She glanced at it, then back at the house he had come to demolish. It was the town's attempt at getting rid of an 'eyesore' that had sat there empty for over two decades. Why they had decided that it needed to be done now, she didn't know. But she was there, as requested, to get it done. Mr. Davidson had answered her call and was surprised that she remembered him. He was eager to earn the money she had promised him for the job.

"Do you want to go through the house to look for anything?" he asked as he noticed her silently staring at it.

She shook her head. She had done her picking long ago, her few belongings in some measly boxes and trunks. There had been a storage unit she had gone through as well with a lifetime of memories and knickknacks that meant nothing to anyone but herself. "Just bulldoze it," she said shortly. She wanted it taken care of so she could leave.

"You'll have to move your car," he mentioned as they turned to head back down the driveway.

She glanced at her Maserati and nearly laughed aloud at the contrast between it and his old rusted out Chevy. She hadn't thought of that when she decided to drive back here. If she hadn't before, she would surely stick out like a sore thumb now. Another reason to get the job finished and get out, get gone. Something she had done years ago and not looked back. She glanced over at the barns and silos. They still looked as solid as the day her great-grandparents and grandparents had built them. Nothing had touched them, not time, nor weather, and they seemed to be as strong and steady as the day they were built. They could use a little paint, but with the weather that came through this part of the country it was amazing they were still standing. She could see they were used well by the tracks that led from the path up to them and down the driveway, but that was all. Everything else – the chicken coop and a few other outbuildings – was abandoned. The grass was overgrown and obviously untrodden with no animals or people to grind it under their heels.

"Can you tear down those, too?" she asked as she gestured to the outbuildings.

"Ahyup," he grunted as they reached her car. She automatically pressed the button on her keychain to open the door and let her in. He glanced at the car as the door opened quietly on its own for her. It was expensive enough to pay a couple of years' salary for someone like him and for most folks around here. It was none of his business, though, so he hurried over to the trailer where another man stood, awaiting orders. "Let's get her down," he gestured, and they immediately began removing the chains holding the machine to the bed of the trailer.

The younger man kept watch out of the corner of his eye as the redhead steered the expensive sports car onto the road. She parked it opposite the driveway so they could drive the front-end loader onto the property. She was definitely worth a second *and* third look and he wondered if she remembered him as she watched his uncle maneuver the heavy machine off the trailer. She caught him staring as she got out of the car and he felt his cheeks redden. He hurried after his uncle to collect any boards worth salvaging and hoped she hadn't noticed. She had said they could take whatever they wanted.

She followed along slowly and looked down at her Prada shoes knowing she should have dressed down for the farm, but after twenty years she had nothing appropriate to wear in such a place. She hadn't thought about it as the miles passed and she had headed for this part of Oklahoma.

❉ CHAPTER TWO ❉

THE ESCAPE

She remembered the reverse trip vividly. She had run away as fast as the bus could take her. Was she running away from her past or running to her future? She didn't know, but to her, getting away from South Oklahoma had seemed like the best thing to do. Her bags were packed and Mrs. Davidson had agreed to send on the few boxes and trunks when she was settled.

"All set?" Sheriff Worley asked as he gave her a lift to the bus stop.

"Yep," she answered. She was frightened out of her mind, but she knew she had no choice but to go. She had to leave it all behind her. Leave the memories, the only home she'd ever known, the problems, and let time fade it all.

He glanced at the young girl; he could see how scared she was. He knew he would be at her age. She was just a week over eighteen and had signed all the papers renting out the farm to the co-op. It would be used as they saw fit by farmers who wanted to use the land and the sturdy barns and silos that still stood on the property. He didn't blame her for leaving as there was nothing left. It wasn't a good time to sell. It never was, not in this economy. Farming was a gamble at the best of times, and this wasn't the best of them. She had lost in so many ways and leaving was about the only option. Maybe some time away would do her good. Some of the boys who went off to school returned a little wiser, some didn't last, and few stayed away for good. He was sure he'd see her back. Small town girls were worse than small town boys for wanting to return to what was familiar, what they knew. There were a few boys around her age and a little older who would gladly marry her. She might be scrawny, but she had the farm and that would draw them like bees to honey.

He didn't know her, though. Avril Christenson might have died that day a couple of weeks back, instead of her father. At least in her own mind she had. Not that day, but the week before. They said lightning couldn't strike twice in the same place. They were wrong. Tornadoes did it, and lightning did it too. This time, though, the tornado had taken her life in this world and left her with the shell of the person that was escaping on a bus. Everyone thought her grief was over her father, but it wasn't. It was for the young woman who had been caught in her Chevy truck the week before. The woman had been her best friend and allowed Avril to be brave in the face of a dismal future. She was the one who had given Avril hope. She tried not to remember how much she had loved her best friend, how much they had planned, how much she had wanted to....

"Here we are, now you want some help buying your ticket?" the sheriff offered helpfully, as he would have any young woman.

"No thank you, Sheriff Worley, I've got it," she said in a flippant, teenage way. She threw her red hair back over her shoulder, her freckles standing out in relief against her tanned face with the sun making them seem unending. "Thank you for the ride," she remembered to say politely, as her mother would have wanted her to.

"No problem. Now you take care, ya' hear?" he spoke in return and watched as she gathered her backpack and two duffels before heading into the office that doubled as a bus stop and cafe. He watched through the door and looked around to see if any undesirables were loafing about. He didn't want this young girl hassled. He would have treated her as a daughter, as any young thing in this area would be treated. Poor young thing to lose her best friend and father within a week of each other, and have to graduate high school all alone with no relatives or close friends to see her off. Mrs. Davidson had been kind enough to take her in these last few weeks until she graduated, but other than that, Avril Christenson was on her own. Maybe she was better off. That best friend of hers had been nothing but a troublemaker since she was born, with unnatural leanings from what he had observed. He had never caught her at anything, but a person knew about such things. He thought her interest in the young Avril a tragedy in the making. It had only been a matter of time until she corrupted that innocent child.

Maybe God had taken her for that reason, to prevent it. That poor child, with a father like Owen Christenson to have been left with nothing like that. It was best that she leave, at least for now.

Avril knew the Sheriff was watching her. He couldn't help himself, nosy bugger that he was. She bought a one-way ticket to California, and when the clerk asked if she wanted the return ticket, she declined. The clerk had graduated from the same high school the year before and couldn't blame her for leaving and not coming back; she wished she could do it. She knew who Avril Christenson was. Everyone knew. The tragedy had been all over Oakley. Losing her father like that, the poor child, and right before graduation and her eighteenth birthday was such a loss. The clerk watched her as she sat down on one of the benches for the bus that was due at any time. Avril looked out and saw the sheriff's car was still there, waiting to see if she got on the bus so that his 'obligation' to the citizens of this small town was discharged. She suspected he was afraid she would stay and expose him for the lecherous fool he was, a drinking buddy of her fathers, who hadn't protected her from his abuse. The many scars on her soul she laid firmly at her father's feet, but that man outside waiting in the sheriff's car could have prevented some of them after her mother's death.

It wasn't her fault that her mother had been poorly after giving birth to a 'girl child' instead of the much-anticipated son and heir. She couldn't have any more children and the blame had been placed solely on Avril, as she had been told over and over throughout her life. Her mother tried to make up for it by shielding her from her father's abuse while she was alive, but he wore her down. He killed her slowly and surely until the shell of the woman blew away in the Oklahoma winds. Her death had been laid firmly at the young Avril's feet, and she was made to feel the abuse that her mother had shielded her from for so long. She was to take over all the duties of running a household. At ten, this was too much for any child. Farm work is tough on a woman at any given time but as a child with no one to teach her, she faltered at every turn. Only her friendship with Ellie had given her hope. Ellie implanted a fierce courage that gave her a will and strength to survive to escape her father's tyranny.

She learned to do her chores quickly and if not perfectly, to hide the flaws so that she would have time to meet Ellie out on the prairie and escape her father's notice for a few minutes every day. She shared all her girlhood dreams with the older girl. With four years separating them, Ellie seemed worldly and wise. She understood what was happening to the smaller, younger girl without being told. She saw the bruises and scratches from the belt she had been given for not finishing her work in a timely manner or not meeting her father's expectations.

Many times, his rage was fueled by liquor and he had no idea of his strength as he yelled at the youngster.

Avril put aside her memories for a moment as she watched the bus come in and one person get off. It looked bigger than the school bus she had ridden for nine years. She bravely got up from the bench and gathered her things, her most cherished possessions, in two bags and a backpack. The rest lay in storage at the Davidsons'. For how long she didn't know, but it couldn't be long as they were charging her for keeping it there. It was their way of profiting from having to 'keep' the minor and not getting enough out of the deal as she had turned eighteen this past week. Had she not been so close to turning eighteen, they would have been appointed her guardians and stolen every dime from her parents' small estate. She slowly approached the bus with her ticket in hand and the driver leapt off to assist her.

"Two bags, miss?" he asked respectfully as he opened the massive storage container underneath the bus. She nodded as he took one bag and gently put it inside the bin before reaching for her second one. He closed the doors behind them. She must have looked worried since he said, "They'll be safe in there." She nodded with a tremulous smile.

"Ticket, please?" he asked, and she hesitated to head for the door of the bus. She handed it to him as she adjusted her overly full backpack on her shoulder. He looked it over, surprised to see the destination, and handed it back to her. "You first," he said politely while indicating towards the stairwell. With a last look over her shoulder at the station and the sheriff car sitting there, she went up the stairs and looked for an empty seat, one where she could watch the container if it were opened up again. All her things were in those bags and she couldn't afford to have them stolen. Sitting down, she put her backpack on the empty seat beside her to discourage anyone from sitting there. She glanced around, taking care not to make eye contact with anyone, and noticed the bus was almost empty. A few people in the back seemed to be traveling together, but most were sitting by themselves like she was. She was close enough to the front to watch for her stuff, and close enough to the driver in case anyone wanted to start something. She watched as he closed the door, sat down, and strapped himself in. She looked for seat belts, but there were none, just like on the school bus. She had often wondered at that. The bus driver had once explained that in the event of an accident, it was so the driver could get the kids out easier. She hoped a bus this large didn't get into accidents. As it pulled away from the depot, she saw the sheriff's car pulling away in the opposite direction with a small cloud of dust blowing up from the tires. She guessed she was no longer Sheriff Worley's concern.

At first, she watched the familiar landscape go by as the bus picked up speed and headed for the interstate. It would take a while as there were several small towns such as hers where it would have to stop.

Sometimes, someone would get on, but not always. Sometimes it was a total waste of time. They had to stop, though, from what she could see. The landscape gradually began to change, and once they were on the interstate it went by rapidly. She gulped. She had never been this far from home and she knew she had to be brave. A lot would change and there was no going back. The hands of fate had been turning for weeks now and she would be brave. She was going on. Ellie would have wanted her to for both of them.

That was the day Avril began to go by her middle name Ellen. To honor her mother who had also been named Ellen, and it was close enough to "Ellie" that it would honor her as well. She gulped, remembering Ellie's sweet face and the plans they had made together. They had just been waiting for her to graduate high school and turn eighteen. They had *so many* plans. Ellie had saved up enough for both of them to start over somewhere else by working at the gas station. The two of them against the world. They had been ready; they were just waiting for the right time.

Her father must have sensed she was getting ready to leave. His drinking had never been worse and his abuse had only increased. He felt he owned her. She was *his* child and she had to do what *he* said. His sense of ownership was truly distorted. Her eighteenth birthday must have bothered him as it came closer, and he started getting meaner, if that were possible. He didn't approve of Ellie May Fredericks or her family – those 'white trash' Fredericks that lived in the mobile home trailer park. They were *better* than anyone living in a trailer park. He had told Ellen often enough to stay away from *her*. The rumors about that girl were positively unnatural. He had laughed when he heard that the tornado had ripped through the trailer park where the Fredericks lived and killed not only Ellie, but many other 'white trash' families. He thought he was better than anyone living in "tornado magnets" as he called mobile homes. He owned a home, he had a farm, and according to himself he was better than anyone in that part of their small town.

Avril had been the one to identify Ellie when the body was found along with her truck. Only her short yet beautiful honey blonde hair with its shaved sides and the designs scored in them gave her away. Avril had run her fingers through it just the night before. Ellie had been caught in the tornado, pulling into the park just as the storm hit. She never had a chance to run to the bunker for residents that was in the center of the park. The terror that she must have felt when the twister sucked up her Chevy must have been horrifying, and her face, now at peace, still had remnants of the dirt and debris that had embedded itself under her skin. The rescue workers that had found her hadn't bothered to clean her up, and Avril had been hard pressed not to throw up at the sight of her beloved best friend mangled by what nature had done to her. She left the temporary morgue after identifying Ellie and headed right for the mobile home park. The mobile home that Ellie had lived in was off its blocks and on its side, but she crawled in anyway, taking one look around to check if anyone had seen her. She knew scavengers would be arrested, but the cleanup crew would be through if she didn't get to Ellie's things first.

She crawled through the debris to find the 'safe place' that Ellie used to hide her money and most treasured things. She found the box after a long search through all the jumble. She was relieved to find the rolls of bills and the various trinkets in the box, and she cried when she found the engagement ring she had known Ellie wanted to give her but was waiting until she was 'legal.' She looked around the room and took a sweatshirt she found, but other than that she left everything as it was and crawled out of the trailer. She was just in time, and she took off when she noticed the other scavengers coming into the park who would be looking for anything they could find and sell. Though they were supposedly looking for bodies, any money or jewelry 'found' would disappear. She hid the box among her own things, hoping to keep it from being discovered by her father.

Owen Christenson didn't care about anything but what he could find in the bottom of a gin bottle. If his friends distilled something a little more than one hundred proof, well, that was fine by him, too. When he saw her after the death of her best friend, he laughed and told her she was better off without that 'trailer trash' and now she could go find a 'real man.' He even offered to find her one. She shuddered in distaste but knew better than to answer. Around her father she was shy, quiet, and respectful, and she attempted to remain as invisible as possible. She kept his house as much as she could and waited for the day when she could leave. She had promised her mother that she would graduate high school, something her mother herself hadn't had the advantage of and regretted her whole life. She wanted to keep from his notice, and the idea of his 'friends,' who looked at her with barely disguised lust made her disgusted. For years, lecherous hands had reached out to her as she fetched beer for them. He never stopped them and never defended her. She had learned to avoid them, for if she ever complained or spilled the beer, her father would berate her. Words were almost worse than the physical beatings, as he harangued her for 'fun' in front of those friends, much to their mutual amusement. Egged on by their silent appreciation of his abuse, he continued his particular style of child rearing.

She watched the telephone poles loop up and down as the sun set and she headed into it. She was heading west – far, far away from the devastation of the two tornadoes that had hit this section of Oklahoma a week before. Ellen couldn't help but wonder if her father would still be

alive if she had woken him when she heard the tornado sirens go off. They had been loud and clear across the prairie, miles from her bedroom. They woke her and she headed to the stairs for shelter. He had been asleep on the couch wearing his wife beater shirt, appropriately named since he had always worn such disgusting things while beating not only his wife, but his daughter as well. He was snoring loudly and she briefly debated waking him, knowing she would be backhanded for bothering him, but also knowing that the sirens were going loud and clear and that they should head for the shelter her grandparents had built. He drooled in his sleep, and his hand came up to rub his crotch before traveling up to rub his nose. She shuddered in disgust at the sight. The sirens grew louder and then fainter, and she realized that they must be spinning around. It was their next circuit that decided it for her, and she headed to the shelter, alone.

It was difficult for her small frame to open the heavy steel door. The wind was blowing so hard she nearly lost her footing as she struggled. She could see the vent spinning around on top of the storm shelter to let in some air to the close quarters. The door was built tough, but she managed to pry it open. The wind caught at it, before she was pulling it shut behind her and bolted it. She was in absolute darkness and she reached for the flashlight kept on the shelf. Something soft brushed against her hand and she didn't know if was a spider web, a mouse, or something more sinister. She squealed in fright at the sensation but determinedly felt for the flashlight through the eternal blackness surrounding her. She wouldn't go down the steps without seeing where she was going. It was a black pit, a void, an absence of any light, and she was frightened. The steel door had shut out the roar of the wind, but the absence of any sound frightened her further. Finally, she found the flashlight. She quickly pulled it to herself and flicked it on. The batteries were old and unused and the beam was feeble. She cursed in her head but stayed silent in case someone could hear her and berate her for her naughty mouth. She shone the flickering beam around and saw another flashlight on the shelf. This one was also weak and unused, but between the two flashlights she felt better. She saw a lantern deeper in the shelter and headed carefully down a set of stairs. The sound of debris hitting the door frightened her and she wondered how long she would have to stay there. She toyed with the idea of going back up to get her father. Remembering how he had laughed at Ellie's death and taken pleasure in devastation on his young daughter's face, she firmly decided that he was on his own. He would punish her in countless ways later, but it was a price she knew she had to pay.

She retrieved the lantern and lit it, noticing that it provided much more light than the weak flashlights. The wind could be heard around the steel door and a little gray through the small window in the door, but nothing she could see beyond an absence of black through it. She looked around the storm cellar. Her grandparents and even her mother had stored things in here, but her father never did. He didn't even use it, only swore that he had to cut around it in the backyard with the lawn mower.

Occasionally she jumped as something fell against the door; she could sense the power of the wind. Suddenly, she remembered she had forgotten Ellie's box in her hiding place. It was all she had, but she'd carelessly left it back in the house. She got up for a moment with the intention of heading back to retrieve it, but a loud crash outside made her halt in her tracks.

❄ CHAPTER THREE ❄

THE AFTER EFFECTS

She must have fallen asleep at some point. The anxiety of hearing the storm, worrying about its outcome, and the noises coming from outside had kept her up for hours. Sleep crept in, exhaustion really, and wrapped her in its blanket of oblivion…for a few hours anyway.

She awoke to the sound of silence – absolute silence. Nothing came from beyond the sturdy door of the storm cellar. She was disoriented for a moment as she looked around and wondered where she was. Then it all came back to her. She looked up at the door and through the small square of the window she saw daylight and a blue sky beyond it. She got up and looked around for the lantern, which must have burned out at some point while she slept. Carefully she put it back where she found it, along with the flashlights, making a mental note to replace the batteries and fill the lantern at some point. She knew if her father found out she had known about these things and not done them, the punishment would be worse. It would be bad anyway; apparently, she must anticipate things like running out of lantern oil or batteries losing their power.

Walking up the stairs, she unbolted the door and pushed on it. It didn't budge. For a fleeting, panicked moment she thought she might be buried alive under debris blown by the storm. She wondered if her father had even bothered to look for her this morning. She glanced through the square of light coming through the window and wondered what time it was. He'd be angry if she had his breakfast late on the table before he could go to work in the fields. He always insisted on hot meals for breakfast and supper.

She pushed against the door again with all her might. She wasn't able to raise it more than a mere few inches, but that encouraged her. She pushed again and could feel the weight of something against the door, holding it down. She kept pushing and resting, pushing and resting, until it got wide enough that she could slip an arm out, then a shoulder. The door was extraordinarily heavy and she felt her strength waning but she was determined. Her continued struggling paid off, and she was able to poke her head out into the daylight. It was then she discovered that a large branch from one of the ancient oaks had come to rest right across the storm cellar door. No wonder it was taking her so much effort to squeeze out from under the door.

She looked around and then it hit her that the yard was devastated. It looked like a battlefield strewn with debris left behind by a bomb. Her father wasn't going to be too thrilled with all this extra work. Where had all that debris come from? She'd seen a movie that had shown an explosion, and that's what this reminded her of; it was as if something had exploded all over the yard. She'd better get started with the cleaning up and soon or he would be furious. She wiggled out the rest of the way, hurting her hip as the door came down on it hard. She pulled her legs through the tight gap and sat there breathing hard from her exertions. It was then that she got up, turned around, and saw it.

The house was nearly gone. It was off its foundations, like the hand of God had taken a finger and pushed it sideways. The second story lay out by the clothesline on the side of the house. The basement was exposed in several areas, but it all leaned precariously.

"Oh my God," she mouthed and then quickly looked around to see if anyone had heard her use the name of God in vain like that.

She realized there was nothing other than the barns and outhouses left standing. Debris was everywhere. The house wasn't quite a pancake, but that was when she remembered her father. She looked back at the house. She couldn't decide for a moment if she should go look for him. Should she go for help first? Had he already gotten out of the house and left her? She glanced towards the shed that held the family truck. It looked worse for wear and boards protruded at odd angles out of the side of the building. They weren't nailed to it, simply stuck in it like needles in a pincushion. She could see the truck inside, nestled behind the door. The windows of the shed were gone but the

truck remained. She was strangely relieved. That meant he might still be around. She was certain he wouldn't have made an effort to look for her.

She looked towards the house again. Cautiously, she walked towards it, stepping over the countless boards and tornado-strewn debris. She glanced again at the barn and wondered where all these boards had come from since their barn still stood. She glanced back at the house; all the boards seemed to be there despite the lean of the house. She skirted a toilet that sat in their backyard. It was rather clean. "*Almost as if it's been sandblasted,*" she thought idly as she walked past it. It even had the tank perfectly intact. She walked closer to the house and peered in where she could. Her bedroom was on the ground floor now, almost where the clothesline had once stood. Wait, no, the clothesline was through her bedroom window. She began to circle the house. The chimney which she had relied on for heat was now splayed out over where the garden had been. Her father didn't see the importance of getting the heating fixed, especially for a girl's room...maybe now he would, she thought. The roof was fairly intact, just a few shingles gone, but it sheltered the second story only, which was now on the ground next to where their house had once stood. Her mother's sewing room was wide open on the other side of the house, the room where she had made all of Avril's clothes until she died was exposed, the dress dummy looking obscenely naked to the elements as it faced the front of the yard. Her parents' bedroom was smashed in on this corner and she could see one of the oak trees had done a thorough job to it. It was missing a branch and she idly wondered if that was the same branch that almost trapped her in the cellar.

She couldn't see the kitchen or the living room where she had last seen her father. She was about to climb into the debris when she heard someone shout from the front and she looked up to see Sheriff Worley and some neighbors drive up in assorted cars and trucks. She could see concerned faces and she had to wonder if they were for her, or for her father who had been well-liked. She knew she wasn't well-liked, as he had convinced them all she was worthless. That she was a nasty little kid with an attitude. No amount of teachers' notes or good grades had convinced anyone otherwise; they believed him because he was their neighbor, friend, or drinking buddy.

"Avril! Where is your father?" Sheriff Worley asked, pulling up his belt. It didn't matter since his beer belly gut hung over it and hid it anyway. He sounded official.

She noted he hadn't asked how she was. He didn't care, anyway, and she pointed sadly inside the house.

"He's in there?" he asked incredulously as stared in horror at the devastation.

She shrugged and headed for it once more, raising her foot to climb onto the wreckage.

"Hey there, let us men folks do it. You don't know how dangerous it might be," he said condescendingly. Some of the neighbors came up to help him search the house.

Avril pulled back and crossed her arms, holding them protectively close to her chest as she watched the men go through the bedrooms. It was easily accessible as every window had been blown out of the house.

"Where was he?" Worley called to her for clarification.

"He was in the living room," she answered in a monotone. There was no expression in her voice. Some would have thought she was in shock. Some may wonder but not many would voice an opinion.

Owen Christenson had been a big blustery man, but well-liked. No one would argue with him when he told them that his daughter was worthless. No one stood up and said those bruises she sported needed looking into when they saw them. The gym teacher at school had sworn she was just a klutzy kid, but only after Owen had visited him when the teacher had mentioned something about her bruises to the Principal. No word was spoken about this redheaded child again.

"It's okay honey, they'll find him." One of the women who had come tried to put her arm across Avril's shoulders.

She maneuvered her torso in a way that caused the arm to fall off. She stood alone and wondered what would happen when he was found. How angry was he going to be that she hadn't woken him? How angry was he going to be that their home was a total loss? He had, after all, gotten it all for free by marrying Ellen Sheehan and taking over her parents' farm. Avril glanced around as the men went further into the house, wondering if they would find him alive, or worse, incapacitated. The thought of taking care of him the rest of her life didn't appeal to her, and she knew she would be judged if she didn't do it right.

The men searched for hours and it grew hotter. Avril ignored the sandwiches that were offered to her but drank the water; she knew that becoming dehydrated was dangerous in the hot winds that blew across Oklahoma.

"Well, honey, you come home with me, and my missus will fix you up right well," Mr. Davidson told her. The sheriff nodded in agreement. They had searched all day and found nothing in the house. The sheriff had looked away as a few of the men pocketed what they found in the debris.

"Yes, that's best. You go along with Mr. Davidson and we'll start looking again at daylight," he said.

Avril looked at him knowingly but agreed in order to avoid the argument she knew would ensue by disagreeing with an adult. She let them manipulate her and make the decisions for her. Mrs. Davidson

was generous, but only because she was going to charge Owen Christenson for the care of his daughter when they found him.

Avril went with Mr. Davidson the next day when they searched the house again.

"Are you sure he was in there?" Sheriff Worley asked for about the fifth time on that second day. He looked terrible, with sweat dripping down from his lobster colored face. It was obviously covered in dust because he left tracks when he wiped the sweat away.

"Yes, sir," she said politely. She and the other women had gathered what valuables they could find as the men ripped apart the house. She noticed some had kept a few things, but she had stolen a few of them back when they weren't looking, packing them away in the trunks and boxes they found. She packed all her clothes in her suitcase, hiding Ellie's box deep inside when she found it. She took everything she could of value to her, and packed her duffels with her most precious items, including her mother's things that she could find and hadn't already been stolen by her father's friends.

"He's not in there," the sheriff concluded by the end of the second day. Those who had participated in the search had to agree. Someone had braved the basement and the precarious tilt of the house to go through the more inaccessible places. He eyed the trunks and boxes she had salvaged and ordered them put in her father's truck and taken to the Davidsons' while they determined what to do with her until her father could be found.

"Honey, I have some bad news for you. Your father's body was found over in the next county," he tried to tell her kindly, but telling a kid that news was much different than telling an adult. Besides, the scrawny redhead unnerved him somehow and he didn't like the feeling. No seventeen-year-old snot-nosed brat of Owen Christenson was going to make *him* uncomfortable.

Avril tried not to look relieved. The days since the tornado had come and gone. She had taken her father's truck and driven it to the house to salvage what she could before the scavengers stole it all. She rented a storage locker to hide it from the Davidsons, and to not let on that she knew they were trying to appropriate all her worldly goods. She'd already overheard that they wanted to take custody of her.

"She'll be eighteen in a few weeks, that ain't gonna work," Mr. Davidson argued with his wife.

"She don't know no better. That farm's worth somethin,'" she argued in return.

"We don't know that Owen's gone," he tried to reason.

Mrs. Davidson snorted. "Owen woulda come roaring into town by now if he weren't."

Avril had determined that she wasn't gonna let them steal from her if she could prevent it. They were all alike, these friends of her father. The sad thing, if he was alive, and it was someone else this had happened to, he would be in it for what he could take too. He wouldn't think it was stealing either. He'd think it was his just desserts, just like his so-called friends were doing. It was a crime of opportunity.

"I don't know that I's should rent you this here storage unit," Carl drawled as he eyed her.

"C'mon Carl, you know I need to put our things somewhere," she cajoled.

"But you're not yet eighteen yet," he pointed out. "It ain't legal."

Avril had thought of hiding the antiques and other things she was finding from the house in the barn, but she knew someone would eventually find it and appropriate it. She needed to save some of the things her mother and grandparents had cherished. Her father's things she didn't care about. "C'mon Carl, pullease," she begged, looking sorrowful.

He spat some tobacco into a can he carried around. It was gross. It smelled, and so did he. But he looked back at the girl and shrugged. No one would look too closely on the contract how old the kid was and he needed the rent. He saw she had the cash money in her hand. He pushed a contract across the counter to her.

Avril sighed in relief as she began to fill it out. At least she could hide things for now. She was sure that the few things at the Davidsons' were already inventoried, and Mrs. Davidson probably had helped herself to them already. The rest of her things at least would be out of sight. "And do me a favor Carl, don't tell nobody that I'm renting from you?" she asked as she finished.

"Nope, I won't say a word," he promised as he finished filling out the paperwork.

Avril soon had a small storage unit and began to fill it from the bed of her father's truck. She was small, but she was strong and sturdy. Hard work had never been a stranger to her, especially on the farm. She filled the unit to the top with dressers, headboards, footboards, boxes, books, and anything else she could find that she wanted. It took her days, and when the Davidsons thought she was just taking off in her father's truck to go have a good cry, she was actually collecting all her worldly possessions and tucking them safely away.

"Yes sir, now what do I do?" she asked Sheriff Worley. He had been watching her rather unenthused reaction to his statement that her daddy was dead.

"Do you know if your Daddy had a will?" he asked. He sincerely doubted it as Owen had been sure he was going to live forever.

"No, sir," she said respectfully. "But Mama did," she added. She had found all of her mother's papers, things she hadn't been allowed to go through before because of her father.

"She did?" he asked, surprised.

"Yes sir, Mr. Mann has them," she confirmed. Mr. Mann was one of the town's only lawyers and Avril had already taken the papers to him in case of this event.

"He does?" he asked stupidly. "He never told me he made up your Ma's will," he said absentmindedly. He was almost sure Owen had said there weren't one so it all had come to him by right of being her husband.

"Yes sir," she said honestly and innocently. She didn't want him to see how much she knew.

"Well I'll be," he said, and rubbed his chin, thinking. Then realizing who he was talking to, he said, "I'll make arrangements for his funeral." He made it sound so magnanimous.

"No, sir, I'll do it," she told him firmly.

He didn't like that, this small redheaded spitfire telling him what to do. No wonder Owen had said she was so much trouble. She didn't respect her elders who knew better. "Now honey, you let me do it, I know your Daddy would want me to," he told her just as firmly.

"No sir, we Christensons take care of our own," she insisted. She knew if she let the Sheriff and his buddies take on the funeral it would be a chance for them all to drink with Owen's estate to footing the bill, and she wasn't having that.

"The little brat!" he thought. He'd let her do it, then, and be done with it. "Now don't forget, you have to be back in school soon. We don't want you truant," he warned her, thinking ahead. He would like that, so that he could tell her what to do and she couldn't do anything about it.

"Yes, sir. I'll be back tomorrow." Now that she had most of her things stored away, she could call the funeral home to make arrangements to have her Daddy buried in the cemetery plot next to Mama.

"You will?" he asked, surprised. What the heck was wrong with this girl that she wasn't weeping and wailing over hearing her daddy was dead like he had expected? She was a most peculiar child. It was unnatural.

"Yes sir," she agreed to get rid of him. She already knew from talking to Mr. Mann what some of her options were.

The funeral was attended by her father's drinking buddies and some family friends who, out of respect for her mother and grandparents, came to console her. They were few though, pathetically few. Owen Christenson had scared off the majority of her family friends over the years. He had isolated Ellen Sheehan from the rest of the world wherever he could, and he had done the same to his only daughter upon her mother's death. Only school had kept him from completely keeping her at home and working her to death. Her free labor had kept him from paying for a housekeeper or cook, much less an extra farm worker.

"What do you mean I don't get to see the will?" Worley asked Mr. Mann, who attended the funeral.

"You don't need to. Ellen Sheehan left everything to her daughter years ago and Owen kept her from it. As a minor, which will change in a few short weeks, she can't do much. But once she is eighteen the whole place is hers, free and clear." Mr. Mann might not be well-liked by some in Oakley, but he hadn't made Ellen Sheehan's will. His former business partner had, and if he had known about it sooner, he would have seen it enforced. Owen had taken full advantage of people's ignorance and shamelessly stolen his daughter's inheritance. Mr. Mann aimed to see that Avril wasn't taken advantage like that again. He also concluded that there were many things kept from him when his partner died, and he had better go through each and every piece of paper in his files. Who knew how many more Avril Christenson's there were out there?

The sheriff knew he could only throw his weight around so much, and while he didn't like the lawyer Mann, he wasn't going to do anything overtly illegal. He huddled with the Davidsons and they came to an agreement, but even then, Avril thwarted them by announcing she had signed the land over to the co-op on Mr. Mann's advice to be rented out to other farmers, and she was going to college and moving out of Oakley. For some, this was a relief, as her continued presence made them uncomfortable. They had contributed to the defrauding of a minor and it didn't set well with them. They had also allowed Owen to abuse her. Avril Christenson was a constant reminder of their own

illegal activities. Many were relieved when Sheriff Worley came back to report that she was on the bus heading west. There were a few who would miss that sprightly little redhead and her bright mind.

K'Anne Meinel

❖ CHAPTER FOUR ❖

MOVING ON

Ellen didn't know why she had chosen Los Angeles, but it was the furthest west she knew of. She did have a vague idea of going on to school; she'd been honest about that idea when she told the Sheriff and the Davidsons. Her grades, which had been useless as far as her father was concerned, had at least allowed her an opening into the college of her choice. She and Ellie had planned to leave that small town and shake off the dust of Oklahoma. Maybe go to Tulsa and start over, and maybe something bigger like New York. Neither appealed to Ellen now without Ellie, so she decided to head west and see what happened there. She was frightened out of her mind as the bus began to enter the smaller towns and cities that made up Los Angeles. There were no breaks in between them and the next town. Instead, town after town became more and more congested as they became city upon city. As the bus pulled into the bus station, she was overwhelmed. There were no green fields or open spaces like there had been in Oklahoma. As far as her eyes could see it was like a vast ocean of houses, businesses, and of course, never ending asphalt. She swallowed nervously as she gathered her things from the bus. Several people eyed her curiously;

she had made no effort to converse with anyone on the trip out. She knew by keeping to herself that she was less vulnerable. She didn't want to give anyone information that they could, or would, use against her. She didn't know anyone in this large city, and she was scared right down to her toes.

Nervously, she made her way to a taxi stand and asked to be taken to the nearest Motel 6. She knew from Mr. Mann that these were usually fairly clean, and while she would have to take safety precautions, she could feel relatively safe until she found something more permanent.

She ate dinner after she stowed her gear in the hotel room. At first, the hotel staff hadn't wanted to rent to a teenager, but she had a credit card that Mr. Mann had helped her acquire, and her driver's license to prove she was a legal adult. The credit card was there in case of emergencies, so she always carried cash on her. She had to be frugal. The rents from her father's land wouldn't be coming in for a while, and the funds he had left in his accounts had been very little. There had been no life insurance. The funeral had cost the bare minimum, but only because she wasn't willing to pay out for the more expensive fripperies that Mrs. Davidson and Sheriff Worley insisted she should have. They had looked at her in horror as she insisted on the basics. He was dead, so why did she need a nickel-plated handhold rail for the casket?

The little money she had left put her on a tight budget. She was used to that, though. Over the years, her father hadn't given her a dime if he could have prevented it. She thought it ironic that now she had all his dimes. Whether he meant for that or not, he hadn't left a will, and Mr. Mann had seen to it that she got around the estate and their death taxes as Owen Christenson hadn't had rights to the Sheehan farm. She owed Mr. Mann a lot, but he assured her that he couldn't do too much; he still had to live there. He never let on his own crush that he had back in the day for Ellen Sheehan. If only she had chosen him, things would have been very different for this little girl of Ellen's.

The next day, Ellen took several city buses to the Los Angeles campus of the University of Southern California and presented herself in the admissions office. After arguing that she needed summer classes and that she wanted to be enrolled for fall, they began her paperwork. She had to authorize them to send for her transcripts from her old high school, but she already had copies of letters of recommendation from her teachers and counselor who had known she would need them. Her new college counselor, who reluctantly saw her, was winding down for the school year, and didn't appreciate this hick from Oklahoma coming in without an appointment and making demands. Actually, Ellen had been very respectful and a bit hesitant, but determined to attend the school. She was still scared, but after a full day of being given too

much information, she at least had a lead on a couple of places she could stay until fall when the dorms opened up.

Ellen managed to get a part-time job while she began some of her summer courses. She also managed to purchase a small motorcycle with a side-car to get her through the Southern Californian traffic. The traffic was like nothing a small-town girl would ever have imagined, but she kept thinking to herself, *"it isn't Oklahoma, it isn't Oklahoma!"*

Ellen made no friends – none at work, and none at school that summer. She sent for her things from the Davidsons and managed to fit them in the small boarding house room that she rented with the meager amount she made at her job. She didn't mind bussing tables or doing dishes, but she competed with people who spoke nothing but Spanish. Although she had seen migrant workers come through Oklahoma and some had even worked on the farm occasionally, these were people who had lived here for generations and still managed to make her feel like *she* was the outsider. Having her things about her, she realized she had no room for them, really. She only sent for them to prevent the Davidsons from keeping them forever and charging her rent for storing them. Her storage unit, though, was still not known about. No one questioned where the furniture and other things had gone from the Christenson farm. Many assumed some of the neighbors had helped themselves, as had the many looters that seemed to show up after such a tragedy.

Ellen kept to herself. She ate alone, frequently dining on Ramen noodles that she bought from a dollar store or on leftovers from the diner. She worked hard at her general studies, knowing she had to get those out of the way before she declared a major. She wasn't sure what she wanted to be. At one time Ellie would have helped her to make that decision. All they had wanted was to get away, to start over together. Now Ellen had to make those plans and make it all happen by herself. She was going to make if it killed her trying.

"Outta the way, outta the way," someone yelled as Ellen found her dorm room. She ducked as someone carrying a large duffel over their head nearly clobbered her with it. Moving day was chaotic and she had more trips to make to empty out her room at the house where she had been renting. Tuition included the dorm room, and while she knew it would be cramped, she had not been prepared for how small and limited it really was.

The room itself couldn't be more than ten feet across. Each side had a bunk bed, and under each bed was a desk and room for maybe a chair. Ellen put her bag down in the small closet by the door on the side she chose. She saw that her roommate wasn't moved in yet. While she had requested a private room, she had been laughed at as she was a 'mere' freshman. They didn't give out private rooms to freshmen. She slowly moved the straps of her two bags off her shoulders and to the floor, sighing with relief from the strain. She hadn't wanted to make three trips; things in the side-car of her motorcycle were not safe to leave out in the open. She threw one of the bags up on the bunk to the right, claiming it for her own. She wondered how she would fit the trunks and boxes she had sent from Oklahoma in the small space under her bunk.

"Hello," a voice said behind her, and she turned to see a striking blonde standing behind her by the door.

"Hello?" she returned, wondering what she wanted.

"I believe this is my room. Are you Avril Christenson?" the girl asked, looking down from her height.

"I go by Ellen, but yes, that's me. You are Blossom?" she asked, trying to keep a straight face at the incongruousness of the name. Who named their child Blossom? This statuesque blonde was so far from a blossom it was even funnier than when she read the name on the form assigning her this room.

"Yep, that's me, hi," she said pleasantly, holding out her hand and coming forward with a perfect smile.

Ellen found herself shaking the hand of the blonde and wondering if she were a cheerleader or something.

"Are you all moved in?" Blossom asked, looking curiously at the bags, one on the bunk, one on the floor.

"No, I have a few things at the boarding house where I've been living, but I'm wondering if they are going to fit," she gestured to the cramped quarters.

"Well I don't mind if you want to stack them up under there. I won't be here much with practice and studies," Blossom answered, and just then someone cleared their throat behind her by the door.

Blossom turned and smiled. "Oh Greg, come on in with those," her voice had changed slightly, and Ellen could hear the coquettish note in her voice that she came to realize later was Blossom's way of getting guys to do things for her.

A large young man came through the doorway hauling a trunk and two bags. The trunk alone looked to be of some weight, but with the bags it made quite a load. "Where do you want these?" he asked, with a dazzling smile of his own.

Seeing these two perfect specimens of humanity made Ellen feel awkward and inadequate. Here she was with her red hair and her freckles, barely coming to the blonde's shoulder.

"Over here will be fine. Thank you, babe," Blossom said, in the same voice. "Hun, I want you to meet my roommate. Av…um…Ellen, this is my boyfriend, Greg. Greg, this is Ellen," she said, in a nice and unaffected voice.

"Hi," Ellen said, and was surprised when Greg shook her hand.

"Where ya from?" he asked, noticing her accent.

"Oklahoma," she answered, and waited for some smart-aleck comment. She'd gotten a few at the restaurant over the summer.

"Cool, we have some great players from Oklahoma this year. Maybe you know them?" he named some guys and Ellen politely shook her head to the negative.

"Well, you will have to come to some games and meet them. They'd love to hear some down-home voices I'm sure," he said.

Ellen could see why Blossom liked the guy. He was genuinely nice and for that alone she found him suspicious.

"I'm a cheerleader," Blossom put in, confirming Ellen's suspicions. "And I hope to make the squad so I can see Greg at the games. You can come and watch with me if I don't make it."

"I'm sure you will," Ellen said generously. She felt out of place already. "I should really go and get the rest of my things," she said to escape.

"Can we help?" Blossom asked.

"Well, I have to go to the boarding house and get them, and I'm sure it will take a couple of trips with my bike."

"You're riding a bicycle?" she asked impressed.

"Um, no. I have a motorcycle and it has a side car," she clarified.

"I have a truck, would that help get it in one trip?" Greg offered.

"I don't wish to impose," Ellen quickly said, she was feeling trapped and not used to someone being nice to her like this.

"It's no bother. We're gonna be roommates and let's hope we can be friends," Blossom put in. Reaching over to the desk for her key, she quickly walked across the small room for Ellen's and handed it to her. "Come on, let's go finish it up for you."

Ellen found herself in between the two of them as they told her they were both from San Diego and they had come to UCLA because Greg got a football scholarship. The fact that it was also an awesome school was a bonus for both of them. Apparently, they had their life already mapped out for them, including marriage and two-point-five children.

With the three of them hoisting the trunks, boxes, and a few odds and ends, they got Greg's truck loaded in no time. Ellen turned in her key to her landlady and they were soon back at the campus.

"You sure you don't mind me storing this crap here?" Ellen drawled, and then remembering her accent she flushed. Red skin on a redhead was not attractive and she knew she got blotchy.

"I'm planning on spending as much time with Greg as I can at his dorm. Our parents insisted we be in different buildings even though this one is co-ed. I don't mind at all. Here, let's put those under here by my desk," Blossom offered, as they carried one of the loads up together.

"What is all this?" Greg finally asked

"It's memories. There was a tornado, and this is almost all that is left of the house I grew up in," Ellen told him, and then flushed. She didn't mention the storage unit or the people stealing from her.

"Oh wow, how'd your folks make out?" he asked. There weren't tornadoes too often in Southern California, so he couldn't relate.

"My Mom died when I was young, but the tornado took my Daddy," she told him without emotion. She didn't want people feeling sorry for her.

"I'm sorry," he said, feeling immediately contrite.

"Don't be," she reassured him, and dropped the subject.

They soon had her stuff in the small room and she placed it as unobtrusively as she could. Without Blossom giving up some of her space it would have been impossible. "Thank you," she said repeatedly to the blonde, and helped her unpack a little after Greg left them.

"He seems nice," Ellen said, to make conversation. Alone with Blossom now, she felt a little intimidated by the good looks and charm of the girl.

"Oh, he is. We've been together for two years. My mom said we should date others in college, but I'm sure he is the one," she gushed. She already had three pictures on her desk of him. One with the two of them, one of him playing football, and one that Ellen was sure was his high school graduation picture. There hadn't been any money for one of her from a professional photographer so the yearbook contained one taken by a school photographer.

They chatted, unpacked, and locked up their room together as they made their way to a mandatory freshman orientation. It was nice to see the admiring looks that Blossom got, but Ellen was amused that they didn't see her at all. A long time later they were released from the hall where the orientation had been held and the same phenomenon happened with people seeing Blossom and not seeing Ellen.

"Want to go for a ride in it?" Ellen asked Blossom, as she showed her the motorcycle.

"Oh no, I'd be much too afraid with all the traffic around here," she protested.

"It's really a lot of fun," she assured her.

"Thanks, I should get to Greg's. He's expecting me," she waved as she walked away.

"Whose bike is that?" a slightly aggressive voice asked from behind her and Ellen jumped a foot.

"It's mine, why?" she returned, in an equally aggressive tone.

"Cause it's friggin' awesome that's why," the guy answered, changing his tone, as he genuinely admired the old bike. Walking around it he studied it from every angle. He started asking a bunch of technical questions and Ellen kept answering, "I don't know," until he finally asked, exasperated, "What do you know?"

She laughed. "I know I got a good deal on the bike. The guy needed to sell it because his wife was having a baby and he needed the cash. I needed a reliable ride around town and it's fun."

"Wait until the rainy season," he warned, as he smiled at her in a friendly way. "I'm Ryan, by the way," he said as he held out a hand.

"Would you like to take a ride?" she offered, and was surprised at her generosity, but he seemed to genuinely like the bike and it didn't hurt to make friends, she hoped. Blossom and Greg had been very friendly and that surprised her too.

"Oh, could I?" he asked almost reverently. "I get shotgun," he said playfully, and she frowned until he indicated the tube sticking up that was meant to carry a machine gun, but now was welded shut.

She laughed and pulled out her keys.

"Do you have helmets?" he asked.

She pulled up the seat and handed him an aviator's helmet. It had the big goggles, and he loved it instantly. She pulled out another one for herself. She had purchased both from a surplus store she had found.

"These are awesome," he said reverently. "And, totally useless if we crash," he added with a laugh.

She joined in the laughter and had to agree. Starting the bike up, she slowly backed it out of the stall she had parked in. Because of the side car, she took up an entire stall. She loved the side car, though, as it allowed her to carry more things when she needed. She had thought of getting a dog and getting him a hat like hers, but children's size, so he could ride in the car with her. But what would she do with a dog while she was in school?

She roared off down the street. The bike was quite loud, but Ryan didn't care. It was fun and he was having a marvelous time. Kids yelled and pointed while others hooted and hollered at the sight of Ryan and Ellen. They made quite a scene. She drove for about a half an hour before Ryan pointed to a coffee shop and indicated they should stop. She'd been about to turn around and head back to the school in a roundabout way, as she had mapped out the school many times and had become familiar with a lot of the streets. She did, however, nod and head for the parking lot before turning off the bike. The silence, such as it was on the busy LA thoroughfare, was mindboggling after the roar of the bike.

"That is one sweet ride," Ryan complimented her on her choice. "How'd you find it?" he asked as he gingerly got out of the side car. He rubbed his aching backside. It wasn't a very comfortable side car, but it *was* fun.

"I worked in this place and overheard two of the guys talking about it, so I asked for the number of the guy who was selling it. He showed me how to drive it and made me promise to let him be my mechanic if I needed repairs. He also made me promise to sell it back to him if I ever had to get rid of it. His wife wasn't as pleased, but it's been fun, and it was a helluva deal," she told him.

"It's sweet," he said, as he opened the door to the diner. They went in.

"Coffee?" the waitress asked them as they sat at the counter.

"I'll just have water," Ellen responded. She found it so odd that in California you had to ask for water for your table, but had been told it was because they were always in a drought. At so many restaurants, patrons often simply didn't drink the water and it was put down the drain. Here, you had to ask for it to conserve water.

"Can't you afford something more?" Ryan asked her thoughtfully.

"I watch my pennies," she assured him. The check from the co-op for her father's crops would be due in about a month and if she could just hold out until then she could budget for the year. The school had helped her apply for federal loans, but she had to pay some of it herself too.

"If you want I can pay…" he began, but she cut him off.

"No, I'm good, really," she assured him, holding her hand up. "I'm just a bit dehydrated," she drawled.

"Where you from?" he asked with a smile, as the waitress brought him a cup of coffee and Ellen the glass of water.

"Oklahoma," she told him, and waited for some teasing.

"That's a bit of a trip," he said.

"Well, where are you all from?" she asked.

"Michigan," he told her with a grin.

"That's an even farther trip," she laughed at him.

"Yep, California is a trip all right." He sugared and creamed his coffee before taking a sip of the hot beverage.

She didn't say anything in response. She wasn't sure she had anything to say. The awkward silence stretched out for a moment between them.

"So, what brings you to Southern California?" he asked, making an effort.

"School," she answered, and then laughed at the incongruity of it.

He laughed with her. "I know that, silly, but why? Are you studying something in particular that only UCLA would offer?"

She shrugged. "I have no idea. I'm not sure what I want to study. For now, I'm taking general courses."

"Good idea. Gives you time to decide."

Making an effort to actually be pleasant, she asked him, "What about you? Why did you choose UCLA?"

"Ah, they have movie studies and other film school courses," he said excitedly.

"You want to be in movies?" she asked surprised.

"No, I want to be behind the camera. I want to direct. I want to say, 'action, cut, print,'" he expanded, gesturing with his hands dramatically. "I also want to do something with computers," he finished almost shamefully.

"Computers?" she asked surprised. "Like what?"

"I have no idea, but you can see the future is computers. Someday I hope to own one!" he said excitedly again.

She laughed imagining the computer that might fit into her whole dorm room. "That would take up a lot of room. You are going to need a big office!"

He shook his head. "No, they have computers they are calling home computers now. Someday, everyone will have one," he told her earnestly.

"Yeah right, and flying cars," she joked remembering B movies she had seen. "What? You think it will be like Star Trek?" she mentioned the popular show from the seventies.

"Did you ever see Star Trek the movie?" he asked her. "It was out in '79!" he enthused.

She shook her head. Seeing a movie with her father being as tight fisted as he was had been a pipe dream. The only movies she saw were on television. She knew of Star Trek from the old black and white TV they had in the living room. She could only watch it, though, when wrestling wasn't on or her father wasn't around. Gawd, how she had hated watching him watch wrestling, like it was real or something!

"I'm sure we can find some theater still showing it somewhere," he told her. "You have got to see it, it's awesome!"

"You really think technology will go that far?" she asked with a tone of skepticism.

"Yeah, someday. I want to be a part of that!"

"And what, film it?" He sounded like a little boy who was so enthused by the idea he had no concept of the reality of what it would take.

"Maybe. I don't know. But meanwhile, I'm in school, so I'll take what classes they offer and see what comes up. Hey, you're almost done with that." He gestured to her water as he slurped at his coffee, trying to finish it rapidly.

"Um yeah, you anxious to get back to school?" she quickly sipped her water, watching him.

"I want to show you something," he told her.

They were soon on their way and he looked at a phone book to find something inside. He directed her to the street. They were quickly in front of a Radio Shack, and they went inside.

"What is this?" she asked, wondering if she had picked up a real weirdo from the school.

"I want to show you something," he repeated, as he opened the door for her.

Inside he directed her to one side of the store where a couple of machines stood on heavy duty platforms. They had keyboards and small television screens. On the side of each of them were two identical slots.

"These are personal computers. They're built by Texas Instruments for Radio Shack," he told her enthusiastically.

"Can I help you?" a salesperson came up to ask them.

"Could you demonstrate these please?" Ryan asked.

He showed them how by putting a flimsy piece of plastic called a floppy disc into the slot on the right of the machine. He called the slot the disc drive, which he could use to play games. Most of them were typed out and he typed rapidly as he played, showing them how the machine worked.

"That's a pretty expensive game piece," Ellen commented quietly to Ryan, as he watched raptly on the screen.

"Yeah but you can also type out reports and things," he said without taking his eyes from the wonderful machine.

"That's a pretty expensive typewriter," she commented again with a grin. It was pretty neat, and it was probably the smallest computer she had seen. Heck, it was the *only* computer she had ever seen outside of television or history books. Some computers she had seen pictures of took up entire rooms, even warehouses!

"Yeah, but technology is coming far and fast and who knows where it will take us?" he said.

"You can even send messages to other computers," the salesman told them. He knew they couldn't afford the two-thousand-dollar machine. They were too young, but it was fun to play on them and show them off.

"But the computer is right there," Ellen reasoned, pointing to the one sitting on the other stand a few feet away.

"I'm talking around the world," the salesman pointed out.

"That sounds expensive," she said wonderingly.

"If you have a phone line, you can dial up on a modem, and send a message to another person on their computer around the world," he told her.

"Uh huh," she said, not understanding a single world of what he said.

"Thank you so much for showing us the computer," Ryan said to the salesman. He hurried Ellen outside.

"That was a neat toy," she told him. "But I've seen advertising for the Commodore 64 and you can play more games on it!"

"That is so much more than a game," he said exasperatedly and shook his head as he put his helmet and goggles on. "You'll see. Computers are the wave of the future!"

K'Anne Meinel

❖ CHAPTER FIVE ❖

LIVING

Over the next year, Ellen found Ryan to be an annoying friend. Despite his behavior, however, she was grateful for his and Blossom's and even Greg's friendship as she navigated her freshman year. It was new, it was exciting, and she even felt homesick, which surprised her. It helped to have her things around. Occasionally she opened the trunk to look at the pictures her mother had treasured. The ones of her growing up brought on the sweetest nostalgia when she saw her mother in happier times.

She had to get the trunks and boxes out of her dorm room, though. She had once found friends of Blossom's and Greg's pawing through them, laughing as their sticky fingers touched her most cherished items. Her anger surprised her and she vowed to never behave like her father again. She knew that anger, that uncontrollable rage, and it frightened her to find she had it within her. They shrugged, apologized, and wrote it off on her being a redhead. The next day Greg and Blossom helped her find a storage locker near the campus where she could store the trunks. They were apologetic, but since she was still angry, all she wanted from them was the use of Greg's truck once again. She had learned to be a minimalist at school.

Ellen couldn't sleep. There was something…she couldn't put her finger on it for the longest time. Then she realized the window to her room was ajar and the wind was blowing. It was a hot wind, too, but the small crack in the window was making it whistle. She didn't realize she had broken out into a sweat until she sat up and felt it pouring off her body. She couldn't allow a noise like that to affect her so. She got up off her bunk and dropped to the floor, swearing as she stubbed her toe on one of her trunks. Limping across the room, she nursed her foot before shutting the window.

"What are you doing?" Blossom asked sleepily, woken by the noise.

"Shutting the window," Ellen whispered back. "Sorry I woke you," she hastily added as she slammed it shut

"It's so hot," the blonde complained, throwing a leg outside her sheets. Her tan was very apparent against the white of the bedding.

"It's these damned winds," Ellen grumbled good-naturedly and turned to make her way back to her bunk, stubbing her toe once again. She swore under her breath.

"It's the Santa Ana's," Blossom informed her, smiling at her swearing. She could hear it and knew quite well what caused it. The room was all out of sorts since they had taken away most of Ellen's things.

"The what?" Ellen asked as she climbed up the ladder.

"They are called Santa Ana's. The winds. They come out of the Santa Ana Mountains and they are usually hot, strong, and go on for weeks," Blossom informed her.

"Great! That's just GREAT!" Ellen thought to herself. She had escaped the Oklahoma winds, the Tornado Alley as it were, only to find hot, strong, Southern California winds! She wondered if she would get ANY sleep as she shook in remembrance and sweated over the heat of the room and her memories.

They kept a fan blowing and the window closed. The air conditioning was on, but it wasn't strong and they both suffered for it. They weren't the only ones, though. Many people suffered allergies from those strong winds. Ellen blamed the winds for her sleeplessness and told anyone who asked about her red-rimmed eyes that she had allergies. They understood – or at least they thought they did.

"Whatcha doin'? Ellen asked as she came unannounced into Ryan's dorm room, chomping on a piece of gum.

"Some highly-intense gaming," he replied absentmindedly as he leaned back and forth over the controllers and avidly stared at the TV screen.

"Ah, I see you have a new boyfriend," she teased.

He looked up with a question in his eyes, missed his shot, and swore. "What are you talking about?"

She glanced at the bottle of lotion on the table near his gaming setup.

Rolling his eyes, he grinned at her humor. It had taken a while for her to start teasing him in return, but he welcomed her humor. "And what are you doing about finding one?" he asked while put down the controller.

She shrugged, not wanting to talk about her own dismal dating life. She changed the subject. "How do you ever get any of your school work done with all the gaming you do?" She glanced at the most intense setup of electronics she had ever seen.

"This is *research*," he assured her with a gesture at his consoles and TV screen. "I need to know what is out there and how it works."

"You realize there aren't a lot of jobs out there as a professional game player?" she asked dryly.

"You realize if I make a computer program or game I could be famous and make bajillions?" he retorted.

"Uh huh," she sounded disbelieving.

"Seriously, I've told you before…" he began.

"I know, I know," she held up her hands in surrender. "Computers are the way of the future," she finished for him. It was a familiar refrain.

❖ CHAPTER SIX ❖

LEARNING LIFE

"Hey sis, what's up?" Ryan plopped down on the couch next to her.

Sighing wearily, she ignored him for a moment, but knew he wouldn't leave until she answered. When she looked, up she saw he was gazing at her with his best puppy dog look. She laughed involuntarily. Sighing again, she answered, "Karl broke up with me, *again*."

Ryan sighed loudly and dramatically. Leaning in, he cuddled up to her shoulder and rubbed his face against it like a cat. "You know, you seem to pick guys who treat you like shit," he commented absently.

"I do *not*," she shot back.

"Far be it from me to argue you with you, but seriously sis, you do," he pointed out.

She thought about his words and started mentally cataloguing the men she had dated over the past couple years. From her psychology classes, she knew she subconsciously chose men who were like her father. As much as she hated that fact, she also knew it was true. Mentally, she was beating herself up.

"Why don't you..." he began, but stopped himself from finishing the question.

"Why don't I, what?" she challenged him, feeling irritable.

He debated asking the question he had been thinking for a long time. She was his best friend and he didn't want to piss her off more than he just had. He sat up and looked her straight in the face and asked, "Why don't you date women?"

She looked at him, surprised. She had been certain her proclivities were well hidden, but apparently not. The anger in her eyes was immediate. She almost spat out a reply and then thought better of it. If Ryan knew, who else knew?

He could see the debate in her expressive eyes. It was a vulnerability he felt privileged to see. Not many people saw this side of her. She kept herself well-hidden for the most part. It was why he didn't understand the attractions to the shits she dated. There was not one she had dated that treated her well. He only knew because he had seen the bruises, both mentally and occasionally physically. He was the only one that she confided in. His eyes reflected compassion and he said gently, "I know, girlfriend, I know."

"How do you know?" she challenged him, not confirming or denying.

"I've known you for years, darlin'," he said, using his favorite southern endearment. The accent she had from Oklahoma was long gone by conscious application, but he couldn't resist teasing her from time to time. "I've seen you try to fit into the white-picket-fence world. Don't you think it's time to embrace your inner woman?"

She braced herself to hear whatever analogies he wanted to share with her.

"Look, it's not for me to say, but I'm your friend. I'm your *best* friend," he said affectionately. He decided against ruffling her hair. Unwelcome affection or touching was not advised. If she didn't ask him in, she didn't want him. "*I know you*," he finished.

She wilted before him in acceptance. "Who else knows?" she asked resigned.

"No one, darlin', I know because I know you," he repeated.

She looked at him, lifeless. "But how?" she asked.

He smiled at her unintentional confirmation. "You only talk about Ellie from back home. No other friends. Her death has affected you. I still think you should talk to someone about the deaths of your parents. Maybe you should talk about Ellie's death, too," he told her kindly.

The pain was immediate in her all-encompassing eyes. They both knew she could tear up in a minute as she thought of Ellie and her untimely death. She swallowed deliberately to help control her emotions.

"Look, babe, you need to deal with it," he gestured exasperatedly. "You need to deal with it all before it deals with you." He'd noticed how she dealt with fights and conflict, either by rising to it and becoming a bit nasty or by shying away from it. It all depended on how loud the people arguing were. He had seen her practically crawl away from a yelling match between two people in the hallway of the dorm. He had also seen her react to a dropped book as though it were a bomb going off.

She nodded thoughtfully, knowing he had her best interests at heart. Swallowing again, she changed the subject. "You have to wait," she said cryptically.

"For you to go to therapy?" he asked confused.

She laughed. "No, before you start your company," she said shaking her head.

Used to her lightning swift changes in thought, he caught on immediately. "But why?" he asked, confused.

"If you start your company before you're out of college, the college will own your work," she said. She reached to the table, slapped a book, then picked it up and tossed it to him.

Catching it, he looked at her incredulously. "You serious?"

She nodded. "I looked it up in the by-laws. I saw something on *L.A. Law* that made me think about it, and when I began to research it, I found out I was right. Look at the Post-it notes."

Opening the booklet, he searched found the yellow notes that tagged the pages she wanted him to read. Rapidly, he read the passages she had used a highlighter pen on. "Shit!" he exhaled. "Shit, shit, *shit*!"

"So, you see, you can't do any more of your work on school computers," she told him seriously.

He looked up and raised an eyebrow in question. "So, what do I do now? I graduate in three months!"

"Me too!" she said sarcastically.

He laughed as she expected him to.

"Look," she said as she took his hands in hers. "Let's both go to graduate school, get our master's degrees, and then see what happens. Meanwhile, we can both refine your plans."

He thought about it for a moment, mulling over the ideas she had proposed. "You'll run the office, and I'll create the product?"

"I'll do more than that," she told him seriously. "I'll market the pants off of it and make us both millionaires."

"Billionaires," he quickly corrected. He smiled toothily at her and pulled her in for an unwanted hug. "And you will get some therapy?" he asked, remembering their earlier conversation.

She nodded her head in agreement.

❖ CHAPTER SEVEN ❖

ADULT TIME

The last few years had flown by. She'd had roommates come and go. Blossom and Greg eventually did marry…and divorce within a year when she caught him cheating. They remained the nicest people to Ellen when they saw her, and she considered them friends. She had made many friends, but few lasted if they got too close or asked too many questions. Ryan was the exception to that, and he learned early on to be patient and wait for her to tell him what he wanted to know. He hoped to lead by example. He was flamboyant, "out there," and very social. Ellen, however, got quieter and quieter as the years went by, and she dated men before trying to date women.

The first woman she actually dated, Lila, had been sweet and kind, and given her the first real kiss that she had enjoyed since Ellie. The men who kissed her treated her badly. They slapped her around both physically and verbally and not one of them had inspired the kind of feelings that Lila did when they kissed. She'd been so loving and so soft, but she scared the hell out of Ellen when she wanted to go further. Sex had scared her. She knew deep down that sex with another woman was a sin. Having sex out of wedlock was one thing, but having sex with a woman…she was convinced it would send her to hell.

"Come on, Ellen! Don't you want to know what it's REALLY like?" sweet Lila pleaded with her. She was so horny that she thought she was going to pop. She had masturbated so much that her dorm roommate had complained about the smell of sex in the air of their small room.

"Of course I do!" she admitted sharply. But she was afraid. So very afraid. She had to admit she was also curious. It wasn't that she was afraid of getting naked with Lila, as Lila was attractive, pert, and provided Ellen with wonderful company. It was the letting go that seemed to be the problem. She enjoyed the kissing; she found she could do that for hours at a time. Heavy petting didn't bother her. She experienced real fear, though, when Lila attempted to get underneath her clothes.

"Look, you like it when I touch you, right?" Lila tried to reason with her.

"Yes," Ellen admitted with a blush. Her freckles had faded as she got older and stayed indoors more. But with the hot California sun, it wasn't easy. The blushes that she experienced weren't so glaring anymore, making the freckles stand out like beacons.

"I want to feel your skin," Lila beseeched her as she petted her through her clothes. It was when she tried to slip her hand under them that Ellen twisted away and grabbed her hands to stop her.

"You do feel my skin," she argued, knowing it was a weak argument. They held hands, they touched each other's faces, but they couldn't go much further than that except outside their clothes. She sensed Lila's frustration.

"I want to taste you, I want to feel your wetness," Lila said breathily to her in her ear.

Ellen could feel excitement at those words, a tingle that started at her neck and went down her spine. She knew she was wet. She was very wet for this woman, but something stopped her. She felt afraid, confused, and vulnerable at the idea. She turned and kissed Lila, hard. She began to touch her. She began to remove Lila's clothes, pulling off her button-down shirt then kissing her way across her bare chest. Lila, caught in the throes of passion and getting what she wanted, didn't realize how Ellen had begun to manipulate her and take what she was giving so freely. Ellen gently reached into Lila's bra and cupped her breast. She the warmth of it, and it felt perfect in the palm of her hand.

"Mmmmm," Lila moaned.

Ellen could hear the quickness of Lila's breath, the catch in it as she touched her skin. It fascinated her to see these reactions and she wanted to experiment some more. She leaned down to tongue one of the erect nipples.

"Oh gawd," Lila breathed, clutching Ellen's head closer to her chest as she arched into the embrace.

Ellen's hand began to squeeze and tease the other breast as she gently tongued the nipple, pulling it slightly into her mouth. She moved from one to the other and when that wasn't enough she reached around to release Lila's bra. Lila was naked from the waist up. Ellen reached for her jeans and unzipped them, and her hand was soon inside reaching for Lila's panties....

"I believe you have aphenphosmphobia," Lila told Ellen.

"What?" she asked incredulously. She too had taken Psychology 101 and knew of the various phobias. "How can you say that after what we just shared?" She wasn't sure she remembered exactly what that particular phobia was, but she wasn't going to be insulted out of hand.

"Look, I'm not saying I didn't have a good time. I'm just saying, you wouldn't let me return the favor and I think you have a problem," she reasoned.

"So you think, based on one experience with me that I have a fear of intimacy?" she asked, remembering some of the symptoms that someone with aphenphosmphobia had.

Lila nodded. "I mean, it was great and all. But, maybe next time, you should let me do something to you?"

"Next time?" Ellen asked angrily. "Oh hell no. There will be *no* next time," she said with finality and began to walk away.

"Ellen, don't be like that. We can work through this," Lila tried, but Ellen kept walking. She made her mind up that she wasn't going to be abused liked that again and accused of something she wasn't. She had made love to Lila. The fact that she didn't want more wasn't her fault. Maybe it was Lila's. How dare she try to "Psych 101" her? She was so angry and hurt, and it was all Lila's fault!

"So do *you* think you have aphenphosmphobia?" Ryan asked when she told him what had happened.

"Watch it, boyo," she warned as she sorted some of her laundry.

"Was it that bad?" he teased.

"No, it was great. It was wonderful, but then she had to ruin it by analyzing it. Like I'm some Psych project," she finished huffily.

"So, you liked it, but she didn't?"

"No, she liked it. Hell, she loved it. I even got brave enough to go down on her!" she boasted. "And then she had to ruin it by accusing me of having some disorder!" she was angry with how Lila had turned her generosity back on her into something negative.

"Oh yeah? She loved it? How much did she love it? Tell me details." he asked with a leer.

"You're sick, you know that?" she asked. He had accomplished his goal – she was laughing, and she threw a sock at him playfully.

"Hey, I have to know what it's like for you. After all, my sex life isn't that active," he said semi-seriously.

"And whose fault is that? If you didn't spend so much time in the computer lab, maybe you would meet someone other than nerds like yourself. And *what* is with these comic books?" she asked, picking up a couple and holding them up to show him. "Shouldn't you have given them up when you were in, say, junior high?"

"I'll have you know, they are for research." He was trying to sound prissy.

"Uh huh? 'The Incredible Hulk,' 'Superman,' and 'Spiderman' are research?" she jeered.

"Again, I'll have you know that research proves that reading comic books stimulates the brain," he told her authoritatively. "Especially with all the bright colors."

"You just made that up," she laughed. She put the comic books back down on the coffee table and slouched against his couch, forgetting the laundry.

"Yes, but if you weren't so smart you would have bought it," he retorted, proving he had indeed just made it up.

She shook her head with a smile.

"So, you enjoyed it, then?" he asked, referring to their earlier conversation.

She nodded. "I thought I would be too scared to go down on her, but the scents and her reactions really excited me." She looked down at the other sock she was holding – another missile to fire at Ryan if necessary.

"Then what happened?" he asked, knowing that he genuinely cared for this petite and shy redhead. She had only opened up to him bit by bit, and he had had to piece her past together slowly. She was so careful about who she let in, and he had thought Lila was a good distraction for her. It had taken so long for her to get intimate with this girl after dating a few other lesbians.

"Nothing, I went down on her. I made her cum, twice," she smiled triumphantly, as though she had accomplished a real feat. "I held her as she was in the throes. It was wonderful," she reminisced. "I really enjoyed what I did to her."

"What about you?" he asked astutely.

"What about me?" she responded stupidly as she glanced away, hoping he would drop the subject.

"Did you cum?" he raised an eyebrow at the question.

She shook her head.

"So, it wasn't that great for you then," he thought he knew what the problem was.

"No, you don't understand," she answered, looking back up at him. "I made her cum, it was wonderful and great!" she enthused.

"But *you* didn't cum," he pointed out.

"I didn't even take off my clothes," she admitted.

"You didn't take off your clothes?" he nearly scoffed.

She shrugged as though it wasn't any big deal. "It's okay, I didn't need to."

"Maybe that's why she thinks you have a fear of intimacy, you think?"

"Just because I didn't want to get naked does not mean I have a fear of intimacy," she objected.

"Why didn't you get naked with her? You know, skin against skin feels pretty damn good," he pointed out.

She shrugged again. "I just, didn't *want* to, you know?"

"Do you have some horrible disfigurement that you didn't want her to see?" he asked, and then suddenly wondered how much abuse she had suffered at the hands of her father. Had he more than mentally abused her as she ascertained with an occasional slap? He really wished the guy was alive so he could beat the shit outta him for her.

"No," she shook her head.

"Do you have a third nipple?" he asked with a grin to lighten the mood.

"A third what?" she looked up, startled.

"A third nipple," he repeated. "You know, another nipple in the form of a mole or something that you don't want the ladies to see?"

"No, I don't have a third nipple," she insisted almost angrily.

"C'mon, let Uncle Ryan see," he offered. "I'll determine if this third nipple of yours is an eyesore," he told her seriously.

"You want me to take off my top so you can see if I have a third nipple?" she asked incredulously.

"Yes, if you would, please?" he asked, trying to maintain a straight face.

"You know, for someone who purports to be gay, you are a letch," she told him, and threw the last sock which he caught easily.

"Just because I'm gay doesn't mean that I cannot appreciate the female body. Maybe I'm bisexual and really am after your luscious self," he said in the same serious vein.

"Luscious?" she asked with a slight sneer.

"Look at you," he said, really seriously. "In the last couple of years, you have actually grown." He glanced meaningfully at her bust. "You're a hottie now," he told her.

"Bullshit," she replied succinctly.

"No, really. I'm not kidding. If you weren't a lesbian and I weren't a possible bisexual…" She raised an eyebrow at his wording. "Okay, okay, if I weren't *gay*. Then we would have some serious horizontal mambo to discuss."

"Mambo?" she grinned at his phrasing.

"Well, I thought the word was apt. After all, it is like a dance when you are in the throes," he continued.

Remembering how Lila's body had twitched, she had to agree it was like a dance. She herself hadn't experienced it, but she had enjoyed watching Lila, and she had enjoyed what she had caused. Though Lila's anger of not being allowed to return the favor had led to their breakup.

"What is the worst that could happen if you get intimate?" he asked, proving his lightning swift brain could run on several tracks at the same time.

"I'da know," she shrugged, not willing to really discuss it anymore.

"Who knows what good could come of it, eh?" he pointed out.

She shrugged again, feeling uncomfortable, but she knew he had come to the crux of the matter.

"Have you ever given yourself an orgasm?" he asked.

She glanced up at him and nearly started to squirm. She slowly shook her head.

"Then giving her an orgasm must have been enlightening," he nodded at his own analysis of her situation.

She smiled, remembering how she had caused those sensations in Lila, how wet it had made her. She had to go change not only her own panties, but her jeans because she had leaked through. The odor had been intoxicating to her senses. She could feel herself becoming aroused again at the memories.

"Did you at least get aroused, if you didn't come?" he asked hesitantly.

"Oh yes," she smiled again over what she had just remembered.

"Well, that's progress," he told her to let her off the hook. Then he added, "Next girlfriend you should let her touch you there," he glanced at her crotch to emphasize what he was saying.

"Yeah, well…" she shrugged, letting the conversation go.

"Oh wow, you know how to play this?" he asked, surprised. Ellen was always avoiding his video games and comics.

"It's one of the few that I know how to play," she said, embarrassed at being caught playing a Nintendo game.

He watched for a moment and saw she really had some hidden skills. "How'd you know about those hidden mushrooms?" he asked as he sat down on the arm of her chair.

"You aren't the only one with mad thumbs," she indicated as she quickly used the controller to her advantage.

"What else you got here?" he asked her after her man on the screen got a fire ball in the face and bounced up. The familiar music came on that told the player they lost; *da da da da da dum*. "You've got Centipede?" he asked, incredulous and impressed as he went through her cassettes. "Where'd you find that?"

"I have my sources," she hedged, blushing at being caught playing a video game after the hassling she gave him at the arcade.

"So, I bet you really know how to play Space Invaders?" he asked knowingly.

"No, that one isn't one of my favorites," she eyed him touching her Centipede game. "Don't wreck that or I may have to kill you."

"Aha, I bet you are a closeted Pac-man player," he scoffed.

"Nuh uh, that's MS. Pac-man to you," she objected as they bickered over the relative merits of video games.

CHAPTER EIGHT

LEARNING CURVE

Ellen's next girlfriend wasn't as patient as the last few. She picked up where the others had left off, had waited, had been disappointed. Ellen wasn't raped, she was ready to take it to the next step, but Marsh, short for Marsha, wasn't willing to wait, to ease into the experience, and took what she wanted from Ellen and her body. It was a frightening and enlightening experience.

"I don't want…" she began trying to resist but Marsha was stronger, bigger, and more determined.

"Sure, you do," she insisted and continued on, ignoring Ellen's protests.

"I don't think I want to see you again," Ellen told her coldly much later.

"Aw, come on, I know you liked it," Marsh returned hotly.

"How do you know I liked it?" Ellen really wondered at that statement.

"You got wet, didn't you? You moved when I fucked you didn't you?"

Ellen flinched at the crudity of the language and then looked at the soft-butch woman, wondering what she had ever seen in her. "You think because you got me wet, hell, I heard you spit on your fingers," she reminded her. "That I was aroused? That I *liked* it?"

"Some women just need a little help," she insisted, feeling a little insulted.

Ellen looked at the woman and backed away shaking her head. She'd had enough and needed to think about the series of events that led up to this awful sexual encounter.

Later, much later, she realized that while she had been attracted to the soft-butch woman, her aggression had been a major turn-off. It wasn't a generalization as she had met plenty of soft-butch women who attracted her and weren't as aggressive. It was just Marsh, she'd been an asshole. She had taken Ellen's 'no's' and ignored them, kissing her into silence and taking what she wanted. She justified her behavior that femmes said 'no' when they really meant 'yes.' There was no way Ellen ever wanted to be with such a woman again.

By the time Ellen was entering her final year of college, she'd had a couple of girlfriends. Some were sweet and nice, some a little less than that. She learned early on that she needed to stay in control to enjoy herself. Her first orgasm was eye-opening. She loved it, but she didn't understand what exactly had caused it. The girl she had been with wasn't particularly important in her world. It came on and surprised them both. However, they were not meant to be and broke up the following week.

"Why do we have to move to the Santa Clara Valley? Isn't that up by San Francisco?" she asked, confused.

"It's where all the tech firms are heading. It's where we can get a leg up on the competition," Ryan explained.

"But why…" she began again.

Holding his finger across her lips he said, "They nicknamed it Silicon Valley."

She blinked, first at the touch, and then as her agile mind thought about the name. "Silicone? As in that shit they put into boobs?" she asked incredulously.

He shook his head with a laugh. "No, as in silicon chips, it's where they make a lot of tech gadgets for the whole country. Hell, the whole world someday," he expounded excited. Just as quickly as his

excitement rose, it fell. "How are we going to afford all this?" he cried over the lists that Ellen was forcing him to make.

"We need plans, boyo. We need to plan this out carefully," she explained. They both knew they were young and inexperienced and could easily be taken advantage of. Between the two of them, they hoped to create a company to make graphics that would knock people's socks off. They just needed the computers to do it with, but the programs didn't exist yet, much less the computers themselves. "Let's work the summer up there. With our degrees that we'll have in June, we should be able to land some pretty decent jobs. Then, when my payments come in from the co-op, we can do a start up," she told him confidently.

"But don't tell anyone," his enthusiasm returned at her plans.

"I know, dummy, it's why I limited who could see what you had already developed," she told him. She'd been labeled his 'bitch' of a girlfriend and hurt many nerds' feelings with her no-nonsense approach to the files that he had developed. Her advice had been heeded, but only because she was right and Ryan agreed with her. His enthusiasm over his gadgets and ideas had to be reined in and he knew it. He had wanted to brag, but they had to keep it quiet. He let Ellen take the brunt of it. Her insight into marketing and development was brilliant, and he hoped they would be successful with what he had hidden away on the computer they had managed to purchase. They'd stayed away from Macintosh products because they were proprietary about their stuff. IBM and compatible products offered a vast array of possibilities and he had jury-rigged amazing things from it. They also had to stay off the school computers so that they couldn't say they were proprietary to school work and get a piece of the action. Ryan and Ellen both were excited about what they could build if they could just keep it under wraps until the right time.

"Be good," he said.

"Be careful," she responded.

Their graduation, which they both attended, was almost anti-climactic. Ryan's parents refused to travel all the way from Michigan and there was no one else for Ellen, but she did see Blossom and thought she glimpsed Greg waving madly. They were far apart so she couldn't quite be sure. They were there for each other, though. And Ryan's current boyfriend, an obnoxious toad by the name of Jeremy who kept hanging on them both, made it seem it was all about *him*.

"*Now?*" she breathed as they went out to dinner.

"I need to do it carefully," Ryan said under his breath.

"You mean, you wanna get laid one more time before you kick him to the curb," she told him succinctly.

He grinned without remorse and nodded.

She shook her head at him.

The next morning as she packed the last of her things from her dorm room she realized it had been four years since she had moved in with Blossom. Four years of practically being alone as kids came and left and she finally had a private room to herself. Being an upperclassman had its advantages. Rarely did people stay in the dorms for six years, but she had, and Ryan had. In the summers, they had even been allowed to stay as they both took classes so that they had master's degrees in more than one field. They had the knowledge that their professors could impart, they had the degrees that would help them get excellent jobs, but they also had the plans of youth that just might get them ahead in this world, and the enthusiasm that could make it work.

"You about ready?" Ryan asked from the doorway.

She looked up from her musing and nodded.

"You aren't nostalgic for this old place, are you?" he asked as he picked up one of the boxes of books.

"Naw, but I'll miss it, you know," she told him as she too grabbed a box and followed along behind.

"It's been a long six years," he lamented. He was eager to start life. His adopted sister, his best friend, was coming with him and he loved her for it. She accepted him without question.

They got to the parking lot where Ryan had parked their truck, a beat up old Datsun with orange faded paint. It ran, which was the most important thing, but Ellen would miss her motorcycle which she had sold back to the owner who originally sold it to her. He had cried when he got it back two days before. It had been in as good as, if not better, condition than when she bought it from him. He had thought it was gone forever. His son, now six, still couldn't ride in it, but he would have it to look at when he was older and perhaps have it handed down to him, too.

Ryan opened up the camper shell of the Datsun and shoved her box in with his, which were neatly stacked at the front of the bed.

"Will we have enough room for my trunks and things from storage?" Ellen asked, reminding him.

"Sure, there's plenty of room," he assured her.

Together they brought the boxes and suitcases down from her room, one by one, trip by trip. It took a good hour or so and finally the room was clean. Ellen ran the vacuum from their dorm floor over the carpet one last time before locking the door behind her and leaving the key in an envelope.

"Did you turn yours in already?" she asked, gesturing with the envelope.

"Yeah, but my room wasn't nearly as clean as yours," he grinned.

She laughed, shaking her head. He was a neat freak about his electronics. None of the expensive gadgets he had acquired over the years were visible in the back of the truck. All of them were neatly packed in their original containers if he still had them, or carefully packed in the boxes they had purchased the other day for their move. She knew he would protect his toys.

They put the trunks and other boxes from her storage locker into the truck last. It made for a tight fit.

"Do you ever look at this stuff?" he asked as they packed the last of it.

"Yeah, actually I do. Most of this is my mother's stuff, pictures and things that were important to her. Daddy didn't want me to see them, but after he was gone, I went and took what I could that hadn't already been stolen."

"What do you mean, 'stolen?'"

"People loot things after a tornado like that. Not everyone does. But how would you know where to return it if it blew into your yard?"

He looked at her strangely as they got into the pickup; she rarely talked about 'the event' that had changed her life, so these little tidbits were enlightening. He drove her to the admin office and she quickly ran in with her key and got a receipt. "Let's hit the road, Jack," she said brightly.

"Dontcha look back," he returned quickly.

"No more, no more, no more," they sang together as they started out on the six-hour drive north to San Francisco.

The dump they managed to rent was barely affordable on the funds the two of them had saved before their paychecks would begin to come in.

"I can't believe this is Silicon Valley," Ryan said as he looked around at what their meager savings had managed to find them.

"Well, we got to start somewhere," Ellen told him cheerfully as he began to set up his electronics and other toys. "Hopefully it's only temporary," she said prophetically.

The apartment only had the one bedroom, so they flipped a coin and Ellen won. It was a good thing since the living room was taken up by most of Ryan's things anyway, including the computers and other electronics that he assured her would make them their fortune.

"I'm betting on you," she told him sincerely.

"Gawd, this better work," he said, just as sincerely.

They both had jobs in different parts of the valley, so they took turns using public transportation and trading off on the Datsun. It was a real eyesore among the up and coming rich of the valley. Those that didn't live in San Francisco and commute, or even the ones who lived in the expensive houses being built in the valley, all drove expensive cars. The Datsun, parked in the same parking lot as these expensive cars, stuck out like a sore thumb. Someone even had the audacity to suggest to Ryan that he park it down the street so that no one would know that he worked there. Ryan gave him hell for the mere suggestion.

Ryan noticed something about Ellen, though, from living with her constantly. She wouldn't allow the apartment to get cluttered. Dishes had to be washed right away. He later found out through a slip she made that her father would start throwing them if he found them lying about, so she compulsively kept washing them as soon as they were done eating. He tried easing the strain on her by helping, but his own cluttered mind and habits were at constant war with the impulse. Still, he tried to make things easier for his friend.

Occasional forays into the Bay Area, which in its entirety encompassed San Francisco and included the counties around it called Alameda, Contra Costa, Marin, Napa, San Mateo, Santa Clara, Solano, and Sonoma, netted both of them a wide scope of friends. Some even became lovers.

"You're busy, you're an important woman, I understand," Sarah said understandingly.

"Stop it!" Ellen said forcefully, shrugging off the kind hand on her shoulder. "You shouldn't take this crap, you shouldn't put up with my behavior!" she raged.

"But, when you love someone..." she began to beseech her.

"Love? I don't think so," she sneered. She ignored the crushed look on her girlfriend's face and turned away.

"I think you have some sort of phobia, you are pushing me away. But I *know* you, I know you love me," Sarah tried.

Ellen didn't dare look at her or she wouldn't be able to keep her resolve. It was time. She shrugged dismissively and started to walk away.

"Ellen! What about us, what about me...?" she asked in a sad voice.

"Do what you want," she dismissed and shut the door behind her.

This had become a familiar refrain as Ellen tried to navigate the dating field of San Francisco and the surrounding areas of Santa Clara, Oakland, and even Napa. It wasn't fun and it wasn't always nice, but the rising executive in Silicon Valley was attractive and mature, and turned quite a few heads, both male *and* female.

"Wait, wait," Allen called to Ryan as Ryan closed the door in his face.

"Didn't work out?" Ellen asked Ryan sarcastically as she looked at him from her doorway. She'd heard the raised voices and had come to see what was going on.

"Did you see the size of…?" he began but Ellen held up her hand to stop his description and failed. "His feet?" he finished with a grin.

"Uh huh," she answered as she dipped into the bowl of cereal she was munching on.

"Gawd," he said ruefully, his hand coming up to rub his forehead. "Why do I let my eye for beauty blind me to their flaws?"

"That sounds almost poetic," she returned as she chewed around a Rice Chex.

"Or cryptic," he returned with a grin and a sigh. Losing that hunk of beef was too bad; he'd been a beautiful specimen of a man.

"Just be safe," she warned him, she had noticed how big Allen was and he could have beaten the shit out of Ryan without even trying.

"I'm careful," he replied, heading for his faithful computers.

Ellen found the weather in the area to be lovely. The only thing she didn't like were the strong breezes that frequently kicked up every afternoon. When they flowed through San Francisco they would bring the coolness of fog with them – a natural air condition. Inland would be baking under the summer sun. She was grateful that South Bay didn't get as much rain or harsh weather in winter that the North Bay including Santa Rosa and Napa got. She was told by those who would know that Silicon Valley had similar weather patterns to those you would find in parts of Italy, Spain, and even France. That even some of the terrain was similar to Mediterranean climates including many of the same trees, flowers, and bushes. She loved how much citrus she was able to obtain. Other fruit trees grew here prolifically, even olives.

But when the wind would blow, it caused Ellen distress. Particularly hard blasts that caused whistling around windows that weren't completely closed or doors that were ajar could give her a panic attack. She knew why, but she didn't tell anyone. But when the sweats came on from the noise, she frequently found herself angry and upset.

Overall, though, she loved living there. They were close enough to the city of San Francisco for entertainment, and within driving distance of the mountains if they wanted to see snow, get away from work, or even take a hike. She was satisfied with how their plans were coming along even if her partner was a bit impatient.

"I can't wait another year," Ryan whined as they began to put together their budget in anticipation of the co-op checks.

"Patience, my darling, patience," she told him. She too was disappointed, but if they wanted to do this right, to do it well, they had to wait until they had enough money in the bank to launch things. Meanwhile, they had to work and save. Although they were both embarrassed to be seen in the Datsun, they knew it was temporary.

"If you need a car loan, I'm certain the company can automatically take the payments out of your paycheck," Ellen's boss told her confidentially one day.

"No sir, I won't go in debt for a car," she drawled, playing up her Oklahoman accent at times like these. It was completely gone after living in California for over six years, but she knew it would make him think she was a dumb hick or something. But her work showed she was good at what she did and the experience was invaluable. She was learning a lot of what it took to run one of these companies and as this one was so far removed from what Ryan and she wanted to do, she didn't feel guilty that she was using them to launch her own company. Not so with Ryan.

"They almost caught my design before I realized what I had done," he told her as he repeatedly struck his own forehead.

"What were you thinking of?" she gasped as she realized what he had almost given away to his employer. Their future was riding on Ryan's brilliant designs.

"I know, but they haven't got a clue of how to do it and it came so easy to me that I almost spilled the beans on that to point them in another direction."

"So, you give them your design and you set them up to be competitors of us before we even get started?" she asked giving him hell.

"I know, I know, I'm sorry," he whined.

"Just do the job they hired you for and no more," she emphasized.

"I know," he sighed wearily. "It's so hard not to share what I know they are doing wrong," he lamented.

She chuckled at his anxiety. It was hard to do the job they were each hired for and no more than that. They knew a lot of startups failed in this highly competitive valley, the stories about them were legion. They didn't want to start out just to fail. Both firms were good firms. Great, actually. They had given Ryan and Ellen a chance right out of college. In fact, the two were better educated than some at these firms with their master's degrees, but that didn't matter in technology. Ambition and know-how got you a lot further than anything else. It was hard not to show off what they knew, what they learned, what they desired for these people. They had to be patient, though.

❧ CHAPTER NINE ❧

THE STARTUP

"Can a lesbian run a tech company?" one reporter shouted out louder than the others.

"I don't know, can a jackass ask inappropriate questions?" Ellen responded, and the room got deathly quiet for a moment. She raised an eyebrow and skewered him with a look. "Apparently so," she answered her own question with perfect timing and the room erupted in laughter at the reporter's expense before Ellen moved on to the next one.

Upon quitting their respective jobs, Ellen and Ryan had promptly moved into the small building they had rented with the money they had faithfully saved from work and the co-op to pay for rent for the next six months. They had enough to cover rent and operating expenses for a year. Ellen had wanted to save up enough for two, but had been unable to curb Ryan's enthusiasm that long. Already they had hired some of the best tech people to work with them. They were hoping to be ready in time for the Tech World's Fair in Las Vegas right before Thanksgiving. It would reveal the patented and copyrighted technology available from their new company before they even opened their doors. The plans had enabled Ellen to send in for these crucial documents to fight for their rights if anyone challenged them and their ideas. They both knew from the companies they had worked for who the best lawyers were to help them win the fight if it got dirty.

Today, the week before Tech World Fair, they were giving their first press conference. Ellen had felt she was too shy, but she found her voice and she found it well as she explained what they would be showcasing at the Fair. They didn't, of course, show it all. They left the consumers wanting to know more. She knew that other tech companies would be watching and clamoring not only for what they had, but to try and discredit them before they even began. She and Ryan had visited the lawyers in the weeks previously to show them what they had, to put them on retainer, and to get ready for a fight for their lives. The months and years of development were about to pay off and they wanted to be ready for it....

"Oh my GOD, did you see how their heads nearly exploded?" Ryan said as he fell onto the hotel bed in excitement.

"I think, since we are talking about nerds upon nerds, you mean imploded," she answered wryly from her own seat at the desk, and they both started giggling. If the first day of the tech conference was any indication, they were a success. There had already been a couple of annoyances, a cease and desist, but having filed for the copyrights, patents, and having some of the best lawyers available, they had covered most of their bases. They still had to produce results, but so far, everyone was excited at what they had presented. Amazed at what Ryan had developed. The redheaded C.E.O., Ellen Christenson, while young, was one hell of a saleswoman. Ellen and Ryan had immediately faxed all the orders to their offices in case their briefcases were stolen or something equally as dire.

Animated Studios, as they had decided to call their startup tech company, was off to a running start. They needed capital and fast if they were going to keep up with the flurry of orders that were coming in, not only from the United States, but from all over the world.

Ellen tried first locally but the banks didn't trust a startup. She'd been prepared for that. She immediately took the idea to Wall Street and the finance nerds that she and Ryan had befriended back in college, and in no time at all they had interest and financing to expand. Within a year they had to move to larger headquarters to allow for the expansion of their firm. This also meant hiring more staff and the added headaches, which included security.

Over the next couple of years, it was a race to see if they could stay ahead of the competition, who were blatantly trying to copy or at least emulate them. Both Ellen and Ryan as well as their team of loyal employees were relishing the competition and with it, the challenge to come out with bigger, better, and bolder.

"You know, it's amazing the technology that goes into our security," Ellen said as she ripped apart a little box she had found under her desk.

"We should have staff that do nothing but security," Ryan said as he put his feet up. He was amused at Ellen and her disrespect for technology, considering that was how they made their money.

"Um, you didn't notice?" she asked with a cocked eyebrow in his direction. She took out a gadget, one that had been made by Ryan, and ran it over her desk once more, up the sides, and even got down on her hands and knees to run it under the desk.

"Notice what?" he asked as he admired the fine view of her ass in the tight-fitting skirt she was wearing. One of her girlfriends had introduced her to some of the finer stores in San Francisco.

She looked up, hit her head on the edge of her desk as she noticed his ogling, and swore.

"Now, now," he said waggling a finger at her. "Didn't your Mama teach you to be a lady?" he asked as he tried in vain to not laugh.

"I'll mother you," she threatened with a dire look as she rubbed the sore spot on her head.

"Promise?" he asked with a smirk.

She just shook her head. That hurt too and she winced. She continued to scan the room for bugs. She had to wonder how the latest got into her private office.

As Ellen drove to their run-down apartment, she realized that they couldn't live there anymore. First of all, it was a horrible place to live. They both made a lot of money at their company and could afford homes of their own, but they came up with the best ideas and brain-stormed at the oddest hours and living together like this made sense.

"Why don't we just buy two houses, side by side, and have close-circuit TV's so we can talk anytime?" Ryan asked to solve the problem. He too had wanted to move for a while, especially because his dates tended to stay over. Ellen tended to go to her dates' apartments or homes and left before the sun came up. They never saw where she lived. They never saw how she lived.

So that is what they did – they bought two of the newer houses that had sprung up in Santa Clara, near enough to their offices in Silicon Valley that they could drive to work in a short period of time, and far enough from the city that they didn't have to deal with the traffic.

"Are you going to order your stuff from your storage locker?" Ryan asked as he supervised Ellen's decorating 'her' new home. It was identical to his, the houses cookie-cutter buildings to each other.

"I only have..." she started and then remembered what he was referring to. She'd arranged to pay them yearly from the checks she got from the co-op which fluctuated in certain seasons due to the economy and whoever was negotiating rents on the properties. The stuff had been in storage for nearly a decade, and she looked around at the modern home she now owned and realized it didn't belong there. The few things she had hauled around with her since college looked out of place. She shook her head as she remembered the antiques her mother and grandparents had cherished. Now was not the time or the place for the rest of the pieces.

"Why are you looking at real estate ads again?" she asked a few weeks later, coming into Ryan's house without knocking.

"It's good to know the market," he hedged, grinning. You couldn't pull one over on Ellen Christenson. She was too astute, too knowing, and she was an excellent front for their business. Her ideas, which she shared with him, refined with him, were brilliant. He really was enjoying their partnership; she understood him despite his quirks and had since the day they met back in college.

She looked around the house. Most people in their position would have nice paintings on the wall, but instead Ryan had framed posters of comic books or the comic books themselves. Some of them were quite valuable, collector's items really.

"Besides, I was thinking we should get an apartment in the city," he told her as he turned the newspaper backwards so he could show her the ads he had been looking at.

"Why do we need an apartment in the city?" she asked. If he thought they needed an apartment in the city she was on board, but to justify the expense she wanted a reason.

"Well, when we party too hearty wouldn't it be nice to go back to our own place instead of a hotel?" he asked.

Smiling at him, she laughed. They both enjoyed the social life in the city. San Francisco was a mecca for the gay life. There were a few seedy places and they had weeded those out pretty quickly. Instead they headed to higher-end places and now with the firm doing so well they could afford them. "So, where are you looking?" she asked, already on board with the idea. Real estate was a good investment.

He showed her and then added, "We can also put up high-end clients instead of putting them up at The Ritz. They'll have privacy and we can use that as a tax write-off."

"Hey, that's my job," she protested, but agreed as the idea began to really take hold. "When are we going?"

The realtor showed them several places but either Ellen, Ryan, or both rejected them for whatever reason. If one didn't like the place, neither of them would take it. It had to be perfect for both of them and their bickering was amusing to the realtor. "How long have you two been married?" Judy, the realtor asked laughingly at their squabbling. She hadn't recognized their names, not yet, but in a couple of years their names would be very well known not only in this area but the world.

The two of them stopped mid-argument, looked at the realtor, then back at each other, and started to laugh. They didn't correct her assumption and went with her to look at several other available apartments.

The one they finally chose had a beautiful view of San Francisco. High on one of the many hills there, it looked out over the bay, had a view of the Golden Gate, and was near enough to the trolleys that their guests could enjoy playing tourist. The apartment itself was clean in its lines with black marble throughout. Two of the bedrooms were effortlessly furnished with Japanese beds. The third was turned into an office with all the latest technology, suitable for whomever would make use of it. The building was built on a type of industrial spring technology that was supposed to help in case of an earthquake, and it was a big plus with their insurance agency. Strict instructions were left with the management as to who would use the apartment. Only Ellen or Ryan could give permission for a passkey to be given out to a specific guest. The passkeys could not be duplicated. The building itself was not as modern as the apartments in it, but it was in an area that the inside did meet the historic outside and both liked that. It would please and surprise anyone they brought home with them or lent the space out to.

"You should see this," Ryan said with a smirk as he showed her a rectangular box-like thing, half the size of a shoe box.

Ellen slumped her shoulders in defeat. "Don't tell me – you found some gadget to invest all our hard-earned money in?" She looked genuinely worried.

"No, I haven't invested *all* our money," he assured her with a smirk and handed her the gadget.

She looked down at the plastic thing in her hand. Frowning she said, "This looks like my car phone."

"Yeah, without the car," he laughed at her as he answered.

"Cellular phones have been around for like twenty years," she told him prissily.

"Not like that they haven't," he pointed at the box in her hand. "That's the future, making them smaller, portable, and without that bag that you have to carry from your car."

She was intrigued despite herself and she looked at the technology before her. She shook her head as she sat down and examined it closer. "Can we get in on this?" she asked wonderingly.

"I already have," he told her as he began to explain about accessories, towers, and other after-market things that would make them more money than the actual phones.

"So, you are saying the technology is changing so quickly it's actually a better idea to not only invest in the main companies that will be mass-producing these," she hefted the rectangular plastic box for effect. "But, we should invest in this," she indicated the papers that showed a network of lines crisscrossing the United States as well as other countries.

"Diversifying, baby, diversifying," he said as he leaned back on his couch, crossed his hands behind his head, and put his feet up on the coffee table they were sitting before.

She grinned at him. "You are still like a little boy with your toys," she indicated the gadget in her hand.

"Oh yeah, and someday I'll be able to watch my cartoons on it," he assured her.

"Yeah, right, like they will ever get a TV screen that small," she pointed to the digital numbers that were on a screen about half an inch high and about an inch and a half wide.

"Maybe not on that screen, but they'll figure it out," he assured her with a knowing smile. "Games, too," he added for her benefit.

"You'll never get any work done," she assured him as she got up to hand the cellular phone back. She went to leave his office and looked around at the clutter, the various jobs in their various stages of completion. A healthy mess, he had assured her on many occasions. There was a sign posted above his desk, it read: "A clean desk is a sign of a cluttered mind."

"Okay, but if they come out with *Centipede* on one of these things, don't tell me you won't be one of the first to go buy one," he said, hefting the cellular phone and pointing the antennae at her.

"Yeah, right," she grinned, knowing he probably already had the inside track on such a gadget. "So," she turned at the door. "Where's mine?" Her eyebrows raised and indicated the box he was pointing at her.

"Should be on your desk," he said with a grin, knowing she loved the gadgets he found or got first shots at.

She stuck out her tongue at him as she left the office.

"Hey, don't stick that out unless you know how to use it," he called.

She flipped him off good-naturedly, giving him her middle finger before shutting his office door.

"But look, if I do this," he showed her under a microscope that was hooked up to a television screen. "I can get more data into the chip," he droned on until his enthusiasm waned and he looked up to see Ellen with eyes glazed over. "What?" he asked, to snap her out of it.

"Can we commercially sell these?" she asked him pointedly. "Will there be a market for it?"

He sighed in exasperation. "Yes, there will be a market for it, if you would please just get on the paperwork to not only copyright this, but to patent it?"

"I'll get right on that, but I'm going to need your schematics and then I will want to discuss marketing. Can you have working prototypes so we can release it at the con?"

"Working prototypes?" he asked stupidly, and when he saw the light of battle come into her eyes he grinned. "Look at this," he said, as he turned around to a keyboard and put something new on the screen.

Ellen watched in wonder as some of the best animatronics she had ever seen came up on the television. "We need a better screen," she breathed.

"We're working on that too," he told her, and she smiled back at him. That's why they worked so well together. They both knew their jobs and ideas had merit, that they complemented each other. "There's a company in Japan that has…" he started enthusiastically, telling her where they could buy the components and be able to put their own brand on it.

"But really, Ryan, what market will pay to have such fantastic visual effects for cartoons? I miss Bugs Bunny, but I'm not paying big bucks to see him up there," she gestured at the screen where some pretty impressive cartoon graphics were showing.

"It won't be just cartoons. With effects like this, with super-fast micro-conductors and chips that can handle the data, we can create realistic photos and manipulate them," he explained. "At this rate, someday, we might not need real actors in the film industry at all. We can generate them like this," he showed her another clip.

She breathed out through her mouth as she realized the possibilities. "Who knows of this technology?" she asked.

"There are a few people here in the valley working on something similar from what I have heard. Japan has an incredible market for things like this. Get me my patents. Get the copyrights and other legal jargon going. Let's hit the con with a 'WOW' feature," he emphasized with quotation marks in the air. "We are going to have to spin off a division or two with this alone," he said, pointing at the graphics on the screen.

Ellen was already ahead of him on that. She could visualize the brochures, the prospectuses for potential clients. Hollywood, Bollywood, London, Tokyo, Toronto, everyone would sit up and take notice as they realized the aspects of this incredible technology. He was right; they would have to have a division that developed this, and only this. "You realize how much work this is going to take to pull this off in secret?"

He grinned. They both knew about secrets and how hard it was to recruit good people who would keep them. They'd taken a page out of a couple of companies play books and started recruiting at the high school and college levels to people who showed the aptitude to develop the technology they wanted in their company. The results Ellen was being shown were by Ryan's team, but he alone had discovered the final elements that he now showed her. His team didn't even know these final things.

"We are going to need a few clean rooms to develop this technology," he warned her.

"How about another building?" she countered, thinking ahead and planning already.

"With high-tech security," he added as a reminder.

She nodded as she quickly grasped the idea. "And then smaller," she indicated the small chip under the microscope as he grinned and nodded. Smaller was better when you were trying to put more things on less space.

Proving his mind was multi-dimensional, he asked, "Did you look into that prospectus on the new Apple since they rumored that Steve Jobs would be returning?"

She nodded, proving her agile mind was up to his. "Yeah, how much do you want to invest?" She was always willing to follow his lead. He hadn't steered them wrong and as a result they both had reserves to reinvest in their own company and make it grow. They'd already instituted a buyback on the stocks they had to give up when they got their initial investors, and as a result they owned seventy-five percent of their company and the employees, while a few investors owned the other twenty-five.

"Let's call this one Gig-a-Tech," Ryan proposed suddenly, his multi-faceted mind thinking of the possibilities it would infer.

"That's brilliant," she put in. "They will think of 'Giga' as in watts or many, and of course 'Tech' for the technology we will develop," she added, finishing his train of thought.

"Here, that's it exactly," he said as he began to show her again how it would work and what she was looking at.

They discussed their investments and got back to the matter at hand, having multiple conversations at the same time. Had anyone listened to them they would have been confused by their jumping from one subject to the next, but both Ellen and Ryan were used to this and with their longstanding friendship, could keep up. They couldn't, of course, develop all their own technologies that they would need but they knew who and what others were developing that would enhance their own.

Several times during the conversation, Ryan interrupted with a hacking cough. Sometimes it was worse, sometimes it was light.

"Are you going to have that looked into?" Ellen asked pointedly.

"I have. They said it's the air here in the valley. It must be too dry or something," he told her dismissively.

Ellen looked at him sardonically. Silicon Valley had some of the best weather anywhere in the world. It was situated between a desert and the ocean. The temperature swung between that of an arid climate with the more moderate temperatures of the seaside towns. It was sunny most days, and on average, two-hundred days of the year! Even the cooler nights that would get down to the forties had a welcome feel to the air, but never lasted very long. Rarely did the summer temps get above one hundred or equally rare the winters down to freezing. She knew it was a line of bull that Ryan was handing her, but she let it go as they moved on to other subjects.

"So, how is Bill?" she snuck in at one point.

Ryan would get a beatific look on his face at the mention of his boyfriend. "God, he is something," he frequently said in wondrous awe that this amazing man loved him. "You should have someone love you as much as he loves me. When he goes down on me..." he started but Ellen interrupted.

"No, no, no, no, NO," she waved at him to stop. "I don't *need* the details!" she finished with a laugh at her exuberant friend.

"But the way he curls his tongue..." he started again to get a rise out of her, she didn't disappoint.

"La, la, la, la, laaaaa," she said, covering her ears to end that particular conversation.

He laughed at her antics. It was only with him that she allowed her guard to relax and he appreciated it. She was better than the sister he had left behind in Michigan. She was closer, understood him, and didn't judge. She had her own demons to exorcise, and while he had exorcised his in college, she hadn't, not yet. What the world saw when they saw Ellen Christenson was the redheaded bitch that ran a tech company. She was good, she hired good people, but she was cold, ever so cold. She discarded girlfriends like she would old or used clothing. "You know, you could have that too if you wanted," he said quietly.

"I have it now and then," she countered as she fiddled with some of his gadgets in the lab. It was obvious she knew what he was talking about and wasn't comfortable with it.

"But you don't. Your longest relationship lasted what, six months?" he asked knowingly, persistently. "And you have got to stop dating 'the help,'" he finished with a grin.

"That only happened twice and I learned my lesson. I am sure Moira now works for one of our competitors, so now the hiring applications include a non-compete clause," she assured him.

"You think she took trade secrets?" he asked concerned.

She shook her head. "She didn't get them from me if she did. I think she thought she had something, but it wasn't from between my legs," she finished crudely.

He grinned. He was also sad for his friend. She had helped him build this company from day one and her not finding love in the many women she dated saddened him. He shrugged. They were still young and the world was their oyster.

"You did what?" Ellen asked incredulously.

"I invited my sister and her boyfriend. They weren't doing anything that weekend and I know she wouldn't be able to afford such a vacation. I knew you wouldn't mind," she added.

"I wouldn't mind?" she repeated dumbly.

"Well, it's not like you can't afford it…" she began.

Ellen looked at Casey, waiting for her to dig the hole deeper. When Casey didn't squirm over realizing what she had done, Ellen remarked, "I thought that weekend was for us, to get away from the city, to enjoy being together?"

"Well, it is. It's not like the place isn't big enough for several couples…" Casey began.

Ellen held up her hand to silence her current girlfriend. "Just because it's *big enough* for them doesn't mean I *want* them there. We planned that weekend for *us*. It was to be the two of *us*," she stressed, trying to make her point.

"But she can't afford…" she began again with a whine, but Ellen waved her protest aside.

"Then let her find a boyfriend who can afford such weekends."

"It's not like we will even see…"

"I don't care, you should have asked me before you invited her. I invited you because we were dating." At the past tense of her phrasing, Casey began to get a clue.

"It's a huge cabin," she said knowledgeably. They had gone away there before and she'd been impressed. Ellen and Ryan had purchased a cabin in Tahoe. It was a great getaway and a tax write-off for clients they wanted to impress, as they both were fond of saying, "you couldn't go wrong with real estate."

"Yes, and I welcomed you there. I didn't, however, sign up for your sister and her boyfriend."

"They could stay in the other…"

"And I didn't want a romantic weekend away with them," she finished forcefully.

"It's not like they would…"

"But they would. I've met your sister. I've met her obnoxious boyfriend. I'm not footing the bill for them to…"

"It's not like you can't afford it."

Ellen looked at the woman carefully, wondering at her previous attraction. She wondered what she had ever seen in her in the first place. It was obvious that she was only interested in what Ellen could provide to her materially. She was disappointed, once again, in another. "I think it's best, Casey, if we don't see each other anymore," she began.

"You are going to break up with me over our weekend away?" Casey was surprised.

"No, not just over the weekend away. That's just icing on the cake of what is wrong with this relationship. Not once during the course of it have you ever done anything for *me*. You expect me to foot the bill for everything and apparently everyone. It's not like I can't afford to but I'd prefer it to be my choice. Not my obligation."

Casey flushed as she realized Ellen was right. She had used her for what she could get out of her. It hadn't been intentional originally. It was just that Ellen made it so easy, picking up the checks with her platinum or black credit cards, buying her little things to make her happy. It had become a habit. She realized that she taken her for granted and assumed she would continue to buy her things. She had been generous, caring, but not loving. She'd screwed up a good thing and wanted to make amends. "I'm sorry. I will uninvite them then!"

Ellen shook her head in resignation. The woman didn't get it. "You do that and while you are at it, uninvite yourself too. I'm done, Casey." She got up to grab her jacket and glanced around her girlfriend's apartment. This one hadn't lasted but a few months, but enough that she had bought her some nice gifts. Nothing too ostentatious but nice things. She was welcome to keep them, they were only *things*.

"So, you are going to end this – end *us* – over a weekend away?" Casey asked feeling, desperate as she realized what she was losing.

Ellen shrugged. She wasn't that upset. The sex had been good but this wasn't the first time someone had dated her for what she could provide. "Have a nice life, Casey. I wish you well," she told her the familiar refrain. Some took it better than others. She walked out of the apartment and closed the door behind her. She hoped Casey would be one of those who took it well. As the elevator closed and she saw no sign of her now former girlfriend. She hoped it had gone well enough that she wouldn't have to deal with a distraught woman. That had happened once too often over the years. She would inform her secretary to not accept any calls from her. It would just be one on the ever-lengthening list.

❖ CHAPTER TEN ❖

LIFE SUCKS

"**Y**ou can't leave me!" Ellen pleaded with Ryan.

"Well, this time, it's neither of our choices that matter," he laughed, but ended up coughing. He grabbed a handkerchief and they both stared in horror at the blood on it when he was done. "Yeah, well," he shrugged philosophically.

"There has to be a cure. This is the modern age for Christ's sake," she raged. She looked at him sadly. He was skinny. No, he was beyond skinny. He reminded her of a holocaust survivor with his absolute lack of fat or muscle. He was paler than she, and that was saying something since she was a natural redhead.

"Not this time, hun, I screwed the pooch and the pooch bit back," he joked, but elicited absolutely no smile from her.

"What the hell am I going to do without you to spar with?" she asked sorrowfully.

"You are going to go on, you are a survivor and you know it," he told her, but looked very intently into her eyes. "I'm leaving everything to you. Take care of Bill for me, okay?"

"Why not leave it to him?" she was incredulous, as she could only imagine what his estate was worth. She already knew how much she was worth.

"Because he would spend it as fast as he could. I want you to keep him on the insurance and make sure he doesn't have this goddamned disease," he grinned as she cringed at his taking the Lord's name in vain, her words from long ago. She didn't swear like anyone he knew and her upbringing kept her from saying certain things.

"How the hell am I going to keep an actor on the books of a tech company?" she asked, reeling at all she would have to do for Ryan in his final days. She would do it, though.

"We aren't *just* a tech company," he pointed out.

"Yeah, yeah, yeah," she grouched.

"Keep him on as an advisor or something. Ask accounting how it's done so that he is fully insured. We still don't know if he caught this," he indicated himself and his chest with his thumb. "I want him to live in the house as long as he wants to."

"Done," she told him without batting an eye. Whatever he wanted, if it was within her power, it would be done.

"And don't be so serious. Live a little," he told her, while he was busy dictating the terms of her life for her and she was willing to listen.

"Uh huh," she grudged.

"I'm serious, Red. You need to give up the past and start living. Find someone you can love. I did and look how happy he made me!"

"Bill is different. He isn't going to screw you over. Do you know how rare that is?" She was getting annoyed, not only over the conversation they were having, but the incessant beeping of his machines.

"I never screwed you either, despite offers," he joked.

She finally grinned halfheartedly. "Yeah well, maybe it's in the gay-genes you two are spreading around."

"Uh huh, like I made you gay?"

"Well, didn't you? It was your idea I start dating women instead of men!"

"Only because those assholes were beating you up! Both mentally and physically and I didn't want to go to jail!"

"Go to jail?" she frowned.

"Yes, from having to kill one of them!"

She grinned again. "Say, tell me something…"

"Anything," he grinned in return. It was really pathetic on his sunken face with the oxygen piped into his nose.

"Did you and Greg ever hook up?" she asked slyly.

"Greg? Greg who?" he frowned trying to remember all the guys he dated over the years.

"College Greg, the football player? My first roommate's boyfriend. Remember Blossom?" she asked, and smiled as she saw a shadow of pleasure slide over his face for a moment.

He smiled showing the loss of many of his teeth. He nodded silently and then, "Yeah, I did, but I'm certain Blossom didn't mind since I also tried her."

Ellen lost her smile in surprise. "You had them both?"

He nodded and grinned impishly, with the tooth loss it was a caricature of his former smile. "Yeah, those were the days. Ah, college. I was still experimenting with bisexuality then," he said nostalgically.

She slugged him in the shoulder, not hard because his frail body couldn't handle the strain.

"Ow!" he said pretending that it really hurt and rubbing it appreciatively. "What? I was young, I was experimenting. Who knows, if she had taken me seriously I might have been a heterosexual!" he said earnestly.

"You know she caught him with someone, that's why they divorced," she informed him.

"It wasn't me. I only knew him during college, I didn't get her until graduate school," he clarified.

"Oh, my, gawd," she drawled, her accent coming out at this odd moment. He grinned appreciatively.

"You know, I might have been a faithful husband and father if you'd given me a chance," he teased. Only he knew that he might have given up his homosexuality for her, but then knowing how men actually scared her, had scarred her, he knew that he was in the relationship he needed to be, and he had loved Bill.

"Uh huh, you were a man-whore for a while there," she told him honestly in return.

"A man-whore? Who, me?" he asked, horrified. He was smiling, though.

"Who's a man-whore?" Bill came into the hospice room with a big bouquet of flowers.

"Your man here was a man-whore until he fell in love with you," Ellen quickly told him. It lightened the room's atmosphere immediately. She knew Bill would be hurt to find out that Ryan had been with a woman, any woman.

"Oh, he could have been," he responded lightly. He was sure they were teasing each other as they always did. He knew he had nothing to worry about with Ellen. Her girlfriends were legendary; she went through them like water.

"I think you two are ganging up on me. You better go and catch that meeting," he said meaningfully to Ellen with a look.

"My meeting?" she asked, confused for a moment.

"Yes, your *meeting*!" he emphasized and when Bill looked at her and her confusion, he made a jerking motion with his head to indicate she should leave.

"Oh, my *meeting*," she parroted. "Yes, I should be going." She made a great show of looking at her watch, chosen for her by one of her lovers; it was a beautiful Gucci with gold around the bezel. "See you both tomorrow," she said and kissed them each on the cheek as she said her goodbyes.

"I love you, Red," Ryan said, trying to give her an additional squeeze of meaning, but he was just too weak to manage it beyond his feeble attempt.

"Uh huh, that's only because I keep you out of trouble," she sallied with him.

"Be good," he said, and gave her a shove towards the door.

"Be careful," she automatically responded as she looked back once more, but the two men were already looking at each other. The love she saw between them caused a lump in her throat.

❖ CHAPTER ELEVEN ❖

DEATH TAKES ONE OF THE GOOD GUYS

Ryan Mahoney died on a Friday night. No one was in his room as he drifted away. The machines that monitored him told his caregivers of the end of his valiant fight. They hurried in but he had a DNR, a 'Do Not Resuscitate,' order in place, and they could do nothing but note the time and turn off the machines and their annoying alarms. Bill was called, but as his 'brother,' which they all knew was bogus. He was one of Ryan's next of kin. His 'sister' Ellen was called as well and she immediately made arrangements including the call to his real sister and brother back in Michigan.

"God, Ellen, how am I ever going to go on without him?" Bill sobbed on her shoulder.

Ellen sighed, knowing that Ryan would want her to be patient with Bill. She held him awkwardly and patted his shoulder. It wasn't like they hadn't known he was going to die. He'd been in hospice for weeks. He had made up his will well over three years ago when they diagnosed him with the fatal disease, and the plans were in place for his funeral. All Ellen needed to do was enact them. She knew what he wanted, what he planned, and what she could do. Dealing with an overdramatic partner was just part of her duties as his business partner and friend. She'd been his 'sister of another mister' for as long as the two of them had known each other. She felt her own grief, her own loss – what would she do without his sense of humor, his irreverent comments, and his more pointed ones? He knew her. He knew most of her story, and she knew his. No one on Earth knew her better. She remembered one conversation in a flashback as she looked over Bill's shoulder and patted his back.

"I refuse to be a victim again!" she had stated angrily.

"Wait a minute?" he asked astutely. "Again?"

Blushing, she had tried to brush it off, but he persisted. It wasn't often he got these nuggets of information and he wanted to pry while he had the chance.

"My father was an asshole. I refuse to let anyone victimize me again!" she had explained. She went on to cite many of the things her father had done to her, from the hitting, to the berating of her, to the sexual abuse that he allowed from his friends. How she wished him dead, and how it happened. How the tornado had come, and she hadn't warned him. She hadn't even tried.

"I'm never going to love again," Bill spoke, breaking the spell of the conversation she was remembering.

"It's too soon to think like that. Think of the wonderful life you and Ryan had," she told him firmly. She knew he needed a firm hand and hoped she wouldn't strangle him. His needs had always been before Ryan's, or so she thought. He was spoiled. Ryan had been indulgent, and Bill was now bereft of that strength that Ryan had been.

"Did you phone Medusa?" he asked with a sneer.

Ellen laughed as she nodded. "And their brother," she added.

"Oh gawd, Homophobia Central here we come," he lamented.

She chuckled. "C'mon, it won't be that bad," she teased. They both knew it could, and probably would.

"You know they are going to only come to see what they can get out of his will," he said knowingly.

She nodded. "Yes, but Ryan tied that up years ago so no one can do anything about it."

"Do you know what's in it?" he asked, trying to hide the eager note in his voice.

She shook her head. "No, not completely, and you don't have to worry," she reassured him. She wondered what kind of actor Bill was when he couldn't even act like he wasn't eagerly anticipating the windfall that he would receive from Ryan's estate.

"How do you know I don't have to worry?" he pushed, looking at her earnestly. It was the sad look that she knew Ryan would have fallen for.

But she was made of sterner stuff and didn't fall for it as she answered, "I'll make sure you are taken care of, no need to worry." She knew that being vague was the best answer she could give him. He was greedy, but Ryan was so wealthy and so charmed by the performance that he had indulged. The clothes Bill wore, the car he drove, and even the film he was in the process of making, were all financed by Ryan.

"Oh God, I'm all alone," Bill sobbed dramatically, and fell back into Ellen's arms.

She rolled her eyes, but it was for her own benefit since they had no other audience. Bill would be back on his feet in no time at all. He'd find another sugar daddy to support him and take care of him. That was unless he became a sugar daddy for some young stud. He wasn't destitute, but the money Ryan had left for him was held in trust and she was the administrator of that trust. He didn't need to know that until the reading of the will. Ignorance was bliss in this case, and she knew pretending not to know much would keep down the questions. She knew she was a better actor than Bill would ever be. She glanced at him in a mirror beside them; his crocodile tears were fading away as his mind worked on the problem of going on without Ryan. Ellen had often wondered what Ryan saw in him. She knew Bill was a very handsome man, and if not so selfish and childish, he would have made a mint as a model. He had been a minor model of sorts when Ryan spotted him in San Francisco. He had helped him, supported him, and given him a home. Bill, unaccustomed to such luxury, had eaten it up and expected more, ever more. Ryan, with no one to spend his money on, spent it lavishly on his younger lover. Except for the sex, Ellen had often thought of Bill as Ryan's child.

The minister droned on and on and Ellen was starting to feel the effects of the overcrowded church and the heat. The church obviously didn't have an air conditioner and while many of the older buildings in Silicon Valley didn't have or need them, it would have been nice today. She was pleased at the turnout. Ryan would have loved to see his peers, competition, and associates all come to pay their last respects. His body would be cremated after the services and Ellen and Bill would be going out into San Francisco Bay to discretely dispose of the ashes. It was illegal to do that, technically, but no one needed to know. They were supposed to go out three nautical miles from the city, but Ellen knew that Ryan would have wanted his remains scattered in the actual bay and she planned to do just that.

She glanced over across the aisle at Ryan's brother and sister. His brother, Rudy, had greeted her cordially, but his sister, Melody, had been the bitch they all expected her to be. She was playing at being the lady of the manor born, letting everyone and anyone know that *she,* and not Ellen, was Ryan's sister. She wasn't nicknamed Medusa for nothing. Her hair was in knots, a style that didn't become her florid face. The mats that the tangles had become she thought stylish and edgy, instead looked unflattering and dirty. Even in ultra-liberal California people were looking and shaking their heads at the mess, and Ellen had to wonder what people thought of it back in Michigan. She shuddered to think of what might actually live in that mess.

"The service was nice, Ellen, thank you for arranging it," Rudy said pleasantly to her afterwards as she chatted with those from the electronics industry.

"Thank you for coming for it, Rudy. I know Ryan would have liked it," she said nicely. She knew Ryan wouldn't have given a care either way. Their parents had written him off long ago as a queer and fag and for many years he had nothing to do with any of them. It was easier after their parents had passed away, but still there was a tension and Melody didn't help things.

"Where is the reading of the will going to be held?" she asked rudely. Her tone of voice was enough to set anyone's teeth on edge.

"Tomorrow in the lawyers' offices," Ellen replied calmly as she eyed the woman distastefully.

"Why isn't it today? We can't hang around here for days, you know. We have lives back home," she said rudely.

"Because the funeral was held on a weekend. The offices of the attorney are being specially opened for us tomorrow rather than today because they had other plans," Ellen patiently explained. She didn't tell her that the lawyers were here at the service out of respect for their wealthy client.

"Are you coming?" Melody asked.

"Yes, the attorney gave me a list of those named in the will so that I could inform a few of them myself. The rest he informed through his staff."

"I don't see why you have to be there, you were *only* his business partner," she stated.

Ellen didn't reply. She thought it prudent not to say a word, but she eyed the woman with the incongruous name of Melody. It not only didn't fit her, but her voice was definitely not melodic. Her parents must have had high hopes in the child before she became the nightmare she was. Ellen and Ryan had changed it to Medusa long ago because she screeched when she didn't get her way. She had visited once out of 'duty,' under the premise of kissing and making up, but really to get the 'lay of the land,' and met all of Ryan's friends at that time.

"Is *that* going to be there?" Melody asked, pointing towards Bill who was chatting with some of Ryan and his friends.

"Bill? His life-partner? Of course," Ellen answered with relish.

"It ain't natural," Melody pointed out.

"Ryan loved him and Bill loved Ryan. There isn't anything anyone can say to the contrary," Ellen answered with a bit of spirit. Most who knew Ellen Christenson and the light of battle that was in her eye would have subsided to the sidelines and not opened their mouths again...wisely. But Melody wasn't wise.

"He better not get it all. I already spoke to an attorney and as his only legal blood-relatives we should get it," she said snidely.

Stiffly, Ellen replied, "Perhaps he left you something." She would have gone on but was interrupted by the twit.

"Something? He was worth billions! We better get it all!" she said, her voice rising as she used her thumb to point to her brother and include him in it.

Rudy shook his head and made a face to Ellen behind Medusa's back to indicate he was out of it and it was only Melody with this point to make.

"Well, thank you for coming," Ellen said instead of saying what she wanted to say. "I'll see you tomorrow at the lawyer's office."

"Why didn't you get us a hotel?" Medusa asked snidely. "I don't like staying at that house with *it*," she pointed again at Bill, who was sobbing dramatically on someone's shoulder. "It's not like you couldn't afford it and I could have used the spa."

Since she was sorely in need of spa with that hair-don't and could probably use it, Ellen generously offered, "We have a spa through the company. I can call and make arrangements for you if you wish."

"Good, and I'd like one of those big fluffy white robes they have at all the spas," she said authoritatively, as though she knew *all* about it. "Make it two, I can take one home to a friend of mine," she said greedily.

Ellen sighed and nodded. "I'll tell your driver," she said and tried once again to get away.

"And make sure that driver knows who he's working for now," Melody nearly screeched loud enough for the driver, Tony, to hear her from the street. Several heads turned as Ellen made her way hastily away to go speak with the driver. As she walked down the stairs of the church and to the limo that had been chauffeuring around the bereaved brother and sister, she pulled out her phone to call the company spa and warn them of Melody's imminent arrival. She quickly gave Tony his instructions and apologized for anything Melody had said to him.

"No worries, ma'am. You get some good ones, you get some bad ones. I just drive," he smiled showing perfectly white teeth in his African-American face.

Ellen smiled up at him, grateful for his tolerance and familiar face. "Thanks, Tony, I'll make sure you are taken care of," she assured him.

He saluted her as he went to open the car door, having spotted Melody and Rudy approaching the car, not far behind his boss. Ellen quickly went to her own waiting limo to have it drive her to the wake that neither Melody or Rudy had been invited to. She had thought of inviting Rudy but didn't know how she could do so without Melody finding out. The wake was to celebrate Ryan's life – not berate it – and Melody would not be welcome there amongst Ryan's true friends and family.

CHAPTER TWELVE

THE WILL

The reading of the will was a nightmare. Melody kept interrupting to ask impertinent questions, to ask for clarifications of certain points, and to generally make a nuisance of herself. Since it was a videotaped will the lawyer repeatedly had to stop the tape to answer her.

"I, Ryan Mahoney, being of sound mind," he began with a self-depreciating little smile and then an outright laugh. "Okay, we all know I've always been a little crazy. All the legalities can be covered in the actual will," he dismissed as he waved a document to the camera. "Basically, it's this. I leave it all to my sister," they all held their breath and glanced at Melody who began to puff up in greedy pride tinged with a bit of surprise, but the video went on. "...Ellen Christenson. The only 'true' sister I have ever had. The only one who actually understood me, got me, and could really understand what this crazy business we have here is all about," he smiled sadly into the camera. "Except for a few trusts I have arranged," he indicated what looked like legal paperwork in his hands. Grabbing his glasses, he read the first one, "To Bill Cartland, I leave the sum of ten million dollars in a trust to be administered by Ellen Christenson as she sees fit, I also leave the right of usage of my two homes, both here in the valley and in the city for his use." He looked up into the camera. "That's tenancy for life Bill, you have a place to stay and Ellen will take care of the taxes, but you," he pointed at the camera. "Have to keep them clean!" he waggled a finger and Bill nodded as though Ryan was talking to him directly.

Switching to another two documents he held up and continued, "I further leave the sum of ten million dollars to my biological sister Melody and my biological brother Rudy to be also held in trust and administered by Ellen Christenson as she sees fit." He looked up into the camera. "Try not to strangle anyone, eh Ellen?" he asked with a grin.

"This is an outrage," Melody huffed arrogantly. "I'll sue!" she swore.

But the video went on as though she hadn't spoken, and as though Ryan had heard her. "You can sue," he shrugged looking directly into the camera. "It won't hold up in court, of course. But you can try," he smiled his smirk. "This is what will happen, though, you will lose it all. The money, the prestige, and the anonymity." It was almost as though he could see through the camera to his sister as he explained. "It is written in my will that you will get *nothing*," he stressed. "If you contest my wishes, my *will*," he smirked again at the double meaning of the word, knowing he had his sister in a bind. "Furthermore, the terms of the will shall become public." He leaned forward towards the camera to emphasize the fatal blow. "Everyone will know Mel, *everyone* will know you lost millions and not the billions you probably bragged you were inheriting," he halted for a moment to let that sink in to his greedy sister. He sat back in the chair. "Everyone will know that I detested you, and you calling me a *faggot*," he spat out the word distastefully. Ellen flinched in her chair as she listened, but she watched Melody out of the corner of her eye. Melody was even more uncomfortable because she couldn't respond, she couldn't argue, she couldn't do anything but take it. "Which you thought didn't get back to me, I know," he grinned wryly. "But I still have friends back there. I still have people who have heard of you and your views," he said with a sneer. "You will have no power. You will live off the interest only, and then your kids will inherit it upon your death. You will have achieved nothing. You will get *nothing* more," he finished with relish, almost as though he could see how humiliated his sister actually was. "You will have to learn to adjust your expectations, Mel, and while I know you aren't stupid, you will imply to everyone you inherited *all*

my money. We both know you won't let this small sum of money slip through your greedy little fingers, now, don't we?"

He went on to address a few other things he wanted done, including a private video he held up for Ellen to view later, when everyone else had gone. Both Melody and Rudy looked at the video as it sat on lawyer's desk. Ellen could see the greed in Melody's eyes; she wanted to know what was in it.

Ryan had a few smaller things he bequeathed to longtime friends as well as a few employees he wanted to generously bestow the funds upon. It didn't take long, the video, but then they had the actual reading of the will and Melody became her obnoxious self once again.

❊ CHAPTER THIRTEEN ❊

WHERE THERE'S A WILL THERE'S A WAY

"Hey, babe," Ryan began the private tape to Ellen.

"I know you would want to argue with me so I'm putting it on tape so you know my personal wishes," he said with a familiar grin.

Ellen glared at the screen. He *knew*, he knew exactly what he had done to her.

"We'd have talked about all this," his hands spread out over the paperwork on the desk he was sitting behind. She could only guess it had been videotaped at the offices of their attorneys.

He began to tell her how much she had meant to him. It choked her up. He also admonished her for not living her life to the ideals she had often touted to him. She wasn't the girl who had been caught up in the drama of her father's making anymore. She needed to grow up and grab life by the horns. He knew she had it in her. He had the utmost faith in her. She had to get therapy, though. If she didn't, his shares would be given to the homeless shelters of San Francisco.

"And you know what a paperwork nightmare that will be," he grinned as he said it but she didn't doubt it would be enforced if she didn't go into therapy. He had been after her for years to do it and she had repeatedly promised, but life had a habit of getting in the way and she'd been busy. Or that's what she told herself over time. She knew she needed help, and without Ryan there as her friend, her *best* friend, she wasn't sure she could do this all by herself.

He detailed his wishes regarding the trusts, not only for Bill, but for his brother and sister. "I'm sorry to saddle you with Medusa, babe, but that's the way it goes. Maybe the attorneys can work out something so your interactions with her are minimal." He gave her a sad look.

"There's one more thing," he looked uncomfortable as he looked up into the camera. "I know I never kept anything from you. But, this one thing came up a couple of years ago and I didn't know how to tell you."

Ellen's heart was in her throat wondering what it was he had to tell her, and her hand reached for the remote control to fast forward the tape. The look on his face was actually frightening her.

"You are probably worrying about the possibilities," he laughed. "It's nothing bad, babe, I assure you. It's actually something good. Something I did all on my own. I need you to take care of it for me, though." He paused as he thought of how to tell her, his best friend, his confidant, his sister-of-another-mother. "I have a daughter, Ellen," he said quietly.

Ellen waited for the punchline of his joke but it didn't come. She blinked as she waited for him to continue. He couldn't possibly…she would have known!

"It happened in college, actually," he continued. "You remember Blossom, right?" he asked, and almost as though he could see her, he waited for her nod.

"Well, you do remember me telling you once that we hooked up?" Again, as though he could see her he waited for her nod.

"Well, I also hooked up with Greg," he grinned, showing the old spark of humor that she well remembered. He looked well in this video, and she absentmindedly wondered when it had been filmed. His will, she knew was old enough that Medusa couldn't win if it was contested. He'd been of sound mind.

"Anyway, that all aside. That time Blossom and I shared…" he looked down, almost ashamed at what he was willing to admit. "Resulted in a daughter." He looked up, as though to see her reaction. "I didn't know though, I swear I didn't until she came to me a few years ago. She was really finding it hard to make ends meet. She wanted me to have a relationship with her." Here he paused again and she saw a beatific and unrecognizable smile come on his face. "She's beautiful El, she really is. She's got Blossom's beauty and my brains, that's a helluva combination," he said modestly. "She's ready to come work for the firm," he bragged. "Don't you let her, though!" he said emphatically. "I want her to travel, see the world, go to school and enjoy life until she settles down. You'll like her, El, she's fantastic."

Ellen shook her head listening to her best friend confess to something that she had had no idea of. She'd never suspected. She knew that Bill had once spoken to Ryan about having children, but her good friend had laughed himself silly at the thought of either of their changing diapers. Even adopting older children hadn't appealed. To hear him talk about a daughter, and one that had to be in her teens, was a complete surprise to her.

"You'll appreciate this El, her name is Iris," he said with a grin into the camera. He knew her beliefs on the California names that came out of some people's mouths. Blossom had been a nice gal. She'd been caught in a weak moment and allowed Ryan a night of passion, unprotected sex that had garnered them both a terrific young woman by the name of Iris who also happened to be his only daughter.

"I left her a healthy trust, administered by you, El. I hope I've not asked too much of you but I know you'll take care of her. When she's old enough to take care of herself you can let Rudy know about her but then that means Medusa will know too, so be prepared for that uproar. We all know that Rudy can't keep a secret to save his life and I don't want Iris exposed to that until she can handle it. They'd go after her share if they could and I want to prevent that. The rest though is all yours, my friend. You deserve it." He smiled sadly into the camera.

"I left something for you at the cryobank too, babe." He held up his hand. "No, not my luscious self on ice, you already know that if you are watching this." Ellen nearly laughed because he knew her so well. "I left some of me, my essence, for your exclusive use. It's been tested, each vial. So we know it's bug free." He smiled with a self-depreciating smile acknowledging the disease that had killed him. "Someday I hope you find someone and that the two of you want kids. I know male-patterned baldness runs in my family so you might not wanna use my fine self but it's there indefinitely. If you don't use it, if you decide not to procreate, I want you to donate it. My brilliance should be passed on. Iris might not be enough," he laughed at his own joke. Then he leaned in and said seriously, "Go out there, El, find her, find *you*. Enough already. Delegate. Please enjoy life before it's too late." With that he pressed something.

Ellen watched until it faded to black and sat there in shock over what she had learned. Ryan had a daughter! He wanted her to have children someday. She was the least likely to ever have a child, she didn't want to pass on the corrupted genes that had spawned her father, and the chances that she would pass them on were there. She stared at the TV screen for a long time before she hit rewind and replayed the tape.

❖ CHAPTER FOURTEEN ❖

MOVING ON

Ellen and Bill took the cremated remains out onto the boat and discretely disposed of them as they had planned. Bill got dramatic, but Ellen managed to calm him and his vapors. She took him to the apartment in the city and they looked around. He took a couple of keepsakes, but overall the place was left as Ryan and she had left it, as a place to escape to when they were in town. Cold, sterile, and expensive. It wasn't a warm or homey place to live, and since neither had lived there for any length of time it wasn't hard to leave.

When Ellen opened the garage door at Ryan's, at the house he had purchased across from their original side-by-sides, she shook her head over the Maserati sitting there. For a moment, she flashed back to the Chevelle that Ryan had driven all the way from Michigan back in 1979. Comparing it to the car before her she grinned ruefully. It wasn't her style – she drove a Toyota Corolla – but as she eased the expensive sports car out of the garage and drove it off to the freeway she felt the power, the expense, and the admiring looks she got. She smiled, realizing she could get used to this. She hadn't needed the show of ostentation or the wealth that obviously went with it, but she knew

Ryan had needed his toys and the more expensive ones were perfect for his frame of mind.   She donated her Corolla to a charity as a tax write-off the next day and took the Maserati home with her.

That next week, Ellen hired a couple of people to help with Ryan's teams. His energy would be missed. She had already promoted several members of the existing team to continue with the development of his work and ideas. They sat in when she interviewed or hired people to complete the teams. She also began to sit in on meetings that she normally would have missed, trusting her business partner to represent them well. Eventually she would have to trust them to hire their own people.

At one meeting she had never attended before, she found that no one realized who she was at first.

"Honey, can you grab me a coffee?" someone asked of her as she walked in the conference room.

Startled, Ellen looked at him, put down her leather portfolio, and headed over to make him a coffee. Carefully she handed it to him, but perhaps she was too careful, or he was a bit clumsy, either way it landed in his lap. He jumped up with a roar of outrage.

"Oh, I'm soooo, sorry," she said insincerely as she looked at the mess she had created. She had dropped two ice cubes into the hot beverage so she knew his outrage wasn't from the heat of his crotch.

"You bitch!" he returned as he grabbed the napkins out of her hand and began wiping at the front of his pants.

"Yes, and you'd be smart to remember that," the redhead said to him with a now steely eyed look. He gulped and then realized who she must be as she returned back to her things and sat down at the head of the table for the meeting. Embarrassed, he grabbed his things and left the meeting.

Later, Ellen was waiting for another meeting to finish and behind a partition she heard two women talking.

"Yeah, she's hot," one of them was saying. Ellen smiled, leaning back and viewing the ongoing meeting through a glass window. It was tinted but she could still see the figures behind it finishing up their meeting.

"Too bad, really," the other one replied.

"Too bad?"

"Yeah, she'd be hotter if she wasn't such a bitch," was said with a laugh and the other one joined in.

"She fired a couple of women here at the company," was confided, with a whisper that Ellen had to strain to catch. She was surprised at herself for listening to such gossip.

"Are you sure she fired them?"

Silence. And then, "Apparently, they made the mistake of *dating* her," was said with such relish Ellen had to wonder *who* they were talking about.

"Isn't that discrimination or something?" Ellen nodded, yes if they were fired for getting involved with a superior who got them fired, that would be a big thing.

"Yes, but do you think they were fired for dating her or for something made-up?"

"Yeah, they'd have to prove it and she has enough money to hire the big lawyers who would protect her reputation," she spoke with such conviction; Ellen had to wonder who it was. Not only who they were talking about but the woman speaking.

"Love them and leave them eh?"

"Still, if I were a lesbian I'd date her," was said with a giggle.

Another giggle was returned and then, "Yeah but that red hair, you have to wonder how hot the fires get," a pause as though she nudged her friend and then, "Sometimes they don't match, the fire above, ya know?"

The two women talking exchanged hearty giggles over that, trying to keep it low with the partitions between the cubicles. Ellen wondered at the redhead remark. Trying to think of her executives who had red hair, were female, and were lesbians narrowed it down to…her. Were they talking about her?

Just then she noticed the other meeting was over and she walked confidently forward as others began to converge on the meeting room. "Hello, Ellen," she was greeted time and again as people took their places. The last two to enter the room were two women and Ellen couldn't help but wonder if they were the two she had just overheard. Neither of the women would be her type to date anyway, but she didn't like the feeling she had that people were speculating about her. These couldn't be the only two. Their telltale blushes made her certain that she had been the subject of their earlier conversations, but she remained a consummate professional as she went over plans that she had for this division of the company.

❖ CHAPTER FIFTEEN ❖

THE THERAPIST

"I hate it when people tell me I have to 'get over it,'" Ellen practically yelled as she made the quotation marks with her fingers. "It's not like they have ever gone through it! Every day for my entire life he put me down some way or yelled at me for something he thought I didn't do, or how I did it." She looked at the therapist with nearly crazed eyes. "You know when I was the most suspicious?" she asked and waited for the answer. Her chest was heaving from her exertions.

"When he drank?" Nancy asked astutely.

"No, when he was *nice*," she explained with devastating finality as she leaned back in exhaustion from bringing this shit out. To a stranger. A complete stranger. But she knew she needed help, professional help or she was going to lose her sanity *and* her inheritance.

"So, do you think your resentment was because of his drinking or his behavior?" she asked, trying to remain professional, but some of the stories that Ellen had told her were disturbing.

"I think my resentment stems from his blaming me for my mother's death. For me having to do all the work in the house at a young age, even though I wasn't ready for it. His anger and put-downs..." she continued on for a long time. She vented until she was exhausted. It helped just to exorcise it from her soul. She'd let slip to a few of her friends over the years, even an occasional lover, how horrific her childhood had been, but never had she told anyone the full extent of the abuse, not even Ryan, although he had suspected.

"Work is always there for you. It doesn't let you down like *people*." That statement told the therapist a lot about her patient. She was a workaholic. That was obvious. She had this driving need to succeed and her reputation as a first-class bitch was well established. Nancy felt that her business acumen, which Ellen stated was due to Ryan's brilliance, was down to Ellen's own innate skills and genius. There was no doubt in her mind that her patient was brilliant but tended to give too much credit to others instead of owning it herself.

"Yeah, I hadn't done the dishes fast enough and I was sitting on the couch and he started yelling at me. I should have known," she shook her head in remembrance as they talked another session through.

"What should you have known?"

"That he had been drinking. I couldn't smell it on his breath but he was acting the part."

"Did he hit you?"

Ellen nodded as she flashed back to the scene. It had been bad. He couldn't seem to stop himself that time. She had been curled up in a ball to protect herself from his blows. Her legs cramped and lashed out beyond her control. They caught him squarely in the 'bread basket,' knocking his breath out of him. He staggered across the living room and hit the wall. They were both surprised, stunned really. Ellen recovered first and got up and ran from the room. Swearing, he ran after her, but she was too quick. She hid very well until he sobered up and 'forgot' the incident.

"And how did it make *you* feel to actually strike back?" Nancy asked.

"I hated it," Ellen replied to Nancy's surprise.

"It didn't make you feel better that you protected yourself?"

She shook her head. "I felt like I was stooping to his level. It was an accident, my legs cramped. It didn't make me feel better at all."

Nancy nodded in understanding. "He didn't recall the incident?"

Ellen shook her perfectly coiffured head. Her telling of these incidents was in direct contrast to the expensive business suit she was wearing. The child she had been was long gone. "He took revenge in other ways but that was just because he was mean, not because he remembered."

This story and many others like it concerned Nancy, but from what she could see, Ellen was a true survivor. She just needed to trust again and that would be difficult.

"But why do you think his friends and even this Sheriff..." she paused as she consulted her notes, "...Worley, didn't help you if they knew of the abuse?"

"Because then they would have had to take responsibility for their own inaction. They refused to see it because their 'friend,'" she made the quotation marks again, "Owen, was their drinking buddy, their bowling buddy, their pal. He wasn't much different than they were, and they didn't want to see their own imperfections so they ignored what they didn't want to see."

And the questions and deepening emotions went on and on, week after week, and at first Ellen was certain it wasn't working, that it was a waste of her time to see the therapist. After all, she told Ryan the same stories and he hadn't heard as much as Nancy and given her better advice. Then at some point, it all changed. She realized she was angry. She was angry at her mother for dying. She was angry at being blamed for it all. She was angry at being demeaned, humiliated, and potentially molested by her father and his friends. The abuse made her angry and she exorcised it all in these sessions with Nancy. Nancy became a healing balm as Ellen realized how much she had bottled up over the years. Nancy didn't judge her, she merely questioned her and helped her vent. Nancy didn't suggest things that would fix the problems. She let Ellen come to them on her own. Their discussions were insightful, thoughtful, and Ellen could feel a weight lifting off her shoulders.

"Do you think all of that is why you are unable to have a successful relationship?" Nancy asked her one day.

Ellen was angry at first over the question. It proved she had spoken too freely to Nancy. That she had opened up too much and given away too much information about herself. Nancy nailed it, though. She hadn't been able to give herself to others as much as she wanted. It was why all the problems that she saw or created in her own mind kept her from trusting them fully. They couldn't understand what she had gone through. They weren't allowed to know the 'real' Avril Ellen Christenson. She'd kept many of them at bay through her lightning quick wit or her sharp tongue. Arm's length was as close as any could get if they did try to get closer, tried to get deeper.

Taking personal responsibility for her adult relationships was a difficult task. At first, she wanted to blame everyone else, to blame her father for his inability to get past the booze and to get past the blame game. To even blame her beloved mother for leaving her with that monster. Yes, it had been a difficult childhood. Yes, he had been a terrible father; he should not have had children in her opinion. She wouldn't be here or been there for him to abuse if he hadn't been responsible for her conception. Since his death, which she had to admit she had contributed to, she had had to step up to the plate and own the fact that she had treated most people badly. She also had to accept that her actions and her ability to make the women who had come into her life feel so bad simply because they tried so hard to love her and receive her love in return was something she *had* to overcome.

As she came to realize how much she had blown away over the years and how many she had blown off, she began to reconcile in her own mind how she might have done it differently. That gaping hole her mother had left in her heart began to heal. She forgave her father for his weaknesses. She didn't forget, she merely forgave him for her own soul, so it too could begin to heal.

Once she forgave herself, she called many of her old girlfriends for whom she still had phone numbers and apologized for how she had treated them.

"What is this? Some kind of joke?"

"Are you in some twelve-step program?"

"You're kidding, right?"

The questions continued as she tried to make amends. They didn't believe her, but then Rae answered the phone.

"Hello?" her sweet-sounding voice came through the line.

"Hello Rae, it's Ellen," she said quietly. She crossed her fingers that Rae wouldn't hang up on her. Some had, and she couldn't blame them. To those she sent a short note, personally written and signed to apologize for what had happened between them. She kept it deliberately short but deeply felt. She hoped they too could begin to heal for the way she had treated them.

"Ellen?" she asked, confused, not sure she recognized the voice. "Ellen who?" she asked suspiciously. It couldn't be...

"It's Ellen Christenson," she said sadly. She had known that this phone call would be one of the hardest. She hadn't had to make any of them, but felt the need to atone, to explain, and ask for forgiveness. Even if none of them forgave her, at least she had tried. Perhaps they too could move on. Each phone call had made her feel a little better, a little less heartbroken, as she analyzed how badly she had treated them. This phone call, though, this one was one of the hardest.

"Ellen? Oh my God, what in the world?" Rae asked, confused.

"I know, it's been a long time," she said sadly.

"You could say that again," Rae said cautiously. She began to wonder why, out of the blue, Ellen Christenson would call *her* of all people. She had seen her, of course. Who wouldn't? She had been on the front of magazines. Many times, she saw her at the checkout counter of the local market, plastered on the front covers with her latest brilliance, her latest amour, along with her.

"I know. I'm probably the last person on the Earth you would want to hear from." She mentally beat herself up a little and tried to recapture the pride she once held dear so she could get through this phone call.

"To say I'm surprised is a bit of an understatement," Rae agreed. This had to be some kind of trick?

"I'm calling to apologize to you. I realized how wrong I was to treat you the way I did," she tried to keep it simple. Going into explanations had brought on disparaging remarks from the others. Some of them had the need to take a little revenge on her, and while she accepted that, it didn't help with the apologies. To be honest, she didn't really remember what she had done to each and every one of them, but she apologized anyway.

Rae had never heard Ellen Christenson apologize for anything, ever. It was confusing. Then it hit her WHY Ellen would be calling. "Are you okay, Ellen? Is everything alright?" she asked with genuine concern in her voice.

Ellen nearly cried at hearing the compassion in her ex-girlfriend's voice. She didn't deserve it. Rae had been nothing but kind. Loving, wild, bold, and beautiful, she wanted nothing more than to please Ellen and be pleasured by her. Ellen's eventual rejection when she got too close, when she got too loving, had hurt her deeply. It had hurt Ellen too but she couldn't think of that now. "I'm fine," she said in a tight little voice.

Rae recognized that voice. It set her hackles up. "I was just asking," she returned in her own tight little voice.

"No, nothing is wrong," Ellen tried to sound sincere. Since her epiphany, she had beaten herself up enough that making these phone calls was her final way to let go of the past she had created.

"This doesn't seem like you," Rae said gently. She had forgiven Ellen a long time ago, realizing that she had to be the way she was to get the most out of her business and to stay at the top of her game. She didn't need the distractions of a girlfriend who needed her to be human too.

"Yeah, I know. I've changed a bit," she said, without bitterness.

"I'd say so if you are apologizing for something that happened years ago," Rae said with a small laugh which soothed the sound of her words.

Ellen grinned wryly. She'd missed the sound of Rae and her laughter. It had been what attracted her to Rae in the first place, that and her fine mind. She remembered seeing her at some party in the city. Her laughter had been like honey to a bee. "Well, I just wanted you to know how deeply sorry I am for the way things ended. For what I did, or rather didn't do in the relationship. I really didn't mean to hurt you." They both knew that last part was a lie; she hurt people all the time. It was part of doing business. Even relationships were part of that standard modus operandi with Ellen.

"I'm glad you called, Ellen," Rae said quietly as memories assailed her. Not the bad ones, only the good. Ellen, when she was good, was very good. Loving, kind, loyal…and passionate.

"I am too, Rae," Ellen returned just as quietly. She sighed inwardly. There was so much more she wanted to say to this woman, but only to this woman and she really didn't know how. She was still too flawed to fix it. Maybe she would never be able to. "Well, I did what I called to do. I'll let you go now…" she began to get off the phone. She didn't want to bother her.

"Do you really need to go?" Rae asked quickly, and then wanted to kick herself for sounding hopeful.

"Well, I didn't want to bother you," she repeated her thoughts aloud.

"Are you sure you are okay, Ellen?"

Ellen smiled. It was so nice when someone cared like that. Rae had always cared and been thoughtful. "How have you been, Rae?" she asked to deflect the question away from herself.

"I've been busy…" she began. Before they knew it, they had spoken for nearly an hour.

"So, are you seeing anyone?" Ellen finally got up the nerve to ask.

"No, how about you?"

Ellen chuckled and shook her head as she answered, "When do I have the time?"

Rae laughed knowingly. She remembered it well. Still, when Ellen had found the time, it had been very magical.

"I'm glad I called, Rae," she said earnestly. She meant every word of it.

"I'm glad you called too," she said softly and wanted to cry. She sensed that Ellen was going to get off the phone and she would never hear from her again.

"You take care of yourself, Rae," Ellen told her and wanted to cry. She really wanted to ask her out again. After their comfortable conversation and knowing she wasn't seeing anyone, but she knew she needed to heal. She needed to finally grow up to the position she was in.

"You too, Ellen, you too," she said gently, sensing her withdrawal.

"Goodbye, Rae," she spoke into the phone sadly.

"Goodbye," she said and waited for Ellen to disconnect the call. When she did, she sat there for a long time listening to the dial tone until it changed to one that sounded raucous, before she hung up herself.

Ellen lay back on her couch and stared at the ceiling, wondering what could have been.

Rae lay back on her bed and looked at the material covering her four-poster bed, wondering why fate had sent Ellen back into her life at this point, even if only for an hour or so.

"How's your sex life?" Nancy asked her.

"My sex life?" Ellen repeated stupidly back to her. She had just told her about trying to make amends to all the women she felt she had hurt. She had expected some sort of 'atta gurl' but instead this line of questioning confused her.

"Yes, how is it? Were you active with these women? Were you passive? Aggressive? What was it like for both of you?"

"You want to know the mechanics? The details?" Ellen clarified a little testily.

"No, I want to know how you saw your sex life with these women."

Ellen thought for a while. "I was in charge. Always in charge," she told her honestly.

"Why?"

"Why?" Ellen frowned as she thought. "Because that's how I liked it. That's what worked for us."

"For both of you or for you?" Nancy asked pointedly.

Ellen stopped to think. She thought for a while as she went over the mental list of women she had been with. "I don't think any of them objected. I made sure they were satisfied," she answered truthfully.

"Have you ever just let yourself go? Let someone else take charge?"

Ellen was beginning to get uncomfortable as she realized the direction that her therapist was going. "No, I guess I haven't."

"What about if it was something they really wanted?"

Ellen looked down at her hands. They were twisting. She steadied them. "I guess if they didn't like how I wanted things, I got rid of them eventually."

The therapist nodded her head. This was all making sense, another piece of the puzzle fitting into place. She could see that Ellen could understand it too. "What if you found someone who didn't allow you to have your own way? Challenged you? Wanted more of an equal footing than what you normally allow?"

Ellen briefly thought of a couple of her past girlfriends, one in college that took her virginity, and how quickly she had gotten rid of them, all of them, and shrugged. "I think I would avoid her because that's not what I want in a relationship."

"Perhaps you are afraid of giving up the control because of what your father did to you. What those friends of his tried to do to you by being condescending, patronizing, and misogynistic towards you. Their sexual innuendo and what they would have eventually done to you, that angered you. From what you have told me, the thefts of your mother's and grandparents' things upset you."

Ellen had to agree, but she was getting sick of this line of questioning and merely wanted to leave. It had opened a door, though, perhaps a window, and over the following week before her next appointment she would think about it…a lot as she turned it over in her mind and self-analyzed.

"Do you think you have philophobia?" Nancy asked quietly.

Ellen knew immediately what the word meant. She shrugged and then looked right in her eyes. Nodding slightly, she replied, "I think I do have a fear of falling in love. I think I'm afraid to love because they will turn on me. They will stop loving me."

The therapist nodded encouragingly, hoping this difficult client would continue.

"I think knowing there was nothing I could do growing up, knowing he held all the power, knowing that my mother was too frail, I simply gave up trying," she confided.

The therapist was amazed. Ellen rarely shared deep feelings and when she did, like this, it showed such intellect, such understanding of her own condition. She was even more astounded when Ellen continued.

"I think I've been repressing a lot of the anger all these years. There was nothing I could do about him, but I can do it about my own life."

"You think controlling your own life…" Nancy began, but Ellen interrupted her.

"I think I've always been a bit of a control freak. Look at me," she gestured at herself. She was dressed in a sleek business suit. Many of the most elite stores in San Francisco would be thrilled at this executive's patronage. "I'm wealthy, I'm fairly good-looking, but I run a multinational multimillion-dollar company…hell," she corrected. "Multibillion," she said modestly.

"So, what are you going to do?" Nancy asked.

Ellen looked at her, her own eyes darting between the therapist's dark brown ones. "I guess I begin to make amends in some small way."

"You don't think it's another way of self-flagellation?" Nancy worried.

Ellen looked resigned and yet, the spirit was still there. "I don't think so. I don't owe apologies to everyone." She had already started making amends. The many phone calls to women in her past had started her on a new path, and she wasn't going to look over her shoulder anymore.

✦ CHAPTER SIXTEEN ✦

GOING BACK

"Ellen Christenson's office, how may I help you?" The receptionist repeated the phrase over and over many times a day, mostly just to take a message. If she didn't answer the phone, the other secretary would, and if both of them were on the phone taking messages or redirecting the call to keep Ms. Christenson from being bothered, it went to voice mail.

"I'm sorry, Ms. Christenson is busy at the moment. May I take a message?" This too was repeated many times in the day.

As she wrote down the message, it struck her how much odder it was than some of the requests they got for Ms. Christenson's time. She diligently wrote down the details as they were relayed to her. Sorting through the mail, she quickly found a corresponding piece of paper to attach to the message. Someone was in an awful hurry and Ms. Christenson would not be pleased.

Ellen looked at the message and the attached bit of mail. She looked again in surprise as she thought over what it meant. Reaching for her cell phone, she stopped herself and pulled up the information on her laptop, using a search engine to find a phone number. Grabbing her cell phone, she quickly punched in the numbers for the number she had found.

"'Ello?" she heard on the other end of the line.

"Mr. Davidson, please?" she said automatically, officially. She was used to dealing with corporate types and her social skills were lacking on a few levels.

"Who is this?' the gruff voice asked suspiciously.

"Mr. Davidson? It's E..." she stopped herself realizing he didn't know her as Ellen. "It's Avril Christenson," she said pleasantly, using the unfamiliar name that no one had used in twenty years.

He paused for a long moment as he processed why the name sounded familiar. It took a while, partly due to age, partly due to the passage of time. Then it suddenly struck him. "Avril?" he questioned to be sure.

"Yes, Mr. Davidson. It's Avril," she confirmed kindly. She knew he must have been ancient.

"Well, Avril Christenson, who'd a thunk," he said, pleased to hear from her. He knew her to be some high muckety-muck out there in Cali-forn-ny-a. He'd even heard that she'd been on some magazines or something like that.

She smiled at his way of speaking. Getting to the point of her call, she didn't wish to be social, she began, "Mr. Davidson, the town is asking that I tear down my folks' house. I was wondering if you still had your equipment and could take it down?"

He mused over it for a moment before nodding. He'd heard that the town was getting rid of some of the old derelicts. But the Christenson place was a way out of town and he wondered why they would even bother. "Yeah, I could do that," he began slowly. "My grandson and I could have it down in no time flat," he said aloud and then wondered to himself if a good strong kick would knock it over. It had been leaning that way for a long time. He wouldn't be surprised if they could just push it over.

"That would be great," she said agreeably. She looked at the paper before her and quickly read. "I can be there," she glanced at the full calendar on her desk and winced at what she would have to cancel. "In a few days. Is that acceptable to you?" she asked.

"Waaall," he drawled out. "You don't *need* to be there," he told her.

"That's okay, I will," she confirmed. "And you can take any of the fixtures, the boards, the wiring, anything you can use from it," she offered generously, remembering that he was a fix-it man.

"That's right generous of you," he said and started thinking of what might still be in that house. It probably was pretty picked over after all this time. But there might be things he could piece out and profit by; she didn't need the money, from what he had heard. That house still

had to have some copper fittings and…his mind wandered off greedily for a moment.

"I'll be there in a few days and I'll call you so you can meet me out at the farm," she told him, interrupting his train of thought.

"Ay yup," he confirmed as he wandered away in thought again.

"Good bye, Mr. Davidson, I'll see you in a few days," she confirmed and when he said 'good bye' too, she hung up. She stared at the phone for a moment before calling in her secretaries.

"I have to clear my schedule for the next week. An emergency has come up," she explained.

"But Ms. Christenson," one of them had the temerity to protest.

Ellen silenced her with a cold stare. Glancing at the other one who stood there with a frozen face, she addressed her. "I can be reached by phone if anything comes up." With that she dismissed them both knowing she had set in motion an unprecedented series of events. Ellen Christenson never took time off and other than the odd day here and there. Her schedule had been pretty much seven days a week. Her energy unflagging.

She looked over her desk and sat down to finish a few things that she could, packed her briefcase with her laptop and a few papers, locked it, and left the office. Both secretaries watched her leave the offices with their mouths hanging agape in surprise. They quickly returned to work as she turned to push the button on the elevator and glanced back at them.

On the way down to her car she pulled up the number for Nancy Keurig to cancel her appointment for the following day. She was surprised when she called it as she got in her car that Nancy answered it herself.

"Hello? Nancy Keurig's office. Nancy Keurig speaking."

"Hi Nancy, this is Ellen Christenson," she said as she used the key fob to open the door to the Maserati.

"Hello Ellen, is everything okay?" she asked, concerned. Ellen didn't call her offices and hadn't missed a session, and Nancy was pleased with the progress they had made over the past couple of years.

"Not really, I have to go away for a few days and I need to cancel our appointment for next week," she told her. Thinking carefully, she quickly added, "I'm going home to Oklahoma to take care of some personal business."

"Oh my," Nancy involuntarily answered before recovering herself. "How do you feel about that?" she asked, concerned.

"I don't know," Ellen answered honestly. She started the expensive car after strapping herself in one-handed and shutting the door. It purred like a kitten and her Bluetooth kicked in immediately so she could put down her phone and talk to Nancy hands-free.

"I think it's time, though. I've changed a lot since I was there. Maybe it's time," she said almost sadly and to herself.

Nancy nodded in agreement and then said, "Yes, Ellen, maybe it's time."

"May I call you if I need to?" she asked, clinging to her lifeline. She hadn't realized how much she had come to rely on these appointments to vent, to use a sounding board, to get past the past.

"Of course. You have my cell if you need it?" Nancy asked, amazed. Ellen had come far. She wasn't the angry, resentful woman who had arrived at her office a couple of years ago. She'd finally started a road that only she could traverse. Nancy could only help her realize it.

"Yeah, but I'm so used to using the office phone I'll probably panic before remembering I have it," Ellen laughed as she expertly maneuvered through the mid-afternoon traffic towards her house.

"No worries, Ellen. I'm here for you," Nancy encouraged. She wondered if Ellen realized how many women were attracted to her for the Ellen she knew, not the cold and calculating, efficient bitch she was known as in the tech world. Her own attraction she kept well hidden, as it would be unprofessional if she ever revealed it.

"Thanks, Nancy," she sighed before she said her goodbyes and hung up. After she parked the car in her garage, she glanced back at it and wondered if she should rent a car for the trip. She didn't want to fly. She wanted the time behind the wheel to think, really think, before seeing the home she had once had. She was hoping the trip back would be cathartic, and she was ready for it.

As she packed her suitcase she wondered how much had changed. She had gotten a notice for her ten-year class reunion, another for the fifteen-year one. The surprise was that anyone knew where she was. She never even considered going to either one. Doing the math in her agile mind she realized that their twentieth should be this year. Where had the time gone?

As she showered, shaved, and powdered she wondered where the resentment she had long felt had gone as well. Was it the therapy? Was it just the passage of time?

She fixed a few sandwiches, grabbed a few boxes of juice from the fridge, and packed them all in her car along with her bag. Gathering a few 'last minute' items, she set the alarm, locked up the house, and got on the road.

She stopped to fill up with super unleaded gas. It was expensive, but it would clean out the system of her Maserati, and besides, Ryan Mahoney had recommended it. It was through her blind autopilot haze that she heard someone say, "Nice car". She nodded and smiled but didn't invite conversation.

As she drove along the freeway down towards Los Angeles she kept to the speed limit, barely. It was easy to speed in this car with its powerful engine and she endeavored to keep it at sixty-nine when the speed limit read sixty-five. The irony of that number didn't escape her and she laughed at the how silly it was as she turned up the radio and drove the long miles. She stopped outside of Las Vegas and got a hotel room so she could rest and eat. Her drink boxes were long gone, as were the sandwiches. She didn't mind eating alone. She frequently did at home anyway when she wasn't working long hours at the office.

"Wanna buy a girl a meal?" a teen asked her, popping her gum.

Ellen looked up in surprise that the girl would even approach her. Most of the time she intimidated full grown women and men, and the teen's obnoxious question astonished her. She examined her briefly as she realized she just might be a runaway. From her straggly hair to her ripped jeans, she could just be a normal kid, but then again… "Sure, sit down and order whatever you want," Ellen offered as the teen slipped into her booth.

"Really?" she asked in surprise, but not one to look a gift horse in the mouth, she quickly obeyed.

Ellen had just ordered and she signaled to the waitress.

"You want me to remove her?" the waitress asked testily, glaring at the girl in anger.

"No, I want you to take her order. Whatever she wants," she told the woman.

Both the teen and the waitress stared at her in astonishment.

"I'll have a hamburger, fries, and a chocolate shake," the teen quickly ordered before the redhead could change her mind.

The waitress hesitated for a moment, but at Ellen's nod she quickly wrote it down and hurried off.

The awkward silence stretched between the two of them as Ellen looked curiously at the teen and the teen resentfully at the well-dressed redhead.

"So, why'd you do it?" the teen asked Ellen carefully. She hoped she wouldn't piss her off; this was the first real meal she'd had in a while.

Ellen shrugged as she glanced away. She had a lot of time to think away the hours she had driven to get here, and looking at the teen, she realized that there but for the grace of God, went she.

The teen looked at her closely. She was dressed nicely; she could tell the clothes looked expensive. She didn't read *Vogue* or *Mademoiselle* for nothing and the woman wore them well. She also looked like she never went out in the sun. Her skin was like porcelain. Her red hair looked real. It was up in a tight bun and she wondered what the woman looked like when she let it down. The teen glanced out the window too; it was dark so all she could see was her reflection. It was then that she could tell that the woman was watching her in that reflection and she flushed at the contrast in their outfits and appearance.

The waitress bustled up with a tray holding their meal. They both ate in silence, the girl smothering her fries with ketchup, Ellen quietly putting a glop of it on the side of her plate to dip her steak into now and then. She ate her salad along with the baked potato she had ordered. As they slowed down from the sheer amount of food the waitress hurried up again.

"Everything okay?" she asked. When they nodded she continued with, "Would either of you like a dessert?"

Ellen glanced at the teen who looked hopeful and nodded. "Whatever she wants," she gestured towards her dinner companion.

"Could I have a strawberry sundae with nuts?" she asked a bit insolently through a mouthful of hamburger. She'd been gobbling it all as though it was going to be taken away from her at a moment's notice.

Ellen could see the annoyance on the waitress's face and nearly laughed. She'd been young once, too. The opportunity to be this insolent had never been allowed. "That sounds good, I'll have one too," she told the woman to lessen the teen's tone. The waitress hurried away but not before asking, "One or two scoops?"

"Two," they both said together, grinning at each other as she left.

"Sure you're gonna have room?" the teen spoke to her again, this time around a few French fries she managed to jam in her mouth.

Ellen grinned and nodded, food had never been a problem for her. She could eat as much as she wanted and still have room. When others in the dorms had been dieting to near starvation she ate more than her own share. People paid a lot of money for the type of figure she had, and she had been too busy building her businesses to care. "Shouldn't be a problem."

"You ain't from around here," the girl as she finished up the food on her plate and drank the last of her shake. The slurping sound from the straw at the bottom of the glass set Ellen's nerves on edge.

"No, no I'm not," Ellen replied as she used her napkin delicately.

The teen watched the redhead silently. She admired how…girlish the woman appeared to be and wondered how she had gotten that way. She didn't look too old, either.

As the waitress hurried up with their desserts and quickly took away their finished plates, they both tucked in to the sundaes with delight, almost a competition to see who could finish theirs first. The teen finished first. She watched as the redhead finished a bit slower but much more delicately, not putting the whole spoon in her mouth or taking as large a mouthful.

"Is there anything else I could get you?" the waitress asked as she came up. She'd been eying the odd pair and wondered why the woman

would pay for the teen's meal. Did she know she was being conned? They'd kicked that same teen out a few times. But maybe she was one of those…she eyed her speculatively.

"The check would be great," Ellen said with a gracious smile.

"Oh, I'll have that up at the register," the waitress pointed at the end of the counter.

"Then thank you," Ellen said as she wiped her face once more and began to leave the booth.

"Yeah, um, thank you," the teen said as she tried to emulate the elegant woman slightly. She could start with her manners she guessed.

The waitress was startled, but she headed up to the counter to ring the lady up. The meal wasn't too expensive and she was startled when the redhead gave her a one-hundred-dollar bill. "Keep the change, and if she comes in here," she pointed with her thumb at the hovering teen who was making a great show of looking at the board in the entrance where local notices were posted. "Maybe give her a meal now and then?" she asked. The waitress looked startled and Ellen handed her another hundred as a tip. Smiling, she closed her hand over it. "You never know where a little kindness will go," she whispered confidentially before she turned and walked away.

"You got someplace to stay tonight?" she asked the girl as she tucked her pocketbook away, well away from any pickpocket or teen that might think she had a chance.

"I thought, um, maybe I'd pay you back for that meal," the teen said awkwardly and then glanced up at Ellen from under her stringy hair.

Ellen was genuinely startled. "Do you do this often?" she asked concerned. The world was a dangerous place and she didn't want to see the girl hurt.

Shuffling her feet awkwardly she glanced up under her hair again and shrugged.

"What happens if I take you up on your offer?"

The teen looked slightly alarmed for a moment and then shrugged again.

Ellen knew a bluff when she saw it. The teen would do what she had to, to survive. Hooking was an honorable profession in Nevada, but not like this. This was pathetic. "What would you do if I offered you a job, an honest one?" she clarified when she saw the teen glance up in alarm.

Another shrug.

This was going to be harder than she thought. Thinking about Iris and Blossom, she wondered if they were doing okay and if Iris could have turned out like this. She didn't know. They were taken care of by Ryan's generosity. She'd lived up to her end of the deal, except she had never even met the teen, she would be graduating soon. She wondered if Iris was as Californian as she remembered Blossom to be or whether she more like this teen, unclean and unmannered. "Well, I will be coming through here in another week. You think about it. I live in San Francisco and I can arrange a job for you if you want it. An honest job," she again clarified. "If you want it, meet me here in a week, maybe a week and a half," she amended to be sure. She pointed back at the restaurant they had just left.

"What'd I have to do?" mumbled the girl.

"What do you care?" Ellen asked. She was walking slowly towards her hotel and she didn't want the teen to know what room she was in or what she drove. "It would be better than this or what you offered," she pointed out.

The teen nodded slowly. "A week?" she asked, thinking. She could survive another week at this, she was sure she could.

"I already arranged for a meal or two back there," she pointed again with her thumb back at the restaurant. "You eat there once a day and when I get back, you be around here and we will talk."

The teen looked at her in disbelief. She was certain that the woman was conning her. But yet, there was hope.

"How old are you?" Ellen asked.

"Eighteen," she replied resentfully. She knew the woman wasn't a cop; she was dressed too nicely for that.

"Are you *really*?"

"I will be," was the sullen reply.

"Well, I will be here next week when I return from my trip. Be here, be alive, and I'll see you then," she told her. She thought about giving her some money but didn't want the teen to know how much she had on her or where she kept more of it. She wasn't sure the money wouldn't be used for drugs. She didn't know her, she didn't trust her, but she wanted to help her.

The teen watched as Ellen walked away. When she turned around the teen was still watching her and then she began to hurry in the opposite direction.

Ellen watched until she was out of sight before she turned back towards her hotel, walking through the lobby. She hoped the teen couldn't see where she went, but once inside the elevator, she wouldn't know where she was staying unless she was in cahoots with someone in the hotel. She laughed at herself as she locked the deadbolt and the latch; she had watched too many movies with Ryan over the years.

She slept well and was up and ready to go early despite the long miles she had driven the previous day. She stretched, showered, arranged her hair and makeup, and packed the few things she had unpacked for her stay. She checked out of the hotel, got in her car, and drove into Las Vegas before stopping for a late breakfast.

It took her a couple of days to drive to Oklahoma. The memories began to assail her as she crossed the border and the rolling hills, the vivid greens. Even the trees brought back memories. She felt her stomach clench up but she drove on gamely. Calling Mr. Davidson, she told him she would be there the following day. Knowing her town had been too small to have a hotel – much less a motel – she stopped and freshened up and went to bed early before starting out on the last leg of her drive.

❖ CHAPTER SEVENTEEN ❖

REMEMBRANCES

She stared at the ruins of a once beautiful farm house and memories came, flashing back in an instant yet spanning years. Over there once stood a beautiful pair of oak trees with a swing between them for her to play on. She could still hear the echoes of her mother telling her to be careful as she climbed them. Skinned knees and scraped palms; she never complained over the slivers her mother had to remove from her tomboyish activities. Their shade provided her endless hours of escape from the relentless sun and still she would burn from it. The wind would part the leaves and the sun would beat down between them. Her imagination could play for hours as she gazed up through them, envisioning them as towering giants and she a mere mortal. She loved those trees.

"I can't believe you climb like a monkey, and in a dress too!" her mother would scold. She remembered that fondly, the inflections, the lilt in her voice was still in her consciousness despite the span of years.

The house still tilted haphazardly. Weather and time hadn't pulled it to the ground and for this she was surprised as she stared at its sturdy build. Her great-grandparents had been among the first to build in this area and had used good wood and stone to construct their sturdy home. Their son and granddaughter had both raised families in this house. She scowled as she remembered she had been the last raised there.

It looked well picked over. The weeds around the place were elbow high and although she hadn't seen it in over twenty years, she couldn't help but wonder why it hadn't been torn down before; which was why she was now here.

"Ms. Avril?" a voice asked her respectfully and she started in surprise. She hadn't heard anyone approach. "Oh, I'm sorry miss, I was expecting…" he began apologizing.

"It's okay, you just startled me," she said in precise and clear tones, not a hint of the accent that was unique to this part of the country and so apparent in his voice. That accent brought back other memories. Ones she'd tried to quash and couldn't. Ones that she'd known needed exorcising, and *that* could only be done by coming here. It was why she had come herself. She needed to stop the dreams that had returned. Her feeling was that it was in the past and it should remain there. Her psyche though was haunting her and she had to face it one last time.

"I was expecting Ms. Avril," he began again, and peered at her intently and wondering who she was. He was shorter than she, his skin brown from the winds that blew here; he was stooped from a lifetime of work.

She smiled, not realizing the beauty that was apparent in her face. Her pale white skin hid the freckles that came out in the sun, but no tan touched her creamy milk white skin anymore. "I'm A…Avril," she answered hesitating over the name for only a millisecond. '*Or, I was,*' she mentally corrected herself, but not aloud, he wouldn't understand.

"You're Ms. Avril?" he asked puzzled. He peered at her for a long time shaking his head, trying to see some semblance of the youth he had known. As her smile faded, he saw a glimmer of recognition. Not of her but of her mother and that was when he took on a relieved look. His hat came off his head in an instant and his weathered face wreathed a smile showing several missing teeth. "Why Ms. Avril, you've all growed up!" he drawled, pleased at his discovery.

"How are you, Mr. Davidson?" she asked pleasantly. The smile didn't quite reach her eyes, though. Not with the memories pushing at her temples wanting her to remember, to relive them; all the while she was trying hard to once again suppress them.

"Poorly," he said honestly. "Right poorly, but I aim to do the job you is needing done. I shorely do. Just like I promised." He gestured to the truck that was parked at the end of the drive. On the trailer attached to it sat a front-end loader, securely chained to its bed.

She glanced at it, then back at the house he had come to demolish. It was the town's attempt at getting rid of an 'eyesore' that had sat there empty for over two decades. Why they had decided that it needed to be

done now, she didn't know. But she was here as requested to get it done. Mr. Davidson had answered her call, surprised that she remembered him. He was eager to earn the money she had promised him for the job.

"Do you want to go through the house to look for anything?" he asked as he noticed her silently staring at the house.

She shook her head. She had done her picking long ago, her few belongings in a few measly boxes and trunks, and a storage unit she had come to go through as well, a lifetime of memories and knickknacks that meant nothing to anyone but herself. "Just bulldoze it," she said shortly, wanting it taken care of so she could leave.

"You'll have to move your car," he mentioned, as they turned to head back down the driveway.

She glanced at the Maserati and nearly laughed aloud at the contrast between it and his old rusted out Chevy. She hadn't thought of that when she decided to drive back here. If she hadn't before, she would surely stick out like a sore thumb now. Another reason to get the job finished and get out, get gone. Something she had done years ago and not looked back. She glanced over at the barns and silos. They still looked as solid as the day her great-grandparents and grandparents had built them. Nothing had touched them, not time, nor weather, they seemed to be as strong and steady as the day they were built. They could use a little paint, but with the weather that came through this part of the country it was amazing they were still standing. She could see they were used well by the tracks that led from the path up to them and down the driveway, but that was all. Everything else was abandoned, the chicken coop, and a few other outbuildings. The grass overgrown and obviously untrodden, no animals or people to grind it under their heels.

"Can you tear down those, too?" she asked as she gestured to the outbuildings not in use.

"Ahyup," he grunted as they reached her overpriced car and she automatically pressed the button on her keychain to open the door and let her in. He glanced at the car as the door opened quietly and on its own for her. That car was expensive enough to pay a couple of years' salary to someone like him and most folks around here. It was none of his business, though, so he hurried over to the trailer where another man stood, awaiting orders. "Let's get her down," he gestured to him, and they immediately began removing the chains holding the machine to the bed of the trailer.

The younger man kept watch out of the corner of his eye as the redhead drove the expensive sports car onto the road. She parked it opposite the driveway so they could drive the front-end loader onto the property. She was definitely worth a second *and* third look and he wondered if she remembered him as she watched his uncle maneuver the heavy machine off the trailer. She caught him staring as she got out of the car and he felt his cheeks reddening. He hurried after his uncle to collect any boards worth salvaging hoping she hadn't noticed. She had said they could take whatever they wanted.

She followed along slowly and looked down at her Prada shoes, knowing she should have dressed down for the farm, but after twenty years she had nothing appropriate to wear on such a place. She hadn't thought about it as the miles passed and she headed for this part of Oklahoma.

CHAPTER EIGHTEEN

A LITTLE REVENGE

"**M**r. Mann, I'm surprised you are still practicing," she greeted him as he shook her hand and gestured her to a waiting chair.

"Yep, I'm still a-kicking and I must say you are looking fine, mighty fine," he told her with a smile. She was even more beautiful than her mother had been. The teenager who had left this burg so long ago was also long gone. He'd read about her in the papers and magazines and he thought she deserved all the good things that had come to her. She'd worked hard and achieved something that few, if any, could do.

"Thank you," she blushed becomingly. Even after all these years, this sort of thing could make her blush. She controlled rooms of people with her business acumen and expertise, yet this kindly old gentleman had her blushing like a school girl.

"Well, what can I do for you today?" he asked. He'd been wondering since she called to make an appointment. He didn't do much these days, but he could still do a bit. His much younger partner was taking the brunt of the work and would someday take it all as he had himself had done so long ago.

"I'd like to sue a few people around here," she said with a wave of her hand.

His interest was piqued. He was also alarmed. He knew the kind of money this woman had and what she could do to their small town. "A bit of revenge?" he asked astutely.

She nodded but added, "And a bit of justification," she added. She then proceeded to tell him of the visits she had made around Oakley. To the former sheriff's house. To several others who had been surprised to have this smartly dressed redhead on their doorstep but allowed her into their homes when her innate good manners and their own civility and curiosity overwhelmed. She had been pleasant, keeping the visits down to a mere fifteen minutes, but looking about their living rooms she had taken note of specific things and handed a list to the attorney now.

"You realize how this is going to look?" he asked.

"I don't care. They didn't have the right and they still don't."

"Can you prove that?" he asked, indicating her inventoried list.

She handed him a photo album where she had carefully Post-it noted specific pages and photos. She handed him her agreement with the co-op that outlined perfectly what they could and would do with the farm.

"You thought this out, didn't you?"

She nodded again, her many miles between San Francisco and Oklahoma having been lost in thought. "I've had twenty years to think this out. Being here brought it all back," she confided. Her own 'guilt' over what had transpired was rapidly diminishing. She didn't know if Nancy would approve but she felt compelled to do this, to get it over with, to put it behind her and move on. Ryan would have approved and understood.

"Well, I can get this in the works and written up over the next few days," he informed her, thinking about the work involved. Inside he was gleefully admitting to himself how this was going to affect the good citizens of their not-so-little town. It had grown considerably in size in the twenty years since she left, but it was still basically a small town.

"I'll await your call. Do you want me to sign anything?" she asked. "Pay your fee in advance?" she offered glancing about the dingy office, knowing he didn't have a lot of funds.

"Oh, that won't be necessary. I'll be happy to get this going. When I call you in a couple of days you can sign our agreement then."

"Do you know why the town suddenly decided to have my parents' place torn down? It's well outside the town limits."

He nodded. "I think they hoped to have you here. Come personally, and so you have," he smiled.

"What for?"

"Probably to hit you up for some town function. You're the most famous person to ever have come from here. Even Billy Maxon the football player can't beat Avril Ellen Christenson and the fact that she came from this part of Oklahoma," he told her with self-depreciating smile.

"Famous? They couldn't have cared less," she said, slapping her hand down on the corner of his desk and a little bit of the old bitterness came out.

"They didn't care *then*," he leaned forward and put his hand on hers in a grandfatherly gesture. "But you proved the lot of them wrong. They want that association," he informed her.

"Association? They'll get an association all right," she said the irony aloud.

"Yes, they will, won't they?" he pulled back and indicated the photo album he had on his desk.

She smiled and nodded as she arose. "If I have a few more things to add, you'll take my call?"

He nodded and allowed a rare smile to cross his face. Her mother would have been proud of how she turned out.

Ellen drove around, looking and remembering. The house was now gone, and even the weeds and the outbuildings bulldozed flat. She arranged for Tempe Painting to paint the barns and the silos and make them whole, patch them, and fix what needed fixing. Might as well protect her family's legacy. Thankful for the work in this depressed part of the state, Mr. Tempe got to work with his small crew immediately. She paid him half up front, knowing he would have to buy the supplies and possibly rent the scaffolding to get up to the higher reaches of the buildings. He was surprised that the check cleared without a problem. He didn't know who Ellen Christenson was, and he was delighted to be able to feed his family for another month. Hell, with this job and the quote he had given her, a few more months.

She stopped at the storage rental place and went through it as much as she could. Calling a moving company, she arranged for it all to be taken out and her rental agreement to come to an end. Carl, the man she had dealt with so long ago, was gone but a similar man eyed her warily as she filled out the paperwork and ended the longstanding agreement. He had never met her but knew of the unit that had been rented longer than any others in their facility.

"Then you will hold it until my house is ready?" she confirmed with the moving company that had arrived to empty the storage unit.

"Ayup, you get charged the longer we hold it, though," he informed her.

"Thank you, that will be fine," she said as she watched the moving men carefully remove the antiques. They started to make her feel nostalgic as she remembered her mother lovingly polishing them, and she turned away to look elsewhere. These were things. They weren't important, and while they had been in her life for a substantial portion, she knew they were mother's things, her grandmother's even. They were now hers and she would do something with them, *finally*. It had been long enough. She had let the past rule her for far too long. It was time to look to the future after a few choicer things were taken care of.

"You remember me from the houses you showed me and my partner?" she asked the real estate agent.

Of course she remembered Ellen Christenson. She was famous in Silicon Valley. Even her partner, that Ryan Mahoney who had died, was memorable. "What can I do for you, Ms. Christenson?" she asked respectfully, remembering her from when she bought the apartment in the city and hoping she didn't remember her gaffe of thinking they were a married couple.

"I remembered seeing a house that I think you represented in Rolling Hills Estates?" Ellen had remembered Ryan looking at the real estate, it fascinated him. She had no interest in it, but he always saw the potential.

Even though she didn't represent any of the properties in that section of the Valley, she'd lie through her teeth to help out someone of Ellen Christenson's stature. "Yes, of course, Ms. Christenson, were you looking for a particular model?"

Discussing what Ellen remembered and what her needs were, Judy Comella soon had a good idea of what the tech mogul had in mind for a home. She promised to get back to Ellen with what she could find as soon as possible. She lived up to that promise, and using her laptop, Ellen was soon the owner of a house she had never personally seen other than in pictures, a video showing the place, and still shots. Transferring the funds to an escrow account, she arranged for a two-week escrow instead of the normal month to six months to purchase the house. Satisfied with her efforts, Ellen smiled, knowing her family's 'treasures' would soon have a home, as would she.

"Ms. Christenson, isn't it?" an unfamiliar voice stopped her as she came out of the small motel in the next town over, as Oakley wasn't large enough for even a motel.

Used to the city and having lived for over half her life in California, she looked up defensively, ready to punch and run. Standing before her was an older gentleman and she relaxed slightly. "May I help you?" she asked frostily, not used to having complete strangers approaching her except for in business.

He took off the hat he was wearing and nodded to her. "I'm Mayor Barnes," he said by introduction.

She waited for him to continue, not offering her hand, not acknowledging his title.

"I heard you were in town and staying over here. I'm sorry we don't have adequate lodgings over in Oakley," he continued, starting to feel uncomfortable by the redheads penetrating eyes.

It was then that she began to have an inkling who he was and what this might be about. Mr. Mann was right.

"What can I do for you, Mr. Barnes?" she asked to get to the point. She had some places that she wanted to see yet and hadn't visited.

"The City Council asked me to approach you. We were hoping you might help us fix up the town square. We'd like to turn it into a park..." he began to drone on with the council's plans and Ellen tuned him out.

She remembered the so-called town square. It was four intersections that had at one time, in her own lifetime, been four dirt roads that came into Oakley and were now bordered with the old, rotting buildings. She knew that a park in that spot, which was dry, dusty, and filling with weeds, would be an enormous boost to the town.

"We would, of course, name it after your father," he said with a toothy smile. "Christenson Park sounds wonderful, doesn't it?"

Ellen stiffened at the mention of her father. "Were you around when my father was alive?" she interrupted him to ask. She didn't remember him.

"Well, no. My wife and I moved here when the canning factory went in the next town. We didn't want to live there and found a right nice..." and he was off describing the house he and his wife had settled in so long ago. She had grown up there; she remembered where the house was. He further told her about his own background, how when he retired he went into politics and became the Mayor of their little town. How proud he and the council were of her accomplishments.

Ellen had stopped listening fully again as she thought over his proposal. When he mentioned a price, an outlandish one at that, she shook her head. "I thank you for coming by *Mister* Barnes," she stressed deliberately. "But I'm not interested in giving any fame to my father. Nor do I think your proposal feasible."

"Well, it would sure breathe life into our little town..." he tried his best sales pitch but Ellen held up her hand to stop him.

"Your 'little' town," she began frostily. "Deserves to die," she told him with a finality and swept by him to get into the Maserati. She had a breakfast she wanted to find and had no more time for this fool.

Mayor Barnes stared at the expensive sports car in consternation. He couldn't believe someone of her wealth, from their very own hometown – he did consider it his home now after all these years – could turn down the proposal. It was a drop in the bucket to someone like her.

"She can't do that!" was a familiar refrain heard around Oakley as the list of people Avril Ellen Christenson was suing began to get served with court orders.

"How could she know?" gasped someone at the co-op.

"She must have had someone spying on us!" another answered.

"Do you think she had a private investigator checking us out?"

"That Laramy kid, I betcha he told!" someone else put in. The Laramy kid, who had nothing to do with it, was summarily fired.

"What? Those fields weren't being used, how the hell did she know...?" was heard in one household.

"I suggest you just return the items she has listed on that there order," Mr. Mann had to tell a few irate people who barged into his offices. Ellen was suing for the return of her parents' things that she had suspected people had. Her well-timed visits to those who thought themselves 'honored' by her helped them soon find out otherwise. Her observances led to a detailed list of who had what – people she had suspected when she left, some she had known, others merely speculated about. The burden of proof was on her; however, she had the money to make these people miserable.

The court order by Ellen's attorney against the co-op who had led her to believe that they were handling the acres owned by the Sheehan family...not only were they being audited on Ellen's behalf, for the past twenty years, but sued for their mishandling of the acreage. There was one more lawsuit pending against a guy who had been using the back acres far from regular roads for his own crops without paying rent to the co-op or to Ellen.

It was amazing what a few well-placed drinks and dollars could net in the information network in a small town. Ellen hadn't had to try too hard, but neither had Mr. Mann. Rumors were being confirmed.

Possessions that had been 'salvaged' in the search through the house were now being returned or were disappearing to never be seen again, after all, you couldn't sue for the return of an item if it didn't exist, right? Ellen, or rather, 'Avril,' had used her camera on her phone to take a few pictures, which Mr. Mann now had in his possession. Mr. Mann had to hire on his partner to help with the lawsuits, as his new client, who had an unlimited supply of funds, was going after quite a few people.

"I was just doing my job!" the former Sheriff Worley protested when he and his wife were served.

Ellen had a long and thorough memory. She had been a frightened teen and they had taken full advantage of her. Having the means of revenge began to soothe the guilt she felt over her father's death. Some of these people could have prevented the situation, and some of them had taken advantage of it. Now it was time to pay. She wasn't waiting for 'judgement day' to let some higher entity deal with them. Fate or karma hadn't bitten these people in the ass so Ellen Christenson was going to mete out the punishment as she saw fit.

Her final days in Oakley had her glared at, practically spit upon, but justice was swift and everyone who had gotten served was now suspect in the eyes of their small-town neighbors. If someone of Ellen Christenson's stature was going after them, they had to be guilty. Money spoke volumes and she was using it judiciously. As her time came there to a close, the need for revenge faded and she let her anger go in many ways. It was time to leave and Mr. Mann and his partner could handle the rest for her anyway. She only needed to be back in Oakley if any of these lawsuits actually went to court, but most would be settled long before anyone wanted to suffer the public embarrassment of what she was suing them for.

Before she left, she stopped at the cemetery to talk to her mama and apologize.

"I tried, Mama, I tried," she sobbed. She started when she thought she heard the wind that always blew in Oklahoma sigh, "It wasn't your place." Looking up and around she thought she had finally gone over the edge. She felt comfort for having visited her, even in this dismal place. Glancing at her father's headstone next to it she felt nothing anymore, no anger, no resentment. She felt that was progress. He didn't have the control he once had over her, and the anger was gone. It had all been so pointless and such a waste of emotions. It was time to go and as she got into Ryan's car, now hers, she realized she could finally leave the past behind her. She looked around the cemetery once more, the wind blowing her hair back from her face. She saw the names, many of them familiar as many people had relatives still in the small town. They would all end up here and she was done – so done with it all.

❈ CHAPTER NINETEEN ❈

PROMISES KEPT

Driving back from Oklahoma she felt the weight of her years peeling off of her. She finally felt free again. Even the storms she encountered on the plains didn't bother as they once had. Ellen was normally frightened of thunder and lightning, yet now she felt exuberant, cleansed of the past that had once weighed heavy upon her and her psyche.

"Hi, Dr. Keurig," she answered her phone with her Bluetooth in her ear. They had come a long way from the shoebox car phones that even Ryan had pointed out would go by the wayside. Phones nowadays did indeed have her favorite games on them.

"Are you okay, Ellen? I was worried about you when I didn't hear from you," Nancy expressed.

"I'm doing great, I have a lot to share with you when I get back," Ellen promised. She had never felt so free before and was actually looking forward to filling in the therapist on what she had done, what she had initiated, and what she felt like.

Nancy was surprised. While she thought it was a good idea for Ellen to go back to the home she had once had to perhaps exorcise some of the ghosts, the Ellen she was hearing through the phone was completely different from the one she knew. She sounded so…almost happy. She had to wonder if it was real. "Well, do you want your normal appointment time next Thursday?" she asked hesitantly, not sure if Ellen was really as happy as she sounded.

"Sounds good, I'll be there," Ellen promised and disconnected the call soon afterwards.

Driving towards Las Vegas, she remembered another promise she had made, so she checked in the same hotel outside of Vegas that she had stayed in a little over a week ago. Going to the same diner, she looked around disappointedly when she didn't spot the young girl she had hoped to help. Ordering dinner from the same waitress she waited until she saw the woman wasn't too busy to ask, "Has that girl been in here?"

The waitress looked at the well-dressed woman trying to remember her and then it hit her, she had been the big tipper a week or so ago. Of course she remembered her. "Yeah, she's gotten at least one meal a day here for the last few days," she said sourly. The kid was a menace. Dirty and disheveled, if this woman hadn't prepaid for the meals they would have thrown her out.

"Did I miss her today?" she asked hopefully.

"I haven't seen her today," she answered. "I don't think I saw her yesterday either…" she finished musingly, trying to recall.

"Thanks," Ellen said, realizing the woman just simply didn't care. She ate slowly, hoping the girl would show up. She wanted to live up to her promises. She couldn't help wondering, though, if something had happened to the girl or if she had given up. She'd been gone over the week, but she had mentioned it might take longer. The filing of the paperwork and the subsequent lawsuits through Mr. Mann had taken extra time. Even with her money, bureaucracy took time. A lot of it would happen now that she was gone, but she had started it and Mr. Mann was more than up to the challenge – he was relishing it.

Ellen didn't see the girl that night. She was worried. So much could have happened to the young teenager that she didn't want to think about. She spent a sleepless night in her hotel room, tossing and turning and wondering about her. She genuinely wanted to help her. She'd escaped her past, her own dismal youth, and she wanted to help this girl escape whatever demons drove her.

She considered staying an extra day just to see if the girl would show up. But she had been gone over a week from work already and someone with a job like hers didn't just drop everything and run. She ate at the diner for breakfast, and then for lunch. Before the hotel could charge her for a second night she packed up and drove around the little suburb of Vegas, hoping to catch sight of the youth that she had promised a job to. It wasn't until she approached the interstate that she

caught sight of the girl; a woebegone figure standing on the shoulder of the on-ramp holding up a sign. It read, "West or bust," whatever *that* meant. Ellen slowed down the expensive car beyond where the youth was standing. With no luggage, the girl soon jogged up and looked in the window that Ellen rolled down.

"You!" she said in surprise. She glanced at the expensive sports car and to the woman who had promised to come back. She had been at the diner or thereabouts for the past week and the woman hadn't shown up. They had given her free meals so she didn't mind; it had been the only food she had left without resorting to her past ways to make a meal. She had figured this woman hadn't meant what she said and yet, here she was.

"You want that job or not?" Ellen asked with a grin and leaned across the stick shift to open the door.

The girl hesitated for only a second before sliding into the luxurious car. She was genuinely frightened now. Men and women had preyed on her in the past, but none with such expensive cars as this.

Looking at the girl, she could almost smell her fear. The stringy hair, the ratty jeans, and the dilapidated jacket hid none of the anxiety. She was putting a brave, if insolent face on it, but she was still scared. "What's your name?" Ellen asked as she effortlessly shifted the powerful car through its gears and accelerated onto the interstate.

"Di," she answered sullenly, looking around the car and wondering who this woman was.

"Well, Di, I'm headed for San Francisco and I'll have a job there waiting for you if you want, otherwise you can do what you like," she indicated the cardboard sign the youth was still holding.

"That was just to get out of town, I couldn't stay there anymore," she explained. She shoved the sign on the floor by her feet.

"You don't have a police record or anything that is gonna have someone coming after you back there, do you?" Ellen asked, pointing behind them with her thumb.

Di's stringy hair waved back and forth as she shook her head. "I just couldn't stay after..." she began but then went silent.

"After?" Ellen prompted.

"You said a week," the teen burst out.

"I said a week to a week and half. Sorry if you felt I was late," she explained.

Di was so relieved that she couldn't argue. This was almost like a fairytale and she would do anything this woman wanted. She was out of that little town. She had considered heading back to Vegas but knew that there were worse places for a girl in her position and she didn't want a pimp. This woman hadn't taken her up on her offer of payment. Instead, she had lived up to the promise she had made, even if it wasn't in the time that she had thought she said. She had been so disappointed. She'd given it one more day out of sheer desperation. She'd not gone back to the diner because she felt she was wearing her welcome out there. She'd been surprised they had given her free food every day for that one week. They weren't very nice to her, though, but then she didn't look that good, even she knew she smelled. She hoped this sophisticated woman with her nice car didn't notice.

Ellen did notice and stopped outside Los Angles at a store to buy the teen jeans, underwear, a couple of t-shirts, new sports shoes, and toiletries. She even bought a backpack for the girl to store the extras.

"Why are we stopping here?" Di asked, looking around at the truck stop and wondering if this was an elaborate scheme to sell her to some trucker.

"I thought you'd like a shower before you put all that on," Ellen pointed at the bag that contained all of Di's new worldly possessions. She had her try them on at the store to see that they fit but Di refused to wear them out in public. The store salesperson hadn't been too pleased to have the smelly youth trying on some of the clothes, but Ellen had bought them for her.

"Here?" she asked, still suspicious.

"I'll stand guard," Ellen promised, and then did.

Di stood in the hot spray of the shower a little longer than she intended. The shampoo Ellen had bought was heavenly. She used it sparingly, but still it made her hair clean for the first time in weeks. Sliding into the brand-new clothes was a luxury she would never forget. They were stiff but they were *clean*. That wasn't something she had felt in a very long time, being this clean.

Ellen was startled at the pretty girl who walked out of the shower at the truck stop. She had to pay extra because the youth took so long and the showers were timed. She didn't mind when she saw the result. For once the lanky locks were brushed out, the teen even smiled timidly at her when she expressed how nice she looked. The backpack now contained her extra t-shirts, underwear, and toiletries. She threw away her battered clothes.

"Sure you won't need those again?" Ellen asked, amused at the gesture.

"That's the past, I'm moving on," Di said with confidence. She had considered keeping them; after all, she had lived in them for months. While they had covered her, she didn't miss them. They were embarrassing and she felt clean and confident for the first time in so long. Her stomach rumbled.

"Hungry?" Ellen asked astutely.

Di nodded. She didn't want to ask for anything, but she hadn't eaten in a couple of days since she didn't want to go back to the diner anymore.

Ellen found them a booth at the diner attached to the truck stop. Ellen knew that most of the truck stop diners served decent food; truckers insisted on it. A few of the truckers eyed the two women alone but Ellen's steely look in return had them paying attention to their own meals. No one bothered them as Ellen ordered her meal and then Di ordered her own.

"What will I be doing in San Francisco?" Di asked.

"What do you want to do?" she asked, she was curious what the teen would answer.

No one ever asked Di what she wanted. The question threw her for a moment. "I suppose I should go back to school," she said resignedly.

"Is that what you want to do?"

Di shrugged. "I don't know," she admitted.

Ellen looked at her and waited. The silence spread between them, but Ellen wasn't going to push the girl. It was her decision. She'd help if she could but she couldn't make the decision for her.

The long drive between Los Angeles and San Francisco took the requisite six hours. Ellen could have cut the time down a bit with the powerful engine under the hood but kept to the speed limit. It must have disappointed her passenger as well as a few cops, but she wasn't about to get a ticket. She took Di to a shelter she had contributed money to.

"This is only temporary until you get on your feet," she assured the scared teen. "Go here on Monday and they will be expecting you." She gave her a card for the office she owned in the city. She'd call them after Di was out of her hearing to tell them to expect her, train her, give her a job, any job, but most of all, assess her abilities. If all else she would pay to send the teen back to school if she was so inclined. She'd win a scholarship if her efforts were enough. She'd seen evidence with her own eyes of people in her companies that didn't have college educations and soared. School wasn't for everyone, but while the teen was making up her mind what she wanted out of life, she might want to go. It would give her a polish that she just might need to get ahead.

"Thanks, Ms. Christenson," Di said respectfully. They had talked a lot on the trip and Ellen had introduced herself. She had liked that Ellen hadn't pressured her about what she wanted, what she was going to do. Ellen had just listened when she spoke and offered her own perspective now and then. Otherwise, it hadn't been a "Twenty Questions" uncomfortable ride. As she got out of the Maserati she felt a sense of loss as no one had cared enough or taken the time to help her before.

"I'll see you in a couple of weeks. They'll give me progress reports," Ellen indicated the card.

Di nodded numbly and looked up at the shelter. It was clean at least, and no one was standing about. She took one last look at the expensive sports car with the unusual woman inside and bravely headed in.

Ellen knew that Di would be safe there. They'd give her two weeks to find a place and by then the job should pay enough that she could be on her feet, running if she took it seriously. It was up to the teen and she hoped she'd make it. She'd known if she took her home that would create another set of problems for them both. She was afraid the teen wouldn't or hadn't figured out who she was but she wasn't taking that chance.

❖ CHAPTER TWENTY ❖

HOME

"And here we have the sun room." Judy, the real estate agent, was showing Ellen the house she had bought, sight unseen. Judy was impressed, but then, Ellen Christenson was a catch. She'd made the mistake once before of undervaluing this client, and she wouldn't again. The commission from this sale alone would be nice, very nice. She'd basically used her own name to take this sale. She normally only sold in the City, but for this client, this 'special' client, she had used every trick she could to make it happen. The salespeople that sold in this area weren't exactly pleased with her, but it was a cutthroat business.

So far Ellen was pleased with her impulsive purchase. She knew that had Ryan been alive he would have been pleased with her. It was a home, not just a house to live in. It felt warm and cozy and the furnishings that would be arriving soon would go into this modern version of an antique house perfectly. She loved it already. She would have to buy some other furnishings, but she wasn't in a hurry. The things she had at her other house wouldn't fit in here and she wondered what she would do with them. Maybe donate them to the shelter, or maybe to some other charity.

The sun room was rounded with beveled windows that allowed sunlight to refract as it came through their slanted edges, dark wood edged around each of the beautiful windows. The effect was stunning, with rainbows abounding in the ornately appointed room. Whoever had built the house had loved rich woods, and the wood glowed with a cornice on each corner which matched molding leading up to them. Wide windowsills meant that plants could be placed on the shelves that stuck out under the windows, and antique latches gave the windows a finished look as their brass was already molded in a way to make them ageless.

Each room in the house had ornate touches, crown molding, and gorgeous woods that despite being crafted in the last few years made the new house old and settled. The wall to wall wood floors did not creak but the walker would listen for that, expecting it in this house. The banisters glowed in the sunlight that streamed through the various windows strategically placed throughout to bring in the Northern California rays. A switch and the windows would be covered in blinds, curtains, or shutters depending on their location. The whole house glowed like it had just been polished and yet the beams of light had dust floating in them. It was warm, rich, and opulent.

It was touches like this throughout the house that pleased Ellen beyond measure. Despite being an impulse, it was fate that had led her to this purchase. This was the first house since her mother was alive that felt like a home and it was hers.

"What would you like to do with your other house?" Judy asked astutely. Almost as though she was reading Ellen's mind. She had watched her client fall in love with this house. She too would have loved to buy it but it was well beyond her means. The builder had several houses in this section, all different, and yet his eye for detail had allowed him to employ the best craftsmen and women. People who knew how to build to last. This house should last hundreds of years with all its modern conveniences, including a state of the art security system, and yet it would always feel like an antique.

"I'm not sure yet if I should rent it out or sell it," Ellen admitted honestly. She'd thought it over on the trip back. It was the first place she had bought and even though Ryan had sold his identical one next door, it had a certain nostalgic value to her. She'd lived in it for years and yet it didn't feel like home. This house, this modern Victorian, this felt like home and it didn't even have any furnishings in it.

Knowing exactly where Ellen lived, Judy recognized the value of the house. While that builder hadn't been too imaginative in his style choices, she thought this house that Ellen had purchased in the Rolling Hills Estates was much better for her image as a techie in the Valley. It

wasn't a mini-mansion and she knew that Ellen could afford one of those, but being a single woman, she thought this an excellent choice. It was still a gated community and would afford her some privacy; it was situated on a couple of acres of land so she didn't have neighbors looking through her windows. The landscaping was extensive and finished exquisitely, and the overall look of the house was complete. Ellen hadn't quibbled on the price either, and although she could afford it, it showed how much she had wanted this place. Judy wondered if perhaps she was settling down as this house was built for a family.

Once given the keys to her new house and the pass-cards to the estate gate (which was also manned part of the time), Ellen was ready to move in since the house had been vacant. She called the moving company to arrange delivery of her belongings as soon as they arrived in California. She smiled into the phone, delighted to hear they could be there the following day. Knowing what her work schedule would have been had she not had to go to Oklahoma, she sighed thinking about the hours she would have to devote just to catch up. She started to pack the things in her old house she would be taking with her to the new house, leaving most of her furnishings at the old house intact. She took great joy in the few hours she took to shop for furnishings and she started hitting up antique stores. Normally a workaholic, she now began making herself take time off and she enjoyed every moment of it.

"Hello, Ellen," a surprised Rae said when they ran into each other up in Napa. Seeing the well-dressed Ellen Christenson in a dusty old antique store of all places was not something she would ever have thought to see.

Ellen looked back at her in equal surprise. Her single forays into these places had become her special indulgence. Nancy had been surprised at the change that took over her patient, including taking time off to get away from her office now and again. She was pleased, though, very pleased, with Ellen's progress after her trip. She hadn't been pleased at Ellen's vengeance on the people of that small town, but Ellen's attitude over it all, even her tiny bit of regret over the lawsuits, showed how much she had been growing as a person. "Rae, how nice to see you again," Ellen answered and truly meant it. The woman she had apologized to months ago was a delight to the senses. Her well-kept appearance, the rich chestnut hair that begged to have fingers comb through it, even her mode of dress, casual but elegant, bespoke class. She had actually meant the apology she had tendered to *this* woman. She thought of it as an almost twelve-step program that had garnered her peace in her world.

"What in the world are you doing in an antique shop up here in Napa?" Rae couldn't help asking. She looked at the redhead and noticed she looked relaxed, something she couldn't remember EVER

saying about Ellen before. She was one of the most *intense* women she
had ever met, which was part of the reason she had been so attracted to
her. Dressed in jeans, albeit designer ones, a checkered shirt, and high-
heeled boots rather than her usual business suit, she looked chic and
dressed down.

"Oh, I'm furnishing a house I purchased down in the Valley," Ellen
told her truthfully. She was looking for a bedroom set for the place.
She was sleeping on mattresses and that wasn't acceptable. She could
find a new bed set but preferred the idea of an antique set if she could
find the right one. She'd already found two unacceptable ones that she
put into the extra bedrooms she had upstairs in the house. They just
weren't right for the master suite.

Rae was shocked. Everything she had ever seen in Ellen's
apartment in the city was modern. Even the furnishings in that house
she had owned next to Ryan Mahoney's had been functional, nothing
dusty or old or antique-ish in sight. Other than a few trinkets she had
from her mother, nothing was personal in that place. "What did you
buy?" she asked, curious.

"I got a Victorian house up in Rolling Hills Estates," she mentioned
and waited for Rae to acknowledge that she knew where that was
before she continued. "I decided I needed a home, not merely a
house," she explained. She knew that this woman of all the women she
had dated would understand.

Rae nodded but she was beyond shocked at the news. *This* woman
didn't care about such things. She was too busy, too much a
workaholic to have time for a home and family. It was one of the many
reasons they had broken up. Rae had wanted to start a family, she had
wanted a baby, and realized after their breakup that Ellen was the
wrong person to want that with at the time. The reason she gave was
that she didn't wish to perpetuate her family's faults. Even if the baby
would be Rae's she didn't want a child to mess up her life. It was when
Rae had analyzed her and told her that she felt she had Gamophobia, a
fear of marriage, that the relationship had really turned sour. "Wow,
that must be quite a change," she stated.

Ellen nodded and on impulse asked, "Want to help me look?"

Rae shrugged and smiled. "Why not?" Ellen was good company
and the change in her she couldn't understand but she did enjoy. After
hitting several antique shops, they went to lunch and Ellen delighted
her, charmed her, and asked her out, which Rae accepted much to their
mutual surprise. After being hurt by Ellen so long ago she had thought
she would never again go on a date with her, but *this* Ellen, this
completely changed Ellen, she could like her. She realized the apology
that Ellen had given her those months ago had been the beginning of a
change in her, and she wondered how much and what had really caused
it.

⚜ CHAPTER TWENTY ONE ⚜

STUDENT EXUBERANCE

"You want to do what, with what?" Ellen asked the group of young students before her in her loftiest tones. She recognized them from their Oklahoman accents, but her own was safely tucked away.

"We want to use your circuits in sensors we're trying to develop," the leader of their little group said enthusiastically. He had to be about twenty-four.

"Then we want to put the sensors up in a tornado," another one piped up and Ellen looked at him dubiously.

"And how do you propose to do that?" Ellen asked skeptically. She really had to have a chat with her secretary at allowing proposals like this to be offered to her personally. Her time was far too valuable for such nonsense.

"We will put them in a machine we intend to build and then put that in the line of the tornado's path and we hope it will suck it up," their leader – a dubious honor she was sure – imparted.

"Hasn't someone already done something like this?" she asked, trying to vaguely remember a movie on this very subject.

They nodded instantly. "But it didn't have the technology we would put in it," he answered with youthful naiveté.

"Do you have the schematics available for your proposed machine?" she asked, she was sure they were unprepared and the six of them would have to leave soon. She was beginning to feel a bit…claustrophobic with all this enthusiasm.

"We do," he assured her. He pulled a folded piece of paper from his pocket and handed it to her.

Ellen nearly laughed. Most engineers or architects had schematics drawn on poster sized or blueprint papers. This was obviously hand-drawn. She looked at it anyway. It was actually intriguing.

"We were hoping your partner would take a look at this and maybe give us a hand?" he asked tentatively.

Without looking up, Ellen dismissed it with, "My partner died." She looked up at the genuine groans she heard from the group.

"Oh, then are there any engineers that could possibly take a look at this?" he asked hopefully.

She looked at him and sat back in her chair. "What makes you think I'm not an engineer?" she asked in a frosty voice.

He blinked. His companions blinked. The girl amongst them smiled a little secret smile as she nodded as though she had just had a secret confirmed.

"I'm sorry, I thought you were the administrative genius of the operation," he apologized, trying to make immediate amends and thinking he had just blown their one and only opportunity.

"I am," she admitted. "But that doesn't mean I don't know what our products do or how to make them," she pointed out.

"Is it possible you could help us with this, then?" he asked hopefully again.

"Why didn't you go to your own engineers? I'm almost certain Oklahoma has several schools that would contain engineers."

He nodded. "We were hoping to apply for a grant or a scholarship to work here, too. It's why we made the trip ourselves and put in for a meeting with you. We were hoping to plead our case. The engineers laughed at us and our plans. We can make it if we have the supplies, but being able to buy the sensors will just about kill us," he explained.

She knew how expensive things of that nature could be; it's what was part of their bread and butter here. She knew her partners on the electronics side of the business wouldn't be too happy if she gave away the product, either. "How many of these sensors were you planning on putting into this?" Her hand slapped at the paper he had given her with his plans.

"We thought about five-hundred per barrel, each," he added belatedly.

"Each?" she asked with her eyes narrowing. They all shifted nervously. "How many of these apparatuses were you planning on making for your little adventure?" she asked astutely.

"Six," he confessed and then held his breath. It sounded like a lot and they all knew it. But they figured if anything happened to one machine, there would be a backup, and they would learn from each of the backups and improve on them. Six had seemed like a comfortable number to work with.

Ellen sat back in her chair again, thinking. "Do you have a resume?" she asked suddenly.

He shook his head. As she glanced at the others they shook their heads too.

"Tell you what. You write out your proposal to me, completely and professionally. You write out decent schematics for your machine, again, completely. I want cost analyses and a budget. Bring all that to me as well as your resumes, and I do mean ALL," she glanced at the group sitting across from her. "Once I look over your proposal I may have something for you, but only if you do your homework," she advised.

They exchanged glances and nods as one by one they agreed to her proposal. Their leader stood up and they all followed. Ellen stood up out of respect. "We'll do that, Ms. Christenson, we'll surely do that," he said enthusiastically and reached out to shake her hand.

Ellen smiled as he shook her hand as enthusiastically as his outrageous proposal had been. As she escorted them out she called to secretary to come in.

"How in the world did they get in here?" she asked, fixing a stern eye on her assistant.

"I, I, I guess they were on your calendar," she hedged and then she saw Ellen's expression and crumbled. "Bobby's my cousin and he begged me to get him in to see you. I didn't really know the whole story and I ..." she started to go on and on but Ellen held up her hand.

"In the future, you tell me what their 'story' is, and I'll determine if I'll listen to their proposal, okay?"

Her secretary, immensely relieved that she hadn't been fired on the spot, nodded. Now Ellen could see the resemblance to one of the group.

"And here," she said handing the folded paper the boy had left on her desk. "Get this back to them if you would?"

"Yes, Ms. Christenson. Right away, Ms. Christenson."

She shook her head as the woman quickly backed out of her office and went back to work.

❖ CHAPTER TWENTY TWO ❖

THERAPY

"**D**o you think that reliving your childhood remembrances has helped you to move on?" Nancy asked her.

"I think I've exorcised the demons. I know I'm happier. Definitely healthier," she answered. She had been wondering if she needed to come to therapy anymore. Ryan's stipulations in his will had been met. All except for meeting his daughter, and she had made that call for next week.

"And dating Rae, don't you think that's a setback?" Nancy had to wonder at her own objectivity about Ellen's dating. She knew if Ellen weren't a client, she would ask this brilliant and attractive woman out. She knew most of her faults, she knew how she ticked, and still the redhead kept surprising her.

"Actually, I think it's fate," she smiled at that admission. Fate, Karma, she knew some people really believed in that. She wasn't sure she did. "She was a good friend back in the day and I'm glad she is back in my life for however long it is."

"That doesn't sound like you think it will last," Nancy said astutely. Inside she was hopeful that Ellen would stay single. It gave her a chance to make a move when they were no longer doctor and patient.

Ellen shrugged. "None of my relationships last," she admitted. "But I have to start somewhere and I liked Rae back in the day. I've grown. She's different, too." Maybe Rae wasn't really different, maybe she just saw her differently, Ellen admitted to herself. She knew she had been a lot of fun to be with as she helped her shop for her bedroom set and once that was found, other odds and ends for the house. She had exquisite taste. Rae had been astonished at the warm and cozy house Ellen was putting together.

"It's fantastic, Ellen," she told her reverently. She'd always wished to have a place like this; she could see children playing in the backyard. She knew better that to suggest that to Ellen, though. She knew her views on children, or she had at one point.

"Do you think that having a past with Rae might affect your future relationship with her?" Nancy was trying to remain professional. She didn't realize yet how her own feelings were affecting this session, but she would later when she analyzed her notes.

"I think it's time I grew up and moved on. Enough about the past, my past actually. I'm ready to move on and enjoy myself. God knows I've paid my dues."

"Which dues are those?"

"I've worked hard since college. I've done nothing but work. It's time I enjoyed the fruits of my labor. Ryan would have wanted that for me. Hell, he always encouraged me to take time off. Now I do." She had made shopping in antique shops a regular thing and having Rae along had made it even more of a pleasure. She did see the woman in a different light now and while their relationship wasn't exclusive yet, they hadn't taken it to a more intimate level. She enjoyed having Rae as a friend, something she hadn't let her be before. Having a friend, one that could potentially be her lover, was a novelty to her and she wasn't going to ruin it, not this time.

"Well, I'm pleased to see the changes." Nancy was trying to be fair.

"I think I'm ready for them. I thank you for your help and listening to me over all this time," Ellen told her with a finality that made Nancy worry. "I think I won't be coming here anymore," she finished, which confirmed the trepidation that had struck Nancy at her tone.

"Are you sure that's what you want?" she wasn't ready to let go, not yet. She enjoyed seeing her for these weekly sessions. They had worked through so much together.

"Yes, I think it's time. I didn't want to come in the first place." She gave Nancy an apologetic look, but she moved on. "I'm both surprised and happy at how much you've helped me, but it's time I think," she said with absolute conviction.

This was the confident woman that had entered her office so long ago. Before, some of it had been bravado. Now it was part of her that was going to break Nancy's heart. Well, she could ask her out now if they weren't patient and doctor. She'd have to wait a bit and she hoped Ellen wasn't too serious with this Rae. She'd have to run across her at some function. Maybe she too would start antiquing. "Well, you know I will always be here if you feel you need a tune-up," she told her professionally.

"I know, thank you for all you've done," Ellen said politely and stood up. She offered the doctor her hand, and after they shook she took her leave.

Doctor Nancy Keurig watched her walk out of her office and her life with regrets. She sighed. It wasn't professional of her to have had these feelings. She must remember that. She had to let her go. Maybe, if fate was in her favor, they would meet again.

❖ CHAPTER TWENTY THREE ❖

RYAN'S DREAMS

"**O**h, Ryan would have loved you," Ellen told the two people in front of her who had just proposed a movie to her.

They exchanged a smile and looked at her hopefully. "With the technology we saw at the convention that Ryan developed, I'm certain your company Animated Studios has exactly what we're looking for."

"Well, what you are proposing, I think we can actually do. We can integrate the live action in a way that our animated art will look natural. It will be like nothing the public has ever seen before," Ellen mused, imagining it in her head from the storyboards they had presented and wishing she could show it to Ryan. He would have loved it and jumped on the idea. It was why she was inclined to do the project so readily.

"Then you will look at our proposal and get back to us with a quote?" he asked hopefully.

"Absolutely," Ellen promised with a handshake as they handed her the packet. "How soon do you need to know?"

"Yesterday," the woman answered with a smile. "Everything in Hollywood is yesterday," she explained with a self-depreciating little grin. "Hurry up and wait," she amended, looking into the redhead's eyes with a bit of interest. There was a little something more there too that Ellen mentally filed but wouldn't pursue without further investigation. It didn't pay to date someone you were going to work for. She had learned that the hard way by dating employees once or twice. Ryan had joked with her, but they'd been lucky that they hadn't been sued.

"Well, I will look at this soon and you will be hearing from me, I assure you," she said, closing the meeting. They had asked for this meeting shortly after the latest electronics convention where Animated Studios along with Gigitech had both shown off their latest to prospective buyers. After all, it was part of Ellen's job to continue to expand the company even after Ryan's death. She had an obligation to her employees and stockholders as well as the minor partners she had picked up from companies she had bought out to do so.

"We look forward to hearing from you," they assured her and left the office. The woman, Sherrie Spotweiler, glanced over her shoulder before she closed the door behind her. That look told Ellen a lot.

"Well, well, well," Ellen said aloud and then sat down and opened the packet. The proposal they had pitched her sounded so much better than the dry words on the paper she was reading. It did, however, serve to emphasize their much more animated and broad proposal that they had verbally presented. She laughed at the little cartoon characters they had drawn in it. Ryan, with his comic books, would have loved this.

Pressing a button on her intercom, she waited for someone to answer it.

"Yes, boss?" she heard a voice come through the line.

"Hey, can you assemble the best of the best and meet me in the conference room?" she asked. She wanted them on this right away. This was exactly the kind of project Ryan had loved and wanted Animated Studios to head into. Not just cartoons, but real movies that had special effects. They could really enjoy this kind of work. The computer-generated graphics, or CG, that they would be able to embrace would make it a reality. The visual effects would be stunning and very, very real.

In the conference room, they spent hours going over the packet, shooting out concepts and throwing them around. By the time Ellen finally brought the impromptu meeting to a close, everyone was excited about the ideas. They were working feverishly to pencil in the proposal and to incorporate their own ideas into it.

"Okay, we are agreed, you will have some working numbers to me by the end of the week?" she asked with a smile. She knew that creative minds such as these needed to expand their horizons, and the work they had been doing, while enjoyable, didn't excite them the way that a project of this magnitude might. Their eyes sparkled, their brains

snapped, and they were all amped up. Ellen knew that her normal ice-princess personality would never work with these employees. It was why she was such a study in contrasts, and why they were so successful with the employees they hired. She let them use her company to let their skills expand and she used their skills to expand the company.

❊ CHAPTER TWENTY FOUR ❊

FRUSTRATED

Rae was a little annoyed. She wasn't sure where her relationship with Ellen was going. She knew they were dating but Ellen made no attempt to make love to her, and as they had enjoyed a healthy sex life the last time they dated, she had to wonder if they were only fated to be friends. Ellen would kiss her, chastely, respectfully, but any attempts to deepen them had the redhead withdrawing.

She enjoyed their dates, though. Ellen was much more adventurous now. They went out more, on hikes, on forays into places that would result in a trip to an antique store, to even a historical monument. It was much different than the clubbing or eating out they would have done in the past. This thoughtful Ellen was a relief. But still, Rae was frustrated. She wanted to be with Ellen. She wanted a future with her. She had fallen in love with her once but to have a second chance like this and finding Ellen changed had made her fall in love with all over again deeper, stronger, and frustrating. The redhead infuriated and delighted her by equal turns.

"When you say, 'the Valley' this far north people are going to assume you're talking about Napa." Rae laughed at the confused expression on Ellen's face.

"When I say, 'the Valley,' I always assume Silicon," she returned the laugh, amused with herself. This too was new; she would have been annoyed at the misunderstanding before.

Overall, she had a lighter feel about her which Rae had noticed, enjoyed, and fallen deeper in love with. The redhead held her heart and hadn't cared before, but now she treated her and it with kid-gloves. But attempts to kiss had never gone beyond a certain point. To say that Rae was becoming frustrated was an understatement.

"Why don't you want to make love to me?" she asked after a frustrating encounter on Ellen's new couch in the living room. It was an exact replica of a 1920's velvet club couch, and Ellen had wavered on buying it as it was a brilliant red in color. Rae had talked her into it and it had just been delivered along with a matching chaise longue that looked fabulous, comfortable, and a tiny bit naughty. They had both sat on it to test it out and Rae had found herself kissing Ellen.

"It's not that I don't want to," Ellen said uncomfortably. "I just don't want to ruin things between us."

"How could you ruin things?" she asked bewildered.

"I royally screwed things up before," she answered, looking away, ashamed.

"I think it takes two to end a relationship," Rae said astutely.

Ellen looked at her sadly. "I've gone through a lot since then," she tried to explain.

"You told me about Ryan dying. I knew that anyway. I read the papers."

"Well, there is that, but he had a requirement in his will..." she started and began to squirm.

Rae noticed how uncomfortable Ellen was talking about this. What could it be that would make this cool and collected woman fidget? "What was it?" she asked simply.

"I had to go to therapy."

"That's it?" Rae asked astonished. Everyone *she* knew had a therapist.

"Yeah, that's part of it," she admitted, she could feel the old bane of a redhead's existence beginning again as she blushed.

"Is that why you called me all those months ago? To make amends because you were going through therapy? Your therapist put you up to it?" Rae was beginning to become angry. This was the old calculating Ellen she had known before. One who didn't care about another's feelings or emotions.

"No, that was me, totally me. I felt, I *needed* to make amends somehow and apologizing to you was part of that." She wasn't about

to tell Rae that she was one of many who received phone calls and apologies.

"Why did you feel the need?" she asked in a gentler tone. She could see Ellen was trying, but for what?

Ellen shrugged eloquently. "I just felt the past needed to be gone from my life, all that negativity. The way I was before is not how I am now."

Rae could agree with that. The old Ellen wouldn't have talked like this, spoken about anything in her past. It was why she had been so intriguing, living in the present. She glanced around the room. Even this room, a modern house, had an 'old' feeling. Like a house from the turn of the 19th century. It had all the modern convenience, stainless steel appliances, but the woods, the rich woods were something that their grandmothers, hell, their great-grandmothers, would have had in their homes. "Does this mean we won't be having sex?" she asked, trying to lighten the mood.

Ellen grinned at the tone. "It's not that I don't want to," she began. "It's just that I wanted to take things slowly so I didn't blow this chance with you," she finished earnestly.

Rae was amazed to see this side of Ellen. She was almost...vulnerable. Something that wasn't often said about Ellen Christenson, the President of Gigitech and Animated Studios. "What if I told you that you won't blow this chance with me by making love to me?" her voice had become husky with the need and want she was feeling for this dynamic redhead.

Ellen fidgeted. "Can you give me a little more time?"

Inside Rae sighed gustily; outside she smiled and said, "Of course."

As they moved the antiques Ellen had stored for so long around the house, tweaking things, making it comfortable, Rae was surprised at the nostalgia that was in Ellen and her furnishings. The stories that Ellen now shared about her mother and the history behind her furnishings were intriguing. The things they found in the antique stores and what drew Ellen fascinated Rae as she helped her. The delightful lunches they shared on their adventures only made her fall more in love. But where was it going? Rae was starting to feel cautious as she began to protect her heart from what she was sure would eventually be the hurt. Yes, it was different this time, but Ellen hadn't let it progress naturally. She had called a definite halt to things beyond a certain point.

"Do you mind being there for the bed set?" Ellen called her.

"No, I have the card and key you gave me. I don't mind," Rae answered, wondering if she was just the delivery girl for Ellen's things. Her schedule was a lot easier to adjust than Ellen's was. She frequently worked from home on the paperwork she entered into the database for doctors all over the bay area.

"I'll bring dinner. Would you like anything special?"

"Oh, you're cooking?" she teased.

"My kinda cookin'," she laughed as she mentioned a few take out places they frequented. They decided on Italian since they both loved the lasagna from one place.

Rae brought her computer and worked from Ellen's house while she waited for the delivery. She was really excited to see it set up in the blank space that had been the master bedroom before. When it arrived, she ran her fingers along the scrolls and embossing of the rich woods. Using a rag and some Murphy's Oil, she shined it up before struggling with the mattress and placing it on the bed. She awkwardly maneuvered the box spring into a spare bedroom as it wasn't necessary with this old bed. Looking through the linen cabinet, she remade the bed with fresh sheets, spread out the comforter she knew Ellen loved – the soft, squishy one that hugged a body – and fluffed up the pillows. When it was done, it looked inviting and she longed to make love to the redhead in it.

At the end of the bed she placed a chest that perfectly matched the wood of the bed, strategically centering it between the upright posts of the footboard. She looked at the posts and thought for a moment and went back to the linen closet to grab some wispy material and drape it across the posts like a valiance. It wasn't really what it was for, maybe for curtains or drapes at one time, but it looked beautiful against the shining wood and made the bed even more inviting.

She looked about the room, the theme of dark wainscoting, crown molding, and other 'old' touches made it look warm. She looked into the walk-in closet of Ellen's. The walls weren't lined with clothes, but what was there was expensive and uniform. She had good taste but the many suits were all similar. Almost as though Ellen had taken a course in Business 101 and bought all the same suits in many different colors. They weren't exactly alike but they were power suits and Ellen always looked professional in them. Even when she dressed down for antique shopping she still looked classy and semi-professional. The slacks that hung on the second rack of clothes were even more numerous than the suits. The shelves containing shoes lined the back wall, and with a flick of her wrist she turned on the light to illuminate all the shelves showing off their many colors and styles. On the left side of the closet, there was open space for even more clothes. She wondered if she would ever share this beautiful house with Ellen, but she wasn't going to push it. She wanted it too much to let herself ruin this.

Turning out the lights in the closet, she looked into the luxurious bathroom. Luxury was a pattern repeated throughout this place. The double sinks were lined with mirrors at their backs. Each sink had a cobalt blue glass base with golden dolphins for spigots. Ellen had confessed that she didn't like the dolphins but had kept them because they looked nice against the blue. She glanced at the warming towel rack across from the toilet and bidet. Seeing the walk-in shower, she longed to take one and try out the recirculating foot massager and many heads along the walls that would insure a relaxing water massage. There was also the large rectangular tub sunk into the floor big enough for two, and it too had jets to massage the user with powerful jets of water. She had never used any of it and wondered why Ellen had never invited her to. Sighing again, she left the master suite and went down to the den where she popped open her laptop to work on some paperwork remotely.

After an hour, she glanced up from the never-ending work and saw that Ellen was due at any moment and she was glad. She was hungry in more ways than one. She already could anticipate the lasagna, and her stomach was growling. She looked about the den and thought about starting a fire in the fireplace to create a romantic atmosphere. She also thought about popping a bottle of wine but knew she would probably drink more of it than Ellen would and that wouldn't be good since she knew she would be driving home later and not staying over. She looked at the leathers of the settee and matching chairs. The brass buttons holding the leather in pockets were a nice touch against the burgundy of the matching leather. She was comfortable with the leg rest up when she heard Ellen come through the back door.

"Hey, I'm here. Where are you?"

"In the den," she called as she quickly finished up where she was in her work and closed the laptop in time to see Ellen walk in. "Hi," she said as she reached for the hidden button to collapse the leg rest.

"Hi," Ellen smiled, walking up to her as she stood up and putting her arms around her for a kiss. "How'd it go?" she asked.

"Oh, the bed looks fantastic," she enthused, eagerly anticipating Ellen's pleasure over the bed and its setup. She knew that Ellen hadn't expected her to set it up for her, merely wait for the delivery but she was happy that she had done it, despite nearly cracking her head on the headboard in assembling it.

"I'll put it together later but I'm starving. Let's eat," she said as she tugged on Rae's hand to lead her to the kitchen where she had deposited the takeout.

"Oh yes, that smells delicious," she said, sniffing appreciatively.

They set out the lasagna, breadsticks, and salad at the kitchenette and sat discussing Ellen's work. Her job was endlessly fascinating to Rae.

"So they wanted an accounting of the sensors, and the boys are working on them in the department. It's funny how enthusiastic and grateful they are," she said with a grin as she cut a slice of the lasagna.

"I'm surprised that you would offer them the grant to do that," Rae stated.

"Yeah, so are my partners in Gigitech but I'm the majority stockholder so what I say goes," she let the flavor of the rich sauces in the lasagna seep into her taste buds and nearly closed her eyes at the flavor. "Besides, an 'anonymous' grant was made to pay for the rest of their research including a truck with seating for six that will hold two of their machines," she confessed around a mouthful of food.

"So, what about you? What'd you do today?" she asked to change the subject, taking an interest in the other woman.

Rae shrugged dismissively. "I just did some online paperwork." She took a bite of her bread that she had dipped in the sauce of the lasagna.

"Why do you do that? Your job is important, too," Ellen said, watching Rae lick the sauce caught on the corner of her mouth, her little tongue darting out, making the redhead want to groan.

"Not as important as yours," she smiled wryly at the comparison, gesturing with a breadstick.

"Rae, I just got lucky. This was Ryan's dream, not mine," she told her quietly. "Your job sounds much more real than mine."

"What was your dream?" she asked.

Ellen looked down at her plate, not as hungry as she once was. She shrugged. "I honestly don't know what dreams I had. I just wanted out of Oklahoma." She paused for a long moment before continuing. "Then when I got to college I met Ryan and the rest is history," she smiled.

That long pause though spoke volumes to Rae. "Why don't you ever talk about it?" she asked.

"Talk about what?" she hedged.

"Your time in Oklahoma," she pointed out.

"It's in the past, let's leave it there," she answered a bit sharply. She saw the hurt on Rae's face but Rae quickly masked it. Suddenly she jumped up from the table. "We need some wine," she said as though just noticing they had no beverage.

They didn't discuss what was bothering Rae. They didn't discuss Ellen's past. They tried to enjoy the rest of their dinner but the issue hung over them.

Rae followed Ellen upstairs ostensibly to 'help' her put together the bed that had arrived that day. She walked in behind her, holding Ellen's hand when she stopped to see that the bed was not only put together but the matching dressers had been placed strategically about the room. It all shone beautifully and the scent of lemon was in the air. The draped linen looked wonderful.

"Oh, Rae," she breathed. "Thank you," she turned to thank her girlfriend and to give her a kiss.

Rae saw the genuine joy in the redhead's eyes. A bit of a tear in them and she was overcome. She put more into that kiss and found she couldn't stop.

"No, Rae." Ellen tried to back away, to put a halt to the impassioned kiss they had begun to share, as the initial 'thank you' had gone on a bit longer than it should have. Like she had been doing for a while now, she tried to stop it, turning and walking up to one of the dressers by the wall.

Seeing her turn away hurt Rae. She got slightly angry as she walked up behind her. Pushing her against the wall, she reached around her and ripped open her blouse. The buttons shot against the wall and bounced off the wainscoting. She was thrilled to find that Ellen was wearing a bra that opened in the front, and she flicked it open with her fingertips.

"Wait, no," Ellen protested weakly as Rae began to lick at her neck and then up to her ear, causing tingles that filtered down her spine.

Rae had had enough. She started caressing down Ellen's front, cupping her breasts, using her hips to grind against Ellen's rear. The moans that Ellen managed to eke out began to drive her crazy. She wanted Ellen as she had never wanted another woman. She slipped off her suit jacket, trying not to release Ellen as she held her tightly, freeing up her own arms to hold the woman and ravage. She wasn't getting away, not this time. Her fingers plunged into the waistband of Ellen's skirt, seeking, investigating, finding….

Ellen bucked against Rae, trying halfheartedly to get her off of her but she was surprisingly strong. She didn't want to hurt her and she found herself excited to be taken like this. Never had Rae shown she could be this aggressive. The touch of Rae's fingers on her front though weakened her resolve; she *didn't want* this, did she? She was always in control, and yet, not this time as Rae held her firmly, not releasing her, kissing along her neck and sucking on her ear lobe. She gasped as Rae cupped her breasts. The feel of the palms of her hands on the nipples was exciting. She felt them harden within Rae's hands.

She moaned, trying to stifle it and failing. She could feel her arousal as one hand left her breast and began to trail down her stomach, the skin clenching at the touch. Rae reached inside the waistband of her skirt and Ellen tried to buck again, unwittingly bucking into Rae's hand.

"You aren't getting away," Rae breathed in her ear as she began to rub between Ellen's legs. She could feel the kernel of flesh harden beneath her fingers as her nipple had against the palm of her hand a moment before.

Ellen was lost. Used to taking command of any situation, including her love life, she was accustomed to being in charge, giving it up though was something new to her and she wasn't sure she could do it. Rae gave her no choice.

Licking along her neck and ear, Rae breathed deeply and warmly inside it. Her tongue followed, making Ellen go weak at the knees. "Oh," she breathed out as Rae expertly began to play with her clit.

Ellen's attempts to pull back away from Rae's questing fingers caused her butt to grind unintentionally against Rae who used it to further seduce her. "I want you," she breathed as she rubbed harder, using the moisture she found to slicken the passage and hold Ellen hostage.

"Hmph," she breathed hard, unable or unwilling to move. Her struggles were used against her and she was held captive by Rae's fingers. It didn't take long before she felt the familiar tingle as her clit released her in an orgasm. "Uh, uh, uhhhh," she moaned as Rae thrust and rubbed simultaneously. She went limp slightly before gathering her wits about her, realizing her need to keep this on a certain level was over. She turned in Rae's arms, looking at her intently, her eyes burning into Rae's.

Rae worried for only a moment before Ellen spun her about and pushed her against the wall, hard. She kissed her passionately and just as hard, demanding a reaction. Already heated by what she had done to Ellen, she responded accordingly. She found her own work suit discarded on the floor along with the rest of Ellen's before she was pushed onto the bed. Her carefully made bed was soon mussed as they expended their passions together on it, dancing the age-old dance of two lovers.

"I love you," Ellen breathed after their second set of orgasms began to wane.

Rae held her close, smiling down into her laughing eyes, not responding verbally. Raising up, Rae lightly teased her nipples against Ellen's and to her fevered mind they seemed to harden imperceptibly. She reached down once again and was surprised to find that Ellen was still hard, her thumb rubbed it and Ellen arched.

"Nooo," she breathed, not meaning a word of it as her body betrayed her once again.

Rae slipped easily inside again, loving the warm feeling of the slick passage. Watching Ellen rise to the occasion, again and again, had excited her beyond reason. She pushed and pushed and Ellen took and took. It was a revelation to both of them as she thrust and rubbed and enjoyed.

Ellen kissed her passionately in appreciation. Her lips slipped from Rae's and buried themselves in the hollow of her neck. Her teeth bit gently along her shoulder until she couldn't remember what she was doing and she bit hard. It was only later that she had to apologize for the bruise and teeth marks that she left.

"Oh my god, no more," she complained good-naturedly after having gone down on Rae and tasted the results of their passion. Cleaning it up had been so eminently satisfying, knowing that Rae had gotten so excited at what they shared.

Chuckling, Rae turned to her. "You've never been like that," she said by way of inquiry.

"I'd worried for so long if I gave up control I wouldn't enjoy it."

"Are you angry with me?" Rae worried for a moment.

"No, not at all," Ellen assured her.

"So, are all your fears laid to rest?" she said with a grin and then turned serious when Ellen's thoughtful demeanor blackened.

"No, I'm afraid if I told you everything you'd leave me in a heartbeat," she said honestly. She had never felt this vulnerable before.

❧ CHAPTER TWENTY FIVE ❧

EXPLANATIONS

Ellen sat up, pulling the sheet with her. She brushed her hair back off her face. Looking at Rae, she knew at that moment what it was to love another person besides Ryan. She didn't want to lose Rae, but she had to be honest with her. They had just shared an incredible experience. She'd had an epiphany of sorts. She could give of herself without giving up her control; or rather she could give up control, and fully give of herself. It was very enlightening. She owed this woman, who she loved, the truth, the *whole* truth.

"What do you mean?" Rae asked almost fearfully as she sat up, pulling the sheet up to wrap herself in it and hide her nudity. Had she gone too far? Was Ellen going to kick her out?

Ellen heard the trepidation in her girlfriend's voice. Smiling, she reached out to cup Rae's beautiful face and lean in to kiss her. She could smell the sex between them. In fact, the room reeked of it. It was the sweetest perfume she had smelled in a very long time. "Please don't worry, babe. I love you," she said comfortingly. "I wasn't just saying it in the throes," she reminded her with a shy little smile.

Rae wanted to laugh with joy. She hadn't been sure that Ellen would remember what she said as she came over and over again in her arms. Her heart had soared at finally hearing her say it, but to have it repeated and so easily made her want to cry with joy. Her eyes teared up at the sentiment. "I love you too," she told her to be clear.

Ellen kissed her again and leaned her forehead against her. "Let's be honest, always," she whispered.

"Always," Rae agreed. "What did you mean a moment ago?"

Ellen wished she hadn't said anything. She'd spoken her thoughts aloud and should have waited for a more appropriate time. Not when they were both naked and vulnerable. "I want to tell you my story. Something I never told Ryan. Something I never told my therapist, even," she started.

"You don't have to…" Rae cautioned her, but Ellen caressed the side of her head. Rae couldn't help but lean into the affectionate hand that pleasured her so well.

"I want to. It's time. I'm scared though that you might not like what I'm going to tell you," she said sadly. She had to take a chance. She had to be honest, perhaps for the first time in her life. She loved Rae too much to keep parts of her hidden anymore.

"What, did you kill someone?" Rae teased to lighten the mood.

Ellen nodded and said, "Yes." Nothing more, just simply, 'Yes.'

Rae waited for the punchline. It didn't come. Ellen's voice hadn't been teasing. She stared at her lover and waited. The wait went on too long and she asked, "You were kidding, right?"

Ellen shook her head. She was waiting for the rejection she was sure was going to come. Her heart was beating wildly and she wondered if Rae knew CPR in case she had a heart attack.

"Is that what you wanted to share with me?"

Ellen was scared and nodded. She swallowed. Rae wasn't staring at her in rejection. The concern on her face was almost worse.

"Do you want to tell me what happened?"

Ellen nodded and tried to swallow again. Her mouth was suddenly dry. She found by looking away she could start. "You know my mother died when I was young?" she began and glanced up to see Rae nod her head. Everyone knew some of Ellen's 'official' biography, a necessity for all the interviews she had given. "I was ten when she died," she told her truthfully.

"I thought you were thirteen?" Rae asked and squinted as she played over what she had read in articles over the years.

Ellen shook her head, her naked shoulders shrugging as she replied, "No, that was just so it didn't sound so pathetic. The PR guys fabricated some of that shit," she told her ruefully. "My mom was pretty great," she surprised Rae by saying. "She was caring, loving, and tried to shelter me from my dad."

"Was your dad bad or something?"

Ellen nodded as she tried to suppress those memories by remembering her mother first. "He never let my mother forget that she had given him a girl child instead of the much anticipated and wanted boy child."

"Your father wanted a son?" Rae laughed at the old-fashioned values of decades ago. She sobered at the distraught look on Ellen's face as she tried to tell her tale. "Go on," she encouraged. Her hand reached out to rub Ellen's shoulder.

The redhead appreciated the touch. She was sure it would be memorable after she told her tale. "He wanted a son he could be proud of, one that could take over the farm for him someday. Mama couldn't have any more children. He blamed me for that," the bitterness crept into her tone. "Mama kept me from his sight as much as she could so he didn't take it out on me. I learned early to become invisible, to hide. That all ended when he killed her by the time I was ten."

"Wait, your father killed your mother? Did he go to prison or something?" she didn't like this tale and could feel it was taking too much out of Ellen.

Ellen shook her head. "He didn't actually kill her. He wore her down. He abused her instead of me until she died and then he turned it on me."

Rae watched as she saw how it was affecting Ellen. She was ashamed, that was apparent. She didn't like the shiver of fear that went down her spine as Ellen continued.

"I was given all the responsibilities of an adult female," she said, making quotation marks with her fingers and losing her grip on the sheet that slipped below her breasts. She didn't notice as she tried to get out her tale to Rae before she lost her nerve.

"All of them?" Rae asked, wondering if Ellen had been sexually molested by that man.

Ellen looked up at the tone, wondering what Rae was thinking. "Not then, but later he encouraged his friends to cop a feel as I began to grow," she said uncomfortably. She looked down at the sheets on the bed, at the rise of her breasts, and began to twist one of the sheets in her hands. "They heaped all sorts of abuse on me, from disparaging remarks, to eventually a backhand now and then. One even tripped me once so I'd fall against him and his hard-on," she confided.

"Why didn't anyone do anything about it?"

"My father told anyone who asked at the bruises and marks that I was clumsy. Someone at school once tried to defend me and lost their job. Someone else said something in high school and after my father visited him he kept well away from me. I tried to say something but the sheriff and others were my father's friends. They began to say I was a liar, so who was there to believe me?" she asked, not expecting a response.

"I believe you," the brunette said quietly.

Ellen looked up and smiled ruefully before continuing. "It was getting worse. I was growing up. Then I met Ellie."

"That was your first girlfriend, right?"

Ellen was surprised that Rae remembered that. She never spoke about Ellie to anyone since Ryan. She remembered that Rae had asked her once about the name of her first. She nodded. "We never actually did anything but we talked about it. We were going to wait until I was legal. Then she died." It had been so long but the pain was immediately fresh in her breast. She could feel the need to cry and the tears began to stream from her eyes.

"It's okay, baby, you don't have to tell me…" Rae soothed, trying to rub her shoulder, hold her, and comfort her some more.

"I need to get this all out. I need you understand," she hiccupped as she pulled away.

Rae nodded and waited for Ellen to collect herself.

"She died a week before…" she tried again and still the pain cut through her.

For a second Rae was jealous of this unknown Ellie who had held her girlfriend in her heart for so many years. She must have been quite a girl.

"I loved her…my father was happy when she died. He knew what she was. A dyke, a queer, a butch," she said the words that had once caused her to flinch. "He couldn't say enough bad words about her," she sobbed a little.

Rae wondered if the memory of Ellie had kept Ellen from making any serious commitment for so long. Her fears that someone else would be taken from her.

"God, he was so mean. Why'd he have to be that way? You know?" she looked up, her eyes full of tears over her losses. The pain fresh, once again. The anger at how he had treated her. Demeaned her. Hurt her. "Why couldn't he have just loved me for who I was? Just because I wasn't a boy…" she finished and turned to reach for a tissue. Finding none, she unabashedly rubbed her tears on the sheet and then her nose.

"Oooh, gross," Rae teased to lighten the mood for a moment.

Ellen grinned and yanked the sheet up, removing it from under the blanket and from Rae, exposing her delightful breasts which she covered quickly with the blanket. She shook her finger at Ellen. The lighthearted teasing helped her to regain control of her anger and hurt. She swallowed and continued, "He was a mean bastard. Drinking. Carousing. His friends were worse as they made plans for me when I was 'legal.' I wasn't interested in any of them. Who wants a drunk for

a husband?" she asked rhetorically. She had wanted to keep from his notice, and the idea of his 'friends' who looked at her with barely disguised lust made her disgusted. Lecherous hands had reached out to her as she fetched beer for his 'friends' for years. She had learned to avoid them, for if she ever complained or spilled the beer, her father would berate her. Words were almost worse than the physical beatings, as he harangued her for fun in front of those friends, much to their mutual amusement. Egged on by their silent appreciation of his abuse.

To Rae it now made sense why Ellen was such a light drinker. Even when they had gone out in days of old and partied it up, she rarely had an alcoholic drink. Other than a glass or two with dinner or afterwards, she rarely drank. Her wine cellar was well stocked and going to waste.

"When he was so happy that Ellie May Fredericks was gone, I had enough. We were going to get out. I stole her stash of money and hid it from him. If he had found it, I'd have been sunk." That money had helped her when she first got to Southern California before she got a job. Lord knew Owen hadn't had much left in the bank accounts she closed. He hadn't approved of Ellie May Fredericks, those 'white trash' Fredericks that lived in the mobile home trailer park. He had told Avril often enough to stay away from *her*.

"Wait, did he kill her?" Rae was confused, her eyebrow furrowing. Who had Ellen killed? Had she heard her correctly?

"No, a tornado did it. Those damn mobile homes are like tornado magnets or somethin'," her voice began to sound decidedly Oklahoman as she told her tale. "She was in her truck when it caught her," her voice caught again.

"Were you the one who found her?" she asked horrified, jumping to conclusions and wondering at the tale.

Ellen shook her head, gathering her emotions she said, "No, but I was the one to identify her when I heard they had found her truck and pulled a body from it. There was dirt on her face, her hair was a mess. There was dirt under her fingernails. I nearly threw up at what she looked like; they hadn't tried to clean her up at all. I left to go to her mobile home to go through her things before the scavengers could. I got our stash, the money we were going to use to start over elsewhere." She crawled through the debris to find the 'safe place' that Ellie used to hide her money and most treasured things. She found the box after a long search through all the jumble. She was relieved to find the rolls of bills and the various trinkets in the box. She cried when she found the engagement ring she had known Ellie wanted to give her, but was waiting until she was 'legal.' She looked around the room and took a sweatshirt she found, but other than that she left everything as it was and crawled out of the trailer. She was just in time as she took off from the other scavengers who would be looking for anything they could find and sell. Supposedly 'looking' for bodies, any money or jewelry 'found' would disappear. She hid the box among her own things, hoping to keep it from being discovered by her father.

Rae could see what this tale was taking out of Ellen. She had never seen her so vulnerable or known her to share so much. She realized now that there were whole sections of Ellen's life that she had no idea about. "Then what happened?" she asked almost fearfully.

Ellen looked at her with unseeing eyes as she pictured the night. "It was a week later. My father had been so happy about Ellie's death; he said she had been unnatural. An unfit friend for any young girl, implying that she had done things. Ellie hadn't touched me that way. Sure, we kissed, petted a little, but she wouldn't touch me that way until I was eighteen and legal. It was only a few weeks away. I was more miserable than I had been at any time in my childhood with him so happy about her death. The sirens went off that night and he was drunk on the couch. That annoying warning was on the television for the emergency broadcast system. It's tone, gawd, I remember that like it was yesterday." She shuddered at the memories.

"You don't have to tell me now," Rae tried to stop her.

Ellen shook her head. If she didn't get it all out and now, she might never get it out. "I debated only about thirty seconds before leaving him there. I went out to the storm cellar in our backyard." Her voice became a monotone as she remembered and told her tale, frequently repeating herself as she told it and relived it. She couldn't help but wonder if her father would still be alive if she had woken him when she heard the tornado sirens go off. She had heard them loud and clear across the prairie miles from her bedroom and headed for the stairs to head for shelter. He had been asleep on the couch wearing his 'wife beater' t-shirt, appropriately named since he had always worn such disgusting shirts to beat not only his wife, but his daughter as well. He was snoring loudly, and she debated briefly about waking him, knowing she would be backhanded for 'bothering' him, but also knowing that the sirens were going loud and clear and that they should head for the shelter her grandparents had built to protect the humans from this very thing. He drooled in his sleep as his hand came up to rub his crotch and then up to rub his nose. She shuddered in disgust at the sight. The sirens were spinning around as they came louder and then fainter, it was the next circuit that decided it for her, and she headed to the shelter, alone.

It was hard for her small frame to open the door; it was a heavy steel door. The wind was blowing so hard she nearly lost her footing as she struggled with it. She could see the vent spinning around on top of the storm shelter to let in some air to the close quarters. It was built tough, but she managed to pry it open, the wind catching it before she was pulling it shut behind her and bolting it. She was in absolute darkness

and she reached for a flashlight she knew they kept on the shelf. Something soft brushed against her hand, she didn't know if was a spider web, a mouse, or what, and she squealed at the sensation, but determinedly felt for the flashlight against the eternal blackness that was before her. She wouldn't go down the steps without seeing where she was going. It was a black pit, a void, an absence of any light, and she was frightened. She had heard the roar of the wind, the steel door had shut that out, but in the absence of sound the dark frightened her further. There, there was the flashlight. She quickly pulled it to herself and flicked it on. The beam was feeble, the batteries old and unused. She cursed in her mind, not aloud, just in case someone could hear her and berate her for her naughty mouth. She shone the flickering beam around and saw another flashlight on the shelf. This one too was weak and unused, but between the two weak beams she felt better and could see further. She saw a lantern further down and headed carefully down the stairs. The noises outside as things hit the door scared her, she wondered how long she would have to stay down here, she wondered if she should go back up and get her father. Remembering how he had laughed at Ellie's death, seeming to take pleasure in the devastation on his young daughter's face, she firmly decided that he was on his own. He would make her pay in countless ways later, but she knew it was a price she had to pay.

She got the lantern lit and it provided much more light than the weak flashlights that she turned off. The wind could be heard around the steel door and a little gray showed through the small window in the door. She could see nothing except an absence of black beyond it. She could see nothing except an absence of black beyond it. She looked around the storm cellar. Her grandparents and even her mother had stored things in here, but her father never did, he didn't even use it, only swore that he had to cut around it in the backyard with the lawn mower. Occasionally she jumped as something fell against the door or window; she could sense the power of the wind.

Ellen skipped some of her story, unable, or unwilling to retell it to Rae. She had consciously chosen to let her father die at nature's hands and the guilt she had lived with for twenty years. Going back, seeing the town, and suing a few of the people who had stolen from her in many ways only helped a bit. It had, at least, started her on a path to healing.

"You didn't kill him, his drinking killed him," Rae tried to reason.

"But I could have tried to wake him," she answered.

"No, Ellen, he probably would have smacked you. He deserved to die. Some people are born to die," she answered.

"It shouldn't have been my choice, I should have…"

"No, Ellen. He chose to drink. He chose to treat you that way. It wasn't your fault."

Ellen looked at Rae sadly as though she didn't understand. "I sued a few of the people who stole our things when I went back to have the house leveled," she explained. Rae knew about her drive to Oklahoma in Ryan's Maserati and the girl she had helped. She had arranged for a job in her firm for her to help Ellen so that there would be no calls of favoritism.

"Do you feel better for having sued them?"

Ellen shrugged. "I got a few things back of my mother's. I just wanted people to know that I knew, that everyone knew what they had done!"

"Yeah, I hope that revenge made you feel better. Did it?"

She shook her head. "No. Having Mama's things back helped enormously," she glanced around the bedroom at the antiques she had purchased. They reminded her of home and they felt right. The revenge had been sweet. She had the means, the scandal she was assured by Mr. Mann had been enormous, but it didn't bring back her mother, it didn't bring back her youth. "I think it helped me to move on, though," she said quietly. She was exhausted. She lay back against the headboard and pillows.

"I'm sorry you went through all that, Ellen. I would never have guessed," Rae said sadly as she began to lean back too. Ellen pulled her close so Rae ended up with her head on Ellen's shoulder. The sound of her heartbeat under her ear was reassuring.

"The thing is, it was all so long ago. I lived with it for all this time. It played a major part in making me who I am." she said musingly as she thought it over. "I think going back and seeing things through the eyes of an adult was cathartic."

"Is that what began to change you?"

Ellen nodded. Rae could feel the bobbing of her head against her own. "I think the therapy helped. I'd started to change after Ryan's death, but seeing it all, realizing it didn't matter anymore. That was what really began to change me. They didn't have a hold on me anymore. Daddy has been dead. He paid for his abuse with his life. You know, he never even really owned that farm? When Mama died it was to come to me but he wouldn't let her will be read. Everyone assumed it was his." She shook her head at the perfidy of it all. "I guess it will always affect how I look at things, but I don't have to let it rule my life anymore."

"Is that why you hate the wind?" she asked in reference to the tornados that took her first love and her hated father.

Ellen nodded. "I love the rain, I always have, but hate the wind," she said ruefully.

"I'll hold you when the wind comes then," Rae said as she hugged her close.

"Rae?" she asked and waited for her to look up. "Will you move in with me? Or is that too long a drive to work?"

"Do you really want me to move in with you?" she verified, her heart leaping with joy at the offer.

Ellen nodded. She had never lived openly with any of her girlfriends. She wanted this, though. She wanted Rae to be there with her every day. To be there when she got home at night, she wanted a lot of what tonight had been like.

"Are you sure?" she asked. "Just because we made love..." she began.

"I'm sure," she said adamantly. She placed her hands on either side of Rae's face and held her still. "I love you. I want you to move into this huge house I have here so we can be together." Her animated face altered slightly as she had a thought. "Unless you don't want to..." she began but Rae silenced her with a kiss.

"I want to," she said clearly. She couldn't seem to help herself though as she asked, "You think this will work?"

Ellen thought over her response carefully. "I've never asked anyone to live with me before," she answered slowly, thoughtfully. "I want to try to make it work. I know I love you. All I can promise is that I will try."

That was enough for Rae. She knew she loved Ellen. This Ellen, who had revealed some of her deepest and darkest secrets. This vulnerable Ellen was the one she loved. She could only hope that the hard Ellen, the not so likable one, was kept at work.

❖ CHAPTER TWENTY SIX ❖

RESTITUTION

The high-definition television had just been installed in the recreation room in what would normally be the basement of the house. Since they were in California, basements were rare. Instead, this 'basement' was a three-quarters underground set of rooms built into the hillside that led out onto a barbeque patio. Within these rooms was the television room, a wine room, a sauna, a workout room, and an elaborately old-fashioned Victorian bar with brass fittings, a full-length mirror, and rich wood appointments. Ellen had taken the posters that had once been Ryan's from his home, the ones of comic book characters, rippling muscles, tight costumes, and the ones of video game characters that she didn't quite understand, and placed them around the rooms as art. She liked having a part of Ryan in her own home. Greg hadn't cared for the framed posters and had long ago started looking for a new boyfriend. He had already gone through several. It annoyed Ellen, the disloyalty, but it had been years and she understood that Greg was easily distracted and probably lonely.

"I think that is crooked," Rae said as the techs eased the flat-screen back against the wall.

"What?" Ellen asked distractedly as she looked at what Ryan had thought of as art. She kind of liked the comic book covers now, but still hated the video characters ones.

"The television?" Rae nudged her to bring her back in focus to the techs.

"You want the surround sound, right, Ms. Christenson?" one of them asked as he bumped the television with one of the speakers, making it definitely lean to the left. "Oops, sorry," he apologized to the other two techs who had measured, even using a level to get it even.

"Um, yes. Surround would be great," Ellen replied as her eyes returned to the comic covers and memories of Ryan.

Much later after the techs had hidden all the wires they left, leaving her with a dizzying array of channel changers, Ellen looked at Rae, her expression a mix of seriousness and humor, and said, "So, how do I watch television?"

Rae chuckled. It was insane. One of the rectangular boxes was for the television, one was for the cable, one was for the stereo and surround sound, one was for the VHS player. It could be confusing if you wanted a 'simple' television program. "Do you really not get what these are for?"

Ellen grinned. People frequently mistook her for 'just' the paper pushing partner of the firm. As much as Ryan had enjoyed his gadgets, he had shown her how to use them and sometimes she enjoyed them more than the techie had. She confidently turned on the television and the cable box so they could watch the local news.

"In national news tonight, a series of tornadoes have swept through tornado alley including Texas, Oklahoma, and into parts of Illinois. The effects can be seen here..." the newscaster's voice began to drone.

Ellen sat up and looked at the map they were showing of Southwestern Oklahoma. She reached for her phone and made a series of phone calls. Several of them had no answer and she repeatedly tried. "Can you get me the governor?" she asked in one phone call.

Rae was sitting there watching her girlfriend take command of the situation. She didn't understand what was going on but it was at that moment she really realized how important Ellen was. Ellen was able to command the attention of the governor, but which governor she wasn't sure as she listened.

Ellen was on the phone for an hour before she had the answers she wanted or needed. At some point Rae had slipped a pad of paper and a pen to her and she gratefully accepted it as she made notes, smiling in thanks at her thoughtful girlfriend before turning her attention back to the phone call.

"What's going on, babe?" Rae finally asked. She'd been ignored for long enough.

"Apparently tornadoes swept through Oakley where I grew up," Ellen said bleakly. She'd used the channel changers to switch back and forth to news stations that had anything on the tornadoes, trying to catch a camera shot of the devastation she was looking for.

"This is the same place you told me about?" she asked gently, remembering how Ellen's father and Ellie had died. She could see that Ellen was shook up.

"Yeah, but it was over twenty years ago and a week apart that the two took…" she swallowed back the hurt and anger that threatened to take over. "This time they came through within hours of each other," she explained.

"Is there something we can do?"

Ellen looked at her. "This is my…" she began but Rae shushed her with a well-placed finger across her lips.

"Tell me what you need," she said quietly.

"Could you pack a bag? I don't know how long I'll be gone." she asked gratefully.

"I'll pack two, and *we* should have enough for a week or two," she said confidently as she rose from the couch.

"We?"

"I'm coming with you," she told her in a no-nonsense voice as she made her way to the stairs to go to the first floor.

Ellen made a few more phone calls and by the time Rae had bags packed for them both, a private car was outside to take them to the airport. They were met by a team of employees from Gigitech and Animated Studios, including the students from Oklahoma that she had given scholarships to. All were carrying their own luggage as they made their way to the private plane that Ellen had hired. "Everyone set?" she asked and there were a few solemn nods.

As the plane took off, a few questions were asked and Ellen told them she didn't know what to expect. They were flying into the nearest airfield, not a major hub, but one that could accommodate the private jet. Everyone was quiet. No laughter could be heard and each kept to their own thoughts. Rae reached out to hold Ellen's hand which told more than one what she meant to the redhead. A few had suspected but no one knew that Rae and Ellen were living together. Ellen had never hidden her sexuality but her girlfriends hadn't lasted long, and it was a standard joke among her employees. This show of affection wasn't precedented. Most didn't really care as Ellen was a good, if demanding, boss. They had unrestricted freedom to explore and create. Everyone benefited. As they made their way east, a few tried to sleep.

They landed in what looked like a farmer's field just as the sun was coming up. Most of the crew stretched from their nearly sleepless night. A row of vans was waiting to take them to their destination.

They had a way to go before they could reach the scene of the devastation. Flights had been restricted to further away. Ellen got in the first van along with Rae, her secretary, and a couple of other employees. Everyone looked a bit scruffy from their last-minute flight. "Let's stop at the first restaurant we come to," Ellen instructed the driver as they began their journey.

They took up a lot of the space in the small café they came to. Ellen told everyone to eat whatever they wanted or get it to go as she wasn't certain what they would find when they got where they were going. She herself ate a hearty breakfast of French toast with bacon and an egg on the side. She gazed out the window of the café as she thought about what they might find and what they could do.

"Are you okay?" Rae asked her for the hundredth time. She knew this trip wasn't easy and wanted to ease the burden of whatever it was that was riding Ellen's shoulders.

Ellen looked back at Rae from her gaze outside and it was at that moment she had a flash of inspiration. "I'm fine," she stated as she quickly finished her meal. "I'll be right back, you all take your time finishing up," she said as she took out her wallet and laid down a couple of hundred-dollar bills to pay for all their meals.

"Ellen…what…" Rae said as she quickly followed her.

"You don't have to come," Ellen said as she rushed out the door and ran across to the RV dealer on the other side of the street.

"What are you doing?" she asked, jogging to keep up.

"Those people are going to need places to stay," she said as she held her side from the unaccustomed exercise. She quickly began to look about at the new RVs that lined the dealer's lot.

Rae looked on astonished. These weren't cheap or small RVs, either. These were the expensive ones that a couple retired in for their golden years.

"Can I help you ladies?" a salesman came up. He had seen them sprint across the highway from the café. They must really be interested in their selection and he was already rubbing his hands together at the possibilities.

"Where is the manager or owner of this lot?" Ellen asked without preamble.

Surprised at her tone he pointed back at the offices in the middle of the lot and watched as she hurried off, the brunette in her wake.

"Hello, I'm looking for the owner of this lot or the manager?" Ellen asked as she entered the building.

"I'm the owner, this is my manager," a well-dressed man stated when he over-heard her talking to the receptionist.

"How do you do? I'm Ellen Christenson," she introduced herself.

"From Gigitech?" he asked, recognizing the name from the papers and magazines he had seen over the years.

Ellen was relieved. She hadn't traded on her fame, ever. Right now, she needed it to help her achieve the impulse she had in the café. "Yes, that's right," she admitted with a smile. "I'm on my way back home and I am hoping you and your staff can help me?"

"Certainly, I'd heard you were from Oklahoma, but the stories never said clearly," he said heartily, trying to be friendly.

"I'm sure you heard of the devastating tornadoes that went through the state late last night?" she asked to clarify.

"Yes, I'm sorry to hear that ma'am. It must be difficult. Did you lose family in the storm?" he sounded concerned.

"No," she shook her head. "My family is all gone. However, the town is in ruins and they are going to have to have places to stay. I'd like to buy RVs to give them a place to stay until the rebuilding can begin."

"Well, we can help you with that," he said with a nod. "How many were you thinking?"

"How many have you got?"

He blinked, not sure he had heard her correctly. "Ma'am? We are one of the largest dealers in this part of the state," he began.

Ellen waved aside his spiel. "Look, I won't bicker with you. I want them all, every…single…one." She let that sink in for a moment before she continued. "I'm going to need help though in driving them down there. I think we can do it in teams," she said as she thought about the particulars.

"Ma'am we are talking about hundreds of RVs and…" he tried to protest.

"Are you saying you won't sell them to me?" she asked, and he was immediately arrested by her cold eyes. The red hair added to his momentary fear.

"No, ma'am, I'm not saying that at all." He realized he wasn't dealing with an ordinary woman. He began to sweat a little…and today had seemed like an ordinary day.

"Will you take a check?" she teased. His eyebrows raised in surprise as she grinned.

Ellen arranged for a bank to bank transfer as he and his staff made out the sales, hundreds of them.

Rae went across the street to tell their crew that there had been a change in plans and they were all going to be driving, *all of them*, and why. "Let's get your company on the phone and arrange for as many drivers as they can spare to get down here to help us get these RVs on the road," she said, taking command and addressing the van drivers. "We will need you and your services for many days," she added, thinking ahead.

Ellen hadn't quibbled about the price of the RVs but she had asked the owner of the dealership to be reasonable, to think of the people they would be helping, and he immediately thought of the news about this, the prestige, and how he would look. He accommodated her, and employees began to call in their wives, husbands, and children old enough to drive as their caravan started out. They prepped the RVs, filing up their gas tanks and the propane tanks as well as the water tanks. Ellen began to send waves of people down to the devastated area and have them line up the RVs on her land for the now displaced people of the town. She told them to lend a hand if they could and sent the vans after them to transport them back for another wave of RVs to be taken down.

"Where have you been?" Ellen asked Rae after a few hours had gone by and she realized she hadn't seen her in a while.

"I went to the local warehouse foods and cleaned them out. They are stocking the RVs and vans and helping us get the food down there," Rae told her.

"How'd you pay for that?" Ellen asked, surprised and pleased at her girlfriend's initiative.

"Well, um," she was suddenly uncomfortable. "You are going to have to go write a check," she told her as she blushed. "I maxed out my credit cards," she added.

Ellen laughed delightedly and pulled her into a hug of gratitude. "I love you," she whispered into her ear and kissed her. Several disapproving stares followed this show but this woman had just spent an enormous fortune and no one was going to say anything if Ellen had anything to say about it.

The caravan of RVs continued to leave and Ellen went with Rae in one of the vans to pay for the enormous amount of supplies that Rae had arranged for. The warehouse manager himself came up to shake the famous Ellen Christenson's hand. "I've called my district manager and the other warehouses will be sending down similar supplies on your orders, ma'am," he informed her.

Ellen looked questioningly at her girlfriend and then grinned at the plan. Providing shelter had been her first priority but Rae had thought of food as well. "Thank you," Ellen said sincerely. She couldn't remember writing a check like this before. Large purchases through her company had always been through the bank and a cashier's check or a bank transfer. Even today's purchases of the RVs had been handled by phone. A special authorization from her personal accounts that only her passcode could enact.

"We also have these for you," he said handing her a large box of gift cards.

"Thank you," Rae said as she took the box from Ellen with a cautionary look.

"We do appreciate the business," he told her sincerely. He had given them a tremendous discount on their enormous purchases.

"Just make sure they spell your name right in the newspapers," Rae teased him.

He smiled in return. She had used that phrase earlier when she told him what Ms. Christenson wanted and needed from his chain of warehouse stores.

As they left the warehouse and got in the now full van, which was packed with toilet paper, dry goods, and water, she asked Rae, "What if I had said no?"

"I saw what you were up to, I thought I was helping?" she said a bit defensively.

"You did help, enormously. What is that?" she asked pointing at the box on Rae's lap.

"Gift cards, those people are going to be needing supplies after they begin to start building. I thought I'd go by the building supply houses tomorrow to see what I can arrange…" she began but Ellen cut her off with a fierce kiss.

"Your talents are greatly underappreciated at your job," Ellen told her sincerely when she set her back in her seat. "I can't believe how much you thought ahead, and I thought I planned…" she said musingly.

"I wanted to help but I didn't know what to do. When I saw you buying not just one RV but all of them, I knew then what you might need help with. Your secretaries were a big help, too," she added, gesturing to those that were riding with them who smiled and blushed at her praise.

They caught up to some of the RVs heading towards the path of the tornadoes and the utter devastation they had left. The long line of them went on for miles and Ellen dozed off for a while as they continued driving for a good hour or more. Rae spotted several of the vans used to transport the volunteer drivers back towards the larger town, and she wondered how many of them would volunteer for a second or third trip in an RV.

"God, what a mess," Ellen said as they began to come to the scenes of the devastation. The van began to weave in between debris that was on the highway leading into Oakley. The RVs began to turn off and head for the land that had been in Ellen's family for years. She had heard that the tornadoes hadn't gone that way at all and that the RVs were lining up on the fields that had held crops forever. They hadn't been planted this year as some of the lawsuits were still pending on the co-op. Their van continued to drive where it could into Oakley. It stopped at one of the only buildings still standing, the gymnasium of the local high school.

"Is this where you went to school?" Rae murmured as she gazed out of the window and they came to a halt.

"Yeah," Ellen said, bitter memories assailing her as she got out of the van. There were people everywhere, all looking worse for wear.

"Ms. Christenson?" a voice was heard.

Ellen turned to it and it took her a minute to recognize Mrs. Mann, the wife of her lawyer. She was relieved to see her alive, if looking a bit despondent. "Mrs. Mann?" she asked to verify her identity. At the woman's nod, she enveloped her in a hug. "Are you okay?" she asked stupidly, realizing if she was standing here, in a blanket like this, that she wasn't okay, not by a long shot.

She shook her head. "We can't find him," she said in an odd, lost voice.

"Mr. Mann?" she asked, knowing the answer before the woman nodded. "Well, we will keep looking," she promised. She had hoped to find someone in a position of authority as she handed the woman off to Rae with a look that told her that this woman needed to be taken care of.

"Avril?" someone said, and Ellen turned to see someone from high school that looked vaguely familiar.

"Ellen," she corrected and then, "I'm sorry, I don't remember…" she began.

"Of course not. I was your American History teacher. What are you doing here?" he asked.

"We came to help if we can," she said as she held out her hands and began to look around the gymnasium. It was worse than she expected. Cots lined wall to wall. People crying. People in shock. There were medical personnel but it wasn't enough. She could only imagine what the local hospital looked like if it had survived the storm.

"We?" he asked looking over her shoulder at the one woman with her. He wondered if that was her special friend. Everyone knew that the famous Avril Ellen Christenson was a lesbian.

"Yes, I have a crew of people here," Ellen explained. She looked around and added, "Somewhere," under her breath.

"What can you do?" he asked kindly.

"Well, we brought food and RVs so people can eat and shower," she told him as she looked around. It was like a scene from the apocalypse and these survivors were zombies. She wondered if what she had done today would even be enough.

"RVs?" he asked. "Where?"

"They are on my family's farm. I wasn't too sure about parking them elsewhere so I thought that was the best idea," she told him. "Do you know where I can find who is in charge?" she asked.

Her old teacher led her and Rae, who was still holding Mrs. Mann, or rather the desperate woman was holding Rae, up to where some

officious people were filling out forms and trying to help the mass of people.

"Ms. Christenson," a voice stopped her as she carefully went around to the front of the line. She looked on at the woman who obviously knew her.

"I'm with the Governor's office. He told us to be on the lookout for you," she said by way of greeting. "I'm to take you to him when he gets here from looking at the other towns," she explained.

"And your name is…?" Ellen asked and smiled gratefully at her former teacher as he stepped back from escorting her.

"Leslie Brach," she said and held out her hand to be shook.

Ellen shook the hand but noticed the manicure that the woman was so obviously proud of. She was dressed a bit inappropriately for this scene and she had noticed her earlier that she was one of the paper-pushers who were officiating here.

"I'm here to coordinate things," she said importantly.

"Well my people have brought food and water and shelter for anyone who needs it," Ellen explained.

"Good, the national guard should be here shortly," she told her with a false smile. "They can inventory what you brought and assess what the people need…" she began.

"No, that won't be necessary," Ellen told her, sizing her up. "My people will be happy to do that as I've already purchased the items."

"Well, we need to inventory them to see if it's appropriate to…" she began again.

"That won't be necessary," Ellen repeated herself. "My people have it well in hand." She turned from the woman to look at her old teacher and said, "If you know someone who has lost their entire place and needs a temporary home and a good meal, please let me know." She watched as he nodded and began to talk to people.

"You can't do that, there are forms to be filled out and procedures to be followed," Leslie sputtered.

"And they can fill out the forms tomorrow and follow your procedures then," Ellen told her in a firm, no-nonsense voice. Rae smiled at the tone. It was the old Ellen and for once she was cheering that person on. "They lost their homes last night; they don't need your paperwork. They need to rest and recover," Ellen told her. "If your governor wishes to object, too bad. He can reach me out at my farm." With that she left the woman's obnoxious presence and headed after her teacher.

"Avril…I mean Ellen, a few folks would like to take you up on your offer," the teacher stopped to tell her.

"Excellent, my people will help you. I can take a few in my van now and send the van back for more," she told him. "Can you coordinate that for me for now while I send back one of my people?"

"I'll stay," Rae volunteered. "Just commandeer us a nice place to sleep tonight?" she asked as she looked around, still holding the older woman.

Ellen smiled at her and nodded as the teacher began to spread the news. There were hot showers, food, and a place to stay out at the Christenson farm. Avril Christenson, now Ellen Christenson, had arrived and brought that with her.

"What am I going to tell the Governor when the National Guard gets here?" Leslie asked Rae when she saw Ellen drive off with a couple of people in the van she had arrived in.

"That they should begin cleaning up the town so these people can get back on their feet as soon as possible," Rae said as she sat Mrs. Mann down on an empty cot and pulled a blanket around her for warmth. "We will continue to inquire after your husband, ma'am," she told her, unconsciously affecting the speech patterns she had heard from those around her.

Ellen was shocked. The town had been totally leveled. Blocks of homes that had been in families for countless decades were simply gone. The rows of businesses on Main Street were now rubble. The town, what it had been, was completely devastated. Nothing stood in the wake of the two tornadoes that had gone through. It was amazing that the high school was even salvageable; the storm must have hopped right over it as the homes around it were gone too. As she directed the driver to her family's acreage she could see the caravan of RVs still arriving and she directed him to where her people had set up a command station.

They looked relieved to see her hop out of the van. "Could you arrange for these supplies to be distributed and get these people some accommodation?" she asked as she thumb-pointed towards the van where people were climbing out and looking stunned.

Quickly and efficiently her staff took care of the few souls she had brought with her and began to bring her up to date. "We are parking the RVs in blocks so that people can still get in and out; I'm having people sign them out when I give them the keys. I've color-coded them and given them identifying tags," she was told by one of her people.

"I've got the barn open and I've been accepting the supplies arriving from the warehouses. The boys are delivering a box full of various foods and asking the people for their clothes sizes so we can get them

at least one change of clothing to change into after they have showered," another employee updated her. Ellen was relieved. She hadn't thought of things like that, but Rae obviously had when she arranged for things from the warehouses. Writing a check had been the easy part.

"Avril, thank you," someone came up to give her a hug. "We don't know where we would be tonight if it wasn't for you and your people!"

Ellen smiled and nodded, having no clue who the woman was. It was odd to hear her old name after all this time. "I'm sure the governor and the National Guard would have helped," she told her modestly.

"No, you got here faster than they did," she was told.

Ellen dug in to help, taking orders from her people, directing the convoy of RVs still arriving by her people who had it coordinated. She was impressed at how quickly they had gotten things organized. She took a moment between arrivals to see that the vans transporting drivers back to the larger town for more RVs were also now transporting people from Oakley and the overcrowded gymnasium. She also arranged for someone to go by the hospital and begin to transport those well enough to leave. Many families had chosen to stay with their injured but they couldn't stay anymore.

She looked around at the farmstead. In the short time since she had been here and had the house and outbuildings leveled, the grass had taken over. Although she knew where the buildings had stood, it was obvious in a short time that there would be no bare spots and Mother Nature would take it back. She felt no remorse for what had happened all those decades ago. She turned back to help her people help the others.

"Did you at least save us some RVs for our own use?" she joked with a couple of her people.

"Yes, we have that block over there for employees of Gigitech and Animated Studios," she pointed. "Here is your key, we are bunking two to four to an RV, and a few can accommodate six. I've made a few phone calls and we will have power out here to recharge the generators that are on the RVs when they run down."

"You guys are fantastic," Ellen complimented them as she marveled at their efficiency.

"You know, this feels good. To help," someone told their boss. "It's like giving back. I'm glad I came." His sentiments were echoed by several others and Ellen grinned. These people were her family now, not close, but they felt like real people, more so than many of the others she had grown up around. The people they were helping she didn't even recognize.

"You can't do this," someone blustered up to Ellen late in the day. She was just about to head to her RV, a hot shower, hoping to see Rae after the hard day's work.

She turned to see Mr. Worley waddling up to her. Raising an eyebrow, she asked, "I can't do what?" she asked.

"Park all these RVs here, you haven't got the proper permits," he said in the same belligerent tone.

Ellen laughed. A hearty laugh. She had heard from Mr. Mann how upset the former Sheriff had been over her serving him and his wife with papers for the items they had stolen from her and her family. What had been recovered, while paltry, had humiliated him and his wife since it showed they had been thieves. He flushed at her laughter. "I don't need permits when I'm aiding these people." Her hands took in the many people walking about. People felt a lot better with a shower under their belts, some were inquiring how they could help too.

"We'll see about that," he said, stomping off angrily.

"Who was that?" someone asked their boss.

"A sad, sad, little man," Ellen answered and returned to work. Handing a little girl a toy, Rae had really thought ahead when she purchased 'supplies.' Children didn't need to worry about the devastation and a new toy could go a long way to forgetting what was going on around them.

Ellen was exhausted as she made her way to the RV that had been set aside for her and Rae. Using the key, she thought at first she had the wrong one as it didn't work right away. She realized she had the wrong key and used the other one on the ring to open up the luxurious vehicle. It was far too much for just the two of them but it would be a helluva place to set up and coordinate while they were here. She had never been in an RV before and she poked and prodded around, discovering the many gadgets that were in the modern vehicle.

The sides extended out and she opened them up to provide them with even more living and bedroom space. The windows could be closed by the blinds with a flick of a wrist on a button. Everything seemed automated and modern. It was a lot larger than she had imagined. The bed was king sized and that surprised her. The accommodations were very much like a five-star hotel and she had seen several of these RVs spread out on her land.

Someone had also gotten them a few ATVs and golf carts from the RV lot, and these allowed her and her people to go out among the rows and help people get around. Her other people had used less ostentatious ones for their own accommodations. They were sleeping

in shifts and she could see through the windows that some were relaxing and watching television screens in their own RVs.

There was a knock on the door, stopping her explorations, and she opened it to find someone with a box of groceries for her and Rae as well as their bags. "Thank you," she told them as she took them in one at a time. She put away the groceries in the refrigerator, amazed that it was full sized and not cramped like she would expect.

There was another knock on the door. Expecting Rae, she got up eagerly to answer it and was surprised to be greeted by an officious looking man in an army green uniform. "Ms. Christenson?" he asked.

"Yes, may I help you?"

"I'm Major Breeds," he took off his hat quickly and respectfully. "May I come in and speak with you?"

Ellen stepped back and he climbed the stairs into the RV.

"This is nice," he said as he looked around at the luxury. "May I?" he indicated the two recliners that were in the pullout section of the RV, extending the living room area by a few feet.

"Please," she replied and asked, "Can I get you a drink?"

"If you got an orange juice, I'd love one," he told her as he sat down.

Ellen pulled one that she had just put away in the fridge and sat down across from him after handing it to him. "What can I do for you, Major?" she asked politely.

"Ma'am, we seem to have a problem and I'm hoping you will help me out here," he said with a slight twang that she recognized as being from Oklahoma.

"And what is that, Major?" she asked raising an eyebrow. She knew what might be coming and he didn't disappoint.

"I'm part of the forces the Governor sent out here to help the fine people here and elsewhere to recover."

She nodded to show she was listening, but she was still waiting for the problem.

"We welcome civilians helping out and all, but ma'am, we've never encountered the like of what you all are doing here and I'm a bit puzzled at how to address it."

"What exactly is the problem?" she sat back, opening her own orange juice for a sip.

"Well, you are a bit overwhelming as most folks don't know how to take the help you all are offering," he sat back and opened his orange juice too, copying her.

She smiled wryly. Shrugging she asked, "And this is a problem how?"

"Well, the Governor mentioned you all might be coming in, but we didn't expect this," he gestured at the RV and nearly sloshed the orange juice out of the bottle. "Oops," he said apologetically.

"Well, I was raised right here. In fact, you are sitting on my family's farm," she informed him, pointing with her bottle.

He nodded. He had known that. "I understand that, ma'am. But we have a tent city set up, and…" he began but she interrupted him.

"And how long will that last? My people tell me another set of storms are due to come in tomorrow night. These people have lost their homes. The government has too much red tape for them to wait for something substantial to hold them over."

"Yes ma'am, I understand that. But you all are taking it upon yourself to circumvent the system we have in place…" he returned a little heatedly and regretted it when he continued, "I'm half tempted to confiscate your supplies and…"

"Now you listen to me," she said, her voice rising and her own Oklahoman accent coming out. "You touch my supplies without my okay, one of my RV's, that I paid for with my *own* money and my lawyers, and the PR department is gonna have a field day with you and yours. By the time I get done with *you* the Governor is gonna rue the day he got elected and you can bet he will be looking to blame someone," she pointed out.

He got the point and gulped. "Now, I didn't say I was gonna confiscate them…."

"You better not," she interjected.

"I just said, you all are confusing people as they expect the state to help them out. Their own government. Why their duly elected officials even are objecting to your kind of help…."

"I'm helping out my old neighbors. They don't have to like it. They don't even have to accept it. But I'm here, I'm helping, and if you all don't like it, you can stuff it!" she said hotly. "I have enough money to buy this state over and again and the Governor knew I was comin'. He knew some of my plans. I came to help here and elsewhere. You all don't move quick enough and if you touch any of the supplies I arranged to come in for the rebuilding, I'll create a shit-storm the likes of which you would wish another tornado would come through."

He swallowed. He knew when he was beat. This woman might be petite but she sure was a redhead. Kinda cute too, all fired up. Too bad she was one of them there lesbians, or so he heard.

They both heard the door open and turned to see Rae looking in. "Ah, there you are," she said relieved as she hoisted a bag into the RV before climbing in. "Am I interrupting something?" she asked as she looked curiously at the uniformed officer who had stood up at her entrance.

"No, no, the Major was just finishing up," Ellen told her with a smile of greeting. She looked back at the Major. "Isn't that right, Major Burns?" she asked.

"Breeds," he corrected automatically and then flushed when it was obvious she had done that deliberately. He wondered if she meant the bumbling Major Burns that had been on that television show so long ago in the 70's. Eyeing her briefly, he concluded she had. "Yes, I'll be going," he said and nodded at both women. He hastily exited.

"Oh, Major," Ellen called before he could shut the door behind him.

He looked back inquiringly.

"You all remember what I said, not a piece of it," she said with a smile, but the warning was there.

He nodded stiffly and closed the door, careful not slam it.

"What was that about?" Rae asked as Ellen took her in her arms.

"Oh, I think I ruffled a few feathers," she said dismissively as she leaned in for a kiss.

"Um, the walls have eyes," Rae protested, pecking her on the lips and looking beyond her to the large windows that lined the RV.

"Well, that's taken care of easily enough," and Ellen started pushing buttons at various intervals along the walls, closing the curtains, drapes, and blinds automatically until they had their solid walls again, hiding them from view.

"Cool," Rae said with a smile as she welcomed Ellen back into her arms for a deeper kiss. "How was your day?" she asked with another smile.

"Exhausting, and yours?" she returned the smile.

"The same, I have a few ideas I'd like to go over with you before tomorrow."

"Fine, how about you take a shower while I cook something, and then while we eat we can discuss it?"

"Have you showered?"

"I didn't get here much sooner than you did before he showed up," she used her chin to point towards the door the Major had exited out of.

"Wanna share?" she offered enticingly.

Ellen smiled a brilliant smile. "That sounds wonderful," she answered and took her up on the offer as she locked the door of the RV. She was pleased that Rae was still playful after what they had seen and done for the last twenty-four hours or so. The shower relaxed them both as they touched and teased and managed in the confined space. Any smaller, though, and they would have had to take their showers one at a time. "It's good that we conserve water like this," Ellen said through the spray as her hands wandered over Rae's form, washing, rubbing, and arousing her.

"I'm thrifty like that," Rae answered and then caught her breath and sputtered in the water that she inhaled as Ellen's questing fingers plunged inside of her.

"Careful, don't want to drown you, how would I explain that?"

"But I would have died happy," she managed to get out as Ellen excited her, plunging and teasing.

"Most accidents happen in the bathroom, I hear," she said in a near whisper as she nibbled along Rae's shoulder blade. Her fingers were thrusting in a rhythm matched by Rae's hips.

"Um, hum," she managed to get out as the feelings that Ellen engineered inside of her overwhelmed her and she began to buck and writhe against the naked redhead. It was only Ellen holding her steadily that kept her from dissolving in a puddle in the bottom of the shower stall. Thinking about that, she let Ellen's fingers slip from her own body as she began to kiss down Ellen's body until she was kneeling before her, the shower spray nearly drowning her as she began to play between the redhead's legs. The finely sculpted hair was darker down here than up above and she carefully took Ellen's clit in her mouth, warming it more than the shower spray could.

"Oh Gawd," Ellen moaned, her hands plunging in Rae's dark brown hair and massaging the scalp, the soap that was in there being easily washed away by the spray. She lifted her pelvis to grind her clit into Rae's eager mouth as she felt what could only be described as a lava of nerve endings centering on what her partners mouth was doing. The sucking, the teeth even, all made her want to scream. Rae brought up fingers to rub and play with the moisture that had nothing to do with the shower and Ellen nearly collapsed, catching her slipping feet on the textured bottom of the shower stall.

"Careful," Rae cautioned as she grinned up from where Ellen was nearly sitting on her face, her voice coming around the skin folds she was holding captive with her lips and tongue and teeth.

"Uh, uh, uhhhh," she grunted as she came, her fingers digging into Rae's scalp. She pulled one hand painfully away to grasp the bar on the wall and hold herself up as she twisted within her lover's grasp. Rae carefully licked away the evident signs of Ellen's pleasure, the taste and texture much different from the water spraying down. For added measure she washed any traces away with the water. Ellen twitched at the sensation, still sensitive.

"That was relaxing," she commented with a grin.

Ellen returned the grin, leaning in for one more kiss as she reached around the taller woman to turn off the water. "I think we should conserve water like this all the time."

"And encourage others to do the same," Rae teased.

"You bring that up at the next meeting," she teased in return.

Rae opened up the shower door and grabbed a towel. There was only one as no one had really stocked the RVs. They both shared and then changed into a set of clean clothes. "We will have to offer the washer and dryer to some of the others," Rae commented as she looked at the stacked set they had in their luxurious RV.

"Yeah, we should," Ellen agreed as she brushed her hair back and then got to starting dinner for them.

"Let's just have something easy," Rae advised. She was tired. She was so tired and they had just gotten here. "So, this is Oaken Oklahoma, eh?" she asked through a mouthful of pasta a while later.

Ellen smiled. "It was a pretty place. The buildings were all old and brick, the ambiance," she said swirling her orange juice as though it were wine. "It really was picturesque," she stated, remembering.

"Are you doing okay being back here?" Rae remembered the stories Ellen had shared of this place.

Ellen nodded through her own mouthful of pasta. "You know, at one point this would have been hard. But not everyone here was bad to me. Some were actually nice. I needed to get beyond that and I think I have. We are here to help and I can do it. It's not like I can't afford it," she said wryly, remember the Major and his threat to confiscate things.

"Well, money like that people don't understand. They get jealous. They want to feel independent."

"These people have nothing and a tent-city isn't going to get them in their homes too quickly," she said angrily, pointing with her fork.

"I'm on your side," Rae mentioned, holding up her hands in surrender.

"I'm sorry," she mumbled, stabbing her fork into the last of her pasta. "They couldn't wait to hit me up when they wanted help, and now that I'm giving it, they can't wait to take me down again."

"Who exactly are they?" Rae asked astutely. "The people haven't had time to get angry at you. It's those in positions of power that are going to object to you taking a position like this," she circled with her fork indicating the RVs around them. It was quieting down as people went to sleep early. A few radios could be heard as some sat outside the RVs assigned to them to socialize.

"Yeah, I got approached by Mr. Worley today," she laughed through her last bite.

"Isn't that the Sheriff that...?"

The redhead nodded. "He don't scare me anymore," she admitted, her twang showing up again.

"How could he?"

"Well, back in the day," she began to tell her about when she left town all those years ago.

"So he also has an axe to grind," she was indicating one of the lawsuits that Ellen had mentioned.

Ellen nodded and shrugged. She wasn't intimidated, not anymore. Although the lawsuits hadn't really netted her much other than satisfaction, it was the principle of the matter that really counted. "What am I doing here again?" she asked her girlfriend.

"Maybe paying a penance for something that wasn't your fault all those years ago?" she asked astutely. She got up to throw out the paper plates they had used even though there was a full set of dishes in the cupboards. She put the forks in the sink to rinse them off. She sat on the side of the table with Ellen, her arm around her. "And maybe, you are a good person at heart and you want to help those that can't help themselves here," she said softly, leaning in to kiss Ellen.

Ellen smiled into the kiss. Rae so got her on so many levels. "You are such a comfort," she told her as she hugged her close.

"Do you want to watch some television?" Rae asked as she looked around at the luxurious accommodations.

"That sounds good, but I've not figured it out yet," she told her.

Between the two of them they figured out the remote control that accessed the monitor that was hooked up to some sophisticated satellite thing on the roof of the RV. They finally found a station that was showing the devastation from above during the day. It was horrible.

"You know, they should come down here for maximum effect," Ellen commented as the camera's panned from a helicopter to show the path of the tornadoes. Deep grooves were cut in the earth through cornfields and the towns. Not only Oakley but several other towns were just wiped off the map.

"Are you going to help them, too?"

"Anyone I can help from here I will help," she asserted.

It wasn't too much longer that they were both yawning from their efforts of the day. It had been a long one and the following ones promised to be just as long.

❧ CHAPTER TWENTY SEVEN ❧

EDUCATING

"**W**ell, Lasbity, Texas or some such town had six tornadoes in one day. It was like some record or something," one of the boys was saying.

"How many tornadoes makes it a record?" one of the girls sitting around the group asked. Several of the locals had joined Ellen and her team, sitting around a fire pit, roasting marshmallows, drinking beer, and chatting before heading in for the night. It looked like rain again from the forecast on the radios and televisions. They were enjoying themselves before another storm hit.

"In 1974 there were 148 tornadoes over a two-day span," someone put in.

"In April of one year there were like 312 tornadoes during a one-week span. 226 of them were in one day," one of the boys said importantly. The others stared at him in surprise.

"That's nothing," someone put in dismissively waving aside the data he was spouting. "There were like 454 people killed in Mississippi and Georgia in like 1936."

"What about the tornado in 1925 that killed like 750 people in seven states?" someone asked.

"How the hell do you all remember that?" Ellen asked as she sipped a beer. It had been another full day and despite pissing off the Major the previous night, they had coordinated their efforts. She was providing better housing than his tent-city to the people of Oakley. He and his men had left some of the tent-city to those who were too stubborn to take Ellen's charity, but the majority of their efforts were still with search and rescue. They were still finding bodies and a few recoveries from basements around the area as they and many of the people of this town searched for survivors.

"We were getting our statistics together for our final exams," one of the interns told Ellen with a grin. "We wanted to impress you, too," he blushed as he quickly sipped the beer Ellen had provided.

"Well, your work in the labs has been stellar and I think you've impressed some of my people," Ellen told him, giving the students that worked at Gigitech a compliment. She'd appreciated them volunteering for this clean up to help the people of Oakley.

"You know, seeing the devastation of the tornado first hand, I think I want to try something different," one of the girls on their team put in.

"What, we aren't going to make the sensors?" someone asked, she was a team-leader and if she wanted to change something it would affect them all.

"It's been done and while our sensors will give us a helluva lot more data than past attempts, I think we should look at trying to stop a tornado," she put out there.

"Are you crazy? How the hell do you stop a tornado?" several voices asked.

"How about we fire something into the spout itself, causing a chemical reaction?" she put out there starting them all thinking.

Ellen was enjoying the conversation. Rae sat on the seat in front of her and Ellen was sitting on the picnic table where she had enjoyed a dinner with her team, sharing in on the hot dogs and hamburgers and any other food people wanted. It was a nice way to relax after their hard days of helping people. No one was turned away and several people had come to meet and thank Ellen for her generosity. It was just like a think tank listening to the students, though. Not much different than the round table discussions they had at the company.

"How does a tornado actually form?" one of the locals asked and was immediately inundated with answers before one voice rose above the others.

"Hang on, hang on, let's start at the beginning," Bob Talmus piped up. He held up his hands to quiet his fellow students who were enthusiastically bombarding the innocent girl who had asked the

question. "Okay, it's like this. The Unites States has the most tornadoes of any country in the world," he began.

"Why?" was heard from several voices.

He nodded as though he had expected that question. "For one, it's one of the largest countries with many temperate zones and its unique geography causes the right conditions for tornadoes to occur."

"But don't other countries get tornadoes?" someone called out.

Ellen leaned forward slightly to hear this answer herself, she was fascinated. Rae felt her surge slightly and leaned back imperceptibly to touch Ellen closer to her back. Ellen absentmindedly caressed along her bare arm.

"Yeah, they get them all over the world. The US though, it gets the strongest, the most violent and probably more than any other place on earth."

"But why?" a voice called out.

"It has no major east to west mountain range to block the air flows. Because of the Rocky Mountains that block moisture and screw up the atmospheric flow, which in turn makes drier air forced into the troposphere. Then you add the moisture level of the Gulf of Mexico sweeping up our country and you have perfect conditions when the two flows meet. It causes what they call a 'dry line' and that's why we have Tornado Alley through our country," he explained.

"I thought I heard that Tornado Alley extends up into Canada?"

"Yeah, it does, but they don't get as many as we do here in the States. They are, after all, part of the same continent and have the same atmospheric conditions that create a tornado," he explained.

"So how many tornadoes do we get?"

"One year I read we averaged nearly thirteen hundred," he told them with devastating effect.

"No way, that would be on the news," someone objected.

Another of the students piped up, "It *is* on the news but you don't hear about each and every one of them unless you had every channel in the country piped into your TV."

"I never hear of Europe getting tornadoes."

"They do, believe me," Bob continued getting back into the conversation. Ellen could see why he made such a good leader for her interns. He had been the one to present her with their initial plans for the storm chasing they wanted to do. "Europe, South Africa, Australia, New Zealand, and parts of South America get them. It doesn't matter where it is, if the conditions are right, they'll get them."

"Does Asia?"

He nodded. "It's so big, I would think it would be on the news more, but its land mass and the mountains that go every which way keep the numbers down on how many tornadoes they get. Plus, a majority of those countries that constitute Asia don't report things like we do," he said sadly, thinking about how much data was lost in third world countries that could help them predict things even better to save more people.

"Hey, didn't I hear they measure tornadoes or something with a Fuji something?" someone threw out there.

One of the girls from Bob's group answered this time. Ellen thought her name was Laurie. "It's called the 'Enhanced Fujita Scale,'" she said, making quotation marks with her fingers. "They measure it by wind speed and how much damage it creates in his path. You can have an EF0 to an EF5."

"How big were the two that hit Oakley?" a voice asked.

The kids shrugged. No one knew yet as they were all too busy trying to recover and save people right now, but it would be their mission to find out now.

How fast does a tornado have to be to register an F0?"

"Upwards to 250 mph," was the answer.

"Anyone know why we get them all summer long?"

"It's the right temperatures that cause them," Bob answered. "You can get them year-round with the right conditions."

"Yeah, but they seem to happen later in the day," someone argued.

"Yeah, but that's when the hot day is cooling off for evening. You can still have them at night, though, and not just in the day."

"I've never heard of a tornado happening in the morning."

"There was a tornado in 1936 that happened at like 8 or 8:30 in the morning once," Laurie put in.

"I bet we get the most tornadoes anywhere," someone put in with pride, meaning Oklahoma.

"Nope, you'd be wrong," Laurie told him. "Florida actually has more. Statistically speaking. But they also get waterspouts and I'm sure they count those as well."

"I'm moving to a state that doesn't have 'em," someone said bitterly.

"Every state can get them. Every state has had one," one of Bob's friends corrected the misinformation.

"I used to think they only happened out in the country," someone said miserably. They were wrapped in a thin blanket despite the heat.

"Naw, they can hit anywhere. Few years back there was one that hit New York City," the conversation went on.

Ellen answered a few questions about the help she would be willing to give. The RVs were still being driven in and had been all day long as well as the supplies. Her people had been busy handing out things and making sure no one was being greedy or hoarding. Already the scavengers had begun to come through Oakley to see if they could profit from others' misfortunes.

Mr. Mann had been found unhurt but shaken up. He had been blown blocks away from where his office had stood, and he and his Mrs. were in an RV not too far from Ellen and Rae's.

Ellen had let the Major 'take charge' on some things to prevent her people from accidentally stepping on too many governmental toes. Some of the calls she had made had bulldozers, tractors, and other heavy machinery coming in behind the governmental ones to help clear Main Street and begin to assess damage. They wouldn't start anything until enough time had gone by to find missing persons.

"We can waive certain building permits but these places have to be sound," Ellen had argued. "We can start building next week," she insisted. People wanted immediate action and she knew they wouldn't be patient. She wasn't coordinating everything herself but she was making it possible for people to help. Her farm and the crops that were on the land were being turned under as the many people in the RVs began to live out of them. Water was being trucked in, and the electric company was putting in emergency lines to power and recharge the many RVs parked there. Waste was going to be a problem but Rae found RV parks that used big sanitation vehicles and contracted with the companies to empty out the dump tanks.

They were there for two weeks, living in the RV, helping many people around town, but Ellen had to get back. Her teams she paid to stay for another two weeks before they were expected to be back in Silicon Valley and back at work. Those that stayed did so on a purely voluntarily basis. Only one employee flew back on the private plane and that was because her mother was ill back in California. Everyone was changed by the experience.

❖ CHAPTER TWENTY EIGHT ❖

NEXT

"I saw a side of you I have never seen before," Rae told Ellen, amazed as they settled into the private plane.

Ellen shrugged dismissively as she put away her cellphone. She had just ordered 100 oak trees to be delivered and planted on Main Street in Oakley. They were pretty large trees and very expensive. It would take less time for these bigger trees to mature and give the community a sense of pride in them.

"I thought you were going to cut off that Mayor's nuts when he started making 'suggestions' in the form of 'demands,'" she laughed.

"Well, I did what I could and I hope the donations that came in from the publicity will help everyone," she answered.

Rae had been amazed at the amount of work Ellen herself had been willing to do, not just writing checks but physically helping people out. She and others organized a door-to-door cleanup of lots so that the builders that Ellen had contracted could come in and begin building. Since the building inspectors were helping, again asked by Ellen specifically, a lot of the rules and regulations were being bent a bit. Instead of waiting on paperwork, the people that had to do the inspecting were there on-site to make sure it was being done right, often for several houses at a time. Many times, they chipped in to help, seeing the mass of people helping out their neighbors. Truckloads of ready-made houses began to arrive after the first week. Walls, windows, and doors arrived ready to be put up on the basements and foundations that were being revealed. The community was coming together to build each other's homes one by one. It was a sight to see, and Ellen and her people planned daily in order to coordinate what they could. The television stations were going wild with the publicity. Ellen had challenged each of the stations to bring their own people in to help for 'just' a day, film it, and then see what the whole story was about. Several had responded and hundreds more of volunteers had arrived to help not only in Oakley but the surrounding communities. Ellen had turned it into a true 'American patriot' instead of a Gigitech or Animated Studios techie. All the businesses who donated people and materials were featured prominently with the television stations – free publicity, but most of all…community.

The town would take months to rebuild, years, really. The camaraderie and sense of community that had sprung up in their worst hours would last a lifetime. Ellen, her team, and the hundreds of volunteers who had responded could be proud of what they had done, what they had started. The 'pay it forward' initiative was taking hold. The grassroots effort that started in Oakley was spreading and people were responding. With the help of the students and the television stations, it had become an internet phenomenon.

"Are you sorry to be going home?" Rae asked her with a smile. They were both exhausted from the two weeks. Each day they had thrown themselves into helping out as much as they possibly could. Each evening they celebrated that they were alive and joined in the impromptu cookouts that seemed to pop up all over the RV village where they now lived. Their nights were for each other, and they filled themselves with the love they were sharing. Rae didn't know for certain if it was because of the sultry air here in Oklahoma or not. But there was no way she was going to look a gift horse in the mouth, either. She was enjoying sharing this time with Ellen and the nights they spent making love.

"We did what we could. It's time for another chapter in our lives," she said mystically.

"Do you have plans?" Rae asked surprised.

"I think I should start a nonprofit," she stated as she put on her seatbelt.

Rae saw her put on the belt and quickly did her own. The employee flying back with them did the same. "And what would that be for?" Rae asked, but she had an inkling after seeing what they had just accomplished in Oakley and the surrounding community.

"This," she gestured towards the ground they were taking off from. "Just what we did here. Have people ready to fly in at a moment's notice following a natural disaster. They would help the National Guard, FEMA, whomever, and since they aren't bound by the red tape those organizations are, they would not get bogged down and can offer help quicker."

"You've got to admit that you might have lost going up against the Governor and the National Guard," Rae pointed. out then gulped; the plane had done that little thing to her stomach as they left the ground.

Ellen smiled, she'd experienced something of the same sensation but she'd been prepared for it. Her chair wasn't backwards and she had been glancing out the window so she knew it was coming. "Yeah, I know we butted heads. But somehow this sort of thing has to be quicker," she said, smacking the arm of her chair. "It was so frustrating watching some of the crap they made people go through. Making them prove who they are when their identification has been lost in the disaster. Prove that they owned their home when all their important papers were lost, too." She shook her head at the bureaucracy of it all.

"There is only so much you can do," Rae reminded her.

"We'll see about that," Ellen replied.

They changed the subject as they flew west towards Silicon Valley. Ellen was eager to get back to work. She had plans and they included Rae but she wasn't so certain she should bring them up until they were more concrete.

A small limo was waiting for them on the tarmac as they flew into the Mineta San Jose Airport. Their baggage was quickly loaded and the three of them ensconced in the back.

"Let's take her home first," Ellen told the driver, nodding to her employee, Joy Macknamara, who had flown with them.

Joy leaned forward to give the driver her address and a few directions.

The three of them didn't talk much, but Joy hadn't contributed too much to the couple's conversation on the flight. She was too worried about her mother, whom she came home to take care of.

"If you need more time off, Joy, you let us know," Ellen told her as the driver pulled her bag from the trunk.

"Thank you, Ellen. This has been quite an experience," she said reverently. "I wish I could have stayed longer to help."

"You did fine. I appreciate you dropping everything and going with the rest. I hope your mother is better," Ellen told her sincerely, and with an uncharacteristic gesture she hugged the younger woman. "Just give us a call and let us know," she reminded her.

"I will, and thank you," she said gratefully. It had all been such an experience to help those people, to make and see an actual difference in their lives from what they had done as a team.

Ellen got back in the limo with Rae, who waved madly at Joy. They sat back, holding hands.

"Well, we are almost home," Ellen said with a sigh of relief.

"Oakley didn't feel like home?"

Ellen shook her head. "No, it wouldn't. Not after all these years." She looked out the window as she thought about the past two weeks. Several people she had sued had come up to her to personally apologize for taking her mother's and grandparents' things. They were ashamed, and to see her come in and help out the community had been humbling to them. She accepted their apologies but she moved on quickly, rallying people to help each other out. They cleared houses one by one into large receptacles that would be picked over to recycle the wood and other things, and the rest would be chopped into small pieces to be recycled or broken down and composted. Ellen was determined not to dwell on the past, but to move forward and rebuild Oakley and the surrounding communities. She didn't want the negativity of her youth to spill over into her life now and this was one of the only ways she could think to do it.

"I'm glad you think of the house we share as home," Rae said quietly, squeezing Ellen's hand. She had seen the ghosts of past memories pass over Ellen's face, and she knew that they were still painful.

"Are you happy?" Ellen turned to look at Rae, bringing the hand that had just squeezed hers up to her lips for a kiss.

"I am," Rae assured her. Seeing Ellen take charge but back off when one of her team had a better idea or had already taken control of the situation was enlightening. She was the most amazing woman and Rae felt honored to know her.

Ellen smiled and leaned in to kiss her. She couldn't seem to get enough of her. The past two weeks they had gone their separate ways to help out the community of Oakley, but met up every evening to share the campfires, and later to share their bodies. Their time together in Oakley was almost a honeymoon amongst the terrible devastation they had seen. They seemed to renew each other with their passion, as they loved each other. Waking up in the mornings, they were both eager and willing to help and start again. It had been amazing. Their present kiss turned passionate and then the limo slowed at their gate and they heard the driver announce, "Ms. Ellen Christenson and Ms. Rae Granger," to the person manning the gate. They broke apart and smiled at each other, for a moment they had forgotten they were in the

car with a driver as they concentrated on each other. Both sets of eyes held promises of 'later.'

"Will you need anything else, Ms. Christenson?" the driver asked as he put their bags on the top step of the porch.

"No, that's all," Ellen said as she held out her hand for him to shake. In it was a discrete large denomination note. "Thank you," she said as they shook hands and exchanged the money.

"No, thank you," he said with a salute to his cap as he quickly went down the stairs to his vehicle.

Ellen watched as the car left before she picked up the bags.

"I got it," Rae said trying to take her own.

"No, I got it," Ellen replied and watched as Rae quickly put the key in the front door. She loved these doors. They were overly tall with large frosted windows in them, and they opened into a small atrium where another set of doors blocked the entrance. These, too, were overly tall and made of rich woods that reminded her of the color of Rae's chestnut hair. She watched as Rae quickly entered the code to the security system and then unlocked the doors. Leaving the second set of doors open, they locked the front ones and headed upstairs to unpack and wash up. Despite showering together frequently in the RV, it wasn't the same as being home and using their opulent bathroom together. The bath gave them both a good soak together and then the shower gave them the massage afterwards. They ended up in bed, asleep before their wet heads could hit the towel-covered pillows, content to be together even if they didn't make love that night.

❖ CHAPTER TWENTY NINE ❖

NEW IDEAS

"I would like you to head this up," Ellen told Rae as they shared lunch in the company cafeteria. She had invited her girlfriend to Animated Studios for lunch to show her some of the animations they had ready for an upcoming film.

She'd loved the graphics, amazed they were drawings instead of real photographs. "They're so real!" she exclaimed over and over.

"That's the point," Ellen pointed out, remembering Ryan's dream and his prophecy. Someday they might not need real actors and actresses in film. He'd been right about a lot of technology and she was sure he might be right about this someday.

"I like my job," Rae said in response to Ellen's statement.

"You told me it was boring just a few weeks ago," Ellen countered, using her spoon to gesture, nearly dripping yogurt on the table.

"Yes, but it's mine."

"This could be, too."

"I work the hours I want, when I want."

"You'd be in charge," Ellen promised.

"Not if you are holding the purse strings."

Ellen had to admit that was a drawback. "We'll set it up as a tax deduction write-off something with the pencil pushers. That way you would have a budget to work with and you can administer it like you see fit."

Rae had to admit it sounded tempting. She'd taken her job so she wasn't tied down to a desk. She worked on her computer for a few hours a day and got paid really well for what she did. She had to admit, though, it wasn't a challenge. What Ellen was proposing was an incredible opportunity. "What about the red tape?"

"That's where your expertise comes in. Look what you did in Oakley. Didn't that feel great? Wasn't it wonderful to just go in and get things done?"

"Yes, it was, but we can't write a blank check for some disasters. That's what the government is for, that's why there's red tape."

"Yes, but donations and such can fill in the cracks. You could have teams ready to fly out at a moment's notice," Ellen enthused, remembering how great it had felt those weeks before in Oakley. Writing a check had made it easier, but having the means to do it went a helluva long way.

"Can I think about it?" Rae hesitated.

"Of course." Ellen stopped trying to convince her to take the job. Seeing how Rae had taken charge and done some things that she had forgotten had made her the perfect candidate for this job. "I just want someone in there that I can trust," she finished with, reaching out to hold Rae's hand.

Rae melted. Ellen was a wonderful girlfriend these days. Kind, thoughtful, and not at all demanding. This job offer was the first thing she had asked for in a long time. She was ready to say yes and then thought about the logistics of the position. "Ellen, I can't afford to not get paid. Non-profits don't pay well. I need to work!"

"Believe me, after Oakley I know there is a job there. You'll work all right! I'll support you until you get it where you think it should be," she offered generously.

"You will NOT support me," Rae said adamantly. Then to lighten the blow of her harsh words she added flippantly, "Not unless you marry me!" She immediately felt the frost in the air, Ellen's hand that had been holding hers turned ice cold before she withdrew it in shock. "I was *kidding*," she said lightly, trying the stem the hurt form Ellen's withdrawal.

"I know," Ellen said in reply with a false little smile. "The job is real, though, and with the budget you can figure out how much you should earn as well as your crew," she said, trying to change the subject away from the one that had caused her heart to beat hard in her chest. "But you think about it," she said, reaching out with her hand to pat

Rae's again, an attempt to further remove the other subject. "Let me know."

Rae knew she had committed a grievous faux pas. Ellen had made it clear long ago, the last time they dated, that she never wanted to marry, never wanted kids. Didn't want or need that kind of commitment. She knew it was best to pretend she had never said it. It would pass, but she could tell that Ellen was a bit jittery about it. "I'll let you know," she said with an equally false smile as they tried to salvage the rest of their lunch together, pretending it hadn't turned awkward.

"Thank you, Dr. Keurig, for seeing me once again," Ellen greeted her after all this time.

"I was surprised to hear from you, Ellen, but pleased. How are you doing?" Nancy greeted her and gestured her to the familiar chair.

"I'm doing well. I got back a few weeks ago from Oakley," she told her as she sat down, crossing her legs.

"I heard about that on the news, made quite a splash," she said admiringly. She glanced at Ellen's nylon clad legs and swallowed her ire over what would never be hers. She had wondered why, out of the blue, Ellen Christenson had called her. Unfortunately, it was for a session, not a date. The disappointment was crushing but she knew better than to show it.

"Yeah, well, I can't do anything without it making the news," Ellen replied modestly. It was true, though, she had shamelessly used the television stations to make a point. The donations to help repair Oakley and the surrounding communities were still coming in.

"Were you okay going back to Oakley?" the doctor inside of the woman came out, worrying about her patient.

"I was fine. Rae went with me as well as a crew from Gigitech and Animated Studios. We kicked butt," she smiled.

Not too thrilled to hear about Rae going but pleased for Ellen and her ability to go back to the scene of such a lifetime of abuse without it affecting her, Nancy smiled a genuine smile. "So, you aren't here about Oakley?" she asked delightedly, surprised.

Ellen shook her head to the negative, her red hair brushing back and forth and catching the sunlight in Nancy's office. Nancy caught her breath at the beauty of the moment and nearly missed what Ellen had to say. "No, I think I may be anuptaphobic," she said succinctly.

"Anupta..." she said wonderingly, her brain not quite catching it. She was bemused.

"You know, a fear of marrying the wrong person?" Ellen said exasperatedly. "I have the right word, don't I?" she asked, now feeling like a fool.

"Yes, yes of course," Nancy covered, realizing what she had done. The view of Ellen had distracted her and her patient's lightning swift mind had caught her. "Why do you think you have this fear?" she asked, trying to become professional again. "Are you planning on marrying?"

"Well, the other day Rae said something and I froze inside. I think she sensed it," she said looking down at her hands; her leg began to bounce where it crossed over the other one.

"Did she propose that the two of you get married?" Nancy swallowed her disappointment. The relationship had gone on much longer than any of Ellen's other ones, and her hope that they would break up like all the others was gone.

"No, not really, but the subject came up," Ellen's hand wiped across her forehead and eyes. "The shock of it, though, nearly had my heart in my throat. I think I hurt Rae's feelings with my reaction."

"What did you do?" She was curious now and cocked her head sideways a little.

"I just froze," she said, remembering the moment. "She turned it into a joke but I know I hurt her," she sighed deeply.

"Do you not want to marry her?" Her own heart was pounding in hope.

Ellen stood up and started to pace. "I don't *know*," she said in an exasperated voice, her hands gesturing outwards in helplessness.

"Do you love her?" she asked quietly, watching the redhead come a little undone.

"Gawd yes," she said with conviction.

The tiny bit of hope that had begun in Dr. Keurig's thoughts died a harsh death. "But you don't want to marry her?" she tried to be professional.

"I love her but I used to say that I never wanted to perpetuate my family. You know what they were like," she said harshly.

"Yes, but you aren't your family. Both your parents weren't like…" she pointed out.

"Yes, but his blood flows in my veins," she pointed out in return. Their conversation was almost like a sparring match as they spat it out back and forth.

"You don't have to have the baby," she returned, trying to maintain a doctor-patient relationship instead of friend who wanted more than the other friend was willing to give.

"I know that, but if she wants marriage, she is going to want children," she said in anguish, looking terribly sad.

"Do you want to break up with her so she can find someone who wants all that?" the friend asked, not the doctor, hopefully.

"No, I don't want to break up with her!" she said emphatically. "I love her!"

Nancy looked at her sadly, puzzled as to why this woman affected her so. She didn't want to care, but she did. As a professional, though, she had to direct Ellen to find her own answers. "Do you not want children ever?" she said softer, kindly.

Ellen thought back to the RV village and the children running about happily. They had nothing, their homes were gone. Their parents had salvaged what they could from their homes, but toys were not a priority. Watching how happy the children were with the little they had been a delight. Ellen had been an only child and had wished as a young girl to have a sibling. Later she had been happy that no one else had to deal with her father and his abuse. Finding Ryan had been such a blessing. Firstly, he was her friend, and secondly, he was her brother of another mother. She had wished she could be straight occasionally just so that he and she could be a couple, but she knew that could never have been. He had been destined to be her friend, her best friend. Now, with Ryan long gone, Rae was her best friend, her partner, her lover. She wanted to make her happy. "No, I guess I thought I didn't, but I don't mind children," she admitted as she remembered the RV village. The kids had been fun, she had enjoyed them. They hadn't been the problem that their parents felt they were.

"Then what really is the problem? You need to find a donor?" she asked with a small smile. She had already resigned herself to the fact that Ellen didn't see her, she never would. She didn't even know of her attraction.

"Actually, we already have a donor. Ryan left me some of his little guys in a cryobank in his will," Ellen smiled in remembrance.

That was news to Nancy. She returned Ellen's smile. She waited for her to continue; sometimes the silence had her patients finding their own answers.

Ellen sat back down, her agitation gone. "I love her," she said wonderingly. "I don't know why the word 'marriage' scared me at all," she continued. "It's not like we don't have the money to raise the children if she wants them."

Nancy loved seeing her patients find their own answers. Her help was minimal and yet they felt she did so much.

Ellen began to realize that being married to the woman she loved wouldn't be such a bad thing. She wasn't responsible for the genes that ran through her veins; she didn't have to pass them on. Rae could have the babies. She realized she wanted children. Not just one baby, but several, and she wanted them with Rae. The smile on her face was beautiful to see. "I do want Rae, I do want children," she told her therapist.

Nancy smiled in return. She was resigned. Ellen Christenson would never be hers but she was glad she had helped her realize what she wanted. "Looks like you had the answers all along," she said with that smile.

Ellen nodded. "I guess I did," she agreed.

"So, what are you going to do?" her heart felt like it was falling but she was resigned to finishing this.

"I think I'm going to propose to my girlfriend and make it something special!" she said with spirit, the excitement of the idea taking hold. She made a movement to get up and end the session. "Thank you, Doctor Keurig," she said emphatically.

"I think you can call me Nancy after all this time," she laughed with Ellen and got up. Then Ellen surprised her with a hug.

"I can't thank you enough for helping me discover my own thoughts and feelings," she said emphatically.

"That's what I'm here for," Nancy said with a self-depreciating smile. She let her hands drop from the impromptu hug, feeling awkward.

Ellen let her go and said, "I think this time really is the last time. Thank you again...Nancy," she told her and with one more smile she left.

"You are very welcome," Nancy told her patient to her back as she left. As soon as the door closed she sat down sadly and thought about everything she had done wrong with this patient. She had done so much right, though, as she moved on from her past. This unprofessional attraction needed some therapy of its own. Nancy reached for her phone so she could call her own therapist.

"Ms. Christenson...Ellen," she began. "I think the project has merit and I'd like to pursue it, a spinoff from the original division," she said with spirit.

"Laurie..." Ellen began but was interrupted.

"Lauren," the girl corrected her.

"My apologies, Lauren," Ellen began again, remembering the spirited girl from the campfire at the RV village. She was a smart girl, she recalled. "The monies were set aside for your team for storm chasing and the sensors and things, not for this," she indicated the proposal the girl had brought to her.

"Yes, and that data will still be necessary," she emphasized. "I think that this further project will help beyond that," she gestured to the

other project they were working on in the lab; she had cornered Ellen when she came to check up on the results of some of their experiments.

"How in the heck are you gonna be able to reverse a tornado?" Ellen asked as she glanced at what the girl was presenting her and remembered her comments at the fire.

"Not really reverse it but perhaps cause the effects to dissipate," she argued. "A tornado is caused by updrafts and downdrafts. You know, when a thunderstorm occurs?" She waited for Ellen to nod before she hurried on, "That unstable air interacts with something like a wind shear, and that tilting of the wind shear forms the tornado."

Ellen was with her, she understood what she was saying. "But how can you stop that? It's Mother Nature. I thought you guys wanted to help with an early warning system and to understand what happens in a tornado?"

"We do, this data," she pointed to the boards of figures and facts as well as the piles of paperwork they were all working on, including models and computer-generated graphics, "this will help me with my theory. If we can shoot into the clouds that form such," she indicated a model of a tornado. "Like they do to make it rain," she explained and Ellen nodded again. "Then perhaps we can decrease the likelihood of such an occurrence."

Ellen realized the idea had merit. "I think you are arguing your doctorate," she said with a smile. "Okay, you work out a budget. You can base your data on what the team has found here," she indicated the work they had been doing for a while on their grants. "If your team wants to continue or anyone else wants to come on board, they better realize the money is drying up," she told her seriously. "I want specs and everything in a few months," she told the excited girl.

"Oh, I will, I will! Thank you, Ellen, thank YOU!" she spontaneously hugged the red headed executive.

Ellen laughed at her exuberance. She knew that sponsoring such technology would have a twofold benefit. While it was being worked on it was a tax write-off. If anything came of it, if it worked at all, they could profit from it. It hopefully would be a win-win situation for everyone involved. She just hoped no one got killed chasing tornados for the data.

❈ CHAPTER THIRTY ❈

LIFE ALTERING

Ellen had never felt more nervous than she had tonight. She had planned it out to the minutest detail. She didn't count on her girlfriend being late and she impatiently paced the bedroom floor, her heels tapping on the hardwood, then the area rug, then the hardwood floor…echoes could be heard.

When she heard a car pull up in the driveway and saw the headlights she rushed down the stairs to open the door for Rae.

"Where have you been? I've called…" she looked at her dripping girlfriend; she was soaked from the rain.

"I'm sorry, I got a flat tire. My phone died as I got a hold of AAA and fortunately they came to change it, but it took forever in that afternoon traffic from the city," she apologized and then stared at the beautiful outfit Ellen was wearing. "We were going out this evening," she said, horrified, and looked down at what she was wearing. "Was it important?" she asked trying not to feel like an idiot for not remembering.

"Yes, it was important. Here," she said grabbing a scarf from the coat rack by the door. "You run up and change and clean up, I'll change the reservations," she offered.

Rae sagged in defeat. "Do we have to go? Can we go another night? I'm just exhaust..." she started and then looking at the look on Ellen's face, the disappointment, she changed her tone. "I'm sorry, I'll go change...."

"No, no," Ellen sighed. "You are tired, that rain takes it out of you. Let's go up and both change. We'll have a quiet night here at home. I think there is some lasagna left in the fridge we can heat up," she said with a smile, hoping that Rae couldn't hear the disappointment she was feeling.

"No, you said this was important, we can go out..."

"No, it can wait, you're soaking and I don't want you to get sick. C'mon," she said putting her arm around her soaked girlfriend, ruining her own silk dress at the contact. "Let's get you out of those wet clothes," she urged her towards the stairs, dripping on the floor.

"But it was impor..." she began again and then sneezed, ruining her argument.

"Let's get you in the shower, turn on the steam, and get you warm inside. I'll change and put in the lasagna," Ellen told her as she helped her up the stairs. Rae didn't argue. She had known that the meeting or whatever it was with Ellen was important and for her to cancel it like this, she appreciated it. She felt horrible; she'd tried to change the flat herself but was ever so grateful when the tow truck showed up. It was too late by then, though. She was cold, tired, and soaked to the bone. Going out was not on her mind, just getting home was. Rae was soon stripped and in the shower. She poked her head out to ask Ellen to get her something, but when she heard her on the phone cancelling their reservations, she felt like a perfect heel.

Ellen was annoyed. She'd stripped out of the sexy silk dress she had purchased just for this occasion. She downgraded to sweats and socks, not exactly the most beautiful thing to wear for what she had planned, but she didn't want Rae to get ill and it only made sense to stay home anyway with this weather. She cursed the weather and went downstairs after cancelling her reservations. She could hear the annoyance in their voice over her cancellation; after all, she had 'name-dropped' to get it in the first place.

She went downstairs and found the leftover lasagna in the fridge. Having turned on the oven to preheat, she removed the cardboard lid from the container and replaced it with tin foil. Sliding the tin into the oven, she smiled in anticipation of eating this delicious concoction. Leaving it she went to the den and lit a fire so at least they might have a romantic ambiance.

She quickly headed to the wine cellar to select an appropriate bottle of wine. In the end, Ellen chose a full-bodied red with a fruity taste which would complement both the lasagna and the occasion. She lit a few candles and placed them around the den. Grabbing a blanket, she spread it out on the floor so they could have a picnic. She hurried back to the kitchen to the check on the lasagna and to butter some bread, slipping it into a pan and putting it into the oven next to the heating lasagna.

"Everything okay?" Rae asked from the doorway.

Ellen looked up and saw Rae in a ratty old bathrobe with Kleenex shoved up her nose. "Are you okay?" she asked alarmed.

"Oh, I think I have the sniffles. There is no antihistamine in the bathroom, so I thought I'd check here in the kitchen," she stated as she shuffled in bunny rabbit slippers towards the cabinet where they kept aspirin and other pills.

Ellen watched her dispassionately, the appearance was very unappealing and she wondered how much Rae would regret her choice in the morning.

"I can smell that," Rae said cheerfully as she pulled the Kleenex from her red nose.

Ellen smiled but wondered if Rae should go back to bed. "Are you going to be okay?" she worried.

"Yeah, I'll be fine," she smiled as she found the pills she was looking for and pulled the box out to open it and pop out a couple of pills. "Do we have any orange juice?" she asked as she reached for the refrigerator door.

"I think so, in the door," Ellen answered watching her. Rae pulled out the carafe and Ellen reached for a glass to hand to her.

"Thank you," Rae said with a nasal twang from her stopped-up nose.

Ellen watched her pop the pills in her mouth and chase them down with the orange juice. A nice, healthy combination. "Maybe you should go to bed," she suggested, disappointed as her other plans crumbled once again.

"Naw, I'll be fine. I want some of that lasagna," she said, smiling around the glass she was drinking the orange juice from.

"I could bring you a tray," Ellen offered helpfully.

"I want to eat with you," Rae sounded petty and childish, almost as though she was about to throw a tantrum.

Ellen chuckled. "I have a fire started in the fireplace in the den, and I'll bring this in when it's ready," she indicated the oven.

"Trying to get rid of me?"

She laughed again. "No, just getting you off your feet. I'll pamper you, baby."

"Aww, that's sweet."

"Yeah, that's me, sweet," she said sardonically and they both shared a laugh. Sweet was not a word that was used in conjunction with Ellen, ever.

"I could just kiss you," she threatened and they laughed again. It was good to be this comfortable with each other.

"Please, don't," she grinned to soften the plea.

"Fine, be that way. I'm going to the den then," she said with a wink and headed down the hallway towards the room, carrying her glass of orange juice.

Ellen watched her go and sighed. This evening, this perfect evening, all ruined by the rain.

The lasagna was done not too much later and Ellen served it up on two plates along with the bread and put both on a tray. Adding the carafe of orange juice, another glass, and some silverware and napkins, she hefted the tray, balancing it in her hands and carrying it along the hall. She saw that Rae had grabbed the blanket off the floor, ruining her plans for a picnic, and was sitting on the couch wrapped in it.

"Hungry?" she asked to announce her presence.

"Cold," Rae said in return.

"This will warm you up," Ellen said as she put the tray across Rae's legs that were stretched out on the sofa. "Here, let me top that off," she said, pouring more orange juice into Rae's glass and then pouring some into her own. She carefully put the carafe on a side table and distributed the plates between them, dividing up the silverware and napkins.

"Gawd, I can smell that despite this cold," Rae breathed appreciatively at the aroma of the lasagna.

"I hope you can taste it, too."

They both dug into the tasty treat and used the bread to sop up the sauces that spilled across their plates. It was delicious even as leftovers. The fire was crackling merrily in the fireplace; they could hear the rain coming down outside and a bit of wind blew it against the windows now and then. Otherwise it was peaceful and quiet.

That was something Ellen appreciated about Rae, she didn't need to chat and keep her entertained. They both relished the peace and quiet, especially after a hard day. Finishing up their respective plates, they stacked the dirty ones on the tray before Ellen offered more orange juice to Rae. When she refused, she poured the rest into own glass.

"Man, listen to that," Rae commented as a particularly strong gust of wind sent large drops of water against the large windows.

"I'd rather not," Ellen said tightly as she moved aside the tray from Rae's lap.

"Oh yeah, I forgot you hate that," Rae said, trying to lighten the moment and feeling bad that she had forgotten. "So, what was tonight that you had to cancel?" she asked curiously.

Ellen shrugged, putting her stocking clad feet on the coffee table. "Nothin'," she stated dismissively.

"C'mon, I know you better than that," Rae tried to cajole her.

"Well, there was somethin'," she said and glanced up at her, wondering if she should go ahead with her plan.

"Well? Out with it? I'm all ears."

Ellen looked up with a grin and glanced at the ears under her chestnut colored hair. "Are you?" she asked.

"I hide them well."

Ellen chuckled like she was supposed to. She'd planned to ask her a really important question and changing her plans twice hadn't been conducive to the romance she had hoped for.

"C'mon, quit hedging. You didn't light the candles for nothin'," she gestured to the votive candles placed strategically around the room.

Ellen knew there was no fooling Rae; she was too astute, too clever, even fogged up with her antihistamine. She still looked horrible, wrapped in the blanket with her tacky bathrobe; she even had the rabbit slippers still on. Sighing, she supposed she *could* wait but she didn't *want* to wait and she hoped Rae would appreciate the gesture. "Well, I had planned this out better," she began, suddenly feeling nervous. "But..."

"I ruined it with coming home late and the rain," Rae finished for her sighing loudly.

"No, you didn't ruin anything," she protested, although secretly thinking it had been ruined. "I just had to regroup."

"Regroup?"

"Re-plan?" she reworded.

"Re-plan what?" she frowned.

Ellen turned to her and slipped off the edge of the couch, getting down on one knee. "Rae," she said grabbing her left hand. "Would you marry me?" she got out quickly before she could think too much.

To say Rae was surprised was an understatement. She realized now why Ellen had been wearing the silk dress. She had planned something much more romantic than this. She glanced around at the finished carafe of orange juice and the dirty plates of lasagna. She realized the blanket she had wrapped around herself that she had found on the floor must have been part of Ellen's alternative plan. She'd ruined it! "Oh, I ruined your plans," she said horrified, her right hand covering her mouth.

Ellen grinned at the expression on Rae's face as she waited patiently for an answer to her question.

"You planned something romantic," she stated, realizing what had happened in an instant. "And then I ruined it," she started to cry. She was feeling crappy and realizing the trouble Ellen had probably gone to on her behalf, she started crying.

Ellen was still waiting for an answer to her question. Seeing Rae start to cry annoyed her and at the same time tugged at her heart strings. "Baby, don't cry, please don't cry," she pleaded.

Rae looked down at Ellen, looking up at her so prettily and the question she had asked finally penetrated her befuddled mind. "Did you...?" she began and started crying harder.

"Did I what?" Ellen asked confusedly. She was still holding Rae's left hand, kneeling at the side of the couch.

Rae swallowed down her sobs, it was messing with her nose, and she sniffed deeply, making a horrible sound that was gross. "Did you just ask me to marry you?" she asked through the tears. She knew she had heard her but she wanted to hear it again.

Ellen rolled her eyes. Even the attempt at proposing to her girlfriend had been screwed up. "Yes, yes, I did," she said exasperatedly. "And what is your answer?" she asked.

Rae began to cry harder and nod, "Yes, YES, YES!" she shouted and then choked on some of the phlegm and started coughing. It took a long while for her to stop and she used her Kleenex to cough into.

"Jeez, are you okay?" Ellen asked, concerned.

Nodding, Rae waved her away as she tried to calm her cough and get a hold of herself. She finally was able to draw a deep breath and shuddered to calm the sobs that wanted to take hold again. Breathing clearly, she coughed a couple more times before she tried to speak. "Did...did you mean it?" she asked, unsure of herself suddenly.

"Of course I meant it, silly," Ellen said as she got up off the floor to sit next to her. "Are you okay?" she asked again, not sure if the tears or the cold were getting to her.

"Well, usually when someone asks someone to marry them, there's a ring," Rae got out and another series of coughs shook her. The phlegm in her throat wasn't helping things, much less the tears.

"Oh shit, I forgot," Ellen popped up, racing out of the room. She had planned to have the ring in her purse at the restaurant and drop it into some champagne. When she had to cancel that plan, she had planned instead to have the romantic meal on the blanket, and she'd forgotten to bring the ring down when Rae suddenly appeared in the kitchen. Running up the stairs, she was out of breath as she searched for and found the ring box in her purse. She checked that the ring was still in the box. With all the snafus this evening, she was worried that something else would go wrong. She hurried down the stairs, nearly slipping on a wet spot from the rainwater that had dripped off of Rae. Swearing under her breath, she entered the study.

"What's wrong?" Rae asked as she craned her neck to look over her shoulder.

"Oh nothin'," Ellen said airily as she rushed across the room. Kneeling again, she nearly groaned at how her knee felt on the hard floor. Even through the area rug it still hurt kneeling on it once again. Flicking open the ring box, she presented it to the woman on the couch.

It was at that moment that Rae realized how inappropriately she was dressed. The ratty bathrobe, the fluffy bunny slippers, her dripping nose...she wanted to cry again as she gazed at the brilliant array of diamonds before her. "Oh, it's beautiful," she said starting to cry again, despite trying not to.

Ellen grinned as she rose up painfully from the floor, her knee cracking as she straightened it out, causing her to cringe. Gently she took Rae's left hand and pulled the diamond ring from its box. "Are you sure?" she asked one last time. At Rae's emphatic nod she pushed the ring on her third finger. "I'd kiss you but..." she began teasingly but found her face being captured and Rae kissing her despite the cold.

"It's beautiful," she said when she sat back to admire the ring, holding out her hand before her, the fireplace beyond it shining brightly.

"Do you like it?" Ellen asked, her arm around the sick woman, holding her close.

"Oh, I more than like it," Rae assured her.

"Good, now my job's done, it's up to you now," Ellen said, the teasing note in her voice making Rae look up at her in question.

"What's up to me now?" she challenged.

"Well, you have to plan a wedding now," she told her smugly.

"Nuh uh, this is a group activity and you are part of this group," she said waving her thumb, pointing at the two of them.

"Team, baby, we're a team," Ellen gently corrected her with a laugh.

"We are," she said, sniffing loudly.

"Why now?" Rae felt brave enough to ask a few days later. Her cold had been halted once she was tucked into bed by a concerned Ellen who snuggled in with her, her body heat providing an appreciated bonus.

Ellen looked up from the work she had brought home. Rae had been typing madly away on her laptop while she looked over some schematics that needed her approval. She'd found three errors so far and was annoyed by them. "Why now, what?" she asked confused.

Rae waved her ring at her in answer.

"Oh, well, you said you wouldn't work for the nonprofit unless I married you," she teased and then stopped immediately when she saw Rae's face fall. "Hey, I was just kidding," she said earnestly.

"You aren't marrying me so I'll take that job?" she asked, hurt.

"Hell no, I want to marry you because I love you." Ellen got up from the desk where she had been working and hurried over to the chair where Rae had been sitting, her feet propped up by the leg rest. "Baby, I realized I never wanted to lose you, I wanted you forever. I'm not scared anymore," she told her gently as she sat on the arm of the chair and leaned over her. "I want you," she said emphatically. "And if someday you want babies, we can have babies," she said gently.

"Babies?" she said wonderingly, her face lighting up in a way that Ellen had never seen before. "You want babies with me?" she asked to be sure.

Ellen nodded and leaned down to kiss her fiancée. "I want a life with you, Rae, I want forever. I want to love and live with you and maybe even have a family if we are so blessed," she smiled into the kiss as she murmured against Rae's lips.

"I think we will have to shop around for a suitable donor," Rae said as she playfully pulled Ellen off the chair arm and into her lap, kissing her in earnest.

"Already...taken...care...of...luv," Ellen told her between kisses.

"What's...taken...care...of?" she asked in return as she began to make love to Ellen. It was too choice having her in her arms, across her lap like this. She gently pushed the laptop aside, closing it and placing it gently on the floor.

"The...donor," she told her as she returned kiss for kiss, deepening them, enjoying the feel of Rae's arms around her in the comfortable chair.

"Wait a minute," Rae pulled back to look into Ellen's face. "You already chose a donor for us?" she asked, insulted. This was a decision that the two of them should make, not just one of them. She wondered if the old Ellen was returning, making all the decisions for them.

Ellen laughed, trying to lighten the moment that had suddenly become so tense. "No, I didn't choose him, he chose us," she tried telling her.

Rae put the foot rest down and Ellen tumbled to the floor as Rae stood up. "He what?" she demanded angrily.

"What the hell?" Ellen replied feeling angry over being unceremoniously dumped onto the floor.

"You let some guy choose us to donate his sperm to?" she clarified.

"No, no, nooo," Ellen said as she got herself up off the floor. She glared at her fiancée and the misunderstanding. "Ryan left me some

sperm in his will. It's at a cryobank if we want to use it," she explained.

Suddenly deflated from the intense anger she had just felt Rae now felt stupid. "I'm sorry, I didn't understand," she tried to excuse herself. She knew how much Ellen had loved Ryan. She had met him once long ago and he seemed endearing.

"I'm sorry too, I should have explained sooner," Ellen apologized taking Rae in her arms. "I wouldn't make that decision without you," she told her earnestly.

"I'm amazed that you even want children."

"You were willing to marry me even when you thought I didn't want any?" She narrowed her eyes at the woman.

"You said…" she began and then thought she had assumed too much once again.

But Ellen had anticipated this. "I said once that I didn't want children. I didn't want to perpetuate my father's bad seed," she finished for her.

Rae nodded, watching Ellen carefully.

"I know, but I've changed my mind on so much," she sighed and began to steer Rae out of the den. "I think having one or two little "yous" running around might be fun," she said mischievously. "Imagine the sounds of children in this house," she added with a grin.

Rae could imagine that but she had given up that dream knowing that Ellen didn't want children. It had never occurred to her that Ellen would change her mind, that Ellen could change. She let Ellen steer her up the stairs before she thought to ask, "Do you want to carry a child?"

Ellen shook her head for a moment and then as she steered Rae into their bedroom she said, "I honestly don't know. I won't go first, but we have all the time in the world to worry about things like that." She smiled as she pushed Rae across the room and towards their bed.

"Why, Ms. Christenson? Whatever do you have in mind?" Rae affected a southern accent with a grin peeking out, as she knew very well what Ellen had in mind.

Ellen silenced her with a kiss as she began to make love to her. Using her body to push her over the edge of the bed and onto it, being the smaller of the two of them she had to have Rae's cooperation, and she was cooperating fully as Ellen climbed on top of her and began undressing her.

Rae couldn't let Ellen have all the fun so she took advantage of Ellen's position to undress her as well, teasing, and kissing as each bit of skin became accessible. They were soon naked and rolling around on the large bed.

❖ CHAPTER THIRTY ONE ❖

MEETING

Ellen knew it had been too many years in the making but she was finally going to meet Iris, Blossom and Ryan's daughter. She was about to graduate high school and Ellen knew it was long overdue. She'd contacted Blossom and had a nice chat with her on the phone and arranged to meet this young lady who would be entering college the following fall.

She didn't know why she had procrastinated so much over this meeting. It had been years since Ryan died and told her she should meet her. She should have been eager to meet the progeny of her best friend, her brother of another mother, and yet she had delayed it for so many reasons, none of which were viable anymore.

"Do you want me to go with you?" Rae asked supportively.

"Do you want to go with me?" Ellen asked in return. She was still hesitant, but with the girl graduating shortly, she felt she should meet her, her final duty to Ryan. Ellen had given Ryan her word that she would not tell 'Medusa' or his brother about the child, now a young woman, and she had kept that promise.

"Well, I just want to support you," Rae began.

"And see if Ryan's seed has borne fruit or squash," Ellen quipped and they both had a laugh. Since they had talked about having children, they had both relaxed about the subject. It was no longer forbidden. They both enjoyed the Sunday papers with the ads for children's things and actively discussed the playsets they would have installed in the backyard of their home.

"He wasn't an ugly man," Rae insisted.

"He was a nerd," Ellen said fondly, remembering his sense of humor and brilliance.

"You're kind of a nerd, too, you know," she was teased.

"Me? A nerd? I beg your pardon?" she tried to sound prissy.

"Yes, you!" they laughed together.

Ellen knew she could be a nerd. She was also still a bit shy although no one would know it to see the things she had overcome. When she gave an interview, a presentation, or when she had to conduct a news conference…no one would guess how shy she was and how much she hated that publicity. It was part of her job, though, and she had done it all willingly, for Ryan, for them, for their companies that they had built together.

Rae ended up flying down to San Diego County with Ellen. Ellen had wanted to drive but it was just too long of a trip for her to be away like that, and flying meant more time to meet with the girl and visit if she was so inclined. They were both curious what she looked like. They only had a few pictures that Ryan had of her that Blossom had shared with him, and the last one was years old.

As they drove up to the house in their rented car Ellen suddenly became nervous again. "What if she resents that I inherited the majority of her father's money?" she asked Rae in a panic.

"He explained that. You were closer to him and her trust fund is more than adequate," Rae pointed out. Ellen had let her see the tape Ryan had left her.

"Yes, but she's his offspring," she pointed out.

"And you were his business partner, best friend, and soul sister," she said sounding like she was trying to 'jive talk.'

Ellen laughed at the last one. She'd always said 'sister of another mister' or 'brother of another mother' but she *liked* 'soul sister.' They had understood each other, right down to their souls.

The laughter did what it was intended to do – relax her so she could get out of the car. The car had been watched for and the front door opened before they got to it.

"Ellen!" Blossom said with a huge smile.

"Blossom?" Ellen returned the smile tremulously as she was enveloped in a hug. The woman she had remembered from college was no longer built like a cheerleader. The years hadn't been kind to her.

"Gosh, you look even better than the magazine pictures of you!" she gushed. "And who is this?" she asked released Ellen from the hug.

"This is my fiancée," she relished being able to say that word and was actually looking forward to introducing her as her wife someday, if they could agree on the date. "Rae. Rae, this is Blossom," she said by way of introduction.

"Well hello, Rae," Blossom said shaking her hand briskly. "Welcome to our home," she said and waved her hand into the house as she led them inside.

"Thank you," Rae said quietly, quite overwhelmed by the blonde who stood much taller than the both of them.

"And this," Blossom said proudly. "This is Iris," she said pulling the teen out of hiding and propelling her forward to meet their guests.

Ellen stared. This was the Blossom of twenty years ago; this was the Blossom she had known in college, except for a couple of things. She had Ryan's eyes, she had darker hair than Blossom had back in the day, and she had the worst case of acne she had ever seen on a girl. "Hello Iris," she said holding out her hand to be shaken. She had no desire to hug the teen as she found the sores on her face repulsive.

"Hello," the teen said shyly, not quite looking Ellen in the face.

"Hello, Iris," Rae said and held out her hand as well.

"Hello," the teen said, equally as shy. She turned away to lead them into the ranch style house.

Ellen was surprised the house wasn't bigger. This was an affluent part of San Diego but perhaps appearances were deceiving. The front of the house hadn't indicated how small or how simple the inside would be. It was decorated nicely and they all sat in the living room together. An awkward silence ensued.

"Can I get anyone something to drink? Iris made some lemonade this morning with fresh lemons from our very own tree," Blossom said enthusiastically. Ellen could remember her enthusiasm and how suspicious she had been at first when she met her.

"That sounds lovely," Rae answered for both of them and gave Ellen an encouraging smile.

"Yes, lovely," Ellen repeated almost automatically, watching as Blossom got up and went through a doorway.

The awkward silence continued as the teen fidgeted. Rae finally nudged Ellen in the ribs and looking up she mouthed 'what?' Rae made a significant look between Ellen and the teen and gestured with her head.

Sighing Ellen attempted to make small talk. "So, you are graduating this year?" She asked the obvious.

Iris shuffled her feet, didn't look up from her hands that were twisting and nodded.

Ellen glanced at Rae and then back to the teen to try again.

"Have you chosen your college for next fall?"

The teen shrugged.

"Iris?" Ellen waited for her to acknowledge her addressing her. When the silence stretched out she tried again. "Iris?" The teen finally looked up. Ellen smiled at her tremulously. "We both know why I'm here. Your father asked me to meet you." The teen looked down at her hands immediately, her feet shuffled again and she nodded.

Ellen sighed and glanced at Rae who repeated her own gestures to encourage her to try and talk to the reluctant teen. Ellen tried again. "Ryan was my best friend. Is there anything you'd like to ask me about him?"

The teen glanced up almost hopefully. Then Blossom walked into the room and she quickly looked down at her hands again.

"Here we are," Blossom said brightly as she carried in tray with a large pitcher of lemonade with lots of slices of lemons floating in it and ice cubes in the glasses. She quickly poured all of them each a tall glass full of the concoction.

Expecting a sweet flavored drink, Ellen took a sip only to discover that it was tart and nearly puckered her lips. She nearly gagged. She glanced at Rae, who had taken a much larger gulp, and struggled not to laugh aloud at her expression of alarm. She couldn't very well spew the drink back in the glass but had to swallow and patently didn't want to. Ellen watched her deal with her dilemma, however short-lived it was. She hid her amusement as she held her glass and looked at Blossom.

"Now isn't this nice?" Blossom asked as she held her own glass and sipped from it. No expression of hers indicated that she found it too tart.

"Yes, it's been a long time," Ellen agreed, to be civil. She wanted to get out there already but knew it would be rude to leave too soon.

"I don't think I've seen you since you graduated, with honors, I might add," she nudged the teen who smiled without opening her lips. "Both Ryan and Ellen got their master's from UCLA!" she informed the teen, who obviously had heard it before.

"Yes, we decided to go and get our master's when we realized we didn't have enough knowledge or money to start the company that would become Gigitech."

"And look how well that turned out. What's the name of the second company Ryan started?" Blossom asked brightly.

"*We* started Animated Studio's so that he could turn his love of movies and comics into something profitable," Ellen informed them, she was kind of irked by Blossom asking it as though it was all Ryan's idea.

"Oh yes, he had those comic books and video games all over his dorm room I remember," she said perkily.

Ellen was getting a headache. She usually avoided people like Blossom like the plague. She could sense Rae's amusement and later they would almost certainly share a laugh over it, but right now Ellen wasn't finding anything amusing in it at all. She had come to meet the teen and the girl hadn't said but two words. "So, what college are you planning on going to, Iris?" she asked, addressing the teen.

Iris eyed her mother who looked encouragingly at her before she looked down at her hands again, twisting them some more and shrugging.

"Oh, we hadn't decided yet," Blossom put in.

Ellen was shocked. Normally you decided in your junior year of high school and attempted to get into the college of your choice during your senior year. "How are your SAT's?" she asked referring to the standardized tests that colleges relied on to determine your eligibility.

"Oh, those were off the chart. She took them twice!" Blossom said chirpily.

Ellen was getting annoyed, genuinely annoyed. She had come here to meet and talk to Ryan's daughter. Not socialize with Blossom. Although she knew she would be here, she didn't want her to do all the talking. She glanced at Rae for some help.

Rae understood the problem and chipped in. "Blossom, you mentioned you have your own lemon tree, do you grow anything else?"

Ellen looked at her fiancée like she had lost her mind and then realized she was distracting the ditzy blonde. She studied the youth while Rae kept up a conversation with the mother and eventually talked her into showing her the garden, leaving the two of them alone. "Not much of a talker, are you?" Ellen asked kindly with a slight grin.

Iris glanced up and through her hair, reminding Ellen of the youth she had 'saved' a few years or so ago. She'd wondered at the time if Iris would be like her. "Well, I kinda don't know you," she said with a shrug.

"That's why I'm here, so you can get to know me. Ryan asked me to," she added, hoping that would help things along.

"He sent nice things," the teen confided.

"Ryan was a nice man. I always wished he was really my brother," Ellen did some confiding of her own.

"Was he really gay?" the youth asked, not using any filters on her question.

Ellen smiled, showing even white teeth as she put down the glass and sat back. "Yes, yes he was. Although there was a time he thought he might have been bisexual. I think that's when he and your mom had a thing." She was trying to be careful of what she said but at the same time she wanted this girl to know who her father had been.

"Do you have any brothers?" she asked next.

"Nope, I was an only child. Ryan, though, he filled that big brother slot very well."

The teen grinned a little. "I always wanted a brother, maybe a sister," she confided.

"Well, someday you might have one."

The teen frowned, which didn't help her pimply marked face look any better. "How? Mom isn't having any more kids…"

"Well, you father…" she felt weird addressing Ryan that way. "Ryan left his essence in a cryobank for me and my partner to use," she explained, she thought diplomatically.

"Oooh," the teen said wrinkling her nose, making herself look even more horrible. "That's gross!"

Ellen chuckled at her reaction. "Well, you know basic biology. You need a male and a female to make babies."

"Then why didn't you marry him?"

"I loved him like a brother, not like a lover or a husband. Besides, I'm gay, too," she tried to explain gently. She'd expected questions from the teen but hadn't been sure what to prepare for.

The teen nodded sagely. "Yeah, that would have been gross, too," she said using her favorite word 'gross' again.

"So, what do you like to do?" Ellen asked her, trying to take an interest in the girl.

"Wanna see my room?" she asked politely.

Ellen could sense the teen had been prompted to ask that question. Something about it didn't seem natural. She nodded and followed the teen to the hallway beyond the kitchen. She saw that there were two bedrooms and a bathroom down the short hallway. Iris led her to the room on the left with bright red carpeting inside. It contained a twin bed and two dressers. The walls were plastered with ribbons and awards for achievements. Ellen read them, most were for academic achievement but a few showed the teen's athleticism. "You're a basketball player?" she asked, surprised.

The teen nodded and then looked awkward again.

"Wow, Ryan couldn't help but trip over his feet," Ellen confided with a laugh. "He would have been so proud of you."

"He would?" the teen asked, sounding intrigued for the first time.

Ellen nodded. "He was so brainy. I think the powers that be couldn't give him brains *and* coordination or it would have been grossly unfair," she laughed a little, using the teen's favorite word.

For the first time Ellen saw Iris smile and saw why she didn't smile with her teeth for the first time. She had wall to wall braces covering them. "Yeah, when I met him he seemed smart. He was a bit awkward

when we tried to play one-on-one. I beat him," she finished proudly. "I always thought it was him just letting me win."

"Probably not," Ellen smiled as she looked at the typical teenage posters of current pop stars on the girl's walls. She was kind of confused, though, as Iris was a little old to still have such things on her walls. "Do you play for the school?" she asked.

"Yeah, I got an athletic scholarship," she boasted.

"Good for you!" Ellen encouraged.

"Well, Mom said I shouldn't accept any scholarships since you will be paying for school."

Ellen turned in annoyance but stopped herself from saying something rude. "That's right; leave them for someone who really needs them." She stopped from saying something equally nasty as she saw the teen's face begin to fall. Before she could retreat into shyness again Ellen softened her words. "You have the brains and I'm sure you probably got offered a few of those scholarships, too," she gestured at some of the achievement awards and saw the teen nod. "And I'm not paying for anything. You father left you a trust fund to pay for these things. I'm just the administrator. You can go to any college you want, anywhere." She remembered suddenly something Ryan wanted for his daughter. "He wanted you to travel the world and experience things. Maybe you could do a foreign exchange program or take college courses in foreign countries."

"That sounds great. But my mom was trying to get me to go to UCSD; she doesn't want me to go far. I don't think she wants to be alone," she confided. "She's willing to let me go up to UCLA but I think that's the farthest away she'll let me go."

"When are you eighteen?" she asked, unsure of the child's birthdate because she hadn't cared before. Having met her she felt a responsibility to Ryan's wishes now.

"I'm already eighteen," the teen responded.

Ellen did the math and realized Ryan must have slept with Blossom sooner than she had thought to impregnate her with this lovely child. Sure, Ellen thought she looked a bit disgusting with all those pimples, but things like that could be fixed if she wanted them to. "What do you want?" she asked her.

"What do I want?" the teen repeated back, almost wonderingly. She looked down again at her hands, realizing she'd been talking too much. To a practical stranger. Her mother had told her a lot about Ellen and Ryan. When Blossom spoke of the company they had started together, she implied that it was only Ryan's creativity that brought success and that Ellen was merely the 'hired help.' Iris knew from the magazine and newspaper articles she had read on this woman that Ellen was more than that, much more. Her vision had taken a small startup tech company and turned it into a multi-billion-dollar company. Ryan's creations had continued well on after his death and this woman had seen to that. "I guess I want to do what my parents want me to do," she finished meekly but glanced up through her hair at the redhead who stood so confidently in her bedroom.

Ellen smiled. That was a nice, neat, and practical answer. This girl needed her horizons expanded. "But what do *you* want?" she asked again.

Iris bit her lip, hesitating about confiding in this woman. She had been her father's best friend, so surely she could trust her. "I'd really like to travel but Mom won't let me unless I take her along," she started out. Her eyes seemed to reflect more sadness as she added, "She doesn't like to go very far from home, though."

"You're eighteen, Iris. Next fall you should be in college unless you decide to take a year off between high school and college. But you should go to college for the well-rounding it will give you."

"Well-rounding?" the teen questioned, looking down at her lanky frame.

Ellen laughed when the teen looked up defensively. "Going to college makes you meet people and experience things you might not realize you need. Look at me, I didn't know what I wanted to do and then I met your father with his video games and comic books and we hit it off. Never in my wildest dreams would I have thought that we could merge our talents and make Gigitech. Animated Studios was just an indulgence until we proved it could be profitable. The combination of his creativity and my talents was lethal and it all started at college."

"My Mom says without my father you wouldn't have made all that money," she confided, not realizing how the words would hurt.

Ellen nodded, conceding that it was true. "No, the talents of both of us made that money. I'd probably have been happy working for someone else," she realized the falsehood of that statement immediately. "Probably not, though," she added. "I like being in charge, in control. I like running the show. It's a challenge to take the ideas that Ryan came up with, that his *teams* create, and marketing them to the world."

"Is that how the two of you made billions?" she asked innocently.

Ellen smiled again at the teen's question. "We came into Silicon Valley at the perfect time. Using our talents that we refined at college we started the company with your father's ideas and I marketed them. The need for what we were making exploded. Staying on top of all that was quite a ride. Now I have so many people working for me to help me stay on top of it all that I don't even know them. We have teams of people who do various functions within the companies to help. You father's dream of creating movies from comic books has become a

reality. The special effects that he helped to develop are incredible. The people came to us because of our expertise."

"So, you had as much to do as my father?"

Ellen nodded. She knew she was frequently undervalued, but she also knew her worth. She had reined in Ryan and his enthusiasm. Kept him from making some really bonehead mistakes. If she hadn't, they wouldn't have been nearly as successful as they were.

"How come I didn't inherit my father's money if you were equal partners? Why did he leave it all to you?" she felt brave enough to ask.

"Your father only found out about you a couple of years before he died. He knew he was dying by then. He made his will with the intention of letting you have a normal life. If people knew about you, if they knew he had a sole heir, you would have been a target."

"A target?" she sounded alarmed.

Ellen nodded as she explained, "His brother and sister. His sister is one of the greediest women you could ever meet. I hope you never do, by the way. Thought they should inherit his money. He didn't want them to profit from his death since they barely accepted him in this life. I didn't know I was going to get the bulk of it. I'll gladly share with you. You have a healthy trust fund. College is taken care of as well as that traveling you might want to do."

"But we've always been so poor," the teen lamented, almost whining. "He could have helped more," she said bitterly.

"He did help. Your mother didn't tell him until you were about fourteen that you even existed. He didn't know," she explained, wondering if she should be the one and why hadn't Blossom told her in the first place.

"That's why I met him then," she exclaimed as a puzzle piece fit into the picture.

Ellen nodded. "Your mother was having a hard time making ends meet and she wanted Ryan to know about you," she finished kindly. She secretly thought Blossom expected him to pay up as he was worth so much then.

"That's why we moved into this place."

Ellen was listening, wondering at Iris's take on this whole situation.

"But she wouldn't let me do anything," she said, sounding bitter again.

"Neither of your parents wanted that money to go to your head. It's why I'm the administrator of your trust until such time as I think you can handle it. Come on, you know there are things you would have bought that a teen simply shouldn't have," she pointed out kindly.

As much as it galled her to admit it, the teen nodded. She would have loved to have driven a corvette to school, some of the kids did have nice cars, but none of them knew who her father was. Only her mother had been visible, active in all the parent activities she could in the school. "I'd have at least gotten rid of this," she said, with genuine bitterness in her voice as she gestured at her face."

"What, you look like your mother did at that age," Ellen said diplomatically.

"Like a moon crater?"

Ellen nearly laughed, the pimples were a bit much and – to use the teen's favorite word – gross. "Time will take care of those," she pointed out.

"I want them gone now," she whined as she glanced in the mirror in disgust.

"Well, maybe we can discuss it with your mom. There are things that can be done."

Iris shook her head. "No, my mom doesn't want harsh chemicals on my face. She says I should just wait it out. It's hard enough being a brain at school but to look like this?" she gestured at her face and then smiled to show off the hardware.

"When do you get the braces off?" Ellen asked curious.

"In a couple of weeks," she answered eagerly. "But having straight teeth doesn't change this," she gestured at the pimples.

"Have you seen a doctor about that?" she wondered.

The teen nodded. "He said that in time I would outgrow them but I should stay away from greasy foods and sugar. That's why I make homemade lemonade. It has very little sugar in it."

That explained why it was horrible tasting, Ellen thought. No sugar? Who made lemonade without sugar? She nearly shuddered at the memory of the first and last taste.

Just then Blossom and Rae walked in; Blossom was obviously giving Rae a tour of the house. "And here is Iris's room," she finished whatever she was saying as they entered.

Ellen smiled at Rae who returned it in equal measure. They didn't realize they had an audience until the teen asked, "So, you two are getting married?"

Ellen nodded as Rae replied, "Yes, we hope to get married in June."

"Oh, you've set a date?" Ellen asked with a hint of humor in the question.

"Yes, *we did*," Rae said in mock anger, but the laughter in her voice won out.

"Uh oh, trouble in paradise?" Blossom teased, obviously at ease with her guest.

"This one is so busy with her work that she has very little time to for herself!" Rae teased, pointing at Ellen.

"I imagine she is quite busy running that company," Blossom said kindly.

They were invited to dinner, which had more flavoring than the lemonade which they tried to serve yet again. Neither Rae nor Ellen touched the drink. It turned out to be a nice visit. They talked over general subjects, learned more about Iris, and before Ellen knew it, Rae had arranged for the girl to visit.

"How in the world did you get Blossom to agree to Iris's visiting us?" she asked as they drove away towards their hotel for the night.

Rae shrugged but grinned. "She likes me," she said mischievously.

Ellen snickered through her nose and then glancing over at her fiancée she asked, "Likes you as in likes you or likes you as in *likes* you?"

Rae rolled her eyes, waiting until they were under a light so that Ellen could see them in the darkness of the car. "C'mon," she scoffed. "That woman hasn't walked on the wild side for about 19 years," she said meaningfully.

They shared a laugh as they discussed meeting Ryan's daughter and their own impressions and observations during the visit.

"For someone getting a fair amount of money from Ryan's estate, why do they live in a house that looks like that?" Rae asked.

"I was wondering that. This area is a good address. You saw the neighbor's houses..." she mused and then, "I bet Blossom bought the cheapest house on the block."

"But why, surely she can afford better?"

Ellen shrugged but she had to wonder, the payments to Blossom directly stopped upon Iris's eighteenth birthday. Having been the one to administer the trust, she should have remembered that Iris was eighteen and in charge of her future, but she dealt with all the trusts and had people to help her with that. She wondered if Iris had insisted that she visit.

The next day they returned to visit some more but when they left, Iris went with them. There had been a tense moment when Blossom suggested that she go along too but Iris had told her mother in no uncertain terms that she was going alone to see what her father had built. That awkward moment was smoothed over by Rae who insisted that they had to go meet their plane. Ellen didn't point out to anyone that their plane was a private jet and could leave any time they felt like it.

As they drove away, Blossom waved madly and Iris waved back, but turned her back on her mom and her home with no qualms and a big sigh of relief. "Whew, escaped," she mumbled.

"What was that?" Ellen asked with a grin. She had heard what Iris said but wanted her to repeat it.

"I thought we'd never get outta there," the teen grumbled a little louder, she knew Ellen had heard her the first time and her eyes twinkled into the rearview mirror. Ryan's eyes.

It was the first time that Iris had flown anywhere. The fact that it was a private jet just was icing on the cake. "This is so cool," she repeated over and over as she experienced luxury for the first time.

Rae had been telling her about their experience with the disaster in Oakley. "And Ellen there told the old sheriff where he could get off," she was saying as she told part of the story.

Ellen opened one eye from where she was pretending to rest in her chair, partially reclined. It was interesting to hear someone else's version of events. To hear Rae tell it, she was one badass customer and it amused her. She was badass, but she had been firm with people but not willing to be taken advantage of.

"And Ellen provided low or no-interest loans to several people in town whose insurance didn't cover what it should have. The teams of lawyers she employed will have a field day," she heard again as she began to drift in and out of dozing.

"So why don't you take the job?" Iris asked Rae. Ellen really wanted to hear the answer to that, but she pretended to still be sleeping.

There was a long pause and Ellen wondered if Rae was making a gesture, perhaps a shrug, and then, "I don't want to be dependent on my future wife."

"But all those people you could help, I'm sure there are still people in Oakley and elsewhere who need it," the teen pointed out.

"Yes, but I don't want to feel that I am the charity case, that my wife made me a job so she can keep an eye on me," she answered low. Ellen nearly had to move to hear her.

"I'm sure it's not like that, sure, she puts up the dough to get it rolling and you have to account for where you spend it. But think of it as an opportunity to help those people. All those stories, it's obvious it made you feel good," she answered earnestly. She mentioned a couple of things that Ellen must have dozed off during because she couldn't remember hearing Rae tell them. "Gawd, I'd love to help," the teen sounded almost worshipful.

"So, if I took this job you'd want to help, eh?" Rae said in a much better voice.

"Yeah," she said eagerly.

"What about you traveling about the world?" Rae teased.

"That can wait if I can help do something like this. It's more meaningful. Maybe you could do this worldwide someday."

There was a long silence before the teen asked, "How much was Ellen willing to put aside for the project?"

Again, a silence where Rae must have shrugged her shoulder, Ellen wanted to peek but was afraid that the glint of her eye would be seen as

she listened unashamedly. "I don't think we got that far in discussing things."

Ellen listened to the two of the chat for the duration of the trip. One thing did concern her, though.

"Do you think you could introduce me to a plastic surgeon?"

"Why?" Rae asked, concerned.

"To get rid of these," the teen answered. Ellen could only surmise that she was gesturing to her face.

Her assumption proved correct when Rae answered, "Everyone has acne."

"Not like this. It's bad enough I sweat playing basketball, which causes me to break out. I don't eat anything with grease or sugar and that doesn't keep me from breaking out. Then to be a brain – you don't realize the teasing I get from it all!" she passionately explained.

"Well, perhaps we could go see someone about your skin," Rae told her kindly, feeling the hurt and angst that teenagers felt.

"Can we do it without my mom knowing?"

"Honey, I don't think that…"

"Please?" she begged.

Rae hesitated for only a fraction of an instant. "Well, you *are* eighteen…" she hedged away from making an actual promise.

"Oh, thank you," the teen said gratefully.

"You are only with us for Easter vacation," she reminded the teen.

"We can do a lot in that short amount of time," Iris said with absolute certainty.

They did do a lot while they had the chance. Ellen led her around Gigitech and Animated Studios, showing her Ryan's legacy. She also saw firsthand that Ellen was an active partner when she listened in on a few meetings, and Ellen was able to not only read the schematics but discuss them actively and make a few suggestions. She reevaluated her opinion of the redhead. She had thought she was merely a paper-pushing partner and that her father had all the creative genes. She saw now that Ellen not only could create, but that she took her father's vision one step further. She wasn't shy about sharing the accolades, either. She made sure if it was Ryan's idea it got promoted as such, and if it was part of his team's they got the credit.

"I'd like to help Rae if you decide to go ahead with the nonprofit," she told Ellen as they sat out on the patio at their home in Rolling Hills Estates.

Ellen cocked open an eye from where she was laying on her lounger, enjoying a rare afternoon off. She had to pretend that she didn't hear the entire conversation between them on the plane. "That's up to Rae if she wants to take it," she told her. She could at least let the teen think that the adults had discussed it.

"Can't you make her or something?" she asked pettishly. She was slathering her face with something the dermatologist Rae had taken her to, had prescribed for her skin. In the three days she had been using it, she optimistically swore she saw a difference.

Ellen chuckled. "Nope, I can't make Rae do anything she doesn't want to do. It's her choice."

"But it's such a good cause," she nearly whined.

Ellen looked with both eyes on her young guest. She was enjoying her visit and her enthusiasm. She did have a great head on her shoulders. For once she was actually looking forward to the idea of using Ryan's essence to create babies from him. She enjoyed the idea that Rae would be carrying their child. She hadn't told her yet but the way she had felt years ago, the fears no longer ruled her. "I don't own Rae. She's her own woman. I love her, I respect her, so I will also respect her decisions."

"She's so hardheaded," Iris lamented.

"We're equally matched," Ellen commented with a grin.

Iris had to agree with her father's best friend. She was as hardheaded as her fiancée. Both women had shown her how to be strong without being an asshole. She'd heard so many rumors about Ellen Christenson both in her company and through the research she herself had done over the years. She realized Ellen hadn't been afraid to meet her, merely busy. She effortlessly ran the two companies that she and Ryan had founded.

Later they met Bill Cartland when Ellen attempted to show Iris the house her father had lived in. The meeting was a disaster as Bill had moved in one of his revolving boyfriends and they had decorated the place like a harem. It was disgusting and Ellen quickly removed the teen from the house. "I'm sorry about that," Ellen apologized as she drove away from the house in the Maserati. "How about I show you the apartment in the city instead?" she offered. They ended up staying the night in the city as Ellen related stories about Ryan and showed her places they had visited. On one of the final few days of Iris's visit, they drove to Tahoe so she could see the cabin they had purchased for getaways.

"This is fabulous," Iris said, unconsciously imitating her father. Ellen nearly laughed out loud at her exuberance. It was a fine cabin with a butterscotch veneer to the woods used inside the building.

Rae put her arms around Ellen as they viewed the lake from their wide porch, whispering in her ear, "Still thinking about doing a charity?"

Ellen turned slightly so she could look into her fiancée's eyes as she answered. "Interested in heading up such an endeavor?" she countered.

"I think I might be," she confessed.

"Really?"

"Really."

"Any particular reason why, now?" Ellen asked in surprise.

"If we are going to have children someday like her," she nodded at the teen talking to some of the neighbors on their dock. "I think I want to do a few things before we settle down to that."

"So, you aren't disgusted by Ryan's cooties?" Ellen teased as she leaned into Rae's embrace.

Rae snorted through her nose in laughter. "I think having children with you, being married to you is going to be an adventure. I'm up for the job, all the jobs." She smiled and Ellen could feel it against her neck. She shivered slightly as desire began to follow the sensation.

"When would you like to start?" Ellen asked cautiously. She reached behind them both to pull Rae's body closer to her own. The days were warm up here but the nights were cool in the mountains. The warmth, the heat of Rae's body was…distracting.

"On the family or the charity?"

Ellen chuckled at her fiancée's sally. "Whatever you want, my love, whatever you want," she promised her.

❖ CHAPTER THIRTY TWO ❖

MARRIAGE

Rae managed to plan and execute a beautiful and touching wedding for the two of them in June. They invited a few hundred people that they both knew. Some of Rae's friends were still leery of Ellen, having known her from the previous time they had been a couple. They were surprised to discover a different Ellen, so much so that she had proposed to their friend.

Most of Ellen's friends were from her companies or were business acquaintances. Her side of the outdoor ceremony was composed of the "who's who" of Silicon Valley as well as all over the world. Their respect for this tech mogul was obvious.

"Do you, Ellen Christenson, take Rae…" the justice of the peace droned on under the canopy that Rae and Iris had erected in the backyard of Ellen's home. The raised platform made the two participants clearly visible to the congregated friends and family.

Ellen had met Rae's mother and father just the previous evening and while they weren't thrilled that their daughter was marrying a woman, they were happy that she was happy. They welcomed Ellen into their family.

"Does this mean we're gazillionaires?" Rae's little brother asked when he was introduced to Ellen.

Ellen looked at Rae in alarm and saw the humor in her fiancée's eyes. She laughed at the young man, who was not much older than Iris, and answered, "Well, when I make gazillionaire status your sister will be one with me, too."

That seemed to excite him for some reason, and Ellen was amused.

"Is there something I should know?" Ellen asked Rae later.

"About?" Rae asked as she looked over the last of the plans for the wedding. They were sitting in the den going over a few last details.

"Gazillionaire?" she reminded her, she was still amused at the enthusiasm of the young man. He'd met Iris, who had been here for the past couple of weeks helping them plan the wedding. In a month, they would be starting the nonprofit charity to help disaster victims. They had decided to call it the Mahoney-Sheehan Disaster Relief Foundation. It would start off on a small scale but would be able to jet in a team when necessary. They could almost consider the Oakley disaster their trial run. Because Ellen didn't want people to think it was named after her, they had decided to use Ryan's last name and Ellen's mother's.

"Oh, that's just Rob being funny," she dismissed.

"You never really told me about Rob," she asked, beginning to feel a little uneasy.

Rae looked up from the list she was going over. She'd checked it twice before and it didn't need her to go over it once again. "What is there to tell?"

"Babe, I'm just curious, he's nearly twenty years younger than you are and he's asking about money?" she tilted her head sideways, feeling the old feelings coming up from long ago. Her distrust of someone this close to her talking about her money made her uneasy. She trusted Rae but she had to wonder about this unexpected development.

"Rob was an 'oops.' I was born when Mom was eighteen; she was thirty-eight when she got pregnant with Rob. They thought she couldn't have any more children," she explained easily. She could hear a tone in Ellen's voice and wondered at it as she gazed steadily into her fiancée's eyes and explained. "Rob is just enthusiastic."

"You signed the prenup," Ellen pointed out; she was still puzzled over the odd conversation.

"Of course I signed a prenup. I don't want your money," she was starting to feel angry over this conversation about money. She knew that Ellen was a billionaire, several times over. She didn't *want* her money. It was why she had insisted on a reasonable sum when they worked out the agreement over the Mahoney-Sheehan Disaster Relief Foundation, so she had her own monies and didn't have to rely on Ellen's.

"I know you don't," of that Ellen was certain. She had never been after her money. She felt terrible for bringing this up, especially the night before their marriage. "I'm sorry, call it wedding jitters or something but he unnerved me with his talking about money."

Rae got up from the desk where she was working. She came over to Ellen and drew her up from the chair she was sitting in. "Do you trust me?" she asked softly, seeing something in Ellen's eyes that she remembered from long ago, almost fear.

"With my life," Ellen confirmed without hesitation.

"Then trust me that Rob is just a young idiot and awed by the money and power you wield. You don't even realize how easily you do it. You are used to it. Rob and my family come from a modest means. He's just fantasizing. I never want your money, I want *you*, only *you*," she said emphatically.

Ellen was relieved. It was enough. She didn't need to dominate this situation. She could be vulnerable, she could make her worries known and Rae wouldn't run from them. She was her mate, her helpmate, her lover, her equal. She loved her without question. The prenup had just been a legal bit of paperwork that the lawyers and Rae had insisted on. She said in ten years it wouldn't matter anyway. Ellen had to agree. She would have given half of everything to Rae, but she insisted that for all appearances she didn't want anyone to think she was marrying her for her money.

Ellen spent the evening with a few associates from work, being feted as the 'groom' but since both brides would be wearing white wedding dresses the following day she found that amusing. They drank lightly, had transportation so that no one would be drinking and driving, and had what Ellen considered totally 'nerdy' conversations. It was a pleasant evening and she was in bed in the hotel before midnight.

"Do you, Rae..." the justice of the peace was continuing. Rae couldn't remember hearing Ellen's responses. Her hands were cold. She couldn't believe this was happening. She was marrying Ellen! Her hands squeezed Ellen's at some point and the returned squeeze allowed her to say, "I do," without too much of a pause between the question and her answer.

Dancing later under the moonlight of the almost perfect wedding day, which Rae assured everyone she had organized, was the end of a fantastic day and evening for everyone. It had been beautiful, it had been heartfelt, and many an eye was full of tears. The worst drama was with Bill Cartland, Ryan's ex-boyfriend who cried copiously as he assured everyone that he would miss 'his' sister Ellen. Rae's parents rolled eyes at his antics and Ellen found herself amused to realize that Rae exactly duplicated that action.

"Well, we're married. Now what?" Ellen asked as she leaned back on the bed of their hotel room. They had wanted to sleep in their own bed but with all the guests in and out of the house they knew they wouldn't get any sleep so they had left home to spend their wedding night in a nice hotel.

"Now," Rae said as she began to unbutton her fine white dress. "Now we begin our wedding night," she said softly with a smirk as she did a small strip tease for her wife.

Ellen was amused. She was also enraptured as she watched the dress come off. Rae was wearing her garters, one of which had been rolled off and thrown at the reception following their late afternoon wedding. As the stockings were slowly rolled down Rae's legs, Ellen found herself licking her lips in anticipation.

"Let's get this off of you," Rae whispered as she saw Ellen freeze from her removing her frilly dress. She had to admit that Ellen had chosen a beautiful Vera Wang dress, and its lace and silk combination with her red hair was striking. Her heart had leapt into her throat when she saw her coming up the aisle in their makeshift outdoor chapel. Her white porcelain skin had actually looked tanned against the sheer white of the wedding dress. Her hands reached for the mother of pearl buttons holding Ellen's dress closed. She felt nervous for some reason, her hands shaking as Ellen made no attempt to stop her, but she made no attempt to help her either. Instead she reached for Rae's nearly naked body, clad only in the white slip that hid her underwear from Ellen's view.

Ellen slipped the full-length slip over her wife's head after hiking it up her body. Her gasp at seeing her wife...her wife's body, was heard by both of them. "Gawd, you're beautiful," she whispered reverently.

"Why is your dress taking longer to remove than mine did?" Rae complained good-naturedly.

"Good things come to those who wait," Ellen quipped with a grin as she reached to unclasp her wife's push-up bra. She nuzzled the cleavage until it was released and she quickly removed the bra despite her wife's attempts at trying to remove her dress. She could hear the frustration in Rae's breathing at how difficult it was becoming to undo the buttons. She now knew why she had almost been late to her own wedding. Getting into this dress had been a nightmare. She couldn't help but touch the sentient skin; she saw goosebumps beginning to form on her wife's skin.

"Help me," Rae pleaded as she tried to hurry. She wanted, she *needed*, to feel Ellen's body against her own.

Ellen breathed deeply from where she was nuzzling between Rae's breasts. The scent of Rae's body was...intoxicating. She could have stayed there for days, nuzzling, licking, and...she stopped herself at Rae's plea and stepped back to help her wife unfasten the buttons that

were frustrating her so. She sheer number of them exhausted them both. As the bodice separated from the waist and then that from the fullness of the skirts, they could slowly remove them from her overheated body. She was already breathing deeply from her exertions.

Rae looked on the petite redhead with sheer lust. She didn't realize until they were removing the many layers that Ellen had played a joke on her, on all of them. One she would never reveal to anyone. Ellen had been totally nude under the many layers of her gown. Rae gasped when she realized that. How Ellen had stood by her after the ceremony for all the pictures that the photographer had insisted on, had danced with her repeatedly, had talked to their many guests, all the while she was naked under the dress, no underwear, no petticoats, nothing to hide her nudity. "What if you had fallen and the dress had flown up?" she asked as she began to smile at her wife's audacity.

"Good thing I didn't fall so the dress could fly up, then," she stated with a smile of her own as she pulled her wife's bikini bottom clad body against her own naked one. Rae's gasp at the contact gave her immeasurable pleasure. "I love you," she told her fervently. She had never imagined her life could be this complete. That she would belong to someone like this. The rings they had exchanged today had only been the beginning of what she hoped would be a lifetime of memories that they would make together.

"I love you more," Rae said as her forehead meet Ellen's and she looked deeply into her eyes.

Slowly Ellen moved her hands firmly down Rae's body, molding it to her own and touching her deeply at the firmness of the caress. The hitch in Rae's breath told her of her wife's arousal, her need to be touched.

Rae began to caress delicately along Ellen's shoulders with her fingertips. Her lips followed, barely touching but caressing in a similar feathery light fashion.

"What say you we meet in the middle?" Ellen suggested breathily as her head nodded towards the wedding bed they had yet to touch.

"I'll meet you there," Rae said in return, equally breathily as she never left Ellen but instead began to dance with her towards the bed, her pelvis pushing suggestively against Ellen's.

"Oh, I like that," Ellen enthused as her hands reached Rae's hips and she pulled them tight against her.

Slowly they danced their way to the side of the bed, hands caressing each other's upper torsos, their lips exchanging breaths between them. "I love you," one would murmur followed by the other's, "I love you too," gently, easily, and profusely.

Kneeling on the bed, Ellen pulled Rae with her as they slowly danced against each other on their knees, touching breast to breast, stomach to stomach, and pelvis to pelvis. Little murmurs of appreciation telling the other that their touch, their fondling, their caress was wanted, needed, enjoyed. Slowly they became prone on the bed as Ellen rolled Rae over to pin her down. Rae welcomed the feel of Ellen's smaller body against her own, wrapping her legs around Ellen's to hold her there as she ground up against her.

Rae pushed Ellen's long red tresses out of the way so she could see her face, her eyes, as she smiled in delight over their loving. "What are you smiling about?" she asked softly in between the kisses she bestowed on her wife's face, her jawline, and into her neck.

Ellen arched her neck to show Rae the places she could put her lips, turning her face away from her wife in her efforts. "I'm smiling because I'm so happy," she told her truthfully. She was happy; she was now forever mated to this woman, legally and emotionally. Now she would be physically as well, and she couldn't wait. She ground her mons against Rae's in a suggestive manner and heard Rae groan back in appreciation. "A little horny, my wife," she teased in her ear.

"Hell, I've been beyond horny for a while now," Rae admitted, whispering when there was no need to whisper. She nipped at Ellen's ear, earning a groan of her own.

Slowly Ellen ground down on her, snaking her hand between her legs to insert itself between her mons. She could feel the heat coming up off Rae's body and her fingers eagerly sought the wetness she knew was there as well. Slick moisture greeted her fingers and she slid in easily.

"Ohhh," Rae mouthed as she tried to keep herself concentrating on arousing Ellen and found herself losing the battle.

"Take it," Ellen told her as her fingers slipped inside, bypassing the thick kernel of flesh standing up and waving for attention. She curled her first two fingers and Rae came nearly undone at the sensation it caused. Using her thumb, she gave the flesh outside a rub and was rewarded as her wife's overheated body began to convulse at the combination. She leaned down to capture an erect nipple in her mouth, tonguing it fiercely as Rae arched, nearly throwing her off, but her legs were locked around Ellen, holding herself to that position. It also enabled her to grind up on Ellen's efforts with her rather nubile fingers and hand which only took a few more 'come hither' motions and rubs with her thumb to make Rae come in convulsive twitches.

"Oh, ohhh," she let out as she felt the waves come over her body. Her legs loosened as her body released itself from its spasmodic throes. It took a while for her to come down from the high and Ellen was delighted in causing this in her wife's body.

Her wife! What an amazing feeling that was. Hers, not anyone else's. They belonged to each other forever. The feeling that gave her was indescribable. She had a hard time putting it into words in her

head. It was almost a feeling of ownership, of proprietorship, of love that was overwhelming. She would have continued to make love to her wife if Rae hadn't finally recovered enough to turn the tables on her.

"My turn," she said delightedly as she began kissing Ellen senseless. Loving every moment of it she fully gave into her wife's gratitude and mutual lust and let her have her body willingly. She kissed her way down Ellen's petite body, relishing at the perfection she found in it. Each pert breast received lavish attention, from petting and squeezing to licking and a sucking sensation that had her capturing Rae's chestnut covered hair and pulling her closer.

"Oh yes," she agreed at Rae's demands. She arched her body in supplication as she offered it to her to do anything she wanted to it. Rae didn't disappoint.

Slowly she kissed down her body, her hands following sometimes, sometimes her lips following her hands. She made her way down until she was hovering sideways over Ellen's manicured mons. Slowly she leaned down for a taste, the essence of Ellen's lust telling her how aroused she already was. Her chin soon became inundated with her juices; her fingers probing told her that Ellen was gushing. She licked her way through the folds, her tongue probing deeply.

Ellen swore there were new nerve endings between her legs. As Rae's tongue went inside of her she could feel every small touch of that agile appendage that her wife possessed. Her mind was ready to explode from the sensations it was causing. As Rae pulled it out, Ellen almost found herself pleading for more and was rewarded as Rae read her mind and thrust as deeply as she could with her tongue.

Reaching up she palmed Ellen's breast, using her palm to warm it and then her fingers to tweak the erect nipple. Her other hand came into play as she reached around to palm Ellen's butt cheek and pull it tightly to her body, helping to spread her legs for her body to settle between them. Her face was a mess with the copious juices covering them. Her tongue plunged over and over inside, lapping them up, nearly drowning her with the amount. Her nose unknowingly hit Ellen's clit, sending her over the edge with the combination of her hands, tongue, and nose.

"Oh my gawddddd," Ellen screamed into a pillow. Her hands didn't seem to be able to reach Rae so she grabbed a pillow in order to feel something, anything of substance against her. Rae's body angle made it impossible and as she came against her wife's face she swore she saw stars behind her eyelids. The feeling of tingles spread throughout her body causing her toes to clasp tightly, her fingers clenched against the pillow, and her body arched. "Oh baby," she cried as the waves continued. Mentally seeing what Rae was doing and looking down as she orgasmed she saw the mess her wife was from making her cum and it excited her more if that was possible. She closed her eyes again and let her body convulse against Rae's face.

Rae smiled, her tongue staying in her mouth as she wiped her face against her wife's thighs. First one side and then the other. She brought her hand up, she could tell her face had been full of the essence of her wife, she had cum so profusely. Slowly she climbed up Ellen's prone body, kissing her way, and rubbing some of the essence off onto Ellen's own skin. Before she got to Ellen's lips she was smiling for making her wife feel this way.

"Happy?" Ellen asked her when she was face-to-face with her once again.

"Very," she replied. She was exhausted. It had been a hectic last couple of weeks. "You?"

"Ecstatic," Ellen replied holding her body against her, feeling the tingles of desire once again in her body. "I think we need a shower," she mentioned.

"Too bad we don't have the small RV shower anymore," Rae teased in remembrance of their gymnastics in that small space.

"I can buy one of those anytime you say the word," Ellen promised as she kissed her wife, because she could.

"Don't you own several of those still?" Rae teased, knowing how many she still did own.

They eventually rolled off the bed and showered, too tired to attempt any of the gymnastics they had in the RV. Washing up and cuddling in bed sounded good to both of them.

❊ CHAPTER THIRTY THREE ❊

CHARITY

"You said I had complete control?" Rae confirmed and waiting for Ellen's nod she continued, "Then let me do what you said I had the autonomy to do."

Ellen sighed and tried hard to keep her mouth shut. "All I said was that buying dogs seemed like a bit of a…" she let it peter out as she saw her wife's expression. She had promised not to interfere with the Foundation. It was Rae's baby and she had done a great job keeping the board of directors informed of her decisions and why. This purchase seemed excessive though.

"If you had waited for the explanation of why I purchased that many dogs and what they were going to be used for, we wouldn't be having this argument," she further pointed out.

"Okay, I'm sorry. You're right. If you would indulge me though before the board meeting this afternoon, please explain to me why the Foundation made such a large purchase of…dogs?" she tried not to sound condescending, demanding, or bossy. She was failing as she could see by the angry expression on her bride.

"Okay, but this time and this time only. I bought the dogs so that they could be trained in search and rescue. I've contacted the local veterans' association to offer the dogs to those that qualify. We will be helping vets returning home and in exchange they can help us with the dogs. The Foundation will pay for their training and service. We also will be using veterans in a 'habitat for humanity' type of effort to help us rebuild in places like Oakley after a disaster. Because they have various skills in the military it will serve us a threefold purpose, retraining, rebuilding, and security. We will be providing them with RVs, many of which we still have the rights to from Oakley. Those that you didn't give away," she reminded the now squirming Ellen who was feeling foolish at questioning her very qualified wife. "We will be repurposing the remaining RVs, stocking them with dry goods and other necessities. It will provide those vets who will work with this program with a home and transportation in the event we need them to go to a disaster site," she explained.

"That's brilliant," Ellen conceded.

"Actually, I thought it was, too. I would appreciate it in the future if you don't jump to conclusions but you allow me to explain at the designated meeting or this. In this case, this afternoon's Foundation meeting. I would have explained in full as I have to you and as I have in this prospectus," she patted one of the folders she had put together for her wife and the other board members. "You hired me for this job, allow me to do it."

Ellen was absolutely contrite. No one dared to put her in her place like this anymore. She was too rich, too powerful, and too knowledgeable. Rae was right. She had been worried when she had been told that her wife had gone out and bought dogs. Many, many dogs, and expensive ones at that. It hadn't made sense but it certainly did now. She had to remember to sign over the many remaining RVs to the Foundation. They had decided that calling it a foundation instead of a charity sounded so much better months ago. "I'm sorry," she offered, knowing it was very little. "I won't do that again," she promised. She wasn't about to explain. Her wife was right. She had been hovering, worrying about the amount of money that was going out and hearing about foolish acquisitions such as the dogs. She should have trusted Rae as she had when she had proposed she take this position.

"Ellen, you wanted me to take this job because you trusted me to do it well. Let me," she pleaded slightly.

"You're right. I will try," she promised.

"You better succeed," Rae threatened and then eased the sting of her words as she moved in for a kiss.

Iris had listened to what she could from the atrium of the small offices where the Foundation was located. They didn't need much but

with the supplies coming in they would need a warehouse soon. Part of the meeting this afternoon was to discuss that as well as the enormous expenditures that Rae had already authorized. She was having a blast this summer helping Rae set up things as they got ready to help people with small interest loans where the government ones failed. When FEMA and the military failed to help, they would go in, sometimes faster, and help where they could. She had already decided to go to Stanford in the fall. Rae had helped her get in when she applied, using Ellen's name shamelessly so that she was closer to help with the Foundation if she could. Blossom wasn't happy as she wanted her nearer to home but already she was talking about selling the house in San Diego and moving north.

❧ CHAPTER THIRTY FOUR ❧

PARENTHOOD

"I honestly thought it would be different," Ellen complained good-naturedly. They had wanted this. After two years of marriage Rae had said it was time. If they were going to have a family, neither of them was getting any younger. They could both still have their careers and hire people to take care of any babies they had, or they could delegate to their people to make their jobs easier and spend more time with their babies.

"What, all flowers and good vibes?" Rae asked as she practiced her breathing techniques. Ellen rubbed the bulge that constituted her belly, the baby inside of it a product of the last few attempts of fertilizing their eggs. They had chosen one of Ellen's eggs and one of Rae's for her to carry. It had required timing and a lot of patience. They had first tried implanting some of Ryan's sperm themselves. Several times actually but the fear of 'running' out had them using the doctors. Then they found that Rae's eggs were few and far between and conception was more likely to be successful if Ellen's eggs were used.

"It would be better if we used Rae's body for the gestation," the doctor informed them. "Her body is ideally suited for this," he informed them, making Rae feel insanely proud of that fact.

"But I don't have enough eggs," she said bitterly, depressed over the idea that their future children wouldn't have any of her genetics.

"That isn't a problem, not really," he gently explained. "If you two are willing we will extract eggs from both of you. If conditions are ideal we will fertilize both sets of eggs and you two can decide which of you will carry your first offspring." He waited to see that they were both following him before asking, "Did you want to choose the sex too?"

"You can do that?" Ellen asked surprised.

"We can here at the clinic, but don't let that get around. Some liberals wouldn't like it that the sex can be chosen and let's face it, some cultures would choose boys every time," he rolled his eyes at this. "Nothing like a type of genocide within their own culture."

"So, we can choose whose egg she carries as well as the sex?" Ellen clarified.

"Why can't you carry the baby?" Rae teased.

"You heard him, your body is ideally suited for this," she said with a grin, proud of her wife and their decision to finally have a baby. "But if you really want me to carry one I suppose I…." she began.

"I was kidding; I don't mind carrying our baby." She took Ellen's hand in her own. "Your baby," she said softly.

"As long as it's okay with the doctors we will do anything you want, babe," she said in a same tone.

"Well, it helps that Rae is the younger of you two. Nothing like leaving this to the last moment," the doctor teased.

"Last moment?" Rae asked with a cocked eyebrow.

"Most clinics wouldn't take you this near to forty. Fortunately, you both are still healthy. I still want you to come in monthly and of course during the eighth and ninth month weekly. I want to make sure this baby, these babies," he gestured towards the petri dishes that might eventually house their offspring, however briefly, "are healthy."

The first implant was not successful and they were moderately upset by those results. The second was a huge disappointment.

"It's my eggs, I bet you!" Rae said dispiritedly.

"It's just the way things go," Ellen tried to console her. She, too, was disappointed but she couldn't blame anyone and certainly not Rae. Privately she thought it was her eggs and the thought of reproducing, that negativity, those horrible genes she had inside of her, plagued her thoughts.

They had talked about it, of course. Ellen had explained her fears but Rae pointed out that it was the parents, not the genes, that would determine how the child turned out. The age-old argument of nature

versus nurture. "Babe, it's a psychology term…just because a baby has your genes, heredity versus the environment of how we raise this baby. We will determine how she or he turns out," she argued.

Ellen argued but lost, pointing out all her father's behaviors.

"But you aren't like that, you have never been like that," Rae argued back.

"I was different before, you know that," she pointed out that as well.

"You were hurting. Ryan was right; you needed to release all that anger, all that hurt. You aren't the same woman you were or I wouldn't have married you!"

"Children don't become their parents," the doctor weighed in on their arguments when they brought them to him.

"The whole point is moot anyway," Rae, feeling depressed about still not being pregnant chimed in.

It took five treatments until Rae began to puke into their fine toilet in the bedroom. She was secretly thrilled but at the same time scared that she would lose this baby. The doctor, in an effort to be overly cautious, put her on total bedrest. Ellen relished the opportunity to take care of her wife, waiting on her hand-and-foot. She wouldn't have even allowed Rae to get out of their bed to use the bathroom if Rae hadn't insisted. "Don't be silly, I don't want or need a bed pan," she argued. She was thrilled that Ellen had jumped on board so heartily, if a bit too enthusiastically.

Which was how they came to taking prenatal classes, learning how to use Lamaze techniques to deliver the twins that Rae was now carrying. They had chosen not to know the sexes of their babies, instead wanting the surprise. The bedroom next to theirs had been lovingly turned into a nursery with neutral colors and two cribs. The two bassinets were already set up in the master bedroom awaiting the arrival of their babies.

"No, I just thought that it would be a room full of panting mothers," Ellen said as she looked around the room full of expectant parents. "Yeah, there would be fathers but this is a surprise," she pointed to the other couples. They weren't the only same-sex couple in the room. There was another lesbian couple as well as two dads who had agreed to use a surrogate who they judiciously spoiled. Ellen was fascinated by how this sort of dynamic had changed over the years. She almost felt the oldest in the group but one of the two fathers was at least ten years older than she. She mentally cheered them on in creating their family as she rubbed Rae's belly and cheered about their own.

"Times have changed," Rae agreed, looking around the room and seeing the same things that Ellen had.

Their teacher was thorough and took them through the many things that they could expect while expecting as well as during the delivery.

"Keep in mind that the birth mother," she said using a term that wouldn't offend most of her clients. "Will not remember most of the birth. They will say or do things that you as the birth partner would never expect them to," she smiled wryly as many had heard of these things. She went on to explain about the personality changes she herself had witnessed citing many examples of improper language and threats that the birth mother could and would use, making them all laugh over her stories. "You must not hold this against her as she may not remember most of it," she explained.

They watched videos on the subject and squirmed through the messy process of birth. It wasn't pretty. Ellen knew if it weren't for Rae she wouldn't have come to this point in her life. She was proud and scared at the same time. Proud that Rae would be giving birth to two babies, one of each of their genetics. She didn't want to know which and Rae agreed with her. They knew that one of each was inside of her, growing healthy and about to be born, and that was enough. They wanted them healthy and they didn't care which sex they were.

It was a rainy Saturday night when Rae went into labor. She had eaten their favorite meal, lasagna, and thought the heartburn she was experiencing was from the spices. When Ellen began to time the heartburn and found them to be six minutes apart, she called the clinic and the doctor agreed to meet them. Driving the Maserati as quickly and safely as she could on the rain-slicked roads, Ellen rethought the conversation they had just the previous week.

"We're going to need a minivan," Rae had pointed out.

"The safest we can find," Ellen promised as she shifted easily through the gears on the Maserati.

"I can't imagine you driving a minivan," Rae teased in a laugh.

"I can't imagine you putting car seats in this," Ellen teased in return, indicating the sports car.

They shared a laugh. They shared a lot of those laughs to keep Rae's hormones from making her a crying mess.

"Oh gawd, if this it..." Rae groaned loudly as they drove carefully and slowly to the clinic in the dark.

Ellen hoped not, she'd seen those emergency deliveries in cars and as much as she didn't care about the upholstery in the Maserati, she didn't want their sons or daughters born in the expensive sports car. It was as she was turning the last corner to the clinic that the accident happened. It wasn't even her fault as she was driving so carefully. Another driver lost control of their car and sideswiped their car.

"Oh shit," Ellen had just enough time to say as the other car hit them. It was over quickly and she turned to Rae to ask, "Are you okay?"

"I'm fine, check on the other driver," she advised doing cleansing breaths. "I'll call 911." Ellen nodded.

"Are you okay?" Ellen got out of the car to ask, getting soaked in the process. There was no one around on the normally busy street.

"I couldn't stop, the road was too slick," the woman stated.

"My wife is having a baby; we have to get her to the clinic," Ellen pointed, "There."

"Are you saying it's your fault?" the woman leapt onto this tidbit of information.

"No, I'm not saying that. I was stopped at the intersection when the light turned green," Ellen said almost defensively. She was angry at the delay and glanced back at her car to see Rae on the phone nodding and clenching her teeth. "Look, my wife is having a baby, we need to get her to the clinic," she repeated pointing again down the street.

"Your WIFE?" the woman asked confused.

"Yes, my wife," Ellen repeated, trying to make her understand. She saw that the woman had a head injury, a small trickle of blood was coming from a gash on her forehead, she wondered idly if it was from the steering wheel and glanced at it as if to confirm her theory. The woman was gripping the wheel tightly.

The woman blinked but obviously didn't understand. Ellen was about to get back in the Maserati and leave the scene, she was drenched from the rain pouring down, when she thought she heard sirens. She was shocked to realize it was an ambulance and it turned at the corner to head for the clinic she was desperately trying to get to. She glanced into the Maserati to see Rae making panting gestures; she looked to be in agony. It was then that she saw a police car coming up behind them.

"Is anyone injured?" he called from the safety and protection of the cop car, his window rolled down.

"Yes, this driver hit me and my wife, she has a head injury," Ellen called back. "My wife is in labor, we need to get her to the clinic," she pointed down the street where the ambulance had gone.

"I'll call for an ambulance," he called back, rolling his window up slightly to protect himself from the deluge.

Ellen stared at him in utter shock that he hadn't gotten out of the vehicle. "My wife is in labor. Can I drive her there?" she yelled through the window and could see him on his police radio. He held up a hand as though to stop her from speaking.

Ellen was furious. First this idiot woman had hit them and now this idiot cop? "What the hell are you playing at?" she yelled at him.

"Now, ma'am, you take it easy there," he said condescendingly.

"Why don't you come out here and do your job?" she asked just as loudly.

He stared at her like she was a madwoman. "Why don't you go back to your car, ma'am?" he advised.

Ellen glared at him one more time, ready to say more, and then took his advice. She checked on Rae. "Are you okay?" she asked her again.

"I…need…to…" she took a deep cleansing breath. "Get…to…the…doctor," she breathed.

"I know, baby, I know," she answered worried. She glanced over at the other car where she could just make out the other driver, now holding her head with her hand. "Call the doctor and tell him we are just down the street," she advised.

They waited a few minutes before an ambulance came from the opposite direction. The police officer got out of his car for that, wearing a rain poncho in the deluge coming down. Ellen was pissed to see them go to the other driver first. She got out of the Maserati to approach the officer again.

"Ma'am, get back in your car," he said pointing back at the sports car.

"But my wife…" she began and he cut her off.

"Ma'am, get back in your car!" he barked. "If you don't, I'm going to arrest you!" he stated and Ellen, despite her need to argue, complied.

"Are they going to send someone over?" Rae asked through clenched teeth, her forehead was beaded with perspiration despite the cold of the car and the rain coming down.

"No, did you get through to the doctor?" she asked pointing at the cell phone.

"No, I got the recording that all lines were busy. I think the storm is causing a…ouch," she gasped as another contraction hit her.

"Oh baby, are you okay?" Ellen asked once again, concerned.

"I…need…to…" she started again but couldn't finish, the pains were too intense.

It was then that the cop finally came over to take their statement. "Holy shit, she's pregnant!" he said unnecessarily.

"That's what I was trying to tell you!" Ellen nearly shouted but tempered it with Rae's presence.

"Is she far along?" he asked, equally as stupid.

"She's in labor, due to give birth at any moment," her voice did rise a bit with this information. She was cold, her wife was in labor, and because of this idiot she was still sitting here. "Look, the clinic is right there, could you follow me over for my statement so my wife can be admitted? They are expecting her."

"I should call an ambulance," he began but she interrupted him.

"It will be quicker if I drive her, you can follow us over."

"I should really follow procedure…" he began again. It was then that Ellen realized how young the guy really was. Usually they had partners when they were rookies…she wasn't sure he was a rookie.

"Look, she's not going to last that long. I'm taking her there, to the clinic. You can arrest me after she's admitted," she said and closed the

door in his face and tried to start the car. It turned over once and died. "Damn!" she swore.

"Ma'am, get out of the car!" he commanded loudly through the door.

Ellen ignored him and tried the car again. It turned over.

"Ma'am, get out of the car!" he shouted once again.

Ellen ignored him again and put the car into gear. Hearing Rae crying next to her, mewling in pain, was breaking her heart. She steered around the other car and sped off down the street to the clinic. Pulling into the entrance bay, she was relieved it was under the building and out of the rain. They had been waiting for them and staff ran out to the passenger side to unload Rae and get her into a wheelchair.

"You can park over there," one of the staff said pointing to some open spots, still out of the rain, and Ellen nodded.

Parking the car, she debated whether she should wait for the stupid cop or to go in after her wife. Rae won out and she quickly went inside.

"Ms. Christenson?" one of the staff greeted her. "These are for you; you can change in there," she pointed to a room, "And get out of this wet stuff. Can I put it in the dryer if it's safe to?" At Ellen's nod, she smiled.

"There will be a police officer coming in here," Ellen told her. "Looking for me. We were in an accident down the road," she said pointing from the clinic.

"That was you? We heard it on the scanner," she indicated the radio behind their desk.

"Yeah, they wanted to order an ambulance but since we were so close…" she began to explain.

"I'll handle it and have him wait. You better get changed if you want to see your babies born," she advised.

"Thank you!" Ellen said reverently and slipped into the room the woman had indicated. Peeling off her wet clothes she was surprised at the amount of water that was in them, but then remembering the amount of water coming down, she wasn't as surprised. She dried her body quickly with a towel she found in the room and slipped into the scrubs, which included slippers of sorts, normally worn over shoes but even her shoes were soaked. She put her hair in a rather unattractive head cap and opened the door.

"This way, Ms. Christenson," another nurse approached her, obviously waiting for her.

Ellen began to follow her and made the mistake of looking back. The police had arrived and were arguing with the other staff member. She turned around and kept walking, following the nurse.

Rae was on a reclining table. The doctor was telling her to "PUSH" in no uncertain terms.

"Oh, thank God, Ellen!" Rae said, relieved to see her wife.

"I'm in time? Have you had either of them?" she asked as she went to hold Rae's hand.

"Nope, just trying to get one out!" the doctor quipped. "If Rae would cooperate?"

Rae chuckled and then winced at the pain as she began to push in earnest.

Ellen was amazed at the grip she had on her hand, it was then she realized Rae should have had her nails clipped; they were digging in painfully to her hand.

"That's it, Rae, push once more and we'll have one," the doctor encouraged her.

Moments later they heard the first cry of their baby. Ellen and Rae exchanged a look and Rae asked, "Is it a boy or a girl?"

"You have to push more so I can tell, they don't put genitalia on their heads," he said to make her laugh.

Rae laughed but the pain made her wince again as she pushed through it. Moments later, she heard, "It's a boy!" from the doctor, who quickly handed the baby to a nurse, cutting the umbilical cord after he neatly clamped it.

"Let me see him, let me see him," Rae ordered weakly. She was exhausted.

"Nope, let them clean him up, we have another one to deliver here and they aren't waiting!" the doctor told her authoritatively.

"Watch them, I don't want them to switch him or anything," Rae said to Ellen.

Ellen looked startled at the suggestion and glanced at the doctor who grinned and shook his head. She did watch as they began to wash him, weigh him, and do other things to him across the room. He wouldn't be leaving it without one of them.

"Now PUSH," he told Rae as he glanced at his monitor, seeing the rise of another contraction on it.

"I can't, I'm tired," Rae whined.

"C'mon, babe, you can do this," Ellen encouraged her.

"You do it, I'm tired," Rae tried to make a joke but she began to halfheartedly push.

"More than THAT!" the doctor admonished her. "Just a little more and you'll be done!" he promised.

"No, I don't want to," she refused.

The doctor sat back and glanced at the now fading peak of the contraction, exhausted.

"Now what?" Ellen asked concerned. Rae had loosened her death grip on her hand, her nails no longer imbedded in her skin.

"Well, unless she pushes, that baby ain't comin' outta there," he said matter-of-factly.

Ellen looked at Rae and mopped her brow using a cloth they had placed there, she hoped for that very thing. "Come on, baby, we need to get that baby out of you. I want to know if I have won the bet or not," she teased.

Rae got a glint in her eye. "What if Iris wins the bet?" she asked as she began to feel another contraction starting and began to bear down.

"That's the ticket," the doctor exclaimed getting ready to catch the baby as it crowned.

"Then she wins the bet, but I'm gonna win it," she promised confidently.

Rae pushed with some more spirit, but she felt like she was being torn asunder. The baby slipped easily through her passage, the previous baby stretching the way. "Bet it's your offspring," she gritted her teeth to mete it out.

"Oh? Why do you say that?" Ellen asked, they didn't care whose genetically they were, they were THEIRS!

"It's impatient," Rae said and pushed, hard.

"It's a GIRL," the doctor proclaimed holding it up, showing it off.

Both Ellen and Rae were crying but neither wanted to hold the yucky baby, it was covered in fluids and he understood as he clamped the cord.

"Do you want to cut it?" he asked Ellen who shook her head. She was staring in awe at Rae who had just expelled two babies from her womb.

"Is she okay? Is she okay? She's not crying," she cried instead.

"She's beautiful," Ellen breathed reassuring her.

"She's perfect, let us get her washed up and you can see for yourself," the doctor told her as he clipped the cord and then held her up, yuck and all.

Rae smiled weakly but she wanted to see the two babies for herself. The doctor got busy between her legs again. "Ow, that hurts, what are you doing?"

"You have to expel the placentas," he told her.

"NO! You lied to me!" she told him angrily.

"What?" he asked perplexed looking at Ellen in absolute surprise.

"You said only a little more and I pushed and the baby was born, I don't want anymore," she whined through her tears, she began to sob in pain.

"C'mon baby, you remember they said you had to expel the placenta," Ellen encouraged her.

"I DON'T WANT TO ANYMORE!" she shouted. "IT HURTS!"

Ellen pulled back, not too far but to be out of the line of fire as she glanced at the doctor. He shrugged and shook his head but waited for Rae.

"Ow, that HURTS," she repeated and pushed against the pain, convinced she had another baby in her. In no time at all she had expelled both of the placentas and they cleaned her up.

"I've put a little numbing here so I can stitch you up," the doctor told her.

"I ripped?" Rae asked concerned.

"Just a little, nothing to be worried about," he explained.

"OH my GOD," Rae screamed.

"What? You can feel that?" he asked concerned. He looked down to where he had made the first puncture with his sewing needle.

"How about I take your foreskin and pull it over your head and see if that hurts you?" Rae threatened weakly.

"Here, let's give you a little shot," he said, nonplussed by her vulgarity or her threat.

The sewing only took a few stitches after the numbing agent took effect.

Rae lay there flitting in and out of consciousness, exhausted from the quick and intense labor she had experienced. Ellen stood there by her side, feeling useless as she held her hand. She woke up enough as they brought the now clean babies to her. Both cried until they were in her arms, where they stopped immediately. The boy baby was wearing a little blue blanket and matching skull cap and the little girl was wearing a little pink blanket and matching skull cap.

"Oh, aren't they beautiful?" Rae asked Ellen, her eyes shining with unshed tears.

Ellen thought they looked squashed and ugly but she wasn't about to argue with her wife now. She nodded and gave a false little smile of agreement.

Later she looked again at the babies through the maternity window and still thought they were ugly and squashed. She wondered if she just wasn't the maternal type of woman. Gazing at them, she realized that biologically one of the babies was hers and the other, her wife's. They both were related to each other through their father.

"I've got a brother and a sister!" Iris said excitedly. She had been out with some of the people from Gigitech, friends she had made from working at the Foundation. Getting the text from Ellen telling her that Rae was in labor had cut her evening short. "I guess you win the bet," she joked with Ellen.

Ellen smiled at the pretty young woman. The acne was gone, the dermatologist had confided in Rae, telling her that the teen would never have it again if she simply kept her face clean and occasionally used the crème she had prescribed. She now looked exactly like a younger

version of Blossom, except for the eyes. Ellen turned back to the twins in adjoining bassinets and realized that three children of Ryan's were here and it was amazing. Winning the bet that they would have one of each wasn't that big of a deal. Iris had been convinced they would have two boys, and just to be contrary, Rae had said they were having two girls. They were here, they were healthy, and that was what counted.

The police weren't very understanding about Ellen's leaving the scene of the accident. They at least didn't arrest her when she pointed out the twins her wife had given birth to. They had wanted not only to arrest her but give her a healthy ticket for the accident. Even the ticket would be dismissed when the woman who hit her was found to have caused the accident. That didn't stop the lawsuit that the woman filed when she found out who she had hit with her car. Ellen Christenson had deep pockets and she felt she should pay.

Ellen wasn't upset, though, not in the least. People were funny that way; she wasn't going to get angry. Not over the accident, not over the car, and certainly not over the greedy woman who was suing her.

She brought her wife and children home in the new, luxurious, and safe minivan. She had gotten rid of the Maserati and was already contemplating replacing it. Ellen looked with pride at the happy, healthy family she had and realized how much they meant to her. They were her family, her accomplishment; not something she had inherited, but something she had made. She was proud of this accomplishment more than any other in her entire life. No amount of money that she and Ryan had made for their inventions could buy what she was holding in her arms as she held one baby, Ryan Allen II, and Rae held the other baby, Ellen Sheehan, giving them both unique and personal names, and unique lives. Ellen thought that perhaps Ryan was looking down and smiling on their proudest 'invention' as she held her wife and babies.

As Ellen escorted her into their home Rae whispered, "We have *got* to do *this* again!"

Ellen was simply Blown Away....

~THE END~

About the Author

K'Anne Meinel is the BEST-SELLING author of LAWYERED, REPRESENTED, SAPPHIC SURFER, DOCTORED, VEIL OF SILENCE, and VETTED as well as several other books including her first, SHIPS which was written in 2003 over the course of two weeks. A gypsy at heart, she has lived in many locations and plans to continue roaming. Videos of several of her books are available on YouTube outlining some of the locations of her books and telling a little bit more…giving the readers insight into her mind as she created these wonderful stories. As of this date she has more than 88 published works including shorts, novellas, and novels. She is an American author born in Milwaukee, Wisconsin and raised in Oconomowoc. Upon early graduation from high school she went to a private college in Milwaukee and then moved to California for seventeen years before returning to the state. Many of her stories have Wisconsin in them as settings for her wonderful, realistic, and detailed backgrounds. Named the lesbian Danielle Steel of her time, K'Anne continues to write interesting stories in a variety of genres in both the lesbian and mainstream fiction categories. Her website is www.kannemeinel.com.

If you have enjoyed *BLOWN AWAY* you'll look forward to a sample of K'Anne Meinels splendid and unforgettable novel:

Small Town Angel

In print and E-book and available at fine retailers.

Small towns are notorious for secrets ... but what if you bring your secrets with you?

Amy Adams arrives in Northpoint, Wisconsin on a Greyhound bus. Small towns are well known for not taking to strangers, but THIS stranger decides to stay.

Amy has a look around and to her, it 'feels' like home. She rents a cabin in the woods outside of town and proceeds to look for a place to open a store. Renting to own from one of the locals, she soon finds herself making friends and making waves. She won't discuss where she is from and has nothing to say about her past.

People are extremely curious. This Southern Belle has them talking.

Abby Shipman, the Chief of Police in this neck of the woods, is intrigued by the decidedly mysterious and straight redheaded whirlwind that has blown into town. It's strange that she won't talk about her past, and she is certainly uncomfortable around Abby ... or is it cops in general?

CHAPTER ONE

As the bus pulled into Port Washington, she wondered if she should get off at this stop or go further up the coast. The bus *was* pretty crowded, having taken on a lot of passengers in Milwaukee, but Amy decided to wait it out, see where it went. She knew the end of the line for this particular section of her journey would be Green Bay but she was searching. Searching for something. Anything. She wasn't sure what, but her instincts told her to sit down and bear with the fates, to put up with the smelly, obese woman who had gotten on the bus back in Milwaukee and overflowed her seat and into Amy's seat. It seemed as if the woman hadn't washed herself in days. *And eaten garlic right before she got on the transport*, Amy grinned to herself. Still, she was polite to the woman. She probably had no idea that she smelled or that she even was taking up part of Amy's seat on the cramped bus. Amy was willing to put up with it. Something kept her in her seat and not just the fact that she was packed in like a sardine.

She watched as more passengers got on and off in Port Washington. The large, noisy bus took off once again and headed up the Eastern coast of Wisconsin toward The Thumb, the appendage-like shape of land that stuck out into the large inland sea, Lake Michigan. They headed into Door County, and the towns got smaller. These smaller towns enchanted her as they pulled in and out of them, dropping off and picking up other passengers. She didn't mind the constant start and stop; it was fascinating to people-watch, to see the different sights, and the changing fall leaves. Occasionally they pulled into a town where she caught glimpses of Lake Michigan. All her life the lake had been nothing more than a feature on a map and now she was *actually* seeing it.

Slowly the bus emptied as more people got off rather than on it. At Sturgeon Bay, they crossed a bridge that separated the 'mainland' from an island on the appendage. They continued north on Hwy 57 through places like Whitefish Bay, Bailey's Harbor, and Moonlight Bay. Later she would become familiar with Egg Harbor, Sister Bay, and other such intriguing and unique names. It was at Northpoint that her inner voice said to get off the bus. Her ticket was paid in full for Green Bay but something told her to get up, get out, and the driver obliged her. It wasn't his lookout where his passengers disembarked, and he helped her get her large bag out from under the bus. Northpoint was his 'turnaround' point anyway. The northern most point on The Thumb where he would turn the bus and go south once again on Hwy 42 this time and hit those little towns that relied on this service. He watched as she hitched her large backpack and managed to pull along behind her the large bag he had just pulled out from the luggage compartment. Fortunately, it was on wheels and had an extendable handle. He wondered if she carried a cast iron kitchen sink in the thing since it was so heavy. He shook his head as he began to pack the couple of bags his new passengers handed him and forgot about her.

Amy headed for a sign she had seen from the bus; the Duck and Swan Inn was charming looking. She knew since it was a bed and breakfast that it would be expensive, but she was tired, and she was cranky. After sleeping several days in various bus seats, she needed a good night's sleep as well as a nice hot bath. She rubbed her arms from the coolness of the evening as she looked around wondering if this was it; this was her last destination. Would this be her new home?

"May I help you?" a pleasant faced woman answered her ringing of the small discreet bell on the counter at the front of the home she had walked into. She had hesitated to just walk in to the inn, but an equally discrete sign had invited her in, and she hoped it was okay.

"Hello, I'm Amy Adams, and I was hopin' you had a room?" she asked with a pleasant smile, returning the one the woman was giving her.

"Oh, you timed it right. It's the end of the season, and we have a few open now during the week. Good thing you didn't come this weekend or there would be nothing in town available; would you like one with a fireplace?" she asked.

"Oh, a fireplace sounds lovely," Amy enthused.

"And how many nights?" she asked as she pushed a registration card across the small counter.

Amy filled it out quickly, and with neat handwriting, the woman noted. "A couple of nights?" Amy asked hopefully.

"That will be fine, but we do need the room for the weekend as we are full up," she replied as she read the details Amy had filled in. "I'll need payment up front and a picture I.D?"

Amy was ready for her and handed over both a credit card and a driver's license, which the lady took and processed efficiently. "I'm Sarah Katzenburger, and me and my husband own this house," she introduced herself as the credit card went through the little pin pad and printed out a receipt for Amy to sign.

"It's a lovely house," Amy commented as she looked around at the homey touches and antique look of the saltbox house. From the outside it was weathered, probably from the storms that must occur due to the lake.

"Well, breakfast is from six to nine a.m. and I can arrange a lunch or dinner at any of our fine restaurants around town if you are interested," she said brightly as she reached for an antique key and handed it with a receipt to Amy. She eyed her guest trying to figure out what a woman alone and with a southern accent would be doing this far north at this time of year.

"That sounds fine," Amy answered and ignored the inquiring look. She knew most people wouldn't ask too many personal questions until they felt more comfortable with a stranger, and she hid behind that for now. Tomorrow might be another day, and the woman curious, "I'll need to find someplace tonight to eat dinner," she commented with a broad hint.

"Well, the burgers over at Chuckies' are fantastic, but he also does a full meal of steak and veggies," she added when Amy first wrinkled her nose at 'burgers.' Grease didn't appeal after a long journey with only bus stop food to tide her over, but a full meal would sit just right.

"That sounds good, um where is it?" Amy asked.

She listened as Mrs. Katzenburger gave her a brief layout of the town and where Chuckies' was in location to the inn. Thanking her hostess, she climbed the stairs to the room that was inscribed on the key and found to her delight not only did it have a fireplace but the wood already laid. She put down her heavy suitcase and looked with delight at the private bathroom. She was looking forward to that deep claw footed tub as she quickly washed up, ran a comb through her thick red hair and lightly freshened her makeup. Looking in the mirror, she examined her detested freckles that had mostly faded along with her summer tan. She had smooth skin otherwise, brilliant green eyes, a fine narrow nose, and luscious 'kissable' lips. She thought her eyes were her best feature, while her eyebrows delicately outlined them along with the double set of eyelashes that made it easy for her not to wear mascara. Most redheads had light brown or red brows and lashes, but not her. Amy's were dark and clearly outlined her features. Though she had been teased over it her entire life, she liked the way she looked. One more run through with the comb and her hair was neat once again, and she headed out of the delightful room she found herself in, locking it behind her and pocketing the key.

Sarah watched as the new guest headed out for the evening and wondered about her once again. She seemed pleasant enough but a southerner, which was going to create a bit of gossip in this touristy town.

Amy found Chuckie's easily enough and was pleased at the selection on the menu written above the bar. She ordered a steak, home fries, a salad, and a Corona and asked if she could sit in a booth. The bartender assured her she could and that the entire meal would be brought to her when it was done. He had frowned when she said she wanted it well done, but her pretty smile with the hint of a dimple charmed him. She took her beer and headed for an out of the way spot where she could watch the restaurant/bar and read the newspaper she had purchased.

Amy started with the want ads and continued on through the 'for sale' ones, trying to get a feel for the area. It covered all up and down the coast, and the towns were all unfamiliar to her. She made a mental note to purchase a map of Door County tomorrow when she was well rested.

"Who's that?" a tall dark headed woman asked as she sat on a stool at the bar. The bartender didn't ask her what she wanted as he poured a beer from the tap and slid it down to her where she expertly caught it in her hand and took a sip.

"Tourist," he grunted, as he wiped the moisture from the well-polished bar.

She nodded as she glanced curiously at the woman from the reflection of the mirror and then quickly averted her eyes to the other patrons of the bar, classifying them by "tourist" or "townie" in moments. Her eyes were drawn back to the redhead though as the light above her booth hit the strands of her hair most becomingly. She could appreciate a good-looking woman, but when the woman either felt herself being observed or just looked up from her newspaper, the brunette hastily concentrated back on her draft.

"Eats?" the bartender asked and at her nod he wrote up a tag for the kitchen and picked up the tray that the redhead had ordered and gave it to one of the waitresses.

"This looks delicious!" Amy enthused as the waitress laid it out for her. It smelled heavenly, and her mouth was watering. She cut a few slices of the steak, delicately put down her knife, and picked up her fork to eat them along with the fries. She reached across the table and applied ketchup to her plate so she could dip. She carefully cut up her salad so she could eat convenient mouthfuls of it. Her left hand repeatedly returned to her lap where she had delicately put her napkin. She unconsciously showed off her manners and breeding to the establishment and anyone watching her.

Amy really enjoyed this first sit-down meal she had in days and when the waitress returned she ordered a second bottle of beer, relaxing over the newspaper, reading it from front to back. She glanced up occasionally to look at the other patrons and noticed one or two observing her as well, but her eyes glanced over them and kept going.

She felt delightfully full as she handed over her credit card and waited for the waitress to return with the slip to be signed. She had no problem leaving a twenty percent tip as she filled in the blanks, kept her copy, stowing it and the extra copy of the bill in her wallet. As she got up she carefully folded the newspaper back, tucked it under her arm, and headed out of the restaurant watched by a few people including the brunette who was eating her dinner at the bar.

CHAPTER TWO

"**H**ello, I'm lookin' for a realtor?" Amy asked the next morning as she presented herself at one of the local offices from the newspaper she had read the evening before. She felt much better after a good night's sleep and an excellent breakfast made by Mrs. Katzenburger. She had met Mr. Katzenburger and a few of her other guests and chatted amiably with them. She implied she was on vacation but found out a lot more about them than they did about her despite their well-meaning questions and inquiries. She eagerly went out into the early fall weather with the sun shining brightly and realized she would have to get some fall clothes as it was a lot colder this far north than she was used to. The lovely fall leaves were changing on the trees around the town. It was rather picturesque.

"Well you've found one!" The older woman told Amy with a smile.

Amy returned the smile as she looked around the well-lit office. Almost all of the small office was taken up by windows that allowed a two-sided view of the marina and the lake. It was light, airy, and perfect to show off the many pictures hanging on the walls over the windows and around them of properties for sale or already sold by this office. "I'm lookin' for a year-round rental, possibly lease to own," she told the woman, eyeing her nametag quickly. Lenora.

Lenora smiled at the possibility of a sale over just a rental and introduced herself quickly and efficiently. "What exactly do you want in a home—a stand-alone, a condo, a fixer upper? Will your husband be joining you? do you have children?" Her voice grew excitedly as she talked.

A brief shadow crossed Amy's eyes, but it was gone in a flash. Lenora didn't notice.

"No, this is just for myself so one or two bedrooms would be fine." Amy hoped her voice sounded natural. "I don't know about a fixer upper but what do you have?"

"Well we have—" Lenora started to speak.

"Oh, I should tell you I'm thinkin' of lookin' into any businesses that may be for sale here in town as I'm thinkin' of stayin'," Amy interrupted quickly.

Lenora thought she had died and gone to heaven but still she was cautious. Many tourists *thought* they would like to stay in one of the many little towns located in this area of the state, but they never stayed. It was all grandiose dreams and 'what ifs' and never came to anything, except maybe a huge waste of her efforts and time. She began to show the potential client the rentals she had on file, but she also surreptitiously noted the woman was well dressed in slacks and a nice blouse with an expensive faux leather jacket that completed the outfit becomingly. Her red hair was a little much and Lenora briefly thought it must be dyed to look that exact color especially with the dark eyebrows and lashes. She did however speak slowly and precisely in her southern drawl which bespoke nice manners and a certain flair. It impressed Lenora who began to discuss the businesses located in the town, both for the tourist trade and for the locals. Most shopped in the larger towns for groceries or even trekked down to Green Bay for the major things. Their town was a jumping off point to the islands that were out on the lake. The ferry, and the fishing trips that were a major income for their little town.

Amy was intrigued. It had started as a small fishing village and grown to accommodate the tourists and still retained its homey charm. It wasn't large and yet enough people came through here to make it worth the locals while to maintain the tourists' interests.

Lenora showed her a couple of houses, driving her in and around the town as she chattered away. Finally, Amy found one she liked. An old hunting cabin that needed some work but was private, discrete, and secluded. The closest neighbor was a mile up the road. The price was low even for a rental. but she knew that was because of its location than anything else. She carefully noted as Lenora showed her around how far it was from the town and determined it was a nice walk although with winter not that far off she would have to obtain a vehicle of some sort.

After reading the papers closely, Amy signed the papers to rent with the contingency to make an offer at any time up to a year from the date of the rental. Then Lenora began to show her some of the empty buildings in town as well as established businesses giving her a little gossip at the same time.

"This one has been owned by the same family for nearly a hundred years, and I know the current owner has no interest in maintaining it anymore," Lenora confessed as they went into a little market store with a few fishing reels on the one wall and a little bit of everything. A house was attached to the store with a police cruiser in the drive. Amy could already see the store was under-utilized and had shrunk from its former glory days, very little of the actual space was used. She could see potential though. It had a wraparound porch that went around the entire building except for the one side against the neighboring house, and one side was out over the marina where a gas pump stood on a dock.

"Hi Lenora, how's tricks?" a little girl of about six or seven asked from behind the counter. Amy blinked in surprise and tried not to laugh.

"Heather, that's not polite," Lenora hissed reproachfully. "You are to call me Mrs. Watson and not by my first name without permission."

"You call me by *my* first name," the girl returned sulkily. It was obvious her mode of address had been a repeat of something an adult had said at one point.

"Where is your ..." Lenora hesitated before continuing, "Mother?" she asked cautiously.

"She's around here somewhere," the little girl replied saucily. She wasn't kept down very long by Lenora's tone and looked around the place as though to make her mother appear magically.

"Why aren't you in school today?" Lenora fired at the little girl.

Amy watched amused as the little girl handled the prickly realtor effortlessly. "Parent teacher conferences," she said distractedly as she called out, "MOM!" making the two adults cringe at the ear-splitting yell that came from the small girl.

"Yeah?" a voice answered from a back room and soon they all saw a brunette swagger into view; it was obvious she had been working on something as she was disheveled and looked like she had just gotten up. Amy was amused as she recognized her as one of the patrons from the bar of last night and wondered if she had been drinking today.

"Abby, I have someone here interested in your business," Lenora began in her best salesmanship voice. She didn't see the startled look on either of the other women's faces. Amy because she wasn't ready to just jump into it like that, and Abby because she hadn't expected to be approached like this.

"Who says I'm ready to sell it?" Abby asked, and the tone was similar to her daughter's sulky one.

"C'mon Abby, you know it's gone downhill since your grandparents passed on, and you don't have the time for it anymore," Lenora responded not in the least intimidated by her tone.

"Maybe, but who says I wanna sell it?" Abby asked again.

"Abigail Shipman, you know you yourself said it not so long ago. Now I have this nice lady who is looking at possible investments here in town, so are you interested or not in the possibility of someone taking it over?" Lenora asked hotly, sick of being toyed with, first by her impertinent daughter and now the mother.

Abby grinned as she shared an amused glance with Amy. "Maybe I am, maybe I ain't," she returned.

Lenora exhaled loudly through her nose at this news and crossed her arms in annoyance. "Well, we won't waste your time then," she said as she gestured to Amy that they should leave.

Amy found herself being ushered out and glanced back amused into the brunette's laughing brown eyes and nodded her goodbyes as Lenora puffed up like a wet chicken. The rest of their morning she showed her empty buildings, and while there were possibilities, most of the 'plans' she had were vague re-creations of what already existed in the town. Amy thanked her for her time, picked up the keys to her rental, and returned to the inn.

Sitting down she made a list of things she was going to need at her new house and knew she only had about forty-eight hours to accomplish them.   She only had the room for another night and couldn't stay longer because of the tourists.   With that in mind, she caught the bus before it left town that afternoon using up her ticket that had been paid until Green Bay to head there.   She got to see the inland side of The Thumb.   Faintly across the water she could see land but not the towns until they got to Green Bay.   She got directions and took a cab to the car centers.   She knew what she would need in an area that got a lot of snow and what would be necessary to survive up here.   The salesmen were like any and her southern accent charmed them all.   She knew as a woman alone shopping for a car that she was at a disadvantage, but she continued on until she came across a SUV she liked.   It got good gas mileage, had a four-wheel drive, and was only *slightly* used with low mileage so that she got a discount off the newer models.   She didn't believe the story that an older couple had traded in the vehicle as it was 'too much' for them, but she did like the four-door vehicle with plenty of cargo area in the back.   She signed on all the necessary lines and took out a *small* loan to establish herself in this area; fortunately it was still early enough in the day that her bank account in the south checked out, and they knew she was good for it.   Driving off the lot she felt powerful as she headed for the nearest home stores.

She bought paint for the cabin, an inflatable mattress, and a hunters sleeping bag until the sheets and pillows and cases she also bought could be used.   She went to a restaurant and ate as she continued her lists and then hit the stores once again.   She was really pleased with the selection and for the first time heard about a place called Appleton and the Fox River Mall that had outlet stores.   Hearing it was an additional hour south, she decided to concentrate on where she was at for now.   In short order she arranged for a beds and mattresses for her humble home as well as a living room set and a television.   She got some of the basics, and with all this piled in the back of her new SUV, she headed back up the coast hoping she wouldn't get lost.   It was a fairly straight forward ride, yet confusing to her in the dark as she was unfamiliar with the area.   Strangely, once she got across the bridge in Sturgeon Bay, she had a feeling that she was heading 'home.'   She was relieved once she hit Northpoint and found the Duck and Swan.   Parking on the street, she went inside for a well-deserved rest after her full day; she was grateful that her hosts had obviously been in to clean the room and lay down new wood that took only a moment to light.   She went to sleep with the screen in front of the fireplace dreamily watching the flames and wondering about her future here in Northpoint.

The next morning, she checked out of the Duck and Swan and thanked Mrs. Katzenburger for her hospitality. She mentioned she had rented a place outside of town and relieved her host's curiosity as she mentioned the location.

"Oh, that place, it's been empty for years. You are going to want to have the heating and vents checked; it gets pretty cold up here," her eyes knitted together. "I can recommend a handyman if you want," she offered.

Amy took her up on her offer. The best people came by recommendation, and she knew if her new friends recommended them they would probably recommend the best.

"Oh, you bought a truck?" was the next question-like comment.

Mr. Katzenburger chimed in on that, "I'm not so sure about them foreign jobs. I personally stick to the adage, buy American."

Amy listened respectfully, but as it was the first vehicle she had ever purchased herself, she was going to stick with it; she was proud of it and that she could afford it. While her hosts had their own opinions, she wasn't going to let them upset her with their comments. As she put the heavy bag containing all her clothes in the back seat, she was pleased she still had so much room in the SUV. It all belonged to her though; it was all *hers* and hers alone. She pulled up in front of her cabin and looked around at the tall trees, the deep layer of years of accumulation below them, and breathed in the silence. This was hers. Rented perhaps, but hers. The pride bubbled inside her while she began to unload her belongings.

She swept out the small cabin first, noting the thick logs and wondering if it would be warm enough to get her through the winter. She had no idea if it would, and the wood next to the cabin in a neatly stacked pile didn't look like nearly enough. She didn't see any other way to heat the small cabin, and thoughtfully sweeping every nook and cranny from the ceiling to the floor, she eliminated dust and debris from years of having no one in the cabin. She raised a bit of dust herself by her efforts and opened all the windows noting how cool it was as she worked. Finally, she felt it was clean enough to haul out the soaps and conditioners she had bought for her wood floors and walls. She started in the kitchen and began scrubbing the walls first and then floors, astonished at the amount of dirty water she soon had in the bucket she used. Throwing it outside beyond the porch, she stretched her back, realizing the time as the sun was starting to set. She would have to leave some of the house cleaning for another day if she wanted it to warm up.

She closed the windows and started a fire in the fireplace only to have the smoke start to choke her out. She tried the flue, but that didn't seem to work well, and she wondered if the chimney had something in it. She shrugged; it was too late in the day for her to do anything about it really, so she brought her sleeping bag and blew up her mattress. She realized she needed to get the electricity turned on in the cabin and get a phone. She made numerous lists as she realized how unprepared she really was.

Washing up with cold water, she checked and found an electric water heater in a closet in the kitchen, so she knew she would eventually have hot water. Having no idea how to turn on the electricity, she shivered from the cold water and rolled down her sleeves and put on a sweater to hide her dirty shirt and headed back into town. She tried another restaurant. This one was a little finer than Chuckie's, and she felt self-conscious in her jeans until she saw other patrons wearing the same.

"Table for one?" the greeter asked her, and she nodded as she was shown to a table near the marina side with a wooden sidewalk separating the window from the actual dock. It was very lovely and picturesque, and she was startled out of her reverie when asked for her order. She had to admit she hadn't looked at her menu and soon ordered the stuffed pork chops, green beans, and applesauce along with a cold glass of milk. She smiled as she realized milk wasn't that sophisticated, but it sounded so good with the rest of the meal she couldn't resist.

She looked out at the marina again and noted that she was in a great place to people watch, she could see and watch the other patrons in the reflections on the windows. She wanted to cringe and hide when she saw that brunette that Lenora had introduced to her earlier in the day. What was her name? Abby or something? She could see she was better dressed than the jeans and t-shirt she had worn earlier, in fact, she seemed to be dressed up, but not for going out or anything, just better. She glanced back out the window and began to mentally categorize what she needed to do to make her cabin habitable for winter.

"Mind if I join you?" Amy looked up startled at the voice; she had been lost in thought looking out at the lights in the harbor. She was more startled to realize it was the rude brunette. "I promise I won't bite..." she smiled and then added softly, so softly that Amy thought she hadn't heard her correctly, "hard."

Amy couldn't think of a single reason to refuse her, and perhaps they had just gotten off on the wrong foot, or maybe it was Lenora. She didn't know how to extricate herself from this awkward situation, so she gestured to the second chair and watched as the woman pulled it out and sat down.

"I'm Abigail Shipman," the brunette said holding out her hand to be shook.

Manners drilled into her from birth had Amy reaching across the table taking the hand that was offered. "Amy..." A slight hesitation and then, "Adams."

Abby smiled noting the hesitation but not saying anything as she firmly shook the woman's hand and then said, "Hello Amy Adams, welcome to Northpoint."

"Thank you," Amy said quietly as her hand was released, and she returned it back to her lap.

"What in the world is a woman from the south doing in so cold a climate?" Abby asked with a grin showing she meant no harm with the question.

"Can I get you anything Abby?" their server was at their table.

"I'll have what she's having," Abby said playfully.

The server grinned in return. "Even the milk?" he asked.

"Milk?" Abby asked alarmed and then shook her head. "Actually, that's probably a good thing; just add chocolate to mine if you would."

"Chocolate milk then with pork chops, green beans and apple sauce?" he repeated back with a smirk.

"Green beans?" she asked and the concern in her voice could be heard.

"The pork chops are stuffed otherwise I'd suggest potatoes," he was laughing at her and showed it.

"I'll take those potatoes, mashed, maybe with a bit of garlic," she laughed back at him as he wrote down her order.

"Will do, have it up in a jiffy, Chief," he said with cheerful good humor.

Abby laughed to herself, and Amy watched amused. "You don't like milk?" she asked.

"I like it; it doesn't like me. Lactose intolerance," she said pointing her thumb at herself before continuing, "But apparently chocolate milk is okay, something about the lactate being negated by the cocoa bean," she explained.

Amy nodded, it made sense. She was fortunate that she had never experienced it herself, but she knew people who had, and it wasn't pleasant.

"So why Northpoint?" Abby returned to her earlier question.

Amy shrugged, "Somethin' told me that I should check it out; you've got to admit that Door County is beautiful."

"The bajillion tourists we get here every season attest to that, but unless you are ready for snow and a lot of it, you are in for a shocker."

Their server brought them two small plates, a pile of butter squares and a basket of warm sliced bread, putting it down between them with a smile as he turned to head to another table to take their order.

Amy reached for the bread; she was starving, but her hand collided with Abby's, and they exchanged an awkward little laugh as they tugged from both ends, the bread hadn't been sliced through. They both soon had a slice and used the butter to smooth over the surface of each of their slices, the butter melting almost immediately with the heat generated from the warm bread.

"I'm hopin' I'll make it," Amy said with confidence she wasn't feeling.

"Well, that cabin you rented is going to need some work," Abby said as she leaned back and bit into her bread.

"How do you know...?" Amy began only to be cut off with a wave of Abby's hand.

"Small town, you don't think Lenora would keep that to herself, do you?" Abby's eyes twinkled as her perfect white teeth bit into the bread again.

Amy laughed at her own naiveté; of course, Lenora would tell all she knew about her. Despite spending many hours together looking at places and discussing things, Amy had told her relatively little about herself. It had frustrated the older woman to no end. Besides, renting a place that had no takers for a couple of years would be a feather in her real estate cap. "Well, I suppose not," she conceded gracefully. Her own mouth watered at the delicious bread she was eating.

"You gonna heat it with wood?" Abby asked knowingly.

Amy nodded and then asked, "You know anyone I can buy some good hardwood from?"

"Hardwood?" Abby asked feigning that she didn't understand.

"Hardwood's burn cleaner, and I don't want to gum up the chimney," she drawled, her southern accent sounding very becoming to the brunette's ears. "I'd like a few cords of wood if I could get them, and I need a chimney cleaner," she added.

Abby smiled; this wasn't some wilting wallflower from the south but some steel magnolia she had heard tell about. She obviously knew she would need wood and a lot of it from what she was saying. Good, she hated when people were ill-equipped to move into the area and got themselves in trouble. "Well for hardwoods I'd contact Jacob Meyers, he's in the book and has cords he will deliver."

"How many do you think I should buy?" Amy asked as she finished her first piece of bread and unashamedly reached for another.

"You have to figure at least one cord of wood for every month of winter and then some," Abby told her as she too reached for another piece so she would get her fair share. The redhead knew how to eat!

"How many months of winter do y'all get up here?" she drawled.

Abby grinned, a slight wrinkling of her nose and around her mouth showing she appreciated the question. "Depends, but it's in the air, so I would suggest you give Jacob a call and see about having him deliver that wood for you. He has others, so you don't want to wait. As for cleaning out your chimney, I'm sure Jacob can recommend someone; the last one that I knew that did it regularly moved away."

"Got sick of the snow?" Amy asked with a grin as she finished her second piece and reached for her third and final.

Abby gave Amy a dubious look. "There was probably not enough business for him, and I'm sure he didn't work too hard." She told her as she grabbed the last piece, the heel of the bread, before Amy could gobble it up.

They chatted back and forth getting to know each other through their delicious meal. Amy wasn't surprised that the woman asked more questions than she answered, but she was prepared for those questions anyway. She wasn't prepared for the next one though.

"You still interested in my store?" Abby asked.

Amy eyed her slightly. "I thought you weren't interested in sellin' it?" She asked as she enjoyed the flavor of the apple sauce; it was an excellent accompaniment to her stuffed pork chops and green beans.

"I might be to the right person; Lenora is right, but don't tell her I said so. I'm not interested in running it, and it's almost like every other store in town. It's been going downhill since Gramps and Grandma passed on. They were the draw anyway." She shrugged.

"Was it your grandparent's place?" she asked, genuinely interested with a gleam in her green eye.

Abby nodded. "Yes, once they were gone I just simply had no time, but we live next door so it was convenient, and I didn't want it just gone. It's time though."

"If it's not too much to ask, what about your siblings or parents, wouldn't they be interested?"

"It's not a secret. I never got along with my parents; they live across the bay in Oconto."

"Ocont what?" Amy asked, grinning unrepentantly at mashing up the name.

Abby snickered at her butchered attempt of the Indian name. "Oconto, it's a town on the mainland. They live there, I live *here*, and we are all fine with that. Besides Gramps left it to me to take care of Grams, and I did until she passed too. I love it here, and my children were born and raised here."

"Children? I met your daughter," she mentioned as she delicately wiped her mouth.

"Heather?" and at Amy's nod she continued with a prideful grin, "Yeah she's something, but Bailey is a bit of a handful; he's ten now and full of pre-teen mouth and angst."

Amy giggled as she was supposed to, and Abby's eyes were drawn to her.

"Do you have children or a husband?" Abby asked noting the faint white line that time hadn't erased from her left hand.

Amy didn't hesitate even a moment as she shook her head. "No, I'm a widow, and we were never blessed with children."

"Oh, I'm sorry to hear that; you're young to be widowed," she observed.

Amy nodded her thanks but didn't say anything as she looked down at her plate concentrating on her food. The two girls sat in silence for some time as they gobbled their food down. Amy enjoyed the flavor of her applesauce, occasionally dipping her pork chop into it when she was sure Abby wasn't looking.

"I didn't mean to bring up bad memories." Abby began to say as she pushed her plate away from her.

"Did you ladies want desert?" their server asked as he took their finished plates away.

"I'll have carrot cake if you have it?" Amy said shyly, thankful for the subject change.

"We do," he assured her before turning to Abby. "And for you Chief?" he asked with a saucy little grin.

"I'll have some chocolate cake with chocolate frosting if Lance baked it, but if Tasha did, I'll have carrot cake instead," she told him, smirking at the grin he gave her.

He nodded as he toted their used dishes away.

"Small town, I guess everyone knows everyone else, eh?" Amy asked hoping to avert the brunette's apology and forget what they had been talking about.

"Yes, it's a blessing and a curse. The tourists make it all interesting though," Abby told her, and while she had noted the change of subject, she didn't bring it up again. "What would you do with the store if I let you have it?" she asked instead.

Amy had seen the other stores in town and noted what they lacked. Touristy items were fine and they were well supplied in the other stores. She herself would carry…some. But she wanted a little more than that and began to discuss it with Abby who proved to be a good listener and nodded as they ate their carrot cakes, which apparently Tasha had baked today.

"Wow, it sounds like you know what you are talking about," Abby said as she finished the last morsel of her cake and the delicious icing.

Amy nodded. "My parents had a small fishin' place on the Gulf when I was growing up," she confided and then blushed

"You didn't want to work there?" Abby asked, noting the blush on the redhead's face.

"They passed away. The bank and my brother sold it before I could say yes or no," she told Abby and looked away.

"I'm sorry for your loss." Abby found herself apologizing again and for some reason it irritated her.

Amy looked up straight into those soft velvety brown eyes. She had been more forthcoming with this woman, and she didn't know why.

"They were old; they had me and my brother late in life, but in the end it didn't matter, as neither the bank nor my brother got the proceeds after my grandmother's lawyer stepped up. It all went into a trust." She grinned ruefully and shrugged at life's intricacies.

"You seem to have had a lot of loss in your life," Abby commented as she finished her chocolate milk. It left a cute little moustache on her upper lip.

Amy resisted the urge to blot at the brunette's upper lip, as she pantomimed it for her dinner companion to make her aware of it without embarrassing her and then watched amused as she wiped her lips clean like a child would with the back of her hand.

"It's just…life. It doesn't always play fair."

Abby had to admit that was certainly true.

"Would you ladies like anything else?" Their server came up with separate bills, which he handed to each of them.

"I'm good," Abby answered as she glanced down at her check.

"It was delicious," Amy said courteously.

"Why don't I get this?" Abby asked her, reaching for Amy's check.

Amy looked up startled at the offer. "Why would you do that?"

Abby seemed surprised that she would question her offer. "Why not? We spoke about business; I could write this off." She grinned at the idea.

Amy shook her head. "Thank you, but no, perhaps another time, and if you are serious about sellin' me your store, perhaps we could do this again?" she offered, hoping to couch her refusal.

"Why don't you come by the store again tomorrow? I'll be…around. We could discuss terms that would be agreeable to both of us. I like your ideas, and I think you'd be successful at it. I'd like someone to succeed at it; God knows I have no interest."

Amy nodded as she slipped a twenty-dollar bill into her hand from her purse. They rose from where they were seated and headed to the cashier together. "I'd like that; perhaps we could have Lenora draw up some of the papers so she doesn't feel left out?" she suggested.

"You've already got her number, don't you?" Abby said astutely, as she watched Amy pay her bill and then catching Mike the server's arm as he walked past, she handed him a five-dollar bill.

"Thank you, ma'am," he said blushingly. Most people left the tips on the table, but he kinda liked the opportunity to thank her personally.

They walked out into the brisk early fall night, and Amy pulled her jacket closer. The air was so clear you could almost drink it, and she breathed deeply in appreciation of it.

"You look like a hound dog smelling the air like that," Abby teased as they walked along.

"Could be worse things that I look like. Daddy had a good pair of coon dogs," she answered with a laugh as she pressed the button on her key ring and unlocked the door to her new SUV.

"This is yours?" Abby asked in surprise. Her car was parked alongside. She noted that the vehicle still had the dealer plates on it. If it wasn't brand new, it was only recently old;it was a Mazda CX-5 and looked sharp. She gazed at it enviously.

Amy nodded proudly. "Yes, I bought it yesterday. I knew I'd need a good sturdy vehicle for the winters up here and to get in and out of the cabin I rented."

"It got four-wheel drive?" she asked as she nearly drooled over the modern SUV.

Amy nodded again. "Yep and all sorts of gadgets I'm gonna have to get used to."

Abby nodded wondering how much the SUV had cost her and smiled ruefully. A new SUV was far in the future for her and her children. In the meantime, she had her cruiser. She watched as Amy got into the SUV, and it smoothly started for her. "Hey, you might want to get a remote starter for it," she suggested to her new friend.

"Already got it thanks," Amy said with a grin. "I'll see you tomorrow." She waved as she closed the door and slowly backed out of the stall. She didn't notice that Abby was getting in the cruiser that had been parked next to her own SUV.

~End Sample Chapter of SMALL TOWN ANGEL~
For more go to www.Shadoepublishing.com to purchase
the complete book or for many other delightful offerings

~ Because a publisher should stand behind their authors~

 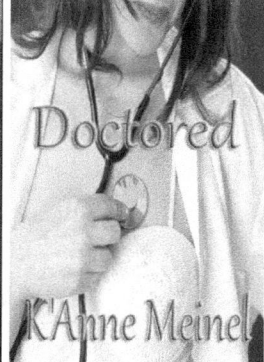 

~ Because a publisher should stand behind their authors~

What do you do when you meet someone who changes everything you know about love and passion?

Paige Harlow is a good girl. She's always known where she was going in life: top grades, an ivy league school, a medical degree, regular church attendance, and a happy marriage to a man. Falling in love with her gorgeous roommate and best friend Alyssa Torres is no small crisis. Alyssa is chasing demons of her own, a medical condition that makes her an outcast and a family dysfunctional to the point of disintegration make her a questionable choice for any stable relationship. But Paige's heart is no longer her own. She must now battle the prejudices of her family, friends, and church and come to peace with her new sexuality before she can hope to win the affections of the woman of her dreams. But will love be enough?

www.shadoepublishing.com

~ Because a publisher should stand behind their authors~

As I watch the wormhole start to close, I make one last desperate plea..."Please? Please don't make me do this?" I whisper.
"You're almost out of time, Lily. Please, just let go?"
I look down at the control panel. I know what I have to do.

Lilith Madison is captain of the Phoenix, a spaceship filled with an elite crew and travelling through the Delta Gamma Quadrant. Their mission is mankind's last hope for survival.

But there is a killer on board. One who kills without leaving a trace and seems intent on making sure their mission fails. With the ship falling apart and her crew being ruthlessly picked off one by one, Lilith must choose who to trust while tracking down the killer before it's too late.

"A suspenseful...exciting...thrilling whodunit adventure in space...discover the shocking truth about what's really happening on the Phoenix" (Clarion)

~ Because a publisher should stand behind their authors~

In the male dominated sport of Formula 1 racing, Samantha 'Sam' Dupree is struggling to make her mark against the boys. She hears about a driver who is making a name for herself in NASCAR and goes to check her out. Little does she know that she's in for the race of her heart.

Addison McCloud wants nothing more than to drive. She doesn't care about fame or fortune; she just wants to be fast enough to get herself and her family away from her abusive father. Meeting Sam, changes her world and revs her life into overdrive.

When the two women meet, sparks flies like the race cars that they drive. Will they be able to steer their relationship into something more and win the race, or will their families make them crash and burn. The boys of Formula 1 are going to learn that Southern girls are a force to be reckoned with.

~ Because a publisher should stand behind their authors~

Carrie flees from the demons of her present, trying to protect the ones she loves.

Frankie hides from the demons of her past, and the memory of loved ones she failed to protect.

A modern day princess thrown to the wolves, Carrie's only hope is the rancher who had spent the better part of a decade in self imposed, near total, isolation. Frankie's history of losing those she tries to save haunts her, but this madman threatens her home, her livestock, her sanctuary. She knows she can't do it alone, has she still got enough support from her oldest friends?

www.shadoepublishing.com

 ~ *Because a publisher should stand behind their authors*~

Amelia Gittens had the credit of being the first and only woman thus far in the United States military of being a sniper in combat, made possible by being in the Military Police unit of the crack 10th Mountain Infantry Division. After retirement she joins the City of New York Police Department, and suddenly finds herself involved in a suspect shooting incident which soon encroaches upon her entire life. In order to protect her therapist who has been targeted as a revenge killing, Amelia takes on the responsibility as if she was still in the Army, treating it as a tactical maneuver.

www.shadoepublishing.com

~ Because a publisher should stand behind their authors~

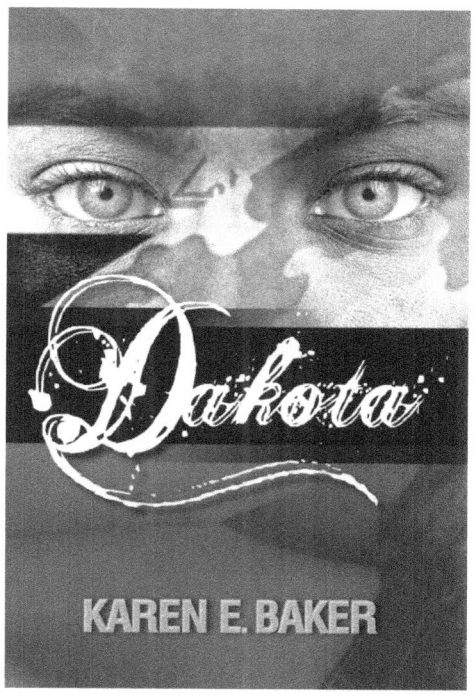

When U.S. Marine Dakota McKnight returned home from her third tour in Operation Iraqi Freedom, she carried more baggage than the gear and dress blues she had deployed with. A vicious rocket-propelled grenade attack on her base left her best friend dead and Dakota physically and emotionally wounded. The marine who once carried herself with purpose and confidence, has returned broken and haunted by the horrors of war. When she returns to the civilian world, life is not easy, but with the help of her therapist, Janie, she is barely managing to hold her life together...then she meets Beth.

Beth Kendrick is an American history college professor. She is as straight-laced as they come, until Dakota enters her life, that is. Will her children understand what she is going through? Will she take a chance on the broken marine or decide to wait for the perfect someone to come along?

Time is on your side, they say, unless there is a dark, sinister evil at work. Is their love strong enough to hold these two people together? Will the love of a good woman help Dakota find the path to recovery? Or is she doomed to a life of inner turmoil and destruction that knows no end?

www.shadoepublishing.com

If you have enjoyed this book and the others listed here Shadoe Publishing is always looking for first, second, or third time authors. Please check out our website @
www.shadoepublishing.com
For information or to contact us @
shadoepublishing@gmail.com.

We may be able to help you bring your dreams of becoming a published author to life.